# DIARY OF AN ORDINARY WOMAN

# DIARY OF AN ORDINARY WOMAN

Margaret Forster presents the 'edited' diary of a woman, born 1901, died in 1995. From the age of thirteen, on the eve of the Great War, Millicent King keeps her journal in a series of exercise books. She records the dramas of everyday life in an ordinary family touched by war, tragedy, and money troubles in the early decades of the century. She struggles to become a teacher, but wants more out of life. From bohemian literary London to Rome in the twenties her story moves on to social work and the build-up to another war, in which she drives ambulances through the bombed streets of London. She has proposals of marriage and secret lovers, ambition and optimism. But then her life is turned upside down once more by wartime deaths.

A triumph of resolution and evocation and with a voice all its own, this is a heartening, beautifully observed story of an unknown woman's life—a narrative where every word rings true.

# DIARY OF AN ORDINARY WOMAN

## 1914–1995

## Margaret Forster

**WINDSOR**

First published 2003
by
Chatto & Windus
This Large Print edition published 2005
by
BBC Audiobooks Ltd by arrangement with
Random House UK Ltd

ISBN 0 7540 7973 2   (Windsor Hardcover)

British Library Cataloguing in Publication Data available

Printed and bound in Great Britain by
Antony Rowe Ltd., Chippenham, Wiltshire

FOR SUSAN MORRIS

WITH THANKS

# INTRODUCTION

In May 1999, I received a letter from a stranger, Joanna King, which seemed at first to be one of those pleasant fan letters that authors are occasionally cheered by, but which turned out to be something else. Joanna King's husband had an aunt, Millicent King, aged 98 in July, who had kept a diary from the age of 13 until she was 94. Neither Joanna nor her husband nor any member of their family had ever been allowed to read any of these diaries but they were sure that, because their relative was a woman of strong opinions, they would be interesting. The point of writing to me was to ask my advice on what might be done with them after their owner's death. Joanna had read a memoir I'd written (*Hidden Lives*, about my grandmother and mother) and, because it was the story of two ordinary women with no claim to fame, it had made her wonder if I might agree that there was some value in Millicent King's diaries as a social document. Could I suggest what might be done with them?

What I suggested was that one of the universities with a department devoted to Women's Studies might be keen to accept the diaries, and I enclosed various names and addresses. I said the thought of anyone keeping a diary over such a length and span of time, so neatly covering most of a century, was in itself extraordinary, and I would love to read them myself. This brought another letter from Joanna saying this was what she had hoped, that is, that I myself would be intrigued enough to want to 'make

1

something of them'. I hadn't, in fact, meant that I'd like to do this but once it had been suggested, in that vague kind of way, I began to toy with the prospect. But what form could this 'making something of them' take? Whatever Millicent King's diaries turned out to be, she was hardly Virginia Woolf. If I tried to edit the diaries I'd be stuck with the problem of how to make the ordinary interesting unless I was very lucky and the content turned out not to be ordinary at all. Or could I use them to write a biography? But who would want to read the biography of someone of whom they had never heard?

I wrote back again saying that I was drawn to trying to use the diaries in some way but that I thought Joanna should think very carefully about the possible consequences of letting me have them. She, and more importantly Millicent King herself, might not like whatever I made of them. I pointed out that it is quite dangerous letting a writer loose in a field of very personal material—I might run amok and trample on sensitive areas. I said that, in any case, I was busy finishing a book and wouldn't be free to consider anything else for at least six months; so why didn't she discuss with her husband's aunt whether it would be wise to let me have a free hand with her diaries, and they could let me know in October. A week later, I had a phone call from Millicent King herself. Her voice was strong and confident and, if I hadn't known she was 98, I would never have guessed. She said she was delighted to hear that I thought her diaries might have some worth but that she worried that Joanna might have given me the impression that they contained exciting material, and she was afraid this was not the case. 'They may be trash,' she said. I said I was sure they would not be; but she said I should not be so sure, and that she wanted to send me some samples and then I would know if it was worth 'putting up with another eighty-odd years'. If I decided it was, I could come and collect all the diaries in the autumn.

The samples arrived a few days later, with a covering note from Millicent King herself, the handwriting a little faint, but clear, even though she apologised for its untidiness (it's true it wavered all over the page). They were, she wrote, from the first diary she ever kept, in 1914, when she was 13. They'd been photocopied from what looked like a lined exercise book with the dates written in the margin. I was fascinated by them straightaway. The writing was fluent and lively, and seemed driven by some sort of inner energy which, though the content was mundane enough, gave it a sense of drama. I kept a diary myself at that age and it was embarrassing to look it out and compare how I wrote with how young Millicent wrote. If she could write with such vigour at 13, how would she write at 23, 33, right up to 93? I was suddenly filled with enthusiasm to find out, and wrote yet another letter, saying that nothing would give me more pleasure than to read all the diaries and perhaps try to edit them. Could I come in October and collect them? Millicent said yes, and we agreed to fix a date once I returned to London from the Lake District.

I have promised the King family not to identify the village in which they still live (or did at the time of writing) except to say it is in the West Country. I got a train from Paddington to the station in the

3

town nearest their village and Joanna King met me there. She told me a little about herself as she drove me to Millicent King's home, describing how she had met her husband Harry and had come to know Millicent herself, who, it turned out, had only comparatively recently moved from London to be near them. She explained that Millicent was living in a cottage at the end of the lane leading to their farm, so it was very easy to keep an eye on her without her forgoing her independence. Joanna passed the cottage at least twice a day, taking her two dogs for the walks they needed, and Harry was always coming and going in that direction as he went about his work on the farm. Millicent was frail but perfectly capable of looking after herself and she resented any suggestion that the time might soon come when she could no longer do so. She had been in hospital recently for a minor operation (Joanna didn't say for what) and had agreed, though most reluctantly, to go into a nursing home afterwards to convalesce. She was booked in for two weeks but after one night had discharged herself, saying she felt fine and couldn't abide being among so many old and sickly folk, and had taken a taxi home. She was, said Joanna, indomitable.

It was hardly surprising that by the time we arrived at Millicent's cottage I had built up a picture of her as a suffragette type, imagining her to be a physically as well as mentally formidable woman, even though I knew that people of 98 are unlikely to fit such a description. I thought she would be tall and imposing so the biggest surprise when she opened her door was to find she was small, quite tiny in fact, I guessed no more than five

4

feet or so. She was not in any way bowed or hunched but held herself erect, seeming to push her shoulders firmly back as she greeted me and holding her head high. She wore gold-rimmed spectacles and I could see a deaf aid in her left ear. She had on a pretty, flowery dress and a lilac cardigan which picked out the colour of the floral pattern. When she turned to lead the way into the cottage she steadied herself with one hand on the wall but then walked (without a stick) quite steadily into her living-room.

It became immediately apparent that she did not want Joanna to stay and equally apparent that Joanna had intended to. Millicent suggested that Joanna was busy and had lots to do, and she did it in such a way that for Joanna not to agree would have seemed rude. Joanna did try to say that she had been going to make me some lunch after my long journey but Millicent said she already had something prepared and that, if Joanna came back about three o'clock to run me to the station, this would fit in very nicely with helping to pack up the diaries. So Joanna left, if reluctantly, and Millicent smiled and said she was a good girl but inclined to fuss. 'Now,' she said, 'shall we get down to business?' Business is what the next hour or so felt like. Somehow, I'd imagined that I'd sit and sip tea and be shown photograph albums while Millicent rambled on about her past. But no. First I was closely questioned about my own life and then about my reading habits. Millicent, it transpired, had been a great reader all her life and warned me that her diaries were full of comments on her reading which I might find tedious. I said that, on the contrary, I'd be fascinated and would read

5

along with her, just as I'd done with Elizabeth Barrett Browning when I had been working on a biography of her. This, I think, pleased her. She then moved on to raise the question of what I thought a diary was for. Why, she asked, did I think an ordinary woman such as herself had gone on keeping a diary all these years? It was obviously a test question and I took time answering it, carefully suggesting several possible reasons, and emphasising that it seemed not as extraordinary to me as it might do to others. I hadn't kept a diary every one of the fifty years since I kept my first, aged 10, but I'd kept enough diaries to know how compulsive the habit can become and what strange satisfaction it can give. We discussed this, the satisfaction, and she said that hers had sometimes annoyed as much as satisfied her and that sometimes she had hated her diary and had felt horribly bullied by the compulsion to keep it.

I was beginning to wonder if we would ever get to the stage when I would be shown these diaries, but after a snack of cheese and biscuits, and some delicious rhubarb tart which Millicent had made herself, she took me into a little room at the back of the cottage which she referred to as 'my sewing-room' (and which did indeed have an old treadle sewing-machine underneath the window, though since there were several pot-plants on it, the machine looked as though it might no longer be in use). There was a floor-to-ceiling cupboard to the right of the window which Millicent unlocked. Odd, I thought, to feel the need to lock a cupboard in a house where she lived alone. Inside, there were three shelves packed with hardback exercise books, most of them red but some black. She stood back and surveyed them, telling me that whenever she looked at them like this, she felt her life must, against all the evidence, have amounted to something after all. She said that there were more than eighty diaries (she'd already told me she'd had to give up at the age of 94) because some years she had filled more than one book. She had never been drawn to the printed sort of diary, she said, with its one page per day, as though every day was worthy of exactly the same space, but instead had from the beginning preferred to put the date in the margin and then write for as long, or as briefly, as she wished. She went on standing in front of the open cupboard, gazing lovingly at its contents, for what seemed like a long time and then she invited me to take out as many as I thought I could carry. Later, Joanna or Harry would bring the rest to me when next they drove to London, which they did from time to time to visit Joanna's sister who, it emerged, lived fairly near to me in North London.

I took out the first ten diaries, feeling it was almost sacrilegious to touch them at all, and then carefully put them into the rucksack I'd brought with me. There was plenty of room still, so I added another ten, and then, testing the rucksack for weight, added yet another five. She herself, clearly counting as she watched, added another one, saying that would take me up to 1939, a good place to get to, a significant year. I assumed she meant the outbreak of the war, but she said that, though this was indeed significant, she hadn't meant the war, but she didn't say what she *had* meant. She closed the cupboard door and locked it again and then said we had time for a cup of tea before Joanna came to take me to the station. She seemed a little sad as we sat sipping the tea she'd made and I worried that, now the moment had come, she might be regretting parting even temporarily with her beloved diaries. I said something to that effect but she shook her head and said, no, she was glad I was going to read them and perhaps be able to make something of them (that phrase again) and that she'd merely been ruminating on what her diaries might mean to someone who did not know her. 'One thing,' she said, 'I never lied to them.' (I noted she said 'to' and not 'in', as though the diaries had life themselves and were not inanimate objects.) She said I wouldn't realise the importance of this until I'd read them and repeated again that she had never lied, never once lied.

Joanna returned promptly, at 3 p.m., and then there was a rather awkward and touching departure. It was clear to me, and, I think, to Joanna, that Millicent didn't really want to see her diaries go, whatever she said. She inquired whether my rucksack was waterproof, and when I said that, though it might not look it, the bag had withstood torrential Lake District rain without any contents getting wet, she remarked, 'Good, because ink runs, you know.' I was careful to keep the rucksack on my knee when I got into Joanna's car, and not put it on the back seat or in the boot, and I thought she looked relieved to see me cradling it like a child. She stood at her door waving as we left and I waved until we were out of sight. I said to Joanna that I hoped she wasn't going to regret this, but Joanna assured me this was unlikely, that once her mind was made up she seldom changed it.

\*　　　\*　　　\*

8

In the following weeks after Joanna had brought me the remaining diaries, I read straight through them completely absorbed in Millicent's growing up and constantly surprised by the odd turns her life took. I still hadn't made a single note nor had I come to any decision as to what I might 'make' of them. By the time I'd read the whole lot, I could see that the obvious thing to do, and what I wanted to do, was edit them. They could not possibly be published in their entirety—the material was far too bulky, and the content varied enormously in interest. Editing would involve a rigorous selective process which, because it would be done according to my particular tastes, might not please Millicent. There would also have to be a certain amount of bridging work and to do it I'd have to research all kinds of background material which I either knew nothing about or of which I had only the sketchiest knowledge. But I had no doubts at all that I wanted to do it, to 'make something', if I could, of an ordinary woman's life, so meticulously recorded. I saw a thread running through it which captivated me and which I hoped would intrigue and captivate others. I hope I have let Millicent King tell her own story and that my editing has not been too obtrusive or in any way unfaithful to it. It has not always been possible to refrain from comment— what Millicent does and says and thinks is inclined to invite reaction—but I have tried hard to keep this to a minimum.

One thing I feel bound to say: there was nothing ordinary about this woman. Indeed, I now wonder if there is any such thing as an *ordinary* life at all.

## 26 November 1914

Father said if I want to keep a diary I must begin it on New Year's Day. He said no one starts a diary in November. But New Year's Day is five weeks away and I do not want to wait. I don't see why I should either. Why should diaries have to start on 1st January. It is tidy, I admit, and I am a tidy person, but that is all.

Father said he doubts very much whether I have it in me to be a diarist. He said I have no sticking power and will soon get bored. He said Matilda is more likely to keep a diary properly. He can see her writing in it every day. She has the discipline. He said he thought even George could manage a diary, though if he did it would be awfully badly written. But Father thinks I am a flibberty gibbet (I don't know how to spell that but I don't care about spelling, it is my diary). Mother told him not to be so unkind but he was laughing and said he was not being at all unkind, he was merely amused and wanted to know what had put the idea of keeping a diary into my funny little head. Mother said there was nothing in the least odd or unusual about it, it is a stage girls go through. She said Matilda had probably already kept one but had been secretive about it. Diaries, she said, are for telling secrets to. She smiled herself then, and Father asked why was she looking so mysterious and had she ever kept a diary and she nodded and blushed and Father said, What secrets did you have to confess, my love, but she would not tell him. They were very merry about it and forgot about me.

11

I can't think of any secrets. My diary, this diary, is not going to be for telling secrets to. Why should I tell myself secrets when I know them already, it is silly. I don't know yet what I want to keep a diary for. In fact, I don't see why I have to have a reason. I want to, and I can do what I like. I don't see why I have to write in it every day either. If I don't feel like it, I won't, and that is that.

I don't want a diary like Matilda's. Mother is right. Matilda did used to keep a diary. I have read it. It is in her stocking drawer, inside an old pair of black woollen stockings she never wears. I know it is wicked to look through my sister's things but I can't help it. I don't see why it is wicked. Matilda often calls me a sneak and I suppose she is right and I should be ashamed but I don't care. I do no harm. I haven't told anyone about her diary and I never will. It is very dull. She kept it the whole year, though, writing every day. She started it on 1st January 1912, when she was 13 as I am now. She wrote exactly one page every day though sometimes left a few lines empty at the bottom of the page. Every day she described the weather and what we had for dinner. There is quite a lot about me in the diary. It hurt me to read so much about what a pest I was, and a cry-baby and a nuisance who caused all the trouble in the family. I don't know what trouble she meant and my heart beat fast thinking about it. I wanted to ask her what this trouble was but of course I could not and had to endure the pain as my punishment for reading her stupid diary.

Matilda always wrote down what she was reading, too. It was pure swank. She tells the plots of *Kipps* and *A Tale of Two Cities* and it is very

12

boring. I never saw her reading those proper books either. I am almost sure she never did. Sometimes I have the feeling I am going to turn out to be something queer when I grow up. Matilda is so ordinary she makes me feel special. I am not like her. I want to be different, I don't know how. Matilda hates to be different. I am different already.

## 6 December

I hate music lessons. I never improve and Miss Bryant thinks I am a dunce, I know she does, and only keeps on for the money, I expect. Today I did scales until I thought I would go mad and then I had an idea. I asked Miss Bryant how scales were invented and she took the bottom out of the piano and showed me all the inside and explained and then there were only five minutes of the lesson left. Before she left Miss Bryant said, You think you are very clever, Millicent. I pretended I didn't know what she meant. I am thinking about it now. Well, I *do* think I am clever. Everyone knows I am clever. Why should I pretend I don't agree. But I know Miss Bryant did not mean that. She meant she knew I'd tricked her and she was cross. I don't care. She doesn't like me and I don't like her and it is unfortunate we have to be together. I don't care if people I don't like do not like me. It makes sense. I am determined to be strong about this. I cannot go through life currying favour, I have decided.

## 12 December

George is 18 today, though he behaves in such a childish way sometimes, it is impossible to believe it. Father gave him a gold watch with the date of his birth and his initials engraved upon it.

Mother gave him a leather wallet. That had his initials on too. Matilda embroidered six linen handkerchiefs for him which I thought a very dull present and I am sure George did though he said they were topping. He asked me where my present was which I thought very rude and I said that because of his rudeness I might not give him anything. He said he didn't care because knowing me it would not be much, he had never seen me go to any trouble for anyone. I thought I might cry and I left the room but Mother called me back and said not to spoil George's birthday so I was forced to go back and give him the pen I had bought at very great expense. He looked at it and asked why I had given him a pen when I knew he already had two and was not fond of writing. I said it was a good pen and could go with him to the war if he went. Mother burst into tears and Matilda said, Now you really have spoiled George's birthday and you are very horrid and mean, Millicent. They are all against me. George did not even look at his pen properly. He did not see it is made of steel and will not break even if a bullet hits it and it has a clip on it to clip on the pocket of his uniform when he gets it which his other pens do not have. If he is killed I hope it will be returned with his Special Effects. I should then keep it as a memento of him. Father took his photograph standing outside the front door. He made Ivy polish the brass knocker before

14

he took it. I could tell Ivy was not pleased. She had already polished it that morning and doubtless thought it clean enough. And it is not really her job to polish but since Pearl left she has had to do it as well as tend to the children.

## 26 December

Christmas Day was a great disappointment to me, I must confess. I could not get in the way of it. I wished I were young again when I heard Baby shouting and the twins running in and out of Mother's and Father's bedroom to show what Santa Claus had brought them. They blew their toy trumpets and banged their drums and it gave me a headache. I did not enjoy dinner either. Being a vegetarian is very hard. I ate only the roast potatoes and parsnips but without gravy they were dry and I could not partake of the gravy because it was made from the juice of the turkey. I was hungry until we were given pudding. Uncle Ernest laughed at me and said next thing he would find was that I would be chaining myself to railings. I do not know what he meant. Father said he was not to put ideas into my head because it was full of too many silly ones already. I asked what were the ideas I had which are silly and everyone round the table shouted 'vegetarianism'. I tried to explain why I am a vegetarian but Father told me to stop before I started because he was not having arguments on Christmas Day. If Mother had not given me more pudding I would have cried.

## 4 January 1915

I have been too ill to write in this diary for a whole nine days. I am not yet fully recovered which is bad news with which to begin the fateful year 1915. It is Father who declared, This will be a fateful year, mark my words, so I am marking them. My illness began with a *really* sore throat, so painful it was like swallowing a sword every time I swallowed, and then began a headache *so* bad I could not turn my head and had to lie in a darkened room. Hardly anybody came to see how I was or to ask me if I needed anything except for Mother and she was rushing and said it was the flu going about and she hoped Baby would not catch it, I must keep away from Baby. I hardly slept for three nights and could not read because I was dizzy and the print jumped about before my poor eyes. It was very pitiful. I would have thought Mother would have sent for Dr Robinson but she said she did not think it necessary and that hot drinks and keeping warm and quiet were all that mattered. I know if it had been George or Matilda she would have had Dr Robinson. George is her precious first-born and Matilda is said to be delicate, though I don't know why. I am most unfortunately placed in this family, coming after Matilda and before the twins and Baby. I am special to *nobody*, and that is the truth.

## 5 January

I feel shaky on my feet but at least I can read again. What would I do, I wonder, if I could not read. My very existence would be unbearable. I had two

16

books out from the library and finished them both today. One was *Pride and Prejudice* by Jane Austen which Miss Bailey said we should read in the holidays because we are going to study another of Jane Austen's novels next term. I dread it. *Pride and Prejudice* I found very slow and I could not be bothered with it. Mother says I will appreciate it when I am older. She is always saying things like that. I don't care how old I am, I will always think Jane Austen dull if *Pride and Prejudice* is anything to go by. The other was *Uncle Tom's Cabin* by Harriet Beecher Stowe, which made me cry, it is so terrible what happens to Tom. I wish Miss Bailey would let us do *Uncle Tom's Cabin* instead of something by Miss Austen. There would be so much to write about and consider. I mentioned this to Father and he said Jane Austen is literature and *Uncle Tom's Cabin* is something different. I do not know what he means. He said Miss Bailey will explain better than he could. I shall ask Miss Bailey.

## 6 January

I was well enough to go out today. It is not so cold and there was a little sun, but I am *not* going to waste ink on the weather. I walked to the library to change my books. I wish they did not have this stupid rule that only two fiction and two non-fiction can be taken out at one time. I want only novels, I have no interest in any other sort of book. I want stories. I wish I knew how to find the stories I like. I read the first page of books but I find that is not a good guide to the rest. Dickens sometimes has good first pages but then he so often goes off and becomes heavy. I wish the Brontës had written more. I have read them all. They are full of passion and I know I am a passionate person. I feel things very deeply, nobody knows how deeply. I chose *The Way of an Eagle* by Ethel M. Dell, but confess it was because of the cover and I do not have high hopes of it. The other is *Tom Jones* by Henry Fielding, but I may have made a mistake because it looks heavy and I only chose it because I liked the name. I felt gloomy coming home. There was nothing else to do except go to the library and I had done that. Mother said I should invite a friend to tea but there is no one I would like to invite and certainly not to *tea*. Tea in our house is dreadful. The twins shout and run about and Baby cries and throws food and it is altogether an ordeal. I could not submit a friend to it. Also, I cannot tell Mother this but there is no girl I really like. I do not have a best friend and I don't want one. I don't *think* I do. Florence Richardson used to be my best friend and I was always having to keep in with her. She cried if I walked to hockey with anyone else. I did not like her house either. It smelled and she has three cats and I hate cats. When she came to my house she annoyed me because she liked to play with the twins or hold Baby and I had not invited her for that.

**10 January**

School began again. Edna swanked about going to the theatre four times as she always does and there was lots of swanking about fathers and brothers

18

going to give the Germans a good hiding. Iris asked me if my brother had joined up and I said no, he wanted to but Father needed him in the business. She said her brother was only 16 but he looked older and he had run away and joined up and been taken and only told them at home afterwards. Her mother hadn't stopped crying since but her father, although angry, was quite proud and said the boy had spunk and no harm would come to him because the war would soon be over and he probably would never see battle. I do not think George has spunk. He would never run away to join up. I wonder if I would, if I were a man. I am sure I have more spunk than George. But I do not agree with war. Father sighs when I say that and he says he wishes it was as simple as that. He said sometimes war is inevitable because if someone attacks you and your country you must defend yourself, what else can be done. I said turn the other cheek as it tells us to do in the Bible. Father groaned and said unfortunately this does not always work. George laughed and said he could see *me* turning the other cheek, he *didn't* think. He said, Milly's temper is so bad she'd punch anyone who slapped her. Then they all laughed, as though I were a child and had said something funny. I left the table in a dignified way.

**11 January**

I wish I had a room of my own. It is insufferable to have to share with Matilda, but I suppose it must be insufferable for Matilda to have to share with me because after all she is older and even more

19

entitled to privacy. I have thought and thought about how it could be managed and I don't see why a wall could not be built in our room. It is a big enough room to divide into two. I have examined the wall where the door is and it would be easy, I should have thought, to knock a hole in it and make another door. There are two windows in this room so we could each have a window. It would make me so happy. I told Matilda about my idea but she was not at all responsive. She said Father would never agree because of the cost and trouble and mess and all for what, and Mother would say that she had shared her room with her *two* sisters and not even had her own bed and had been quite content. I suggested it to Father all the same when he was in a good mood. He laughed very hard and said, What would I think of next and why did I want a room of my own, did I hate my sister so much? I said no, I only sometimes hated her and that mostly I wanted my own room because the presence of another person unsettles me and makes me irritable. You are a funny little thing, Father said in a strange voice. I said I knew I was and had accepted it. He frowned and said he did not want to hear any more of this kind of thing. That is how it always ends with Father. I wish we were not such a big family. If it were not for the twins there would be enough bedrooms for me to have my own room. I would like to have been an only child, or at the most one of two.

**15 January**

Mother has gone to see Aunt Jemima taking Baby

with her and I have been forced to look after the twins the whole long day because Ivy has left to work in a factory. Mother is horrified. She dreads Gladys leaving too. Matilda has First Aid class all day. I do not know why she needed to give her hair such attention if all she is doing is going to First Aid class. She has bought a bottle of Danderine because she has dandruff and believes it will cure it. She spent hours last night taking a moist cloth with Danderine on it through her hair, one strand at a time. It cost 1s 1d a bottle and frankly I cannot see it has made any difference, but she is convinced her dandruff has gone (it has not) and that her hair is now glossy and wavy. I am glad I am not vain. I have no dandruff either. I believe I will never have children. I do not see the point. They are so much trouble and for what? I took the twins to the park in the morning and let them feed the ducks and run around, hoping to tire them, but it did not tire them and when we came home they were noisier than ever and fighting all the time and doing damage for which I will be blamed. It is a very terrible thing to say but the twins wrecked my life. I do not see why there was any need to have them. Matilda says I am a ninny if I do not understand how babies happen and cannot be helped sometimes if people are married, but she misses the point. I do know what happens but I have heard at school that there are ways of making sure it does not happen. Edna found something in her father's dressing-gown pocket which she said was like a balloon before it is blown up and her brother told her what it was for when she showed it to him. She was very shocked and disgusted and dropped it and could not put it back and her brother did so, saying he did not know why she was looking in her father's dressing-gown pocket. Edna said she was looking for a cough sweet. At any rate, Edna only has one brother. She is so lucky. The twins spoil everything. When Mother told me something nice was going to happen soon I thought she meant that we were at last to have a dog, but it was twins. And then there was Baby, as if twins could not be an end to it.

I am very tired and discontented about my fate in life.

**10 March**

Gladys has given in her notice. Mother is distraught. She says she thought Gladys, unlike Ivy and Pearl, had more sense. Now we will have nobody except Mrs Norris who comes on Fridays to scrub the floors. I don't blame any of the maids. I would rather be anything but a maidservant, especially in a house like ours. Father says that in the present circumstances we will be unlikely to engage new maids and so we must all help in the house. I asked if he included himself and was told not to be impertinent.

**2 April**

Father has read an article about how garden patches can conquer the Germans if they are used to grow vegetables. Instead of importing food, we must grow it, Father says. He started straightaway on our garden, which is not very big. Jack Peel usually comes to do it, but he has joined up and Father has to manage himself. Mother could not believe he was going to dig up the grass and asked where would the twins play, but Father said the grass must go, it was the supreme sacrifice. He dug it all up, peeling the turf off with a spade and then breaking the soil up with a fork. Then he dug holes all over and dropped some silver sand into each hole and then he planted potatoes. Mother dared to ask if it was the right time of year and Father said it was. I could tell he was not sure. When he had finished with the potatoes he planted radishes in between the rows. Mother said had he forgotten that he himself did not care for radishes and neither did anyone else, but Father said it was no time to be faddy and that at least she could make soup. Mother said she had never heard of radish soup and she would rather he planted onions. The garden looks awful now, all muddy and black. Mother cannot let the twins out into it because they jump on the plants and get all filthy. It is altogether a disaster and Mother cannot believe any vegetables will grow.

**4 June**

I had a fight with George today. We are too old to fight, it is undignified, but George provoked me beyond endurance. He says I have no sense of humour but what he did, or rather instructed the twins to do, was not funny. What is there to laugh at when one's plaits are tied to a chair? I was sitting reading at the dining-room table, which has not got comfortable chairs but it is the only quiet room in the house except for my bedroom, and Matilda was there tidying her drawers so noisily, and I had just got to the bit in *Oliver Twist* where Bill Sikes murders Nancy and I was nearly crying and did not hear the twins creep in and tie one plait each to the chair. Half an hour or so later, I am gleefully told, I stood up and dragged the chair with me as I tried to walk. George and the twins were watching and screamed and laughed. The pain in my head was intense and I had to shout and shout to be freed.

## 6 June

Today I got my revenge on George. I know it is petty to want revenge, but all the same I relished it. George could not find his cricket bat. Well, of course he couldn't because I had hidden it. It was almost time for the match and he was frantic. Have you seen my bat, he asked, and I said dear me, no, have you mislaid it, what a pity, you are late already. I then said I would help him search for it, and called for the twins to help too, and we rummaged through the house making a fearful mess. George was almost in tears before I said I knew where it was and that I would only produce it if he apologised for setting the twins to tie my plaits to the chair. He said sorry, and I gave him the bat, which I had hidden in the laundry-room, and he immediately slapped me and said he was not sorry at all, so I snatched back his beastly bat and threw it out of the window. It landed in the water butt and George vows it is ruined. Mother came to see what the commotion was and said we should both be ashamed. I am ashamed, but only slightly.

George isn't, I'm sure.

## 6 August

Father says he cannot come on holiday with us this year, the business will not allow it. They are already short-staffed because of men going to the war and he is training replacements. George cannot come either. There was a fearful row last night because George wants to volunteer. At least, he does not really *want* to, in my opinion, but most of his pals are in uniform and he feels embarrassed not to be. I am sure that is it. Father told him not to be a fool. He asked him, Have you no imagination do you not know what war is? I do not think George does have any imagination whereas I have plenty and I know what Father is talking about. I have read his newspaper, about the trenches and the poison gas and the Germans mowing everyone down and I can see it all in my head. Edna's brother was wounded at a place called Ypres and he told her what it was like and she told me. He has lost his sight in one eye and Edna says he screams at night. I thought I should tell George this but he would not listen.

## 7 August

Father is furious because now Matilda says she does not want to go on holiday, she wishes to join the Voluntary Aid Detachment. Father says he has never heard such selfishness and that her place is at Mother's side in these difficult days when we have lost Ivy as well as Gladys and Pearl, and there is so much to do in the house. He says if Matilda wants to do her bit she can do it right here at Number 25 Victoria Road. Matilda cried and said she was not selfish, that Mrs Pankhurst herself had said women want to fight just as much as men, and Father interrupted her and said he did not want to hear that dratted woman's name. Then Matilda said she had been to a big meeting last month and she had been persuaded it was her *duty* to become a VAD and she wondered at Father not wanting her to do her duty. But it did no good. Father just repeated that her duty was at home. Matilda cried all night, which was very wearing for me, but I bore it well because for once I agreed with Matilda. If I were as old as her I would want to be a VAD even though I do not agree with war and have decided to be a pacifist. The atmosphere in our house is not pleasant. Father scowls and cannot be spoken to and Mother sighs and is very tired and does not want to go on holiday either, but the house is taken so she is bracing herself. Father says he wants us out of London because there are rumours that there will be more Zeppelin raids and it is no place for children. He is going to look into renting the holiday house in Westmorland for the duration of the war. I cannot believe he means it. We have rented that house before. There is *no library* for miles and miles, and no school for me. I would be entirely at the mercy of the twins and Baby.

**12 August**

We are in Westmorland, only Mother and I and the twins and Baby, and I am so unhappy. I cannot think of one single thing to be glad about. It is raining and the house is cold and I have been made to play with the twins for hours and hours. Baby has earache and cries all the time and Mother has been sick and says she depends on me. I do not want to be depended on. I am weighed down with the responsibility and there is no one to share it. I wish Matilda was here. I never thought I would say that. Mother says I ought to be happy because I have my own room here but what good is that when I am tied to the twins and have no chance to be in it. There is no peace or time to read and in any case I must be sparing with what I have to read because there is no hope of getting to a library. I have made *Lorna Doone* last for ages and I do not even like it.

## 13 August

There was a letter from Matilda today. It was addressed to Mother but began dear Mother and Milly so it was partly mine and I was glad she had thought to include me. Her life as a VAD is very hard, just as Father said it would be if she defied him. She rises at 5.30 a.m. and walks to the hospital and works until 8 p.m. or later. She rolls bandages and empties slops and does much other unpleasant menial work but she is glad to do it and feels useful and that is all she wanted to be. The plight of the men in the wards is distressing, with so many of them missing limbs and in great pain, but there is no time to waste being in tears if you are a VAD. Her legs ache but otherwise she is well. Mother says she will get varicose veins with all the standing

27

and suffer from them the rest of her life. I said I did not know how Mother could worry about such a trifle when there is a war being fought and men are losing legs and Mother burst into tears at what she said was my unkind tone.

**1 September**

Father has come to take us home in three days' time. I am vastly relieved, and so I think is Mother because she has not liked it here any more than I have. We have had some fine days since the rain stopped but the twins had chicken-pox and were quite ill and we could not take advantage of the good weather. Father looks very worried and thin. He is afraid that there will soon be new rules and that George will be called up and he will not be able to claim exemption. Even worse, he himself may be eligible for service if the war continues. I was astonished and said, But Father you are surely too old, and he smiled sadly and said I might think so but in fact he is only 42. I have never known Father's age, or Mother's. I thought about it afterwards and felt shocked to realise he and Mother must have married when he was only a little older than George is now. I suppose Mother must have been near Matilda's age. How sad everything seems. What we will do if Father is called upon, I shudder to think. I wish I understood why we are fighting. I have tried to understand but it makes no sense to me.

## 6 September

We are home, hurrah. I am so glad to be back in London I have not complained once about standing in for Ivy as nursemaid to the twins. I am sent to do the shopping now so there is some respite from them, but this is no easy matter. The queues outside every single shop are long and my legs get tired standing. Mother said I was to go to the butcher's first and if possible buy 2 pounds of the best pork sausages, but to take anything if sausages have run out. I did not know what she meant by 'anything' but when I asked her what she meant she was cross and told me to use my intelligence for heaven's sake. I dreaded finding there were no sausages but there were. I hate sausages. I hate meat. It is cruel of Mother to make me go into that loathsome place of slaughter. I almost fainted at the sight of those bloody carcasses swinging from hooks. The knives make me shiver and the dirty aprons are disgusting. It was a relief to go on to the greengrocer and buy fruit and vegetables. My basket was very heavy and I had to stop and put it down often. When I got home Mother was lying down and the twins and Baby were screaming and she said she couldn't stand the noise and I was to take them to the park. My life is one of drudgery but because of the war I am supposed to bear it without complaint.

## 10 September

Mother is expecting! It is too awful. Baby is not yet 1 year old and now there will be another. I am embarrassed and I am angry. I am reminded all the time about the war and now this happens and I would like to remind *them* about the war. What will happen if Father is called up? They should have thought of that. When Mother told me I could not believe it and was horrified. I blushed and wanted to run away. She said she would need me to help her and then she wept a little and said she felt weak and sickly and did not know what she would do without me. I was her treasure. I do not want to be her treasure, or anyone's. I have told no one at school. I am ashamed. It is so careless to have *seven* children. It is too bad.

*       *       *

*These extracts, taken from the very first of Millicent's diaries, give something of the flavour of her personality—outspoken, quite selfish, restless, ambitious and inclined to self-pity. During the rest of 1915, the self-pity gets a little out of hand. She spends pages complaining in her diary of how put-upon she is because of her mother's pregnancy. Her indignation is often so fiercely expressed, and so out of proportion, that it becomes comical. The twins, 7-year-old Albert and Alfred, particularly annoy her— 'sent by some malevolent force to be a burden upon my weary back'—and yet she is obliged to be constantly in charge of them. Michael, the baby, she resents less but she cannot see 'any charm' in him. School provides an escape, but she is not entirely happy there either. There is no mention of its name, or exactly what kind of school it was, but it sounds like a small, fee-paying establishment. No exact location of her home is given either—there are thirty-*

*six Victoria Roads in London—but from internal evidence it was clearly in South London, possibly Peckham. Also not revealed is the nature of her father's business, but he was obviously engaged in either the making or selling of furniture (perhaps both) and was quite prosperous. Millicent is clearly very fond of her father and continues to worry that he will be called up. But it is her brother George who, in the middle of September 1915, goes off to the war and then the tone as well as the content of her diary changes. She says she writes regularly to George and tries to be cheerful.*

\* \* \*

## 6 November

George is still in this country, being trained how to fight. Father says he will be forced to grow up quickly, he is very young and immature for his age. Mother bridled at this and defended her darling son saying he was very loving. Father said not loving enough to write what I would call a decent letter. I agree with Father. George has only written once and his letter was full of food. He wrote that the *grub* was fine, and listed all his meals, every one of them, enthusing over bacon and tomatoes and eggs for breakfast and trays full of bread slices and butter and jam and oat-cakes for tea. He wants cakes sent to him and Mother immediately got out Gladys's recipe book and began making gingerbread, but we had no treacle left and it was essential. I think George thoughtless to ask for cakes.

## 10 January 1916

A letter, at last, from George, only the third in four months, though we have all written to him every single week. He is in France, under canvas, and says he likes it fine. The camp is on sandy soil and in spite of the incessant rain he is dry. He wants cigarettes to be sent and is most particular about what kind. They have to be Three Castles (Star), and sent in a tin box. Apart from that, he only wants butter. He says army butter is frightful stuff. It all sounds so trivial, as though he was at school camp and not in a war. I said so, and Father frowned at me, and made a gesture to indicate I should not say such things in front of Mother. Afterwards, he said George was doing a good job pretending, for Mother's sake, but that he himself was not fooled and he was surprised that I was. I suppose he is right. Things can't be as jolly as George makes them sound.

## 25 January

To our great surprise, another letter from George. He is billeted in a small village back from the firing line. The owner of the house is a voluble French woman. He writes that when she gets in a state, which is often, she rambles away at a terrific speed in a mad, high-pitched voice 'just like Milly when she is in one of her tempers'. My eyes filled with tears as Mother read this out. She was *laughing* as she did so. I swallowed hard and tried to bear this insult bravely.

## 4 February

Mother got a beautiful postcard today from George. It is so pretty. There is a border of pale cream thick paper with little flowers all over it and in the centre there are three pansies embroidered in silk and all around the purple flowers are green leaves. Above this flap, for the embroidery is done on a gauze flap, are the words 'To My Dear Mother' also embroidered, in pale blue, and underneath 'From Your Loving Son'. And that is not all. When the flap is lifted it reveals another card, very small, resting in a kind of pocket. This card has a castle on it but we do not know where this castle is though we studied it for ages. The words 'loving greetings' are printed in ink, and George has written 'from your own boy' beside it. Mother was quite overcome. On the plain side of the card it says *Carte Postale* but though there is space to write George has only written that he is well but the weather not very good, and he trusts we have got his letters. I wonder where George bought this card. Mother examined it closely and there is no doubt the embroidery is genuine and of a high standard. It is strange to think that among all the mud and fighting in France which we hear about someone is making these beautiful cards.

## 1 March

George arrived home today for three days' leave. We were not expecting him until the afternoon and so when the bell rang at eight in the morning and I had to go and open the door I got a great shock when I saw him standing there. I hardly knew it was him, he looks so thin and worn. Worse than that, he looks old, his face all drawn and his cheeks hollow. I stared at him and words would not come and I was for once glad when the twins came shrieking into the hall and saw him and started shouting his name. He picked them up and seemed glad to hug them though never when he lived here did he show them particular affection, being of my opinion with regard to them. Mother was breakfasting in bed but hearing the commotion rose and put on a wrapper and came to the top of the stairs. I was afraid she might collapse when she saw George but though she was startled she made her way carefully downstairs and held out her arms and embraced him. I saw George's face as he beheld her and he was alarmed at her vast size and I'm sure uneasy about touching her. He had breakfast, which I made. I have become quite proficient since Gladys left. I used all the bacon for the week and three precious eggs, and then George went to bed. Mother asked him if he was not going to take a bath but he said he was dog-tired and had dreamed of his bed for weeks and longed to go to it.

### 3 March

George and I and Father have had a long talk about the terrible battle at Verdun. We sat in the drawing-room after dinner when Mother and the children had gone to bed and George and Father drank whisky and smoked. George told us how everything was chaos, orders being first given then cancelled, and no one knowing what was happening and all the time the Germans shelling the trenches and the fear of gas very strong. He said his rifle was not a good one and twice jammed in action but that the second time this had saved his life because he had been obliged to halt and look to his rifle and the soldiers in front of him were killed and he would have been where they were. He said he would not talk of the sights he had seen or the sounds he had heard in front of me, though I begged him to and said I wanted to know and was not afraid to hear. Father sighed a great deal and said it was common knowledge that the war was not being conducted as it should be and it was not going our way.

## 4 March

George's last day at home. He screams in his sleep. I do not know if anyone else heard him but I did. I woke and heard him moaning and then he called out 'No! No!' and screamed and my own heart beat fast and I got out of bed and listened at his door. The door was closed but I opened it and at first thought the room empty but then saw he was on the far side of his bed, hunched on the floor. I went to him and crouched down and stroked his back. He had no jacket on, only trousers, and his skin was wet and sticky with sweat. I do not think he was properly awake. I could not lift him, so I took the pillow from the bed and put it under his head and then wrapped just a sheet over him. Presently, the moaning sounds stopped and he seemed to sleep deeply and I left. In the morning, he said nothing and neither did I. He did not want to leave and we did not want him to leave. Everyone cried, Mother most pitifully. He had hardly left the house with Father before her pains began and I was sent for Mrs Allardyce. She is here now, and the nurse, but all is silent.

## 5 March

At four o'clock this morning my new sister was born, while we were all asleep, even I. I did not intend to sleep, nor did I think I ever would, but I was so very exhausted I could not help it. I slept in the same bed as the twins, with Baby in his cot beside us, fearing that they might waken in the night and try to run in to Mother's. I knew nothing until seven o'clock when Baby woke and I got up and went to the kitchen to make his bottle. It was a shock to find that Father was there standing by the kettle and about to make tea. I have never seen him in the kitchen before. You have a new sister, he said. His tone was not, I thought, joyous. I asked if Mother was well and he said she was well but very tired and that I could go in to see her but must keep the boys out for the moment. I did not know how this could be managed, but Father astonished me by saying he would give Michael his bottle and stay with the boys for a few minutes. I went up to Mother's room half fearful though not knowing why I should half dread seeing her. She was lying propped up on the pillows with her eyes closed but when I tip-toed in she opened them and said 'Milly!' and looked pleased. I went nearer, thinking I must kiss her, and it was not so difficult. She looked pretty, her cheeks not pale as they have been but quite flushed. She pointed to the cradle at her side and I peeped in and saw my new sister who is the smallest baby I have ever seen but with thick yellow downy hair like a chicken's when it is first hatched. The hair was so funny I laughed and Mother said George's hair had been the same. She asked what I thought we should call her and did I care for the name Hope. I said no. Mother said Father had suggested it, thinking of the war and how we must all hope. He had suggested Faith, and Mercy, too. I said I disliked symbolic names. Mother said she had wondered about Helena, or Grace. I like both. I did not go to school today, of course. There was too much to do and no one else to do it. How I longed for Ivy to be still here, and Gladys. Mother has the maternity nurse only for three days and was fortunate to get her. Nurse Tranter is old or she would be working among the wounded in the hospitals. Matilda has managed to get two days' leave and comes to take over from Nurse and after that I do not know what we will do. I cannot stay off school forever though Father does not seem to think my absences important. I wish more than ever that I were in Matilda's shoes and already away from home.

## 8 March

The baby is to be named Grace Helena. Matilda came today and I was very thankful. She has come to look after Mother and not us but she has made herself generally useful and we have not quarrelled at all. She looks different but I cannot put my finger on why or how. She is happier, I think. She

37

says the work is very hard but that it is rewarding. I think that must be it. My work in this house is very hard but it is not rewarding, it is tedious and I do not like looking after the boys and trying to cook meals and do all the things Mother has been obliged to do since all the help left. I am the wrong age for this war. I said this to Father and he was cross and said that may be true but that I was the right sex. I suppose that is true. I would not like to be George and if I were a boy and nearly 16 I should be very near the age of being called up if this war goes on. I think often about that. I am a pacifist but I do not think I could be a conscientious objector all the same. It would not seem right. I am in a muddle about it.

\*         \*         \*

*Millicent was in a muddle about lots of things throughout the summer of 1916. She agonises over religion, and what she believes, wondering if in fact she believes in anything at all but afraid to say this out loud, and she is suspicious about whether there is such a thing as true romantic love. Her teacher, Miss Bailey, is very fond of Robert Browning's poetry and Millicent learns yards of it while doubting that any man can mean what is said. One verse in particular irritates her, beginning:* The moth's kiss, first! / Kiss me as if you made believe / You were not sure, this eve *(from 'In a Gondola'). Miss Bailey thinks it is beautiful but Millicent thinks it is silly and challenges her teacher, who gives her a disorder mark for impertinence and—this hurt more—insensitivity. Millicent collects many disorder marks, all of them, according to her, grossly unfair. She hates the school*

38

*uniform (long black woollen stockings, long-sleeved, high-necked winceyette blouses whose white collar and cuffs soiled easily, black serge skirts and black beaver hats in winter or hard 'straw-bashers' in summer) and is always in trouble for not wearing it properly. But she is obviously, as she records without a trace of false modesty, clever, regularly having her name read out on Friday mornings in Assembly for gaining more than five stars for her written work (stars were only given for exceptionally good work and only girls with five or more had their names read out). There is a great deal about the content of lessons in the diary at this time and very little about the domestic life of the King household. Her aunt Jemima (Aunt J.), her mother's eldest sister (aged 42), a spinster, arrived to help out the week Grace was born, to Millicent's intense relief. Then, in July, the diary is solely concerned with George and her already noticeable taste for the dramatic is given free rein.*

\*　　　\*　　　\*

## 2 July

Father says a great battle has begun on the Somme and he is sure George's regiment will be part of it, but there is no way of knowing for certain. He told me not to mention this to Mother or she will worry more than she already does. I could hardly get on with reading *The Mill on the Floss* for thinking about George. Half the time at school now girls are weeping because some relative has died and it has become so usual hardly any notice is taken. It is very dispiriting. What is the point of anything. Miss Bailey talked to us about School Certificate and the importance of the examination for our future, but what future is that? I tried to talk to Father about my going to college to be a teacher and he said no plans could be made in the present circumstances and I should not count on going to college. I dared to ask what these circumstances were apart from the continuation of the war and he said there was no apart, everything was to do with the war and his business being affected and money scarce. So it seems that there may be no money to pay for me to go to college. My head was spinning to hear this. I felt resentful. I burn still with resentment. I *will* go to college.

## 4 July

News has come that George is alive but wounded and we are all frantic to know the worst. It came in the post, on a Field Service postcard. I was the first to see it when I collected the letters and though it was addressed to Father and Mother I read it, being an open postcard, and so was the first to know George was wounded. I stared at what was printed on the card for a long time, not understanding why so much seemed to be crossed out. On the top it explained that nothing was to be written except the date and the soldier's name and if anything else was, then it would be destroyed. Then underneath was printed 'I am quite well', 'I have been admitted to hospital sick/wounded', 'I am being sent to base', 'I have received your letter' and two or three other choices. George had crossed everything out except 'I have been admitted to hospital wounded and am going on well'. His signature was very shaky and hardly looked like his. I took it in to Mother and Father and Father read it first and said, Thank God he is alive, before reading it to Mother. He laid great emphasis on 'am going on well'. Father was right, his regiment was in the front line of the battle at the Somme which was a victory for our side but at great cost. First Mother wept with gratitude that George had survived then she wept with fear at what his injuries may be. Father has gone to see if he can find out more but I do not know where. He says we must prepare ourselves for George having lost a limb or his sight or something equally terrible. I try to imagine George without a leg. What will he do? He will not take easily to having only one leg and not any more able to play the games he loves so much. I hope if he has a limb missing it will be his left arm which would be inconvenient but better than a leg. I see him in my mind's eye without a leg and then without an arm and I am prepared. I will try to be a good sister and help him and never complain.

## 6 July

George has not lost a leg or an arm and he is not blind. News came today that he was shot but that he was very lucky for the bullet missed his heart and his lungs and went into his spleen which has been removed. I do not know what a spleen is but Matilda says it can be done without and she should know. She came home just for an hour or two when she heard we were expecting news of George's condition. George also has a broken arm from how he fell when he was shot. I cannot help wondering if my steel pen saved him from more serious injury, but I have said nothing. He will be in the field hospital for some time yet before being sent home. Mother gives thanks all the time for his safety and hopes that by the time he is recovered the war will be over and he need not go back to the slaughter. Thousands and thousands have been killed at the Somme. We are preparing a parcel to send to George.

**20 July**

We are not going on holiday this year. I am not sorry. Everything is dreary here but it would be more dreary in the country. The reason is that George is expected home soon and we must of course be here to look after him. He is still very weak because he lost a lot of blood and will be in bed a good deal so his room is to be moved downstairs into Father's study. Aunt J. and I cleared Father's books away into the dining-room and Father moved his desk into the drawing-room with the help of Mr Baty next door and they have brought George's bed down and set it up there. We have tried to make it look as much like his old room as possible. I am going to move upstairs and have his old room which will be bliss because sharing with Aunt J. is worse than sharing with Matilda ever was. I hate to see her undress and cannot always avoid the unpleasant sight. She is so fat, her corset is huge, and she will insist on demanding my assistance to unfasten it. She says her fingers are stiff and cannot manage the tiny hooks whereas mine are nimble. She will have to get Mother to help her now. I will be too far away up another flight of stairs and she will not bother, I hope, to call me down. I am ashamed of my feelings towards Aunt J. She is so kind and cheerful and loves us all so much and will do anything for us. Mother says she was very pretty when she was my age but I cannot believe this. I search and search in her lined face for any trace of prettiness and cannot find it. Her nose is too big and can never have been small and she has no lips. Her lips cannot just have disappeared. I feel sorry for her but pity does not do away with irritation at her fussiness. I wonder if it is not being married and not having children that has made Aunt J. so pathetic. I cannot see that she has anything in her life to make it worth living. I suppose she has her garden, and her tortoise.

## 5 August

George is home. Father and I collected him from the station and brought him home in a cab though we had trouble procuring one so great was the press of people also wanting one. It was a long wait for the troop train on a very crowded platform. I held Father's hand for fear of becoming separated. When the sound of the train was heard approaching a cheer went up and my heart began to beat very fast with excitement. There were soldiers hanging out of every window as the train came to a standstill and some of them, nearly all of them in fact, had bandages on their heads or were

43

wearing slings. Then the doors opened and the crowd grew suddenly quiet when the stretcher-bearers began bringing out the badly wounded. People began crying when they saw their loved ones lying there. One woman with a little girl of the twins' age rushed forward to a stretcher upon which lay a man covered up to the chin with a blanket and when she kissed him and held the child up he threw back the blanket without speaking showing his two stumps where his legs had been and she screamed and screamed. There were such scenes all along the platform and I began to feel faint. The stretcher-bearers shouted 'Clear the way, clear the way' but people were desperate to find their relatives and would not be orderly. We began to think George was not after all on the train when, far down its length, I saw his face at a carriage window. He was just sitting there, his face pressed up against it, looking helpless. We went onto the train which was by then almost empty and at first he did not seem to know us and was startled and shrank back into his seat, cowering away from us. Then when he recognised us he began to cry, the tears rolled down his bony face and would not stop though he smiled too. We had to help him up, he was so thin and weak, and I carried his kit-bag while Father guided him off the train, half carrying him. It took a long time with many stops to get to the cab rank. George had to sit on his kit-bag while we waited and he shivered all the time although it was not in the least a cold day. I crouched down beside him and took off my cardigan and wrapped it round his neck. It was my new mauve cardigan and looked silly against his uniform but he pressed my hand and said he was glad of the warmth at his

44

neck. He slept once he was in the cab and it seemed cruel waking him when we arrived home. Mother was standing on the steps with Baby in her arms and Michael clinging to her skirt and the twins dashing up and down the steps waving their flags. George was half asleep and overcome. When she saw him, Mother rushed down the steps and pushed Baby into my arms and embraced George and cried and cried. Michael fell trying to follow her and cut his head and bawled and the twins ran into the road in their excitement and almost went under the wheels of the departing cab. I was glad when we were all indoors. George soon went to bed and Mother sat at his side all day, sewing, and I of course had to look after the boys and Baby. There was such a strange atmosphere in the house, not at all joyful.

## 15 August

Today George went out for the first time. I walked with him to the park. We walked slowly and he held my arm, still being unsteady on his feet. He walks like an old man. Mother has been feeding him up but he is still so thin though he devours everything she gives him. His arm is mended but it is not entirely straight because it was not set properly in the plaster but George says it works well enough. The doctor says it is only a matter of time now and that George will soon be his old self but I cannot see that happening. He has nightmares all the time and now the whole house hears him and his screams frighten the twins and Michael. Mother goes in to him and finds him drenched in perspiration and crouching under his bed. There is no need to ask what his nightmares are about. I tried to talk to him today on our walk but he does not seem to want to talk. He has become very silent, not at all like the old George. We sat on a bench in the park, beside the duck pond, and he took some pleasure, I think, from watching children feeding the ducks. It was a lovely day and the water and sky were very blue and the children bright-faced and noisy and happy. George closed his eyes after a bit and I thought he was dozing off as he often does but when I said his name, to check, he said he was just feeling the sun on his face. We met Angela Smythe on our way home and she stopped and exclaimed at seeing George and asked how he was, very eagerly. But George almost ignored her though he used to be sweet on her and once took her to a dance and said he thought she was the prettiest girl there though I myself never thought her pretty. Poor Angela was most put out and I whispered that George was still ill and she looked very concerned. I do not know what is going to happen to him.

## 1 September

George had an army medical today. Father took him to the place where they give them and stayed with him. There had been little doubt that George would be declared unfit for active service but still it was a relief when this was confirmed. He had a strange outburst when he returned home. When Father was telling us that for the moment George was unfit, George started shouting, Not for the moment! For ever! For ever! I will never go back! Never! I will top myself first! Then he cried and would not stop and it was queer and embarrassing. I do not know if I am the only one embarrassed. Is it wrong to feel like that? Also, and this is dreadful to write here, I feel a little ashamed of him. He has suffered more than I can know but he is home and alive and yet he shows no appreciation or gratitude for that. Sometimes I think he is not trying to get better. We all rush to do everything for him and perhaps that is not healthy. I would like to discuss this with Matilda but I am never alone with her on her visits and they are very brief and it is too delicate a subject to bring up without being sure of privacy.

## 10 September

School again, and how glad I am to be there. There is a new girl in our class, Mabel Crowthorne. Her father was killed at the Somme and her mother has now moved to live with her sister, also a widow. I was asked to look after Mabel and found I liked her immediately which surprised me. She is serious, like me, and loves reading. She lives three roads away from us so we walked home part of the way and we have arranged to meet at 8.30 a.m. on the corner of the main road. I felt quite light-hearted for a change when I left her.

\*　　　　　\*　　　　　\*

*The diary for the remainder of 1916 and into 1917 is devoted almost exclusively to Millicent's growing*

47

*friendship with Mabel Crowthorne. Apart from both being serious and voracious readers, it soon emerges that the main attraction for Millicent is Mabel's feelings of resentment at her lot in life which mirror her own. But whereas Millicent has no clear goal, Mabel does. She wants to be a lawyer. Millicent wonders in her diary if this would be fun and then chastises herself for being so frivolous. Mabel has no interest in fun. She is politically minded and has always bought* The Suffragette *(each Friday, price 1d) ever since she was allowed pocket money. Millicent borrows her old copies, but finds them hard going. Secretly, she prefers the trashy, brightly coloured women's magazines left behind by her sister. She knows that though her ambition is the equal of Mabel's, her sense of purpose is not. Nor can she quite scorn clothes and self-adornment the way her friend does. There are some telling reflections on how spotty Mabel is, how ungainly, how unfortunately short-sighted, how badly fitting her clothes are, 'so it is lucky' comments Millicent 'that she does not care how she looks and thinks the state of one's mind more important than one's appearance'. She does not doubt that Mabel will one day be a judge, 'whereas what shall I be, I have no firm intent'.*

\*     \*     \*

## 20 April 1917

Dreadful, dreadful news. Mabel was in a great state about it, even to the point of tears and I do not blame her. Her mother says she must leave school in July because her father's money has run out and

48

she must go to work in an office to earn some at once. Mabel had been crying half the night, her eyes were red-raw, and I felt truly sorry for her. It is a tragedy, all her plans shattered. Miss Bailey says she has a chance of Cambridge and would be the first person our school has ever sent there if she were to be accepted. I wonder why Miss Bailey has never said to me that I might go to Cambridge. I know she has never liked me, but it seems queer, and unjust. But I have said nothing to Mabel. At least I know I can train to be a teacher even if I would like to aim higher, but Father would not stand for it. I was so afraid there would be no money to pay the college fees after he had said I was not to count on it that I did not dare ask if I could go to university. I know he only believes in higher education for girls if it leads to definite employment as soon as possible. I am lucky business has picked up enough to make Father less worried about money.

## 28 April

Mabel's mother has bought her a typewriter. It is not new but is in good working order. Mabel is to teach herself how to type so that she will be able to get a job in an office as soon as term ends. Her mother says that since Mabel is a proficient piano player learning the keys of the typewriter will be easy for her. This makes Mabel angry because there is no comparison. But she is doing her best to learn from the chart which came with the machine. She showed me the exercises she does and I tried them. It is much more difficult than it looks. Each hammer needs to be struck quite hard to make an impression. It took me ages simply to write my name. Father says Mabel's mother is very wise and that she has the right idea because, with so many men at the war, offices need girls to type and Mabel will get a job easily. He made my blood run cold by asking if I had not thought myself of becoming a typist and earning money straightaway after leaving school instead of more studying. I said no, very firmly.

**2 May**

I stayed at Mabel's house for the night which was not the pleasant experience I had hoped. Her mother did not seem to want me to be there although she must have agreed or Mabel would not have invited me. I think Mabel is very lonely. There is only her mother and her aunt and her aunt's son who is five and not much good as a cousin. The house is very quiet and tidy, even the little boy does not run around or shout like our twins but then he must miss his father, I suppose. Both Mrs Crowthorne and her sister wear black from head to toe. Mabel talks about her father sometimes and it is obvious she loved him very much. She has shown me photographs and he looks a kindly man. He was an officer and led his men into battle and was killed in an instant. He was awarded a medal posthumously for gallantry but that is no comfort to Mabel. Her mother gets a pension, but it is not enough to pay for Mabel's further education, or so her mother tells her. She says she feels the war has wrecked her life and all her plans are useless. I do not know what to say to comfort her. She says she envies me and I do not like the feeling this gives me. It makes me uncomfortable to be envied. I wonder what I would do if I were in Mabel's shoes but there is not much point in wondering because there would be nothing that I could do. What can a girl in Mabel's circumstances do? Nothing. She is stuck. She must do what she is told.

**26 May**

There has been a bombing raid. Five people killed and ninety-five injured. Father has begun again saying we must get the children out of London but so far has made no plans. He wishes the Americans would go into action now that they have committed themselves. Mabel and I have heard that there is to be a rally organised by the Women's Peace League and we intend to try to go if at all possible. We would like to work for the League if we knew how and were not thought too young. Our mothers would not give us permission to go to any such rally so we must keep our intentions secret. We are allowed to go to the National Gallery if we go together and so we will pretend that is what we are doing when we go to the rally if it is held in Trafalgar Square which is where most rallies are held. I do so want to *do* something in this war to make people see it is useless and wrong. Mabel has stopped getting *The Suffragette* and now buys *The War Paper for Women*, which also comes out on a Friday and costs 1*d*. She says it is the official paper of the United Suffragists and that the Suffragists are more sensible than the Suffragettes because they want to work for the vote within the law. Mabel is so smart.

**6 June**

Mabel told me her aunt is going to a seance to get in touch with her husband. Mabel's mother is scandalised and has tried to convince Amy (that is her sister's name) that she will be hoodwinked and that there is no such thing as a spirit world but Amy is determined. Mabel says that her Aunt Amy knows someone who went to this medium and was put in touch with her son who was killed at Ypres. She had not told the medium her son's age or his regiment or where he was killed or when, so all these details proved it really was her son. The medium spoke to her in his voice and he told her he was happy and in good company and she was not to grieve and now she is greatly comforted. Mabel's mother is scornful but Mabel herself, to my surprise, is tempted to believe in spiritualism. She asked what I thought and I said I would like to believe in it but would take some convincing. But I would like to go to a seance and so would Mabel. Her Aunt Amy has suggested Mabel might accompany her but Mabel is afraid of her mother's anger and does not see how she could keep such a thing secret.

**10 June**

Mabel's Aunt Amy has been to the seance but came back bitterly disappointed though very willing to talk about it. Nothing happened. She told Mabel the medium was a very coarse sort of woman whom right from the start she did not take to though great claims are made for her. She had her hair in a net. The seance was held in the basement of a house in Suffolk Place and though it was a fine evening the room was very cold and dark with shutters closed and heavy velvet curtains drawn over the windows. It was lit by one candle set on a small table and beside the table the medium sat on a straight-backed chair which Aunt Amy said looked very uncomfortable and may have accounted for why the medium squirmed all the time and could not settle. The house belongs to Mrs Hatch, who has lost her husband and all three of her sons to the war but who speaks to them regularly through this medium and they are all well though one has a cold at the moment. Attendance is by invitation only and soft-soled shoes are requested to be worn. There were ten people there, all women, and some were weeping even before the medium was brought in. There was music playing in another room, a harp, or so Aunt Amy thought, but otherwise no sound. Mrs Hatch said everyone must close their eyes and keep very still and think hard of a loved one who had passed over. Aunt Amy did as she was told and after a while the medium began moaning and Aunt Amy peeped between her eyelids and saw she was rocking. Then in an odd, very gruff voice the medium called, Jack! I have Jack and he is looking for ! and she was interrupted by a woman calling out, Me! He is looking for me, for Cissie!, and the medium went on, Cissie, yes, he is looking for Cissie and wants her to know he is thinking of her and of how he left her, in the state he did, and this woman cried, Oh! I knew he knew, I knew it, oh thank God he knows about our baby. Aunt Amy said this is how it went on and that even she, hopeful though she was and ready to believe, even she could see the trickery. She will not go again, she feels worse than ever now and is ashamed. Father says these seances are everywhere now and that they should be stopped. He asked if Mabel's aunt had had to pay anything but I did not know and would not like to ask. If she did, it makes the whole thing worse.

## 1 July

The examinations are finished but I do not feel as happy as I should because I do not think I have done brilliantly in every subject and I may not after all get a distinction which I want so badly. Mabel probably will. She has studied so hard even though there is no point when she is doomed to office work. She says she likes to study and that it is worth doing well for its own sake surely and that one day in the future it may do her some good to have matriculated well. I do admire Mabel. My maths will have let me down. I have no doubts about the other subjects but mathematics have always been a problem, alas. It is not fair that a poor performance in one subject can spoil one's chances of a distinction overall. Mabel is good at maths. Her grandfather was an accountant and she imagines she has inherited his facility with numbers.

## 2 July

Mabel has got a job! In only one day. She went for an interview this morning, feeling very nervous and not knowing what to wear, not that she has much choice. Even Mabel's best clothes are rather shabby though I would never comment on them. In the end she wore her grey school skirt and a pale blue blouse she got for Christmas and a black velvet jacket of her mother's. The jacket, needless to say, does not fit her, with her mother being much bigger. I walked with her to the Town Hall and felt sorry for how she looked but her appearance did not tell against her. They gave her a typing test first which she said was easy and she did it in a trice and the result was perfect. Then she had to read a letter in a very difficult hand and that was harder but she understood every word except one which she had to guess and luckily her guess was correct. She waited with four other girls and then after a bit was called into an office where a man asked her questions which she said were an insult to her intelligence though she could not remember exactly what they were. She expected to be told they would let her know and that she would then be dismissed but they told her to wait again and afterwards offered her the situation. She starts work in a month's time.

## 3 July

I thought all night about Mabel getting that job. I do not envy her and know I would hate to have to give up dreams of college and go to work in an

55

office but still she will be earning money when I will not and this will give her an independence I will not have for years. She will be a working girl and it makes me feel somehow inferior. I dare not say any of this to anyone, especially not Mabel who would think me very ungrateful when I have all the opportunities she does not. Of course, almost all of Mabel's money will go to her mother and aunt, for her upkeep, but she is to have 2s a week to herself and later 2s 6d, which is not nothing. She is going to save it and maybe one day pay her own way through college. I am sure Mabel could win a scholarship. Miss Bailey said she would inquire, but Mabel said even a scholarship would not be enough and she would rather not know about one at the moment.

**10 July**

Father says I am going to cost him a fortune. He did not say this jokingly either, but with a frown and crossly. It is because my book list arrived today from Goldsmiths' College and it is very long and the books are expensive. Father says he does not see why I cannot use books from the library but he has not been in our public library for years and he does not know that its stock is very limited. He says I must try to decide which are absolutely necessary and then attempt to procure second-hand copies. He said I could spend Saturdays going round the second-hand shops in Charing Cross Road and look at the barrows of books in Gray's Inn, but Mother immediately spoke up and reminded him there was a war on and the centre of London was a dangerous place. I think Father was a little ashamed. He said to make a copy of my book list and he will look himself. Then he said maybe it was something George could do, it would give him some purpose because he no longer seemed to have any though he was quite well. Mother flushed and said on the contrary he was not quite well and had Father forgotten that at the last medical they had declared him permanently unfit for further active service because his lungs had been damaged by the mustard gas. Father said, Slightly, and Mother said, What? and Father repeated that George's lungs were only said to be *slightly* damaged but not enough to incapacitate him in civilian life. There was an atmosphere. Mother knows that Father thinks George should, as he puts it, stop lounging around. It is a year since he was invalided home and he still mopes about the house and, Father says, he cannot do that forever. At this point Mother usually weeps.

## 15 July 1917

My birthday. Sixteen today. I used to long to be 16 but now it does not seem so wonderful. I thought at 16 that I would be free of childish restraints and able to enjoy my own life and do what I wanted, but it has not turned out like that. I am not as chained to this house as I was once, because Aunt J. does such a lot, and has even found a girl to help, but still I cannot count on much time to myself and worst of all I have lost George's room since he moved back into it and am once more sharing with Aunt J. which is almost unendurable. I asked Father to let me have his study but he said it had only been made into a bedroom as an emergency measure for George and it had been very inconvenient, was certainly not to be given up to me. I am worse off than when I was 13. And I do not have the fun I had expected at 16. I do not mean having a beau or any such thing. I have no interest in boys. And I do not wish to go to dances even if there were any to go to, but all the same I should like some fun and there is no fun because of this war. Everything is dreary. No one talks of anything but how there is no food to be got and all supplies are short, and who has been killed or wounded. I am tired of it. I know this is a very selfish attitude but I cannot help it. It has been a miserable birthday though Mother did her best and managed to get hold of the ingredients to make a cake which was very nice. Baby loved the candles.

## 18 July

I wish, this year, that we *were* going on holiday. Mabel, before she starts her job, has gone with her mother to a cousin's farm in Devon and I miss her. I do not fancy a farm holiday, but I would like to be out of London at the moment. I would like to go somewhere exciting like Paris or Rome, except all of Europe is spoiled by this war. It is so hard always having to tell myself that I am lucky to be alive and to have all my family alive when I simply do not feel lucky. Mother is always reminiscing about how perfectly lovely it was to be sixteen and what a good time she and her sisters had. My generation know none of that. It is beastly to have been born in 1901. I am very sorry for myself, which I know is wrong but I cannot help it.

\*　　　　\*　　　　\*

*Millicent's gloom continues throughout the summer of 1917 but lifts in the autumn when she starts at Goldsmiths' College, then the largest teacher training college in the country. She is a day student, one of those without a free place, and her father pays £14 for her tuition and £7 for her dinners (which have to be taken). There are 314 women enrolled in October 1917, and only 17 men, all studying for a two-year certificate of education which will entitle them to teach in an elementary school. To Mr King's relief, men and women are kept strictly apart, with separate entrances and common rooms. Lectures continue all day from 9.30 to 5 p.m. Millicent is very young to be allowed to enrol but perhaps because the previous year has seen the lowest enrolment ever since the college's foundation in 1891 (though it was not until 1904 that it became an official teacher-training college affiliated to London University) her youth is overlooked. She has, at any rate, the necessary qualifications, having matriculated not with the distinction she craved (and Mabel gained) but with merit. She finds the work hard, much harder than at school, but at the same time is excited to be at College.*

\*     \*     \*

## 15 October

I have so much to do that I have little time to write in this diary which is ironic because I actually have something of interest to record. Goldsmiths' is such a splendid place, the very buildings I mean. I have never seen the colleges at Oxford or Cambridge but surely they cannot be more grand. I said this to Father and he roared with laughter and said there was no comparison and that I could have no understanding or appreciation of architecture if I fancied Goldsmiths' so magnificent. I thought it was very unkind of him to say so. Why can new buildings not be as beautiful as the very old? Father said it was not worth arguing about and that one day, when I have been to Oxford and Cambridge, I will understand. Well, I feel very proud to be educating myself in such surroundings though I am overawed too and keep getting lost because the corridors are so long and look the same and I am always having to ask my way which can be embarrassing. I wish I was not so very small. I look positively childlike compared to the other students and some of them treat me like a little girl which is infuriating. I know I do not look as if I could ever be a teacher but I mean to be a good one.

## 18 October

There is a girl called Phyllis who has made friendly overtures. I am not good at making friends so I am always glad when I don't have to. Phyllis is very attractive and lively and a bit noisy. She was reprimanded yesterday for talking in a lecture and was not a bit put out whereas I would have been mortified. She is a day student too and pays her own fees so we are in the same situation. We both wish we were boarders living in one of the hostels, especially Surrey Hostel because the girls there seem to have such fun and form quite a clique. It would be heaven not to have to go home to Grace crying and Michael shouting and the twins running around like wild beasts, but I must not complain. I could be Mabel, stuck in an office. I hardly dare meet Mabel now. She asks me about Goldsmiths' and is so envious. I think it would be cruel to tell her how I love it so I just say it is terrifically hard work. I do not mention the fun we sometimes have, as we did yesterday, when somehow a dog got into the lecture room and grabbed Miss Spalding's notes and we all gave chase and ran ourselves ragged trying to catch it. It was the loveliest dog, a spaniel, and it thought it was a game and we were laughing so much we kept falling over. Eventually, it was cornered, and I was the one able to get the notes out of its mouth. They were all soggy and ruined but Miss Spalding was sporting about it.

## 19 October

Phyllis has invited me to go home with her tomorrow. Not for tea, though. She said her mother does not understand about tea. I don't know what that means but didn't like to ask. She has a brother at home at the moment. He is called Tom and has been wounded twice in the war, once at Verdun, and again at the third battle of Ypres where he lost an arm from the elbow down. I imagine he will be in an even worse state than George and I am prepared.

## 20 October

Phyllis took me home with her yesterday. Her mother, it turns out, is American though she has lived in England since she married Phyllis's father. I was surprised by their home which is not a house but an enormous flat in a block. There is no dining-room at all, the drawing-room does for everything. I cannot describe it properly except to say it is quite unlike a conventional drawing-room. It is one huge, beautiful room with big settees and tables with books on and a massive desk and it is altogether more like a stage setting. I don't know why I am writing so much about the flat, which Phyllis's mother calls an apartment, when the people were even more interesting and worthy of comment. Phyllis's mother is called Carrie and is girlish. She and Phyllis could pass for sisters easily. She smokes, which my mother would find very shocking and which I did not altogether approve of myself, though Carrie (she said she would not answer to Mrs Hart) makes smoking look elegant. Mr Hart is in the navy. He is Welsh. They have a proper house too, in Wales. In civilian life he is a doctor who specialises in tropical diseases. Then there are two sons, William who is also in the navy and was just finishing at Oxford when war was declared and Tom who was just about to go there. They must be a very clever family. Carrie was very friendly and asked about my family and as usual I was embarrassed having to say I was one of seven children but she exclaimed how lovely and seemed to mean it. I said it was not at all lovely but she only laughed. Then Tom came in. Because Phyllis had told me about his arm I was prepared to find he would be like George and very morose but he was not. He seemed very cheerful, unless it was for show before a stranger. It is his left arm, which is lucky. Phyllis had told me he is to have an artificial limb fitted but that it cannot be done yet and that anyway he says he does not know if he wants one. He is bored and wishes he could return to France and the fighting which I found extraordinary but I kept quiet about George. We all sat around and had cocktails made by Carrie. Cocktails are much nicer than tea. I don't know what was in them but they looked so pretty in delicate, wide glasses and they tasted nice, though the taste may have come from the cherries floating in them. Afterwards, Tom said he would see me to my bus and I protested there was no need but he said he wanted some air. We walked together to the stop and he stood with me chatting very amiably. I have to confess that I enjoyed standing there with a young man instead of on my own. He was wearing his army greatcoat and I was pleased about that too which I know very well tells me I wanted to be seen with a soldier.

## 28 October

There have been four successive air-raids over London and it has felt dangerous going to and from college. Mother worries if I am not home directly and so I have resisted Phyllis's invitations to go home with her again though I would like to. I should invite her here but I cannot bear to. It is not just the thought of how trying all the children are but it is this house. It is stifling, and crowded and the rooms are so small and everything in them ordinary and mostly shabby. Phyllis would find it claustrophobic. It may be that I am a snob.

## 15 November

The newspapers are saying that peace is really in the air at last but they have said it before and it has not been true. Father says, as he is always saying, once the Americans join the action, which should be soon, the prospect of victory will be real. Tom says the same, though he does not like the impression (even if he is half American) this might give that the war cannot be won without them. I cannot understand how he is so untouched by all the horror he has been through. He says he is not untouched and that he relives terrible things he has seen all the time and he will never forget the suffering he has witnessed but that all the same he is alive and well and he has the rest of his life to live and it does no good to always be looking back and that for the sake of his friends who have been killed he thinks it his duty to be as cheerful as he can. I wish George thought like that.

## 29 November

Tom has asked me to a dance next month. I thought Father might refuse me permission to go, especially as he has never met Tom, but Mother persuaded him by saying she would ring his mother. I don't know what Carrie will think of that. The dance is to celebrate a friend's 21st birthday. This friend is one of those soldiers granted a whole two weeks' leave because he has served a full year in France. I did not tell Tom I have never been to a dance in my entire life and I do not know how to dance properly. Miss Lewin taught us some dance steps at school in games lessons when it was too wet to go out but I am in a panic that I will not even remember how to waltz. Phyllis is going too and I am sure she will be an expert at quicksteps and every other sort. And I have nothing, *nothing*, to wear. What can I wear? Mother is as concerned as I am. It makes her tearful to think I have no dress in which I can go to a proper dance. She has looked out all her old dresses and thinks something might be done with a white silk gown she had made before the war for a club dinner she went to with Father, but I will *not* wear white, it is too childish. I look infantile as it is. Mother says she has never heard of anything more absurd and that white is the proper colour for young girls. I would like to wear something bright instead. Aunt J. asked why did I not have the white silk remade and wear it with a blue bolero and sash. She has a royal-blue silk jacket which she said I could give to the dressmaker to see if it would make a bolero and so I took it to Mrs Walshingham with the white silk and she laughed and said she could make ten boleros out of Aunt J.'s jacket for someone my size. So that is what I am to wear, the white silk restyled and a blue bolero and sash. I don't know what I will look like. The only shoes possible are black and will look all wrong. It is all such a bother. I am not the right sort of girl to be going to a dance. I said to Tom it did not seem right to be going to a party when we are at war and he said that kind of attitude made him angry and that on the contrary having a jolly time was important and good for morale and that it was just a pity everyone was not afforded the opportunity.

## 20 December

The dance is over. It upset me.

## 21 December

I don't know why I wrote that the dance upset me. I think I was just very tired and felt funny after all the unaccustomed excitement. I am not used to being among people of the type who were there, quite well-off people I now realise. They all seemed perfectly comfortable to be dancing to a band and having such rich food to eat. There was very little to tempt a vegetarian. I cannot think where the hams and chickens came from and indeed do not like to puzzle my brain over it for fear of the answer. I suppose the trouble was that I was out of place and overawed. I hate to think I may have looked it. I know I was quiet most of the night and not laughing and roaring like Phyllis and the others who all seemed to be let in on some huge joke I did not share. I managed the dancing fairly well, though. Tom is not much good at it either and was content to smooch about. Phyllis is a brilliant dancer as I knew she would be. She danced with practically every man there. She looked lovely in a silver sheath dress which had sequins all over and glittered when she moved. She said it was her mother's dress and that it had not needed to be altered. I felt dowdy. I wanted to be the life and soul of the dance and I was not. Then afterwards, Tom and I walked all the way home, to their flat of course, because it had been agreed between our mothers that I would stay with Phyllis to avoid the bother of getting home. It was a very cold, clear night though not snowing. The air was frosty and beautiful, and the stars were gorgeous. We held hands, with gloves on, and it felt nice. I was glad to have left the dance and apologised to Tom for not being much fun there. He said he was sorry I had not enjoyed it more and I said it was as I had suspected. I was not a dancing sort of girl. He squeezed my hand. When we got to his home there was no one else yet there. His mother was out with an old friend and Phyllis still at the dance. I felt apprehensive and thought how Mother and Father would not approve. I thought I should go to Phyllis's room and go to bed but it seemed so rude to leave Tom like that. He put on some record on the gramophone they have and asked me if I would like a drink. I said some cocoa or Bournvita would be nice if they had any and he laughed and said he didn't mean a nursery drink, he meant a proper drink. I said I had drunk enough at the dance where I had had champagne for the first time in my life. He came over to where I had sat myself down and said I was so sweet and would I slap his face if he kissed me. I was a coward and said nothing. He put his good arm round me and gave me a very gentle kiss and said, First dance, first champagne, first kiss, and though I liked the kiss I did not like his saying that. It made me feel like a baby. I am quite sure it was not *his* first kiss. Then Phyllis arrived home with a young man called Arthur who goes back to France in two days' time. They started kissing on one of the settees, in front of us, which I did not like. I said goodnight to Tom and went to bed. It was ages before Phyllis came to bed. I pretended to be asleep.

**2 January 1918**

Aunt J. is going home tomorrow. I don't know whether she wants to or not. She shut her little house up to answer Mother's call and I think she may be a little worried about how she will find it though there have been no bombs anywhere in that area. She says she is tired, and no wonder, with all she has done here, and at her age. But Mother says that with my help and Dora's, the girl Aunt J. has found, she can manage and that Aunt J. deserves a rest. I hope and pray she will not expect me to pick up where Aunt J. leaves off. I will be at college all day so cannot help then and I must study at night and cannot be expected to put Grace or Michael or the twins to bed. I feel sorry for Mother but not sorry enough to want to take on any of her burdens especially when they are of her own creation. I know that makes me seem hard but surely Mother could have limited herself to three children at the most. I will never have more than two, if I have any at all, and I have no plans to do so, quite the reverse needless to say.

## 11 January

College began again and I was glad. I have not seen or heard from Phyllis all this holiday but I know she has been away somewhere in the country. So has Tom. I did not ask her about him. I have not heard from him either. I sent him a thank-you card after the dance, thinking I should, but did not expect a reply. I worry that Phyllis seems a little distant. Maybe she is going off me. I tried to be friendly but she was abstracted and not her usual self.

## 19 January

Now I know why Phyllis was not herself! It was nothing to do with me. I can hardly credit this but it seems she let Arthur take advantage of her the night of the dance. I was so shocked I could not help giving a little scream when she confessed this.

She said she had drunk too much champagne and hardly knew what was happening but I do not believe her. *I* would have known what was happening I am sure. I do not think much of this Arthur either, taking advantage. It puts Tom in a good light I must say. Anyway, Phyllis has her Visitor now so all is well, she says. I am surprised she thinks so. I would have thought relief that she is not carrying Arthur's child would not be enough to set her mind at rest. What about when she marries and her husband finds she is not untouched and that she has spoiled herself. It would worry me most dreadfully but it does not worry Phyllis. Suppose, when the war is over, Arthur comes back and tells people about Phyllis. Her reputation will be ruined.

## 2 February

Tom was waiting outside college. I thought he was waiting for his sister who had not yet come out because she had an extra lecture but he was waiting for me. I am afraid I was so pleased that I blushed. He said he was sorry not to have seen me since the dance but that he had been for fittings for a false arm and hand and it was a beastly business and he had not been good company for anyone. The false arm chafes the stump of his remaining arm and hangs like a dead weight and he hates it and has persisted only because he felt he ought to. He hates to give up when things are difficult, but he is going to give this up. He never wanted a false limb in any case. He is so very frank about all this and I admire him for it.

70

## 3 February

Tom was waiting for me again today and again walked me to my bus stop. He said he had nothing much to do and felt restless cooped up inside with nothing better to do than read. He has studying to do before he goes to Oxford in the autumn but cannot seem to settle to it. He hopes by October that the war will be over and like Father believes it will be. He asked if I like training to be a teacher and I said I did but that given a choice I would rather have tried to go to University if Father had allowed it. He told me that Phyllis has no intention of becoming a teacher, she is just playing at it for something to do that will please their parents. I think he is right. Phyllis takes nothing seriously just as I can't seem to take anything lightly.

## 17 March

The Americans have joined in the action at last. George has no interest. Tom and Father are jubilant. They both follow the progress of the war in great detail and read every day about what is happening. I know I should do the same but I cannot apply myself to that sort of reading and rely on them for information. I am more interested in what Matilda has to say about the state of the hospitals and the different sorts of injuries the wounded now have. When the war is over she intends to train to be a proper nurse though Mother says she thinks she has surely been trained already. It is curious the way Matilda no longer seems part of our family. She has her own life

71

about which none of us knows much except what she tells us. If it had not been for the war this could not have happened so there has been as much good in it for her as there has been bad for George. I don't know what would have become of George if there had been no war but I am sure he would not have ended up in a permanent state of collapse as he is now. Father takes him to the office and sometimes to the workshop hoping to make him take an interest but he reports that George just sits at a desk in the office and stares into space and cannot bear the noise in the workshop. Father gives him very simple things to do but he seems incapable of doing them. It is as though he is in a trance and this maddens Father who is convinced George is not trying. I don't know what can be done. I have talked to Tom about it, even though it is such a personal and private matter, and he says he knows many men like George and that he needs treatment. Tom says there are doctors for the mind as well as the body and George should see one of them. I tried to tell Father this but he would not have it. What do you want, he said, your brother certified a lunatic and put away.

\*　　　\*　　　\*

*The diary entries for the rest of 1918 contain a great deal about the Goldsmiths' lectures, many of which Millicent finds difficult to follow, so much so that she begins to think she should have waited another year to enrol, and a great deal about Tom, though she does not see much of him since he is now at Oxford. Very little of the events in the war that year are mentioned but there is a long account of the armistice celebrations in November when she and Phyllis are among the excited crowds in Trafalgar Square. It seems to her that now life can really begin.*

\* \* \*

## 2 January 1919

Another new year, and it ought to be a happy one with the war over and peace to look forward to but it is all so disappointing. Everything seems to go on in exactly the same dreary way. Food is still short and now there are all kinds of strikes, I don't know why. Father says business is not picking up as it should. I do not like the expression on his face when I have to give him the termly bill for my fees. He says I am the most expensive member of the family. I would like to contest that but I dare not.

## 8 January

Father is ill. He came home last night shivering and went straight to his bed and today he has stayed there in a fever and Mother has sent for Dr Robinson. I tried to buy him some grapes on my way home but they are 12*s* a pound! Mother says shopkeepers are Kings these days. I had such a struggle getting home. The omnibuses are crammed to bursting, with crowds waiting at every stop. Getting about is worse than before we won the war.

73

## 9 January

Dr Robinson says Father has the influenza. Mother said she thought the epidemic was over but Dr Robinson said that he had attended four new cases that very day. There is nothing to be done except to keep Father warm and make sure he has plenty of fluids. He has given him something for his cough. His cough can be heard throughout the house, it is so loud and comes from deep in his chest and racks him.

## 10 January

Father has pneumonia on top of the influenza. Dr Robinson says he must be moved to hospital and put in an oxygen tent but that there is at the moment no space. Matilda, who came home as soon as she heard about Father and has stayed, says it is true, all the London hospitals are overflowing. But Dr Robinson was able to arrange for oxygen to be brought here and has fixed up a tent for Father. What a blessing it is to have Matilda here. Mother is quite frantic. I feel it is a judgement on me for complaining about how dreary everything is and now it is worse than dreary here, it is frightening and has happened so quickly.

## 11 January

Father is worse. I did not go to college of course. I sat with him, taking turns with Matilda. Mother hardly leaves his side. The children cry and shout for her but she shuts them out and ignores them and sends them away with Ivy, who has just come back, thank goodness. Father has eaten nothing for three whole days. He cannot swallow and even thin soup is too much. He takes tiny sips of water and that is all. He tries to talk but cannot manage to make sense and then his cough breaks out. It has begun to dawn on me that he may not recover. I cannot write what I really mean by that, but it is too frightening and I am frightened. Mother does not seem to realise what may happen but I am sure Matilda does though we have said nothing to each other. If *the worst* happens, what will become of us? I cannot help thinking about this though it is too awful to contemplate the future. The days are so long and the nights longer and we are all so exhausted. Father's bedroom is so hot, with the fire kept up all the time and the rest of the house so cold in comparison. The ghastly atmosphere in the sickroom is not much worse than the bleakness in the rest of the house where nothing is being seen to. It is all Ivy can do to keep the children occupied. I went out today to the shops to get some necessary provisions and though it was bitterly cold and miserable it was such a relief to escape and I felt I wanted to run away which was disgraceful. I am full of such unworthy thoughts and yet I love Father dearly. Tom writes complaining that I have not answered his last two letters but I cannot.

**13 January**

Father passed away in the early hours of this morning. May he rest in peace.

## 21 January

I have not been able to write in this diary and it has not seemed right to do so. This has been the most dreadful week in my life, in all our lives, and I feel I will never truly recover. Father was only 45. He was not ready to be taken. So many men have been killed in the war but who could have expected to die of influenza. Mother is in a state of paralysis. She does not seem to know what to do and looks bewildered and sits with Grace on her knee and Michael clinging to her and does not reply when spoken to. If Aunt J. had not come and arranged the funeral I do not know what we would have done. I am sure there would have been no funeral which I cannot help thinking would have been a mercy but I suppose there had to be a funeral. Aunt J. said it had to be done and so we were measured, even Grace, and now we are all dressed in black. My dress is frightful but I am quite glad to look so wretched for I feel it. We had six black cars to take us to the church and then to the cemetery. It all passed in a blur. The tea afterwards was painful with so many people pressing in and saying they were sorry and I did not know half of them and cared nothing for their sympathy. Yet when they had all departed it was worse. We did not know what to do. I had never thought to welcome the noise the twins make but for once I did, and did not try to restrain them. Matilda slept with Mother. I could not have done so.

## 22 January

Mother has come out of her becalmed state and is in a frenzy over what will happen to us. She is worried about money. Then there is the business. It must continue to be run but by whom. George should take over but he is incapable. Matilda went down to the workshop today and Mr Riggles assured her he would keep things going until some arrangement was made. Meanwhile Aunt J. compelled George to go with her to the bank to inquire how much money Father has left. She came back white-faced and George looked terrified. It seems Father has left no more than a few hundred pounds in total in a deposit account and a mere £80 in his current account. All of this has to go through probate before Mother can draw on it, but the bank manager advanced £50 as a loan. I do not understand how this can be a loan when it is now Mother's money but that is what Aunt J. called it. She has searched the house and discovered another £40 in pockets and drawers and Father's brief-case. I do not know how she brought herself to go through all his clothes and belongings but she said it had to be done.

## 23 January

Another shock. I had thought at least we have a house, even if it is not a very grand house, and so we have no worries about having a roof over our heads but now it turns out that Father remortgaged it during the war and money must be found to make the mortgage repayments or the house can be reclaimed. I do not understand it all, and neither I am sure does Mother, but I know this is bad news. It hardly needed Aunt J. to point out that there will be no money for my college fees. I hated myself for realising this even while Father was dying. I will have to find employment immediately and so will George. Matilda will continue to live in nurses' quarters. There is some special scheme to which she has applied to cover her maintenance fees and she has been told the authority administering it will look favourably on her application. But I cannot claim the same benefit. I know of no scheme to which I could apply and even if I did I could not avail myself of it because someone must bring some money in and it would not be fair to Matilda to make her give up nursing when she is so far on and will soon qualify and be earning a wage. If only George was earning. Mother seems to imagine he will run the business but Aunt J. can see this is foolishness and that George far from taking charge will be a burden as he has been since he was injured. I could shake him.

**24 January**

Aunt J. is going to sell her house and move in with us. How good she is. I wish I had never had unkind thoughts about her and will try to make up for it. Also, she has some savings and is prepared to use those for us to survive on until Mother can get Father's money and pay her back. I flung my arms round her and kissed her when she told me and I am afraid I wept with relief. She wishes she had the means to keep me at training college but it is impossible, as I quite understand. I am resigned to never becoming a teacher but having instead to accept some menial employment as poor Mabel had to do.

*       *       *

*There follows a miserable period when Millicent searches for a job. To her disbelief, she cannot find one in an office, as she had expected. Unlike Mabel, she cannot type, and finds that men back from the war are in any case filling office vacancies.*

*       *       *

## 14 March

I begin work tomorrow at John Lewis in Oxford Street, and lucky to get the situation. It makes me bitter to have to acknowledge that, for I do not feel lucky in the least, but after all these weeks of trudging around applying for jobs for which I am overqualified, or rather not qualified at all, I know I am indeed fortunate to be able at last to be in a position to earn money. It is not much money. My salary is to work out at 8 shillings a week when fares are deducted. Mabel was getting that years ago. I must provide my own frock, black, but this is not an expense because my mourning frock is perfect. I start work at 8.35 a.m. and continue until 6 p.m. six days a week, except for Saturday when I finish at 1 p.m. The journey there will take about 45 minutes, buses permitting, either way. There is half an hour given for lunch. The worst thing was having to pretend to be grateful that I had been taken on, and indeed I *was*, for a moment, grateful, or rather relieved in a mortifying sort of way. I have been told I was not suitable on so many occasions, and sneered at in the telling, that to be appointed to any situation seemed miraculous. But it was not a miracle which lasted long. I soon saw how I had learned to disguise my education and through omitting to mention what I had been doing since I left school therefore made myself appear suitable to serve in a shop. I learned not to look people in the eye, too, and not to hold my head up, or risk any but the most minimal and humble response to any question. All that was important was to look clean—my hands were carefully inspected and I was glad I had just cut my nails—and docile, and to be able to add up correctly. My maths have never been good but at least I can add up. How low I have sunk. I have not yet written to Tom. He says it is immaterial to him what work I am compelled by my changed circumstances to do, but I do not believe him.

## 6 May

I don't know which part of the day I hate most because there is reason to hate every dratted minute. I hate the very entry into the shop. The air smells stale, after it's been shut up all night and there is something so deadly about the racks of clothes, and the way we shop girls trudge carefully between them as though they might harm us. I long to sweep them all off in one vicious movement and imagine myself stamping on them and tearing the fabrics with my teeth. I hate the next hour, when it is too early for any shoppers yet we have to pretend to be busy and are told to look alert and welcoming. I practised smiling excessively in front of a mirror, to amuse myself, and Mr Anderson caught me and asked if I wished to keep my job because if so I must learn that working in a prestigious store like John Lewis was not a pantomime. He said if Mr Spedan Lewis had caught me grimacing I would have been dismissed on the spot. I hate serving customers, the stupid, stupid women who have no intention of buying anything yet make me bring half the shop to them in the changing-room and never once thank me. I long for the lunch hour but hate it when it comes. We sit at two tables in the basement and grace has to be said before we eat and the silence while we wait for the food makes me want to scream. I scream in my head all the long afternoon. My legs ache but we are not allowed to sit even for a minute. The boredom is dreadful. I hate most of all the *ache* the boredom gives me, an ache right through my bones to the very tip of my toes.


**20 May**

There was a victory march through London today. It was brilliantly sunny and the crowds were delirious with excitement. We were allowed to stand outside the shop, taking it in turn, while the main part of the procession passed along. I found myself in tears but not, as my two companions thought, either through happiness or memories of men lost in the war. No, it was for myself. I am forced to admit that during all these scenes of jubilation I snivelled in an orgy of self-pity. I will never get out of this hateful existence. Even if I were to be offered it, I do not want promotion within the shop. It would make everything worse to become a supervisor and I would be more obliged than ever to act as though this employment was of some importance. At least as a mere assistant in the dress department I am invisible and can keep myself remote and so protect my own dignity. The words, Can I help you, madam? come out of my mouth automatically and I select and hand over frocks to be tried on in a manner that is respectful but distant. The others dislike me for what is seen as my aloofness, of course. I come and go without making friends, though I am always polite. I let them think I lost my father in the war and also my young man, and they leave me alone.

**21 May**

Sundays are somehow worse than weekdays and yet should afford some sense of liberation. I hate to be at home with no privacy whatsoever. Aunt J. and Mother are glad to have me around but I am not glad to be there. The only hour in the day when there is some respite is when they take the twins and Michael to church and this mercifully coincides with Grace's nap. Today I sat in the garden in the sun, with my eyes closed so that I would not be compelled to survey the mess before me. Poor Father, with his attempt at a vegetable patch. I wish the grass would grow again. George is supposed to have sown seeds but if he did there is no evidence of any growth. Mother likes to refer to him these days as a gardener but of course he is no such thing, he is only a labourer who needs direction at every turn and he was only taken on out of pity for what he had suffered and because Mrs Baty feels sorry for Mother. But he is quite content digging, and pulling out weeds, and doing what he is told, so that is something. I wish I were content. I have not accepted my lot in life and never will. I do not want to meet Phyllis or anyone else from my old life. I have declined all invitations.

## 11 June

Tom turned up in the shop today. I was so furious, even though I confess my heart leapt when first I saw him. How dare he! My humiliation was agonising, to the point of almost fainting. I hissed at him to leave immediately but he would not. He persisted in playing the part of someone wishing to buy a frock for his fiancée and I was obliged to go along with it because Mr Anderson was hovering near, alert to the chances of a lucrative sale, and the shopwalker was doing his rounds. Tom whispered that I should meet him when I finished work, at the main entrance, or he threatened to come in every day. I was nearly in tears but had to agree. The moment I stepped out of the shop after finishing work and saw him, I was at last at liberty to tell him what I thought of his outrageous behaviour. I said I never wanted to see him again, though this was of course a lie. He walked along with me and when I had finished he asked me what

I had expected him to do when I would not reply to any of his letters. I said he knew perfectly well someone at Oxford could not have a shop girl as a friend and he positively shouted at me, Don't be so silly! People passing turned to look and my face burned. Tom grabbed me by the arm and pulled me into Lyons Corner House and almost pushed me into a seat. He leaned right across the table and said with real feeling that he hadn't fought in the war to come home and find a world in which one's occupation dictated whether one could be friends or not. It excited me to see him so passionate, and I blushed as I said I was sorry, but breaking off our friendship had seemed to me the right thing to do. Tom sat back then and said, Well, it wasn't and isn't, and unless you agree to spending the day with me next Sunday I shall haunt you and tell you so every day. I hope the weather holds. There has been no rain for six whole weeks.

**17 June**

This is the first happy day I have passed since Father died. Tom took me to Oxford. We went by train and when we got there he showed me his college which is Magdalen and I was dazzled by it and all the colleges and the whole place. It must be like being in heaven to be here. I said so to Tom, and he sighed and said yes, that is how it must seem, and that when he was in France among all the filth and squalor of the trenches he had imagined himself here and yearned for that day but that now this had come to pass something was lacking. I asked what, and he hesitated and said studying seemed irrelevant in view of what had gone before and he was finding it difficult to concentrate. He was not enjoying himself. He was tense and hostile to those who had not fought, and that was no good. We talked like this all day. Tom took me to an area through which the river runs which is called Port Meadow where we followed a tow path to an inn and sat outside and drank cider and ate sandwiches. Tom held my hand on the way back. There were some trees near a little bridge towards the end and we stopped in the shade and he kissed me. It was not like after the dance. This was sincere and I felt myself trembling and though I was half afraid of this feeling I wanted it to continue. But some people came past and we went on walking and nothing was said. Tom came back with me to London, the long vacation having begun, and wished to take me home but I would not let him, knowing Mother and Aunt J. would get ideas.

## 2 July

Tom waits for me every day but not outside the shop. I could not bear it. We have found a teashop which is very quiet and he waits there and reads his newspaper until I arrive. This shop stops serving tea at 6 p.m. and it is after 6 before I get there but Tom is there just in time and orders tea and crumpets and it is very welcoming. He is going climbing next week, with his cousin, to Wales. He asked about my holidays and I said I was not entitled to any paid holiday until I have worked a year so I would not be having one. I tried to say this in a matter-of-fact way and to smile and not be self-pitying. Tom hates self-pitying people. He told me that Phyllis was to come to Wales while he and his cousin were there, staying in their family home. She would probably only stand it for a weekend. I said I hadn't seen Phyllis since I was obliged to give up college and wouldn't feel comfortable with her now even if we did meet. He seemed despondent at this. I do like Tom. I more than like him. I am afraid to think how much more. I no longer dare breathe a word of why, but of course it is because I know I must not set my heart on him when there is such a gulf between us, whatever he says. Even if Father had lived and things been otherwise I would have felt this and it is no good Tom being angry about it.

## 1 August

The days are so hot. It is stifling to be confined in the shop in such heat and to have no opportunity to take advantage of this good weather. The thick carpet on our floor makes the heat worse and ladies trying on clothes make perspiration marks under the arms which ruins them. I had to consult Mr Anderson as to what should be done about this which was very embarrassing but I do not want afterwards to be blamed for letting expensive frocks get in this state. Some of the new frocks are made of such delicate materials and show even the faintest mark really glaringly. I tried one on myself this afternoon. I was so very hot in my black frock, and there was no one at all in the department and Mr Anderson had gone off early so I took a frock which my last customer had tried on and tried it on myself. It is such a beautiful garment, in the new shape, hanging loose and straight from the shoulders and the new length, mid-calf. It did not look right on me, though it fitted well enough. I could not at first think why, and then decided it was because of my hair. The customer who had selected it had had her hair cropped. The frock needs a boyish figure, which I have got but it also needs cropped hair. I wonder if I dare cut my hair off.

## 2 August

The more I think about it, the more tempted I am to get rid of my hair. On the bus today I counted four girls with cropped hair and very cool and smart they looked. I have so much hair and it has always been a bother to braid it and pin it up. Mother, of course, would not approve if I cut it off. She is of the old-fashioned opinion that it is a woman's crowning glory. I do not think Tom would approve either. He has paid me several compliments about my hair.

## 6 August

A postcard from Tom. He wishes I were in Wales with him. He says the weather is marvellous, as it is everywhere, and that they all drove to the coast and swam yesterday. I can picture the scene, and thought about it all the long, close day. I wonder if I will ever live anywhere but London. It is so long since I saw the sea. I daydreamed about it all the way home.

## 8 August

Mother and Aunt J. are to take the children to stay in Brighton for a week. Aunt J.'s old friend Muriel is going away and has kindly suggested this. It will cost nothing except the train fare and that can be managed. I wish George could go too and then I would have the house to myself but our neighbours, his employers, are away and he has guaranteed to work in their garden every day and keep an eye on the place and since I doubt he would ever get another job he cannot afford to let them down. I hope he will not expect me to look after him, as Mother and Aunt J. do.

## 10 August

Saw the family off to Brighton. The children were so excited and Mother too was quite flushed with the pleasure of getting away. It is awful to think how different holidays used to be for her, with Father in charge of all the arrangements. I went straight from the station to the hairdressers' in Oxford Street. I have passed it every day on my way to work and have seen girls coming out with cropped hair and I had made my mind up to have myself cropped as soon as Mother had left. I went in last week in my lunch break and made an appointment. Unfortunately I forgot to ask how much it would cost. I worried it would be expensive and I would not have enough money though I had all my week's wage with me. A girl washed my hair but it was a man who did the cutting, quite a young man, dressed all in black, which was a bit intimidating, but he was friendly and gentle in manner and very concerned that he should understand what I wanted. I had no idea, of course, beyond wanting it cropped. He said I had beautiful hair and that because it was so thick and strong it would not do to cut it too severely, it would not lie straight and would be better layered all round. He produced pictures to show me then he began the cutting, chatting all the while and I found myself chatting back, much to my own surprise. Heaven knows what I told him, but whatever it was it amused him and we became quite giggly. Because we were so easy and merry together, I was not really paying attention to my hair and got a shock when he said he had finished and asked what did I think. I looked in the mirror and did not know what to think. It was not me. I did not want to hurt his feelings and quickly thanked him but I was almost afraid of how I looked. He produced a hand mirror so that I could see the back. My neck looked so *bare*. I had not thought my neck would be so exposed. He asked if I wanted my hair. I looked down at the floor where it all lay and could not imagine what he might mean, why should I want it. I shook my head and left. Only later did I wonder if he had meant my hair might be of some value and he would have bought it. But perhaps not.

## 11 August

I am delighted with my short hair. It felt so good this morning not to have to brush it and pin it up, and so cool and light. I had not realised how heavy hair is. George did not even notice. I cannot wait to see what people in the shop will say. No one else has yet been cropped and they would never have expected me to be the first. I am pleased with my own daring though it is not so very daring. It made me see how timid I am in all other respects and I am ashamed of myself. I should set my sights higher and somehow rise above being a shop drudge. But how? Suppose I were to learn to type, would work in an office be much better? Only a little. Tom said I should not give up the idea of training to be a teacher and that he was surprised I had not carried on studying on my own through a correspondence course. But he does not understand how tired I am in the evenings, which I do not even have to myself, or that such courses cost money and that every penny I earn is needed for urgent necessities for our family. Perhaps when the children are bigger I will be able to resume my training, but Grace is only 3 and in any case the more the children grow, the more expensive they become. I can see no way out. It is all very well for Tom, whose family is well-off.

\*       \*       \*

*But then an unexpected development begins to give Millicent hope. At first, she does not see the significance of a new contact of her mother's, a Dr Marshall, who has been consulted over Michael's*

90

*earache while in Brighton. She notes how Aunt Jemima mentions him frequently, with a smile and a raising of her eyebrows, but presumes this must be because the doctor was young and handsome and Aunt J. is teasing her sister. But it turns out Dr Marshall is neither young nor handsome. He is a childless widower, aged 50.*

\*　　　\*　　　\*

## 20 November

Never did I think I would be writing in this diary that Mother had received a proposal of marriage. I was so overwhelmed with embarrassment I hardly knew where to look, and I think Mother was in a similar state and found it hard to look at me. I simply did not know what to say and when I did speak it was to come out with the most stupid question. Does he know how many young children you have?, I asked, which was foolish of me considering it was through treating Mother's children that Dr Marshall had made her acquaintance. He loves children, Mother said, he is never happier than surrounded by them, and they love him. She paused and added that he would make a very good father for the twins and Michael and Grace, and then she faltered over the word 'father' and was upset. My head was spinning by then with the implications of this proposal if Mother should accept it. She had not yet said she was going to. I could not help wondering why a man of 50 should want to marry a woman in her forties who had seven children, four of them under

91

the age of 11. I tried to look at Mother then as though seeing her for the first time and felt a little shock at noticing she was so attractive. Grief has made her shed the weight she had gained after the birth of Michael and Grace and it suits her to be slender once more. I remembered how she had come back from that holiday in Brighton quite refreshed and happier, and looking younger than her years. It was wrong of me, after all, to wonder at Mother being desirable. But that thought in turn troubles me. It is not seemly, even here, in private, to speculate about whether Dr Marshall finds Mother *desirable* or, even worse, whether she desires him, or indeed anyone. I can see she wants my blessing. She has not told George or Matilda yet, only Aunt J. She reports Aunt J. as being very happy for her, and indeed claiming some credit because it was she who found Dr Marshall when Michael's earache raged. I took a deep breath and told Mother I wanted her to be happy and that if she truly cared for Dr Marshall that was all that mattered and she should accept. She wept a little and said she could never love any man as she had loved Father and had told Dr Marshall so and he had understood perfectly having been very much in love with his own wife who had been taken from him at such a young age. Then Mother said she was lonely and tired of struggling and that accepting this proposal would ease her life and that this was hard to resist. She liked Dr Marshall very much and he was a good man and she felt they could be happy together. So it seems she is going to accept.

## 20 December

Events have moved so fast I can hardly keep up. Whereas up to a month ago all was dreariness and drudgery now there is dramatic change ahead and every day decisions to be made. Mother and Harold are to be married on Christmas Eve and after the New Year move to his house in Brighton, leaving this house to be sold. I have been to see Harold's house and it is a fine house in Kemp Town with plenty of room for all the children and they are thrilled to be going there. Better still, so is George. It was my great fear that George would be left behind and become my responsibility but Mother told Harold she could not desert George and he said he did not expect her to and that if George would come he would be very happy and could find work for him. So it is arranged. Strangely, George has quite taken to Harold, who has examined him and put him on some medication for his nerves. He thinks that, as Tom told me ages ago, George would benefit from treatment and he is to see to it. Everything is in a whirl! I am to stay in this house until it is sold and then I am to be given some of the money to find a place to live. Harold is insistent that the younger children will become entirely his charge, if that is the right way to put it, and that the money from the sale of this house and from what comes from Father's business should be divided between George, Matilda and me. It is very fair of him. But by rights, something should go to Aunt J. I have said so to Mother and she agrees, for if it had not been for Aunt J.'s selflessness we would have been ruined. But Aunt J. has declined any share, and intends to move to Brighton too, near to Mother and Harold, and has enough money left from the sale of her house to buy somewhere modest. Everything is working out so well, I can hardly believe it.

## 21 December

I have given in my notice at the shop and never been so glad about anything. Mr Anderson said it was inconsiderate of me, with the sales coming up, but I simply beamed and agreed. I have applied for a grant to return to Goldsmiths' and am hopeful of obtaining it but even if I do not I will be able to pay my own fees. The only problem is that there is now a great crush of applicants and of course I have missed a term and a half, but fortunately my special circumstances, and the fact that I had an excellent record while there, are disposing the authorities to make an exception for me and find room though they are bursting at the seams. I can hardly sleep for happiness.

\* \* \*

*The entries over the following Christmas and New Year weeks are brief and clearly written in haste. The wedding of Constance and Harold was quiet but there was a party afterwards though Millicent spends no time describing it saying only that it was 'jolly'. Suddenly she is on her own in the London house (though Mr Baty next-door comes in when she has to show prospective buyers round), and spends her time catching up on the work she has to do to go back to Goldsmiths' in mid-January. Curiously, since the bombshell of Harold's proposal, there has been hardly a mention of Tom.*

## 6 January 1920

Three sets of people came to view the house today. I have never cared much for this house but I do find it hurtful when folk are contemptuous of it and criticise the decoration, and Mr Baty agreed with me that some people are impertinent. One woman said of the parlour that it looked as though the wallpaper had been up since the house was built some forty years ago and I was angry and told her it had been wallpapered the year war broke out. There were tears in my eyes because I remembered choosing it with Mother. It is true, however, that the parlour looks forlorn without pictures, and the little chaise-longue has gone, as well as the two oak chairs Grandfather made, and the Indian rug. I do not go in there except to help show people round. The other rooms are more or less intact, with the furniture to be sold at auction once the house has been sold. Mother asked if Matilda or I wanted to take anything but Matilda is in a hostel and I too am going into one of the women's hostels at Goldsmiths' so we have no use for any furniture. It is an odd existence being here alone. Mother worries about it, but I have assured her I am quite happy and safe. Tom came over on his bicycle to visit. I do not mind his coming now the house is empty. I cannot think it is entirely safe for him to cycle with only one hand but I did not dare say so. He is looking very well after spending Christmas in Switzerland. For the first time I have begun to think that such outings maybe within my own reach, given time. I am not absolutely poverty-stricken any more, even if poor enough by comparison with Tom, and I am not obliged to help support my family. Harold has lifted all that worry from my shoulders and I can feel the weight of it lifting as surely as I felt the weight of my hair leave me. Tom, by the way, does not like my short hair. Or rather, he does not put it that way but says he always loved my 'beautiful auburn mane'.

## 9 January

An offer has been made for the house, a very low offer, only £300, but Mother is going to accept it. When everything is sorted about the business and all debts paid, Matilda, George and I will have about £150 each. I shall put it in the bank and try hard not to touch it. Meanwhile, with the grant I am to receive to pay Goldsmiths' fees I will need very little to live on and I am going to accept Harold's kind offer of support until I am earning, when I will repay him. Tom cannot understand why I worry about taking money from a man who is now my stepfather and who is clearly well-off. He has never needed to fret over finance. I think sometimes of all the other young men coming back after the war, unable to find employment, and being as a consequence bitter and resentful. Tom asked me once if I was a communist. I said no, certainly not, and that I know nothing about politics. Father supported the Liberals and so I have always thought I would be a Liberal too. From things he has said, I thought Tom was a Liberal, but it seems he is a Tory. He says he believes in an established order in society and a culture of responsibility among those fortunate enough to belong to the upper and middle classes. It is beyond me. Father said never argue about politics or religion and I am not going to.

## 15 January

I am now settled into St Michael's Hostel and very happy to be here. It is like a large country house with a pretty garden all round. I have been told that the Pentland House hostel is the most desirable but I like St Michael's. There are so many women students now but there are also far, far more men than when I was last here and their presence is very noticeable. They are boisterous and noisy and can be quite overwhelming in the lecture halls or if one meets them in the corridors. They seem so much older than us women though in fact I don't think they can be. Everyone seems to be taking different courses. I myself am to do a new one-year course preparing me to teach in elementary schools. I can do it in one year because of my previous one year's study though really that was so different I can't see how it connects at all. The Education Act last year created different sorts of schools and Goldsmiths' has designed a new course for them. There are only twelve of us women. Every moment of the day is filled with lectures and essays and reading and it is hard work, but I remind myself all the time of what it was like serving in a shop all day. If I am tired or just sometimes the least bit bored this recollection revives me. For the men who have been in the war, it must feel like an escape from hell. I can't help being curious about all of them, finding myself speculating at Morning Assembly as to what exactly each man has been through. The men stand quite separate from us but all the same we can see them, and they can see us (how some of them stare!). I study their faces intently, wondering what lies behind one man's ferocious frown and another's rather silly smile. Some of them have disturbing facial tics from which I avert my gaze.

## 14 February

St Valentine's Day. Someone has sent me two dozen pink tulips. Tom? I don't think so. I have not written to him since I settled here and he has not written to me. But who, then, can they be from? They arrived while we were all having breakfast. Girls were opening cards and smiling and showing them to each other. I had no cards, and had not expected any. Then there was a knock at the front door and Phoebe was sent to open it and returned with this beautiful bunch of flowers tied with pink ribbon. Of course we all thought they were for Pamela, who has so many beaux, and she half stood, expecting to be given them and already blushing with pleasure in anticipation. Then Phoebe said 'For Miss Millicent King, from an admirer' and gave me the flowers. I was bewildered, and blushed. Everyone crowded round me, wanting to read the card, and clamouring to know who my admirer was. I said I had no idea, and they all began speculating. Clara declared it was Hugh Jamieson who she maintains stares at me whenever he sees me and has told John, Clara's boyfriend, he thinks I am divine. Too silly. But it was exciting. I expect they are from Tom, but how can I find out? It would be awful to make a mistake.

*     *     *

*They were indeed from Tom, who cannot resist writing to ask if she has received any flowers on Valentine's Day. Millicent is touched, but warns herself not to read too much into this gesture, and she reminds herself that she has no time for romance, if that is what Tom intended, because she has to concentrate on her studies and do well. She does, coming first in the end of course examination. Now qualified as a teacher and, against strong opposition, she is appointed to an elementary school in Surrey. She is elated to be starting on a career and thrilled to find herself independent. Her share of the money from the sale of the family house comes through, enabling her to rent a pleasant room near the school and still have enough to support herself. She buys a bicycle (£7) and spends weekends exploring the countryside, describing the landscape in great and, it must be admitted, sometimes fulsome detail. The school is small and run by a kind and dedicated headmaster who helps her greatly at first. Her class of thirty 7-year-olds is on the whole obedient and she has little trouble maintaining discipline. The whole of 1921 and 1922 pass without her recording any significant new friendships and her always uncertain relationship with Tom Hart seems to be fading, though she mentions occasional letters.*

*     *     *

**15 July 1923**

My birthday. Twenty-two is not a significant birthday, heaven knows, but for some reason it seems so. By the time Mother was 22 she was married. I have not so far wanted to marry but on the other hand I do *not* want to be another Aunt J., though Aunt J. always seems happy enough. The only man I have cared for is Tom and I knew it would never come to anything. We are still friends but hardly see each other and there is no hint of romance, in spite of those Valentine's Day flowers. The last time I saw him was in September when he visited me here. It was like a visit from a brother or some other male relative. We chatted easily enough and enjoyed a walk and I made him a splendid tea, but that was all. He said I was quite the dedicated school marm and I said, I hope with dignity, yes, I was, and glad to be. But I think that what he implied was that I was not much fun and was in danger of becoming a dried-up spinster. He kissed me when he left but it was a peck on the cheek and I cannot say my heart beat faster. I think the truth is, as I now see it, that Tom was the only young man who came my way and I responded instinctively. Since I came here I have got to know only the male teachers at the school and all three of them are married. And singularly unattractive. Out of school hours I keep myself to myself so it's hardly surprising if I meet no men. I am struggling to be absolutely honest with myself, but I think it is perfectly true that I don't yearn for a lover, or even a pleasant male friend such as Tom. For the

101

moment, I am content with my own company. And yet, would I be writing down these kind of thoughts, if I were? It *is* a puzzle.

**18 July**

The school holidays begin in a week or so and I have not yet made any plans. I must go to Brighton of course and spend some time with Mother and the children but I would like to have something different to look forward to. I fancy a cycling holiday, staying in B & Bs or hostels along the way, but I have not yet decided on any route. It might be a little gruelling too. Then there's Matilda's wedding. I feel I hardly know Matilda now, we are certainly not close, but she has asked me to be a maid of honour. I have not even met her fiancé yet, which is rather shocking considering they have been engaged all this long time. Mother is so happy about this wedding, especially because she approves of Charles and thinks Matilda has made a great catch. I shall reserve judgement till I meet him. I refuse to be swayed by the fact that he is the youngest paediatric consultant at his hospital. Still, I must give him a chance.

**10 August**

I was too exhausted to write about the wedding yesterday, though it was not the exhaustion of having danced my feet off or anything like that but of talking to so many people I did not know and of shepherding elderly relatives around. I did not know we had so many relatives. Where have they been since Father's funeral? I must say, Matilda enjoyed her own wedding. She was not a bashful bride but was confident and beaming. Harold gave her away which surprised me. I thought that in spite of his problems George would manage it. Mother cried, predictably, but was soon over her tears. I noticed that Charles is very attentive to her. He seems intelligent, a good man, but a trifle overbearing. He takes command of any situation instantly. Matilda and Mother like this in a man but I find it irritating. The twins worship him. They looked rather fine in sailor suits and are growing into such big boys. Albert is taller and heavier than Alfred so it is easy now to tell them apart. Grace was adorable as a flower girl in the prettiest of dresses which Mother had made for her. I had an interesting conversation with Matilda when I was helping her get ready. I said something about wondering if she would have as many children as Mother and she said, firmly, that she would not. When I asked how she could be sure, she said there were ways . . . things, that Mother never knew. Haven't you heard of Marie Stopes, she said. Well, of course I have. Matilda did not go into further detail, though. I must say that anyone looking at Mother yesterday surrounded by all of us for one of the photographs would have judged her the proudest and happiest of women to be so blessed. Perhaps she is.

## 17 August

I have made my mind up to visit Paris the first week in September. After the wedding, it did not seem so enticing to go off cycling after all. I have never been abroad and suddenly I feel adventurous again. Sometimes now I feel bewildered at how settled and placid my life seems to be. I never thought it would be. I don't know what I thought I would do or how I would live. I think I had dreams of things just happening but when they did happen they were not what I dreamed of, not happy things.

## 2 September

Yesterday I took the boat train to Paris via Calais—oh, how my heart was bumping. Just going to the station and boarding the train was thrilling. It wasn't like getting on a train to Brighton. The other passengers were so interesting, many of them beautifully and expensively dressed, and with mountains of luggage. I sat beside a French woman returning home and practised my poor French on her. She was very kind and patient, and when I got my guide book and map out showed me how to get to the hotel I had booked in Montmartre. I felt much more confident after her directions but all the same I was terribly nervous when we arrived at the Gare du Nord and I had to leave my new friend and make my own way. I felt quite triumphant when I reached the little hotel. It is a strange place, not at all what I imagined. They serve no food, and the bathroom at the end of the corridor is hardly what I would call a proper bathroom. It is just a lavatory, and a very peculiar one, with a tap beside it. But my room is clean and has pretty blue painted shutters which, when I opened them, looked onto a courtyard full of earthenware pots of flowers. I went out straightaway and walked all the way to the banks of the Seine and across the bridge to Notre Dame and I felt elated. The weather is perfect, sunny but not too hot, and it was a joy just to sit on benches and watch and listen. I keep trying to decide why Paris looks different from London. I think it is all to do with colour. London, or the London I know, is greyer; there are no pavement cafés or bright umbrellas and nothing like so many flower pots everywhere. I was exhausted when I got back to the hotel, and hungry and thirsty. I thought about stopping at a café and dining but did not quite have the courage. It is a bother, being a young woman on her own, I should feel self-conscious. So I bought some bread and cheese, enjoying the simple transaction, and some fruit and also a bottle of vin rouge which made me feel wicked. I had a picnic in my room, with the window open, looking out onto the courtyard, and didn't feel lonely at all.

**5 September**

I ate in a café today and managed well. I chose it with care. It was one I had passed and repassed and had noted the clientèle included quite a few women, some with children, and I felt I would be comfortable if I sat at a table beside such a group. I also bought a copy of *Le Figaro* so that if necessary I could hide behind it but I never needed to. I had fish soup, quite delicious, with crusty bread, and then a kind of onion tart with a salad and a glass of white wine. No one paid me the least attention and the waiter was matter-of-fact, and altogether I felt sophisticated and confident. I liked hearing French all round me, too. My understanding increases rapidly though I am still hesitant about speaking. I went on a *bateau-mouche* on the Seine afterwards and tomorrow I am taking a train to Versailles. I sent postcards to Mother and the children, and to Matilda and Charles, and also to Tom. I wrote them while I was lunching at the café and had trouble with Tom's, finally settling on mocking myself a little but I hope making it clear I really was having an exciting time.

## 15 September

It won't do. Paris has had a disturbing effect. I feel discontented, with the school and my rooms, and oh with everything, whereas before I was happy, or thought I was. Suddenly I see that this town is dreary and the school old-fashioned and my room nothing special and that I am not so glad after all to be independent if it means I have no stimulating contacts. I can't stay here for the rest of my life. I think I must give in my notice and move, but that is a step of such daring, it takes my breath away. I cannot leave one job without having another to go to and somewhere to live. It would be folly.

## 20 September

I went to stay with Matilda and Charles for the weekend. Their house is small but nice, near enough to Regent's Park to walk there. It was fun. They are such an unusual couple, I know no other like them, and I suppose I envy them. There is something so free and easy about how they live, quite differently from how we were brought up. Their little house is so informal it almost feels foreign to me, and a constant stream of friends passes through it. They both work hard but this does not seem to make them tired or hold them back from being hospitable. They seem to drink and smoke an awful lot. All their friends do. They have a piano and there is always someone tootling around on it. Mother would declare it was bedlam. I was complimented on my singing, though all I sang was 'Alice Blue Gown', my party piece. Everyone joined in, and then they all began 'April Showers', except for me because I did not know the words. Perhaps I have misjudged Matilda, who has now become Tilda, if you please. Father would never let her be called Tilda, and she never was, any more than he liked my name being shortened to Milly. At any rate, Tilda was very friendly and took a real interest in my dilemma and gave good advice. She thought I should not get stuck in a rut and that I should be more ambitious, as once I was. She asked why did I not go to university and study English Literature, since I am always reading. I am only 22 and not too old to consider it. But I don't think that is the answer. It is not study I want— though I plan this year to attend a course of lectures I have heard about—it is *action*. Tilda says

I can stay in their guest room any time. She is not a housewife of Mother's variety but then she has a career too. Everything is *not* immaculate or just so but she doesn't seem to care. I wonder what Mother thinks. She would be horrified at the state of the house, but then she is horrified anyway that Tilda continues to work. She is surprised the nursing home allows it and even goes so far as to wonder if Tilda has told them she is married. I asked Tilda that, and she smiled, and said good nurses were always in demand and there were ways of getting round rules. I don't know what that means.

\*　　　　\*　　　　\*

*Events conspire to prevent Millicent from ever making a move to another school. At the end of 1923, when she has begun to apply for several new posts, her stepfather Harold dies suddenly of a heart attack. She goes at once to her mother in Brighton, dreading that yet again she, as the unmarried daughter, will be called upon to support her siblings and keep her devastated mother company. She writes in her diary that Harold's death 'seemed like another judgement' because she had dared to feel discontented and restless. But it quickly becomes obvious that the situation in Brighton is not at all as it had been when her own father died. Constance inherits the house, on which there is no mortgage, together with a substantial income from Dr Marshall's investments. Financially, she has no worries. Then there is the changed nature of George, who had benefited both from the psychiatric treatment Harold had arranged for him and also from Harold's own support. He is ready to assume responsibility for the younger*

108

*children and for his mother. So instead of being obliged to move to Brighton and once more be sucked into family life, which she had always found so burdensome, Millicent finds herself under no such obligation. She goes back to school but starts attending a weekly course of WEA lectures in London.*

* * *

**4 April 1924**

Last lecture tonight. I have enjoyed them very much and feel I have learned a great deal, enough to think again about whether I could go on somehow to study for a degree in English Literature after all. I was thinking about it when Matthew Taylor caught up with me and insisted on accompanying me to Tilda's. I wish I had never told him of my yearning to go to university and even more do I regret mentioning my foolish literary ambitions. I cannot imagine what I was thinking of because of course he has pestered me ever since to show him something I have written. I will never do that, never. I could send stories to strangers but would never show them to someone I knew. Matthew says he admires my critical faculties, though all he means is that he has heard me giving my opinion in class, and asked if I had ever considered journalism. I said no. Mother would die if I took up journalism. This did not stop him urging me to leave teaching and become a journalist. I was sharp with him then, pointing out that I have trained to be a teacher, at considerable effort and expense, and it would be wicked to waste my training. And besides, I told him, teaching is fulfilling and worthwhile. I sounded priggish even to myself. He said 'and boring'. I denied this hotly, but he keeps on and on. He sneers at Surrey too, saying London is the only place to be. I don't know why I put up with him. He is like a terrier, never letting go. He is very energetic, and I suppose quite good-looking, though I don't care for his moustache. Well, after tonight I will have no reason to see him again and he will not be able to find me. He has asked for my home address but I have avoided giving it. He has asked to see me, too, but I have said I am too busy. He never seems offended by my rebuffs, I must say.

## 6 April

It's unfortunate that I am staying at Tilda's for most of this Easter holiday. It means I am a sitting duck for Matthew Taylor's attentions. Tilda doesn't know why I am so unkind to him: she thinks him amusing and lively, and worth getting to know. Since she has only met him on the doorstep I fail to see how she has formed this opinion. She thinks he has a lovely smile. She doesn't understand, either, why I am resisting further acquaintance with him, but then that's not surprising because I hardly understand myself. I have felt as though he is trying to *capture* me ever since first he came into my life three months ago. I know it is odd, but the reason I didn't write his name in this diary until a couple of days ago is because I am superstitious. It is absurd to have to admit this to myself. I wrote about Tom and now it makes me embarrassed to remember that I did and I would really wish to go back over my diaries and erase whatever it was that I wrote, and yet that cannot have been anything very revealing because we were never intimate friends. I felt if I described Matthew when I first got to know him, much the same thing would happen, which is nothing, and then I would have begun on a pathetic course of listing men who meant nothing. There was also the odd thing that I don't know when I did first see him. It was not like being taken to Phyllis's home and being introduced to Tom. I suppose I saw him several times before I noticed him and certainly before we ever spoke. Matthew is not very noticeable, unlike Tom. Among a group of people there is nothing to single him out, which is strange because his character is forceful even if his appearance is not. He says he noticed me at once. I am not sure if that is flattering, or intended to be flattering. There were twenty of us in the class, thirteen women, and he may have noticed me because I was the only woman who asked a question, and the lecturer was not best pleased. Or because of my red hair. Matthew says I looked very striking, standing there in my green dress, 'so slight and fragile' as he put it, but with this challenging question. I don't recall what it was and neither does he which shows it can't have been very challenging. But from then on he haunted me and contrived to sit beside me, even once asking another man to move because he claimed to have something he wished to tell me. He never stops talking. Half of what he says I don't catch because he jumbles his words and speaks so hurriedly. It's extraordinary that he is not put off by my reserve. I have hardly told him a thing about myself, not that there is much to tell, but he has told me so much about himself that there cannot be much left to tell. He trained as a pilot in the war but it ended before he saw any action and afterwards he went straight onto his local newspaper and from there he has somehow come to be the editor of a small magazine. He told me the name of it but I've now forgotten it. He lives in a room above the office in which he runs this magazine. It is in Soho somewhere, which sounds rather louche and glamorous, but I think he is quite poor. His clothes are well-worn and he makes frequent references to the cost of things.

**10 April**

I supposed it must be a coincidence, but I was suspicious. I set off to Brighton today to see Mother and who should leap onto the train and sit beside me but Matthew Taylor. I could not help wondering if he had followed me from Tilda's house, and almost accused him of doing so. It's lucky I didn't because the true coincidence is that *his* mother lives in Hove and he was going to visit her. I felt ashamed of my suspicions and tried to be more friendly and we ended up having an interesting conversation about *The Forsyte Saga*. Matthew is thinking about writing something on Galsworthy's earlier works which I have never heard of. We passed a pleasant half hour talking about writers. We've both been impressed by Katherine Mansfield's stories. He admires Aldous Huxley but I have not read him. By the time we

112

arrived in Brighton I had decided I do like Matthew, after all. He asked me when I planned to return to London and I told him. I hope I won't regret it. He's bound to get the same train.

## 18 April

Term starts on Monday so I must go home tomorrow. I am struggling with the dismal feeling that I don't really want to. It's alarming to confess the reason and to know it is not to do with leaving London and returning to Surrey and the monotony of the school day so much as leaving Matthew. I would not like him to know. He has made no secret of his desire for me to stay in London. Ridiculously, he even suggested I should work for him, or rather his magazine. This was my own fault because I criticised some of the book reviews it has carried and even dared to correct some of the grammar and punctuation. I thought it would annoy him but he only laughed and said a school marm's expertise was just what he needed. It has become a joke that I take a red pen and go through each issue. I still haven't told him, though, that I have sent a couple of stories to other magazines like his of which there seem to be dozens. My stories are always returned, without comment.

## 24 April

It has felt so strange this week being back at school. I felt I was spying on myself and wondering who this young woman was. I could not get into my own head. I saw myself making a sandwich and wrapping it in greaseproof paper and putting it into my bag and I wondered where the sandwich was going and who would eat it. More confusing and dangerous was seeing myself mount my bicycle and ride away and I could not work out which road I would take, but luckily the bike knew. This is how I have felt all day, every day. I feel so detached and yet seem to function adequately. I stand in front of the children calmly and write on the blackboard and ask and answer questions, but I'm in a trance. The other teachers say nothing. We are a quiet bunch, of course, none of us except Muriel Gill given to chattering. I watch her fat, animated face but don't hear a word. How peculiar we must look, all four of us sitting in that dismal little room, each of us like Jack Horner, clinging to our respective corners and munching away at our sandwiches, or in Alan's case his carrots. It's all he ever brings with him and we suffer acutely from the crunching noise he makes. Usually I am irritated by it, and by Muriel's droning, but not this week.

**2 May**

Today, when the children had gone, I stayed in the classroom, intending to inspect the verse they had been set to write out this afternoon. Instead, I sat motionless, staring ahead. There was a thick beam of sunlight coming through the high window at the back and the motes swirled and danced in it. The battered desks, covered in ink stains and scratched names, were bathed in its light and no longer a dull brown but positively golden, and the black iron supports gleamed. I tried to picture the pupils who had just vacated them and it was impossible. I could not conjure up more than two or three faces and yet I have taught Standard Three now for nearly a year. Something has happened. The pride and pleasure I had in teaching have evaporated and I must get them back. It is too awful to think about.

**10 May**

Shall I go for the weekend to Tilda's? It's no use lying to myself. I know why I want to go. Two magazines have arrived from Matthew, sent on by Tilda, and they contained notes from him. He says circulation has increased, though he gives no figures, and that he is serious about wanting to engage someone to help him produce it and not simply in a clerical capacity. He says he can offer me a salary only slightly less than I told him I was getting as a teacher with the prospect of a substantial rise as the magazine flourishes. He says he is run off his feet doing everything himself and if I will not join him he must find someone else.

He doesn't realise that I am not a risk taker. I've always wanted to be, but I'm not. He doesn't know what it's like to be out of work and afraid of being penniless. But if I did give up teaching—not that I will—I could always go back to it, I suppose. I am trained, I have experience. It is not at all the same as when Father died and I had no qualifications.

**16 May**

I think I will do it. It's madness, and Mother will be horrified, and I'm slightly horrified myself, but another part of me is excited. Matthew says life is about taking one's chances when they are presented. Do you want to look back at your life at 60 when you retire from teaching, he asks, and think that is all that you have done. I defended teaching stoutly, when he said this, but I knew that the answer was *no*. I'm no longer sure that teaching really is my vocation. I have never thought of journalism as a career but Matthew makes it seem *very* attractive. I can try it.

**17 May**

I have given in my notice. I thought I would feel wretched but I don't. Mr Williams was surprised but very understanding. He said I had not been myself this term, though he had no criticism of my work. He says he will give me a good reference so if, after my little adventure, as he put it, I wish to teach again I should be able to find employment. Far worse will be telling Mother. I hope that Tilda will back me up, though I cannot be sure even of that.

**20 May**

Mother is angry and distressed. She reminded me, as I knew she was bound to, that Father had made considerable sacrifices to pay for my training and that Harold had been very generous too. What kind of repayment is this, she asked, quite trembling with indignation. There was nothing I could say in my defence. I suppose there is a man at the bottom of this, she went on, Tilda tells me it is all to do with a man. I was furious and knew I was blushing. So much for Tilda's support. I said it was true that a man had offered me the job but I had no attachment to him. Grace came in and saw her mother's tears and went to her and hugged her and said I was naughty and I should go away and not be given any tea, and she said it so sweetly and amusingly—amusing to us not to her—that Mother and I could not help laughing. Yes, she agreed, Millicent is being very naughty but I love her all the same. I felt so ashamed then. Mother has had enough to put up with without my causing her anxiety. She so liked having a daughter who was a schoolteacher, boasted about it even, quite forgetting that at one time she had never wanted me to have a career at all. George, through no fault of his own, has been such a disappointment and now I am too—and it *is* my own fault.

*When term ends in July 1924, Millicent goes first to
Brighton then, at the beginning of September, moves
in with Tilda and Charles, taking over two small
rooms at the top of their house. This is meant to be
temporary until she finds somewhere to rent but by
mid-September when she is about to start working for
Matthew Taylor's magazine she is still there. Nowhere
in her diary does Millicent mention the title of the
magazine and I've been unable to identify it, though
the proprietor, Alison Hooper, did later invest in
Lilliput. But this was the era of small literary
magazines, many of which ran for only a few issues
before disappearing. During the 1920s and 1930s
there were dozens of them, all produced on a
shoestring.*

\* \* \*

## 12 September 1924

I start work tomorrow. I am so nervous, and yet
excited too, far more excited than when I began
teaching. Matthew took me to his office today, just
so I would know where to come and what to expect.
I had trouble hiding my dismay and perhaps
did not entirely succeed. The word 'office' to
me means a business-like, efficient-looking place
with filing cabinets and desks and typewriters.
Matthew's 'office' is above a café, run by Italians,
and the uncarpeted staircase leading to it is
perilous, the boards are loose and creak
alarmingly, and at one point, on the turn, the whole

staircase seems in danger of coming away from the wall. The room itself is tiny and smells, though I couldn't identify what of. Something not quite healthy, maybe just damp. The walls have Russian posters on them. Matthew says they are not his, they were here when he rented the place, but he likes them and so he left them in place. I rather suspect that they cover crumbling plaster.

I don't know where I am to sit. There's no desk, only a wooden table, with one chair in front of it. The floor is covered with untidy piles of papers and along one wall are piles of unsold copies of the magazine's past issues, a great many of them. There is a telephone on the floor near the grimy window, out of which it is impossible to see anything clearly, and beside it there is a kettle but no sign of a gas ring or suchlike upon which to boil it. There is a minute fireplace, rather pretty, with blue and white tiles round the iron work, but all that lay in the grate today was some orange peel. Heaven knows what the room above, where Matthew lives, is like. He did not invite me to visit it, though he dashed up there to bring down another chair and made a great fuss of cleaning it with his handkerchief. I felt helpless standing there, and was filled with a growing dread that I have been taken in. If so, it is by my own vanity and I will have been taught a harsh lesson. There will be no point in wearing a costume, or worrying about clothes at all. I will be able to wear any old thing and will probably look as shabby as Matthew in no time at all.

## 26 September

Things are not so bad. Going to the office is a lot more interesting than cycling to school. I get a bus to Oxford Circus and then I walk, zig-zagging through Soho to Greek Street. The people in the café are usually just opening up when I arrive and they are friendly and cheerful and call me *bella signorina* without sounding impertinent. Matthew is never up at that time so I have my own key and for the first hour, before he stirs himself, I settle in and like the feeling of being in control. Already, in a mere two weeks, I have made a difference to the office. Everything is clean and tidy for a start. I have banished the left-over copies to a cupboard on the landing outside and Matthew has purchased another second-hand table, a long narrow one, which fits neatly along the back wall and upon it I arrange everything to do with the issue he is working on. I sit at the other table which I have covered with a bright yellow cloth brought from Tilda's. And I have found an old jug in which I intend always to keep a few flowers. It is not office-like to do this, but since this room could never resemble a proper office it is of no consequence. Matthew doesn't care what it looks like. He cares more about the standard of my typing. This is coming on but I still make so many errors. I think often of Mabel and her expertise and envy it. But as I have said to Matthew, I am not a secretary and made it plain before I accepted this job that I could hardly type. My job is to be an editorial assistant not a typist. What I do is read copy as it comes in and mark grammatical errors and then, if necessary—and it is nearly always necessary—I cut it down for length. I like this part. I always enjoyed précis exercises at school and that is what it amounts to. At first I worried that the authors of the articles and stories would be furious at having their precious copy interfered with, and not even by the editor, but Matthew said none of them is important enough to mind; they are just glad to be published and paid. There are some very peculiar contributors who come to hand in their pieces. One man came in today wearing a long black coat right down to his ankles and buttoned right up to his neck even though it is a beautifully sunny and warm day. I remarked on this afterwards to Matthew and he said that very likely Vernon, the man's name, was naked underneath. Vernon was in a great hurry, slapping his copy down and exiting without a word. It was written in an atrocious hand and my job was to type it all up. I thought Matthew should insist that all submissions be typewritten but he said Vernon was a special case and had had to pawn his typewriter and it was a brilliant article worth the bother of deciphering and typing up. My bother, of course, though I couldn't see what is brilliant about it. It is about trade unions and what they should be doing. Vernon didn't look as though he would know anything at all about workers. I noticed his hands were soft and very white. He is no horny-handed son of the soil.

**30 September**

Matthew was in a bit of a tizz today. His patron, Alison Hooper, came to inspect the premises, or maybe it was to inspect Matthew, or even me. She finances the magazine. Matthew says it is not just a plaything and that she is quite serious in wanting to be involved in a good, small literary magazine. She is a writer herself and has had a novel published under a pseudonym. I wonder what it is. Matthew doesn't know. She writes short stories too and of course wants them to find space in her own publication. She uses a pseudonym for those too, but changes it all the time. They are quite good. She brought one with her today, already typed. It is called 'The Lady and the Lap Dog'—very Chekhovian, as Matthew commented—and is very sharp and sarcastic and sneers at the exaggerated affection women have for their pets. I liked it, but I cannot say I liked its author. She was disdainful and cold, I thought. She ignored me, though I saw her hard little eyes, and they *are* little, take me in. Matthew was nervous, and ingratiating, which I have never seen before, but then of course everything depends on Mrs Hooper's willingness to go on advancing money. I wonder if he finds her attractive. She is not glamorous but she has good taste and she is slim. She was wearing the most beautiful day dress underneath her coat, I longed to see it properly but she never took the coat off. The dress was of a fine orange worsted material flecked with cream, and trimmed with black and white rayon braid and tassels. The skirt was quite narrow. I couldn't, of course, see the sleeves. Her legs are excellent. She wears spectacles of a type I have never seen before, with red frames. And she smokes through a tortoiseshell cigarette-holder. She started questioning Matthew about expenses, but then stopped suddenly and said she hoped he was going to take her out to lunch. Matthew looked horrified, but said yes, of course. As they departed, I found myself wondering if he had any money in his pocket. Often, he hasn't. I couldn't imagine where he would take her, either. The only place he ever goes is downstairs, where he owes Franco a fortune, but I thought surely he would not take her there. She looks as though she is used to the Ritz. Turned out he took her to the Café Royal, where he had never been in his life. What daring! He had that morning drawn money to pay the printer and used that. He said it wasn't so very expensive because all she wanted was a gin and tonic beforehand and then a thin slice of grilled liver. She is apparently pleased with the magazine and told Matthew she had heard several people at a party singing its praises and saying it was witty and the stories and articles lively and different. Best of all, she said these people thought the magazine had a point to it, unlike so many others around. I wonder what that point is. I cannot see it. I must ask Matthew if he can.

## 1 October

Matthew was offended when I asked him if there was indeed a point to his magazine. He said, very crossly, that of course there was a point or why would he be doing it at all. To earn a living, I said, which was why most people worked. He told me not to be so ridiculous and said there were easier ways of making a much better living and that he would never do anything just for the money. I said that was very high-minded of him but that it showed he had never been put to the test and then we got into a silly argument which went on and on and still he hadn't told me what the point of his precious little magazine is.


## 2 October

There was an atmosphere between Matthew and me all of today. How funny we must've looked, Matthew huffing and puffing over the pages he was pasting up, his back turned to me pointedly, and I pretending to be relaxed, typing in a deliberately languid fashion which I know infuriates him. It is awkward when two people who spend all day together in one small room have had a disagreement. It was only about milk. Matthew had left yesterday's in the bottle and it had gone off. He said there was nothing wrong with it and that I was too fussy. I refused to use it in my tea and he ostentatiously drank it from the bottle. I could tell from his contorted face that he then felt sick, and I laughed. He didn't. We went out at lunchtime as we always do but I said I had some shopping to do and did not join him for a bowl of soup. I needed to be away from him. It bothers me that this is true. However much I like him, and I do, I am often relieved to part company. He likes us to go out together after we have finished work for the day and I like to go to the plays and concerts he suggests but sometimes I worry that he is making assumptions which I do not share. We went to a jazz club the other evening and he introduced me to someone as his girlfriend. Afterwards, I asked him why he had said girlfriend and not colleague, and he seemed surprised. He said girlfriend was

124

accurate enough, wasn't it, and *friend*lier than colleague, and I said the term girlfriend implied a connection between us which did not exist. He looked puzzled, and shrugged. Is he being naive, or am I being priggish? One thing I know, I am not attracted physically to him. He has begun kissing me goodnight and I do not enjoy it. I hope he has realised this. He would have to be dumb not to. Why else, pray, would I have turned up my coat collar, so that he ended up kissing hairy tweed? His mouth must be full of it.

## 1 December

I reminded Matthew that tomorrow my three-months trial period is up. He looked astonished and wondered aloud why I was mentioning it: did I want some sort of written contract, because if so he'd have to consult Mrs Hooper. I said it wasn't that I wanted a contract but rather the reverse, that I was thinking of admitting I'd made a dreadful mistake and so it would be better to give in my notice and return to teaching which was humiliating but had to be faced up to. He asked if I were mad. What has brought this on, he said, I thought you were enjoying the work, you're good at it, we have fun, don't we? I said I had enjoyed it at first but now it had started to feel like playing, just a game, and I needed the sense of purpose that teaching used to give me even when it was monotonous. Oh for heaven's sake, he said, and hit the table with his hand. I reminded him that I'd asked him a few weeks ago to tell me the point of the magazine which still eluded me and it was what

I kept on missing, the *point* of it all. I felt no sense of mission or achievement, and I'd come to realise I needed to. Very well, he said, and began ticking off reasons why his magazine was of value and had a point. One, he said, man cannot live by bread alone, he needs cultural stimulation and our magazine supplies it. Two, it is full of outspoken and controversial views which cannot find an outlet in mainstream journals and which should be heard. Three, it is a cradle for the development of the talents of writers who will go on to influence our society. Is that enough, he said, enough *point* for you, madam? He was so cross his face was red and his eyes bulging, and he suddenly looked like a caricature of An Angry Man, the sort seen in *Punch*, with steam coming out of the ears. I said there was no need to be sarcastic. He had been provoked, I suppose, to speak very sharply but then he changed tack and said he hoped I wasn't serious about leaving because he couldn't imagine how he would manage without me, we were such a good team. A team, I echoed? Well, he corrected himself, a partnership. No, I said, that's not true. I am your employee and no longer comfortable about it. I would rather you were something else, he said, I would rather you were my wife.

Oh God, I should never have allowed him to say that because once said it could not be unsaid and there was no way in which I could conceal my dismay. It seemed best to leave him quickly. Matthew, I said, I am handing in my notice and I want no more mention of, of what you have just said. That was what I said, or something equally stiff and formal, and then I bundled all I owned into my bag, though not Tilda's yellow table-cloth,

126

and rushed to the door. But he was quicker. He stood with his back against it now looking not so funny, but quite threatening, like a villain in a melodrama, and said he thought all girls wanted marriage and why was I so offended and hadn't we been good friends and surely I had known what the natural outcome would be. I said not at all, that on the contrary I'd thought we were good friends and colleagues and I had in no way led him on. His reply was, I am only human. What that meant I cannot fathom. You are really just going to walk out and leave me, he said; and I said no, I would of course work out my notice. Don't bother, he said, and suddenly stood aside and let me pass. Then *I* felt bad, as though I had wronged him, and now I am sitting here weeping without knowing why. I am not at all sad to have given in my notice. Worried and mortified but not sad. Yet I can't help weeping. It is the mess, the way things have turned out, which makes me cry. What on earth is to become of me if I never settle to anything and never like any man enough. I have been such a fool and must face the consequences. I don't know if I should go to the office tomorrow or not. Did he mean it when he said don't bother? I think I should go, and show I am reliable and ready to work out my notice, but I dread it. I know I have hurt Matthew but I would like our parting of the ways to be civilised.

*       *       *

*But there seems to have been nothing 'civilised' about it. Millicent is shocked to arrive at the office next day and find the lock has been changed. There is a note from Matthew pinned to the door saying he will forward the money she is owed to Tilda's address and repeating that, 'in the interests of all concerned', she will not be required to work out her notice. She never sees him again. Her diary, while describing this, is curiously restrained and matter-of-fact and for two days afterwards she writes nothing at all. She remarks on Tilda's kindness, but she is aware that in spite of their sympathy her sister and her brother-in-law feel that she made a stupid mistake coming to work for Matthew Taylor in the first place and has been responsible for landing herself in a mess of her own making. When she resumes her diary, it is to wonder if she has taken 'a wrong turn' in her life from which she will never recover.*

## 3 December 1924

How dreadful it is to have no work. I woke this morning with a sick feeling in my stomach and thought how much worse I would be feeling if I were a man and had a family to feed. It was not much help counting my blessings in this fashion. I kept myself busy, tidying and cleaning the house for Tilda, and making a good job of it, and then I looked again at the *Times Educational Supplement* but there were no new positions advertised. There are too many teachers available, it seems, and those in work do not lightly give it up, as I did, or move around. I don't want to have to teach in an elementary school in London. The classes are big and the pupils not particularly desirous of learning. How childish I sound.

## 11 December

I cannot go on like this—a whole week of doing nothing, or nothing that counts. It does not suit me to be unemployed. I can't persuade myself that it is just a little holiday. I don't feel on holiday. I feel lost and frightened, almost in a panic of uselessness. I *must* have work. Even being a shop girl was better than this. I never, ever thought I would say that. I am going to Brighton for Christmas, as I always do, and will be busy there helping Mother which will take up time. It is sad to write that. I thought, when I was young, that I was going to do something special with my life and I am doing nothing. Self-disgust will soon eat me up.

## 14 December

On the train down to Brighton today I saw an advertisement in The Times. This one was for a teacher for a 10-year-old girl but what caught my eye was that the post was in Italy. The choice of 'teacher' not 'governess' was interesting to start with. I would not like to be a governess with all that implies. I don't know Italy of course, so the address meant nothing to me, but 'a charming country residence near Rome' was referred to. Is he a widower? It does not say, but it does say 'no domestic duties required' so there must be a housekeeper, or some female relative in charge. The pay sounds generous. I think I will apply. I would like to live in Italy.

## 15 December

I have sent my letter of application off, but now worry this is another example of rashness. What am I thinking of? I dare not mention it to Mother.

## 16 December

George is to be married. I can hardly credit it, for who would want to take on George? I know it is very unkind of me to say such a thing, and indeed I would never *say* it, to anyone, but I think it. Mother is delighted. It seems that Esther Holt is exactly the sort of girl she always wished for George. When I asked her what that meant, for I have not yet met this Esther, she said she is kind and dependable and motherly. Motherly! Mother is George's mother and yet wishes his wife to be *motherly*. I feel that tells me everything. She wants George to be looked after by someone other than herself. They are to live here, George and his Esther. Mother declares Esther herself wondered if it might be possible. How peculiar.

## 17 December

I have met Esther. She is a little dumpling of a girl, almost as round as she is tall. Grace had told me beforehand that she was very nervous about meeting me because I was held to be the clever one and she knows herself not to be clever but I saw no sign of nerves. She seemed to me quite complacent and very sure already of her place in this family. She looks after her mother, who is a widow like Mother, and is happy to do so. Her father, a gentleman farmer, was killed in the war. He left Esther and her mother well provided for. After the wedding, Mrs Holt's sister is to go and live with her. Her sister is a twin and the two of them have long planned to live together when their respective children are settled, as it seems they now are. All this Esther told me as though it were the most riveting information. She has such a droning sort of voice, and she nods her head when she speaks. She reminded me of a toy puppy Michael loves, it nods its head when the key in its ear is turned. I longed to stick a key into Esther's ear and turn her off. We

131

have nothing in common. She asked me to be a maid of honour but I protested I was too old and she seemed quick to let me off. It will be a spring wedding, she says. I wonder what the financial arrangements will be afterwards. George, I am sure, earns hardly anything and if Esther does not work at all, what will they live on? Mother? It seemed indelicate to inquire, especially when Mother seems so content about the arrangement and prattles on about gaining another daughter, one who wants to live with her, and how nice it will be for Grace. What Grace herself thinks I do not know. I am not at all certain that she will be pleased.

*　　　*　　　*

*Christmas and New Year receive little attention this year in her diary. Mrs Holt spends four days with the Kings and irritates Millicent profoundly with her constant questions about her personal life and whether she has an 'intended'. On 4 January, just as the holiday period is over and Millicent is beginning to panic over what on earth she is going to do, a letter arrives inviting her to an interview for the teaching post advertised in* The Times *to which she had replied.*

*　　　*　　　*

**5 January 1925**

I don't know what to tell Mother. Nothing, I think. I will just say I am going to stay overnight with

Tilda but I must think of a reason why I am going to London. I do not want to lie, but if I say I am going for an interview for a job, she will naturally wish to know more and I do not wish to tell her. I have not yet even told her I have left the magazine. The interview is at 10 a.m. and I will fix a dental appointment for the afternoon. It will relieve my conscience. The interview is to take place at Claridges Hotel in Mayfair, which sounds a rather grandiose place for such a thing. The man, a Mr Russo, is staying there. I wonder if he is Italian? The name sounds Italian but would he not refer to himself as *Signore* Russo? I have never even walked past Claridges never mind been inside. What on earth shall I wear? There is little choice, really. I have my plain grey coat and underneath it the cream woollen dress I bought three years ago. I have hardly had occasion to wear it in the life I lead and it looks new. Should I wear a hat? Probably. I don't want to look as if I have come to apply for the job of chambermaid.

## 14 January

That is the strangest interview I have ever had, more like an encounter than an interview. I was so nervous, I could hardly bring myself to enter the hotel at all and walked up and down Brook Street several times before I did so. It is every bit as impressive as I imagined it to be, with its shiny marble floors and all the glowing honey-coloured wood, and mirrors everywhere—how I hated seeing myself in them, looking like a little shadow in my grey coat. There seemed to be so many beautiful, delicate tables to avoid and I was terrified I would knock over the elaborate floral arrangements. I wandered around hoping to find a reception desk but I could see no such thing and came to rest in the most enormous room, utterly bewildered by the grandeur of it all. I felt an almost irresistible urge to hide behind the heavy swag curtains, but then I was rescued by a man who, I suppose, was a waiter, though he did not look like one in spite of the tray he was carrying. I told him I had an appointment with a Mr Russo and he told me to wait a moment and then went off, returning with the instruction that I should follow him. I trotted behind him like a little lamb. He took me to a small sitting-room opening off a larger one, and there was Mr Russo. His accent was American, not Italian, and he was as casual as Americans are reputed to be. He was lounging on a sofa when I entered and did not get up, but merely waved a hand at me and said, Hi! Come on over, pour yourself some coffee, though it isn't very good. I didn't know whether to pour myself some coffee or not. Was it a test? I smiled, and shook my head, and declined the coffee. Well now, he said, what do you make of this weather? There was nothing remarkable about the weather so I did not know what to say. It was not snowing or raining, it was not anything extreme. I decided to say that it was quite mild for January. Mild, he repeated, and then thought for a while and said, Mild . . . and mused about it. There was a photograph album on the table in front of him and presently he pointed to it and invited me to look at it. It contained very beautiful photographs, of a sort and quality I had never seen, nothing like our snapshots. They were mostly of a house, set on a hillside with steps leading up to it and great urns of flowers on every step. There were only two people in the frame. I recognised Mr Russo and presumed the girl beside him, who looked about Grace's age, was the daughter for whom he wanted a teacher. What do you think? he asked, Nice house? I said yes, it was. A very nice house, he said, a lovely place to live, don't you think? Again, I agreed. He got up, abruptly, and began to prowl around the room. My daughter Francesca needs teaching, he said. She doesn't need looking after, she doesn't need a nanny, what she needs is to *learn*. She needs her mind set to work, that's what. I want an English school marm. What do you think she should learn? She's 8. She can read and write real good and there's nothing wrong with her math. She needs some mental excitement. What's exciting? That isn't quite how he put it, but near enough. He threw his words down like a challenge. I floundered a bit, saying it was hard to know what would excite his daughter without having met her but that most children of her age found stories exciting if they were introduced to the right ones, and that learning about the natural world could fascinate them, and they liked to learn about other countries, foreign lands, which one day they could travel to. Have you travelled much?, he asked. I said no, only to Paris, unfortunately. He got up then, and began pacing about the little room, and I saw how tall he was and how thin. His clothes were strange, a mixture of formal (the black trousers) and sporty (the yellow waistcoat). I stared at his bow tie, which was *spotted*! Heavens, Father would've had a fit. I've travelled, he said, I've travelled far and wide, believe me. But not Francesca. She stayed with her mother. Her mother didn't like travelling. He walked around the room once more, deep in thought. To travel, or not to travel, what do you think? he asked and stopped and stood in front of me with folded arms. I didn't know what he meant, what he wanted of me, so I merely said that I would really like to travel and broaden my experience of the world. You wouldn't see much of the world living in my house with Francesca, he said. It's a remote spot, you've no idea how remote, very isolated. Think about it. Could feel like you'd been entirely cut off from the world. I felt he was waiting for me to respond to this and murmured that I'd thought his house was in Rome and that to be there would be thrilling. He laughed and said Rome was thrilling for sure, or certain aspects of it, though there were some unpleasant things happening there at the moment, but that his house was twenty miles outside the city and a different proposition. It struck me then that it might sound as if I had no interest in his daughter other than as a means to get abroad and so I rushed to ask who had taught her up to now and why she did not go to school and in general I tried to show an interest in the girl herself. He said she was delicate and not strong enough to go the long distance involved to school and that there were no children living near and therefore she lacked company. He said that for both these reasons he was going to move her to America, to where his family were, but that he could not do so for another seven months. The post of teacher, he said, was only for that length of time. He wanted Francesca prepared for school. Then, quite suddenly he said goodbye and he held out his hand, and I shook it. I left the hotel feeling

136

utterly confused, and yet somehow elated. I have always wanted something unusual to happen to me and this is certainly that. Had I been dismissed with the understanding that I was being offered the post? Or quite the reverse? I had no idea, but inclined to the latter conclusion. But I went to the dentist feeling optimistic and even excited.

## 15 January

Mother inquired after my visit to the dentist so it was as well that I had truly been. I cannot stay here much longer, especially now that Esther seems always to be around, chattering pointlessly away. I think there is a mock-innocence about her inquiries as to how I like living in Brighton after what she calls the 'hurly-burly' of London.

## 16 January

There is a vacancy at Grace's school for a teacher with experience of teaching 7 to 11-year-olds. I do not want to return to that but I am qualified and I need work and I think I should apply. There is no alternative.

## 17 January

I have applied for that teaching post without telling Mother, who thinks I am still on holiday, though I don't know how she can, why she is not suspicious. Grace likes the school so perhaps it will not be so bad teaching there, if I get the post. I must think how to explain why I left teaching and also why I wish to return. It will mean lying and the lies must be convincing and somehow work to my credit.

## 19 January

Good heavens—a letter from Mr Russo offering me the job of teacher to Francesca! I can hardly believe it. The post is, as he said, for seven months and I must begin next week, returning with him and motoring all the way through France to Italy. My spirits leapt at the thought and I found myself grinning idiotically at the breakfast table. Good news, dear?, Mother said, smiling herself. The smile disappeared when I blurted out first that I had given up journalism and then that I had been offered a teaching job abroad. Abroad is such a frightening word to her, never having been abroad in her entire life. Abroad to her means the war, I think. I said, hurriedly, anxious to reassure her, that it was only for seven months and only in Rome, which was not so very far away. Then I rushed to reply to Mr Russo, by telegram, as he had requested, ignoring Mother's questions about who exactly this Mr Russo is and whether he is married and his age and profession, because, of course, I don't know the answers and frankly I don't care. I *want* to be reckless. When I got back from the Post Office, Esther was there. She wondered aloud, and frequently, why ever I should want to go to Rome which she had been told had a very smelly river, and she lamented the fact that I would, by going there, miss her wedding. I hadn't thought of that, but now that she had pointed this out I could hardly conceal my relief and had to struggle to express regret.

## 22 January

Said goodbye to Mother with uncomfortable feelings of guilt quickly followed by assurances to myself that she would hardly miss me now she had Esther. You are always going away, Grace said, accusingly, I thought. It's true, so there was nothing I could say.

## 24 January

Shopping all day for clothes. I spent far too much money but I cannot accompany my employer looking dowdy and shabby. I have no idea what kind of clothes I will need, or even what the weather will be like. I suppose they have a winter there, but I am expecting spring to come much sooner than here and for the climate to be sunny and warm by April so I bought mostly light dresses. They were hard to find at this time of the year with the shops still full of furs and tweeds. I bought a valise, too. It is rather large and I think I should have bought two smaller ones. I may not be able to carry this one when it is full, especially with so many books in it, some for myself and some for Francesca. I forgot to ask Mr Russo, well, I never had the chance, what books Francesca has already, and whether there is an ample supply of exercise books and pens, but I suppose there will be, or that they can be ordered from Rome. It is not as though I am going to end up at Dotheboys Hall.

## 25 January

I dreamed last night that I did end up at Dotheboys Hall, only in a sunny place. I lay for a while suddenly anxious, realising how little I do know about what I am going to. I have asked no searching questions. I have been too eager and accepting, and Mr Russo will have noticed. But it is too late to do anything about it. Wherever I end up, yet again it will be my own fault. I hope Mr Russo has no designs on me. That is a ridiculous thought, a vain thought, but all at once I am full of suspicion. Perhaps there's a mad wife in the attic? Such thoughts are absurd. Tilda doesn't at *all* like the notion of our motoring all the way and asked pointedly if Mr Russo and I were to be alone, and where we would be staying and who would be paying for the hotels? I had to say I had no idea, that he had said he would make all the arrangements. I feel naive not to have checked such details, which are not so very minor. But I have some money. I am not Jane Eyre, and if anything unpleasant transpires, I can simply come home. Mr Russo is to pick me up at Tilda's address, tomorrow.

## 26 January: Paris

Only the energy to scribble a few lines. Mr Russo and I are not alone. In the car with him when he arrived to pick me up at Tilda's were *two* other people, a middle-aged woman called Mrs Harris and a young man called Kenneth. Tilda was relieved. But I know nothing yet about either of them.

*　　　*　　　*

*The drive to Italy through France (quite an undertaking in those days, but Mr Russo was evidently a keen motorist) took a route via Dijon then down the Rhone Valley to Marseilles, but there's not much in the diary, because Millicent is writing long, descriptive letters to her mother. All she notes in it are observations which she obviously feels she can't make to her mother. Most of them concern Mr Russo, who seems to her a very strange man though she likes him very much. She speculates frequently as to whether he is attracted to her and whether she is attracted to him, deciding that if there is attraction, on either side, it is not 'physical'. According to Millicent, he is not good-looking. Apart from being tall and too thin, he is very nearly bald and she cannot abide bald men. His complexion is sallow and he has a prominent Adam's apple. But he is kind and chivalrous and has a quirky sense of humour which appeals to her. Sometimes they catch each other's eye when Mrs Harris makes some ridiculous remark and she feels they share the joke. Mrs Harris, it emerges, is the wife of Mr Russo's cousin and is going to stay with him 'for a rest', though a rest from what is not divulged. Millicent thinks her a snob, an overdressed and haughty woman, who ignores everyone but Mr Russo. The other passenger, Kenneth, is the son of an old friend. He is going to learn Italian and be initiated into the*

141

*wine trade (Mr Russo's business). Millicent sits in the front with Mr Russo, because Mrs Harris prefers the back, and thoroughly enjoys herself except for the headaches she experiences when Mr Russo sings songs from his favourite operas too loudly and for too long.*

\*     \*     \*

## 2 February: Pisa

Our first stop in Italy. We visited the Leaning Tower, which really does lean alarmingly, and Kenneth and I climbed the crumbling steps to the top. It was the first time we had been alone together and he took the opportunity, which shocked me, to call Mrs Harris a bore and to wish she was not in our party. I refused to agree. I am not going to be rude about anyone and I will certainly not let Kenneth think he can make an ally of me. He is rather a callow youth, though I suppose handsome in a very English way, tall and slim with floppy fair hair and very blue eyes. He is very curious about me, quizzing me all the time. I give nothing away, and let him think what he wants. He would like to take a turn driving the car, but Mr Russo was horrified at this suggestion. He loves his car, and is so proud of its performance, with never a hint of any mechanical trouble.

## 3 February: Rome

We are outside Rome, near a very ancient road

called the Via Cassia, on a hillside, as I had seen in the photographs. The villa is beautiful, with glorious views of open countryside. My room, when I was shown into it, had the shutters closed, so it was dim and I could not see much but then when the shutters were thrown open, I gasped at the dazzling scene framed in the window. I had not realised that the villa was so high up above the surrounding landscape, which is flat, no, not flat, undulating and open, a great expanse of rolling green. In the distance this green is taken over by the deep, deep blue of the sky with a line on the horizon so sharp where they meet, the blue and the green, that it might have been drawn with a ruler. All this is far off, and in the foreground there are gardens sloping down from a stone terrace. There are not many flowers at the moment but many different shades of green. I stood there for ages, simply transfixed. There was a bell, tolling somewhere far away, and a donkey braying but otherwise all was still. Still enough for me to be startled when I heard a voice below. My room is large but very nearly empty, with only a bed, one chair, a desk, and a chest of drawers and a cupboard in it. The floor is tiled. The bedcovers are white, the chair has a white cover on it, the walls are white. There are no curtains or carpet. It echoes. I love it.

**4 February**

Mr Russo said I must regard today and tomorrow as a holiday and if I wish he can arrange for me to visit Rome, but I said I was happy to get to know the house and garden and of course his daughter first. This seemed to please him. Francesca was not what I expected. I had imagined a girl much like Grace, from the shadowy photograph which I had seen. But Francesca must have grown since that photograph was taken. She is much taller than Grace, which means I am not so very much taller than she is, being small myself. She is what Mother would call well covered too, quite heavily built and, again, since I am so slight, it had the effect of making me feel somehow at a disadvantage. She is nothing like Mr Russo so she must take after her mother. Her mother has never been mentioned. I asked Mrs Harris if she knew what had happened to Mr Russo's wife and she looked offended, or maybe it was alarmed, at any rate she looked uncomfortable, and said that was for him to tell me. I felt I had shown vulgar curiosity, but surely it is natural to want to know how my pupil comes not to have a mother.

**5 February**

I woke this morning bewildered, quite unable to decide where I was. The sun was coming through the slats in the shutters, casting lines of light across the tiled floor, and I lay there for a while feeling somehow out of myself, as I sometimes have the habit of doing, as though it were not really me in the bed. Opening the shutters, when I did get up, gave me the same shock I think it always will, the shock of the sheer *difference* from what I have been used to. I cannot get enough of it, all that glow of sun, all this colour. I saw Mr Russo walking on the terrace in a dressing-gown, smoking, but he had gone by the time I had dressed and made my way there. Perhaps it was just as well. He might not have liked being approached when he was in his dressing-gown. He might have thought me too bold. The custom in the morning is to breakfast on the terrace. Coffee and fresh rolls and fruit are brought out and set on the white-painted iron table. The coffee is poured into beautiful blue cups and the rolls come in baskets covered with blue linen napkins. Kenneth joined me, complaining at the lack of a real English breakfast and wishing there were at least eggs on offer. I did not respond, except to say I thought the breakfast delightful. Privately, I was thinking this was absolute heaven.

## 8 February

I love waking up here: early morning is quite the best time of day. I try now to walk through the gardens before I go to the terrace for breakfast. Sometimes I see Mr Russo watching me. He waves, but never joins me. In fact, I hardly see him all day, though we all eat together in the evening. He asks me how I am getting on with the teaching but always in front of Kenneth and Mrs Harris and this inhibits me. I just say quite well, thank you, and that we are making progress, and this seems to satisfy him. Perhaps next week I will have the opportunity to talk to him in private and then I can confess that I am finding Francesca perfectly obedient and ready to learn but somehow hostile. I had better not use the word hostile. It is not quite what I mean. I mean that she has no interest in me

145

as a person and looks at me blankly and refuses to be friendly. She never smiles. She is unlike any 8-year-old I have ever come across. Is she unhappy? Is this blankness something to do with her missing mother?

## 11 February

It rained today, positively poured. I woke feeling cold, and there was no light in the room. The lack of sun changes everything. No breakfast on the terrace, and I am told it is not usual in any case to have it there before the middle of March but that this year there has been an exceptionally early and warm spring. We breakfasted instead in a small room beside the schoolroom. Luckily, Kenneth was late up, and Mrs Harris always has breakfast in bed, so I had it to myself and nobody saw me shiver. The schoolroom was cold too, but I had by that time put on a jacket and some thicker stockings. It is the tiled floors and all the marble surfaces which make the rooms seem colder. This villa is built for sun and doesn't know what to do about cold.

## 12 February

Today we had the most delicious meal, starting with what Mr Russo told me was *farce à raviolis*. It looked so pretty on the green plate, and tasted heavenly. I asked what the stuffing was, and Mr Russo asked Sofia and then translated her answer: spinach, onion, herbs, white wine and *lean veal and raw ham*! So I have eaten *meat* and loved it and can no longer call myself a vegetarian. But then, if meat was in any dish that tasted like the ravioli, I would never have stuck to being a vegetarian. I hardly feel ashamed at all.

**14 February**

The sun is out again, thank goodness. I had letters from home today, from Tilda and from Mother, and a sweet note from Grace. I suggested to Francesca that she might like to write to Grace, to have her as a pen-friend. She did not seem to understand that term but when I had explained she showed little enthusiasm. That's the trouble with Francesca in general, she never shows enthusiasm for anything. She has so little vitality, never shouts or screams, never runs or rushes about. She is a self-contained, silent child but not placid. She pays attention to my teaching and does her work conscientiously but she is too dutiful. It's not normal. I never thought I would think of our twins nostalgically, but suddenly I long for their ebullience and some of the high-spirited chatter they indulge in so endlessly. I asked her today what she does in the afternoons. We finish school at midday and I never see her after that, or hear her. She told me that after siesta she rides some days, with an instructor. She has no children at all to play with. If I were her father, I would make more effort to find playmates for her. She will find America a shock, I am sure.

## 20 February

I'm trying hard to learn some Italian with the help
of a dictionary and a teach-yourself book I brought
from London. I have no need of the language to
converse with Mr Russo or Francesca or Kenneth
or Mrs Harris; indeed English is the language of
the villa with even the servants speaking a little, but
it is because of them that I wish to learn Italian.
Drifting round the villa as I often do, when I'm
unsure how I might spend my free time, I hear
Maria and the others talking volubly and I long to
know what is being said. And, besides, it occurs to
me that the servants must know about Mrs Russo
and it would be easier to ask them than Mr Russo.
I dislike not being able to speak to people, and
dislike even more not understanding them. Passing
the open kitchen door as I walked round the villa
this afternoon, I heard a man's voice shouting and
realised it was coming from a radio. I could not
make out a word except for '*Italia!*' repeated over
and over again, but the whole tone sounded
furiously angry. I asked Maria later to tell me who
the voice belonged to and what it had said, but she
shook her head and said it was '*il Duce*' and she
didn't know what he had said. How ignorant I am
of what goes on in this country.

## 25 February

My first day in Rome. I have resisted the lure of the
city for three whole weeks, mostly because I
wanted Mr Russo to see that I put his daughter
before my own pleasure. But three weeks has been

long enough, I think, to establish my credentials and really I longed to see Rome and could resist the temptation no longer. I knew Mr Russo's manservant, Giorgio, who seems to do all sorts of jobs as well as act as chauffeur when required, was to take Mrs Harris to tea with a friend of hers who lives near the Piazza del Campidoglio. So I asked for a lift and arranged to be picked up two hours later at the same spot.

Two hours is not long to see a city like Rome and I have barely touched a quarter of it, and been inside no churches or art galleries, being determined to stay outside and get a feel of how the city looks, but it is a start. I have written a long letter to Mother describing what I have seen. I have asked Mother to keep my letters, though I am sure she would anyway, so that I will have a record of my time here. What I don't put in my letters, because it would alarm Mother, is anything about the strangeness of Mr Russo and Francesca. I just say that Francesca is a good little girl and a willing pupil and that my job could not be easier. I don't pass any comment on Mr Russo, except to remark that he is rarely around but pleasant enough when he is. I make sure to bring Mrs Harris into my letters, knowing Mother will find her presence reassuring. I wrote nothing, though, about the gangs of young men I saw everywhere, strutting about and looking like soldiers, but I don't think they were soldiers. People were wary of them. I noticed they stepped aside to let these swaggering young men pass. I must ask Mr Russo about them.

# 1 March

For the first time I feel comfortable here. I am part of the routine of the villa and accepted as such, more, I can tell, than either Kenneth or Mrs Harris are. The day runs smoothly at last. I get up, walk in the garden, breakfast on the terrace, then go to the schoolroom where Francesca is waiting and spend the morning teaching her, always making sure that I am varying the work. At 10.30 Sofia brings in fruit juice for us and I make a point of us taking it outside and drinking it on the terrace so that it feels like a proper break. We have a little exercise before we go back, sometimes with a skipping rope I brought from England. I had to teach Francesca how to skip. She thought it most peculiar but has grown to enjoy it. Then we continue lessons till midday. Francesca has something to eat in her room and then sleeps, or rests, till 3 p.m. This seems to be a custom that cannot be broken though, since the weather is not at all hot yet, I cannot see the sense in it. I am brought a tray of food, delicious ham or cheese and always a plate of fruit, and then I set off and walk for an hour, returning to read until Mr Russo and Kenneth return. I bathe before drinks on the terrace and then we dine. Dinner takes a very, very long time. It is a lazy life. I never do anything except teach Francesca. My clothes are washed for me, my room is cleaned, I am waited on as though I were a guest like Mrs Harris. What Mrs Harris does all day is a mystery. She stays mostly in her room and when she emerges complains constantly of exhaustion. She rarely speaks to me. She thinks of me as one of the servants. I can't say I care.

I asked Mr Russo at dinner tonight about the gangs of young men I had seen. He said they were fascists, members of the *Fascio di Combattimento*, headed by their leader, Mussolini. He gave me a little lecture on what was happening now in Italy and I was grateful to be given the chance to learn.


**4 March**

I had a meeting with Mr Russo today, which I was glad of. He had requested it, at the unusual time of before breakfast. It was a glorious morning and we sat on the terrace, but round the corner of the main terrace, in absolute privacy. Mr Russo often sits there, in a little bower constructed out of wrought-iron screens up which buds of purple and pink bougainvillaea have begun to climb. It seems to be generally known that when he is there he does not wish to be disturbed. He asked if I was bored. I said certainly not and stressed how much I loved the villa and the whole atmosphere of it and what a pleasure it was teaching Francesca instead of a large class of children. I hoped that would lead into a discussion about my pupil, but it didn't. Mr Russo went on to comment on my youth and the lack of company. I said I had always been of a solitary nature and did not crave company and that I was twenty-three and not so very young. He smiled, and said, Twenty-three, in a tone of mock-awe, I felt, and then, You are certainly very mature for your age, if I may say so. A wise head, I think, on such young and very pretty shoulders. Well, I know I'm not especially pretty, but men think it such a compliment to say one is *pretty*, and Mother was

151

always telling me I should accept it as such and be glad, but I never feel glad. It makes me suspicious, somehow. At any rate, I ignored it and turned the conversation, saying Francesca seemed so very withdrawn and would not respond to friendly overtures. He said, Ah, and got up and lit a cigarette and stood, not quite with his back to me, looking down the garden. There was a silence. Francesca, he began, and then there was another pause, before he went on, Francesca had a shock. A very great shock, a year ago, when she found her mother dead. I am afraid she was alone with . . . she was alone with her for some time. She is much better, but still suffering. It will take time. Sadly, there is no mother substitute, no one who can begin to take her mother's place. I was paralysed with the shock of what he had told me and yet instantly my head was full of questions as to how Francesca came to be alone with the dead body of her mother. I asked none of them, hoping Mr Russo would continue, and enlighten me. But no. He didn't. I managed to whisper how very sorry I was to hear this, how shocked, how I felt for Francesca. He acknowledged this with a bowing of his head, and terminated our meeting by pushing his chair into the table and gesturing that we should walk round to the main terrace.

I felt quite shaken, and later, when I went to the schoolroom, I was sure Francesca saw a difference in my face. She must have seen that I looked upset and my distress made an impression, without her knowing the cause of it, and she responded to it. Her expression changed. She looked not quite so blank. I wondered if I should say something but decided it would be a mistake. We went on as usual. I was ashamed to think I had begun to be impatient with her refusal to respond to me and realised that perhaps the fault was mine, that *I* had been too distant. At any rate, at last I felt a subtle shifting of the relationship between us, but maybe that is fanciful. I suppose my new knowledge made me compassionate and that I relaxed more and so the tension between us evaporated a little. I don't know. She is only 8. When this awful thing—but what, what exactly?—happened she was only 7. It is too awful to imagine myself, or even Grace, at 7 being alone with the dead body of Mother. It was dreadful enough being with Father when I was 17, and I was never alone. I cannot get it out of my mind.

## 10 March

George and Esther's wedding day. I sent a telegram, managing to travel into Rome and do it myself which made me feel proud. It is no easy thing dealing with the post office here. I found myself not quite as relieved not to be at the wedding as I had thought I would be. I am not in the least homesick but on the other hand family gatherings are not so plentiful that I want to miss them. It still seems extraordinary that George has managed to marry at all. I think more and more that I shall never marry. Mother asked in her last letter if I had made any friends of my own age. I know she means *men* friends. Of course, I haven't. I see no one but the people in this house. She sees me as next in line for marriage and waits for news of a romance. Unless I run off with Giorgio, I can't think where it could come from, though Mother may fantasise about Kenneth, which makes me shudder. It is impossible to convince her that I am perfectly happy single. Well, I ask myself if this is really true, or if I protest too much, and I am sure that it is true—*for the moment.*

**19 March**

Long letters from Mother and from Tilda about the wedding—and something much more exciting: Tilda is expecting a baby in early September! Mother is practically hysterical with joy. Tilda wants reassurance that I will be home for the birth and wonders if I could come for a week or so after the birth to look after her. She says Mother wants to, but she has Grace and Michael and the twins to think of, and she does not know the house and the area as I do. I feel quite flattered to be asked, though also a little wary. I'm not sure that I want to move into the role of unmarried sister called on to be nursemaid. That's a mean thing to think, and uncalled for. Tilda has been kind to me, and generous, and I will be the same to her.

**20 March**

Spent most of the day writing letters home. Already Mother wants to know what I am going to do next, after I return from here. I wish she, and others, were not forever wanting to know that. I am not so obsessed with the future that I have to look months ahead all the time. It is so irritating when people expect me to.

*      *      *

*And yet the diary for the following two months suggests that Millicent was indeed thinking about her immediate future and not relishing the prospect of a return to England with no job in prospect. Stuck in the diary for this year is a cutting from the* Times Educational Supplement *with teaching vacancies marked with crosses and ticks. It is unlikely that this paper was on sale in Rome in 1925, which means she must have subscribed to it and had it sent out. Then, in June, shortly before her situation is to come to an end, her employer makes a suggestion.*

*      *      *

### 19 June

Mr Russo, who has been away from home for over a week, asked to see me this morning. He asked me first how I was getting on with Francesca now. I said that I thought she was warming a little towards me and that we were beginning to be friends as well as teacher and pupil. He nodded. Then he told me that he had now arranged the move to America, which was to be in August, after my contract ended. He said he would be glad to leave Italy, that it was no longer a country in which someone half-American by birth could feel comfortable. He has bought a house on somewhere called Long Island, and has already engaged a housekeeper and found a school for Francesca where he hopes she will be

155

happy. He said he thought I had prepared her well for schoolwork and she was ready for it. I did not interrupt, but firstly wondered how he could know this and secondly I doubted he was right. Francesca has had no companionship of her own age, and is still very withdrawn, and I am sure will find going to school in a strange country completely bewildering. Then he amazed me by suggesting I should travel with Francesca to America and see her settled in. I blurted out immediately that I had to be in London in September for the birth of my sister's baby, and that I had promised to look after her. He accepted the news graciously but was obviously disappointed.

I like Mr Russo. I haven't got to know him at all, but I like him. There is something sad and something brave about his oddness. I like him better than his daughter, though I spoke the truth when I said I was becoming more friendly with her. They are both somehow fragile. They move about this villa and its gardens as though in a dream, and it is not, I think, a pleasant dream. Sometimes, each of them can look at me, directly into my eyes, and there is nothing there, they look vacant, and then with what I feel is a great effort consciousness returns. But partly this may be due to the atmosphere here—so sleepy, so slow, the very air enclosing us, making all action an effort. It is what Kenneth hates about the place. He says he feels drugged, half-dead.

**25 June**

It has been so hot today, fiercely so. Francesca and

I sat inside this morning with the shutters half closed against the brilliance of the light. The stones on the terrace burned my feet even through the soles of my sandals and there was not the slightest breeze. Mr Russo and Kenneth rode off very early and the house seems heavily quiet. Francesca does not like it. She gave me odd little anxious looks and asked would there be a storm and would her papa be back before it. I was reading to her but barely had the energy to continue. Sofia brought us iced water with lemon in it and Francesca took out the ice cubes and laid them one on each cheek. Mama did that, she said, she put ice on her face and ice down the front of her dress and ice in her armpits, when it was hot like this. I hardly dared to breathe. She has never mentioned her mother to me before. She went on, Mama said it was too, too hot and the only thing to do was sleep till the storm came, and she sent me for the tablets to help her sleep, and we slept. What could I say, what was fitting to say? I did not believe it would be right to question her and yet longed to take the opportunity. There was a clap of thunder then and a great rumbling, and Francesca sat up straight, the water from the ice cubes running down her face like tears, and said the storm had come; but it hadn't, not then, and we waited an hour or so for the thunder to come nearer and the blessed rain to begin to fall. Mr Russo and Kenneth arrived back soaked to the skin soon afterwards.

**26 June**

Kenneth did not go with Mr Russo today. He

157

stayed and hung about and was in general a nuisance. After lunch, when Francesca had gone for a siesta and I was hoping to follow suit, he kept me on the terrace talking, constantly begging me not to leave him or he'd go mad with boredom. I do not care at all about his boredom, and despise him for being bored, but he grabbed my arm and pushed me back into my chair, in front of Sofia who was clearing the table. He is an odd cove, Kenneth said, don't you think so. I did not inquire who he meant. My father says he always was a bit crackers, Kenneth went on, though I had given him no encouragement. He likes you, I can see. Do you like him? He's a very eligible widower though of course much older than you, but still . . . I was outraged and tried to get out of my chair in order to leave Kenneth's odious company but he stood in front of me, one hand on each arm of the chair, and I could not get out. You are blushing, he said, oh you *are* blushing, well, well, do you have hopes of being the second Mrs Russo? I spat in his face. I know that was a very vulgar thing to do, and that it might even convince Kenneth he was right to suspect that I had designs on Mr Russo, but there was nothing else I could do. And at least it succeeded in releasing me. He put his hands up to wipe his face telling me I was a little bitch, so I called him a repulsive little worm, and ran back into the house. I boil with resentment. Mr Russo has been nothing but good and kind to Kenneth and this is the thanks he gets. Why is it that young men like Kenneth cannot see a girl like me without believing her head must be filled with thoughts of ensnaring every man around. Next he'll be imagining I plan to trap *him*. What a revolting thought.

**15 July**

My birthday. I told no one until the late evening.
Such a hot, still day, hotter than ever, too hot by
eleven in the morning to continue teaching. I
longed to be beside water, beside the sea at
Brighton however cold and grey, but we are miles
even from a river or lake. Mrs Harris who goes
home tomorrow lay all day in a hammock under
the trees in the lower garden and Francesca sat
with her feet in the pond reading *The Secret
Garden*. I went to the summer house on the far side
of the garden, the shadiest spot, and read *Gone to
Earth*, which Mother has sent me. Mother has read
it with much enjoyment, but I found it somehow
absurd and laughable. I couldn't believe in Hazel,
the heroine, who is supposed to be wild and shy as
a wood nymph. She does not behave like my idea
of a wood nymph and does silly things. I knew from
the beginning what would happen. I do wonder if
Mother sent me this novel as a warning, in case I
became like Hazel, seduced, pregnant and ruined.
It made me laugh to think of it. After I'd finished
the book, I lay daydreaming. I lay full length on the
cushions and looked down through half-closed
eyelids on the surrounding countryside, all golden
and shimmering in the heat-haze. I felt drunk,
though since I had never been drunk, just a little
tipsy at that dance with Tom, I wasn't sure what
that would feel like. I told myself I should be
thinking of my life and what I should do with it, but
found I could not think of anything but the heat,

159

and surrendered to it happily. We ate dinner on the back terrace, where there is no trellis and where, if there is the faintest breeze, it catches the cool air. There were fireflies everywhere. Kenneth looked quite desperate with boredom. I ignore him completely now, never so much as glancing in his direction. I couldn't resist telling everyone that it was my birthday. Mr Russo immediately sent Fernando to his cellar for champagne and made a great fuss about chilled glasses. After two glasses, I really did know what it is like to be truly drunk. I floated to my room and fell asleep, still dressed.

**16 July**

Terrible headache all day. Mrs Harris who left directly after breakfast was surprised, saying good champagne such as we drank last night does not normally cause headaches and that she, prone to headaches, did not have one. It is extraordinary to me that I can have lived with this woman in the same house for nearly six months and yet feel she is a total stranger. She has no interest in me, or indeed in anyone. It is as though this house were an hotel and we are all guests (or in my case a servant) who have nothing to do with each other. She has no curiosity and, as I learned very early, if people are curious about her, she is offended. Mr Russo does not seem to mind but I mind, and on his behalf as well as my own. I think she does not deserve his hospitality. Kenneth is tiresome but at least does not sit like a fat sphinx, as she has done.

## 17 July

Mr Russo and I ate alone tonight. Kenneth was away in Rome for the night. Though I like Mr Russo, I rather dreaded dinner, feeling self-conscious, but I enjoyed it. He talked about his father, who was Italian and moved to New York when he was a young man, and about his American mother who never really liked Italy and would not agree to live here when his father had made his fortune and wished to return. Mr Russo said his father was pleased when he himself married an Italian girl. He said this so easily that I felt I could, at long last, venture to ask the question I had longed to ask from the beginning, which of course was what exactly had happened to his wife, how she had come to die. I asked hesitantly, ready to apologise if I could sense he felt it an intrusion, but he answered readily enough, speaking very quietly. It was dark, and the candles had burned low, and I could not see his expression. He told me that his wife had been ill for some time after the birth of Francesca, and that, though she had seemed to recover, ever after she had spells of profound depression which completely incapacitated her. These were made worse by two miscarriages she suffered later. One day, when he was away from home and the nanny who cared for Francesca was away for the day, his wife took an overdose of sleeping pills. He said he was certain she simply miscalculated the dose and did not intend to kill herself but that she had done so. Francesca was asleep beside her when she did it, but woke soon after and stayed beside her mother trying to rouse her. It was four hours before the nanny returned.

So now I know, and I wish I did not.

## 18 July

I hardly slept last night for thinking about Mr Russo's wife. All these tragedies people have in their lives, hidden from the eye, and time rolls on over them leaving no visible trace whatever of the hurt and wounds inside. How could she do it, with her child beside her, but then all she may have longed to do was sleep, not die. I cannot believe she did it on purpose; it would have been too cruel. I wonder why she was so depressed. She had everything, surely. I think and think about her, and am ashamed of how much I long to know. There are no photographs of her in this villa and I want to see what she looked like, though her appearance has no relevance to anything. It seems so strange to go in and out of people's lives as I seem destined to do, part of their history for such a brief time and never becoming intimate in any way. They will hardly remember me, but I will always remember them.

## 19 July

Felt so unsettled today, disturbed even. Francesca went riding with her instructor after her siesta. It is not nearly so hot, though I am told this is a brief respite and the fierce heat will return at the weekend. I started to walk, following the dirt track which leads from this house to the old road, but it was so dusty, the track, and even walking slowly I threw up little clouds which coated my legs and felt uncomfortable. How still it was as I rested where the track meets the road. I stood motionless, gazing at the rolling land, so green when I arrived and now burned and yellow. There is a cypress tree, just one, far down the road to the west, and in the distance, to the east, a group of these trees are huddled together as though in a meeting. No houses, no people. Mr Russo says his house is very old and that he merely renovated it. It was never part of a village but was once fortified with a wall round it and outside the wall were two or three small, primitive dwellings in such bad condition he had them knocked down. I wonder what effect this had on his poor wife, living here, without any company, and no other houses to walk to. It is a very strange place for a man like Mr Russo to choose to live, going as he does most days to Rome. But it will surely be a safe place if, as Mr Russo predicts, civil war breaks out. It is only in Rome that there is any sense of violence. Here, it is so peaceful and calm. I hope Mr Russo is wrong. I hope there will be no war of any kind.

**21 July**

Went to Rome, with Kenneth and Mr Russo, feeling I ought to, since I have so little time left and have hardly been at all. Giorgio drove because Mr Russo has a mild eye infection. On the outskirts, we passed a long line of ragged-looking men digging up the road. Giorgio said something and I asked Mr Russo to translate. Giorgio apparently had said there had been nothing wrong with the road. I was puzzled and asked why in that case it was being dug up. To employ as many men as possible, said Mr Russo, it is *il Duce*'s policy. He smiled oddly when he said this. The city was crowded and noisy, quite vile I thought, and I could hardly cope with the crowds and heat and became bad-tempered and wished myself back in the isolation of Mr Russo's house. I sought the cool of a church, the Santa Maria Maggiore, which was mercifully mostly empty of sightseers. The mosaics either side of the nave, showing scenes of the Old Testament, are beautiful. I thought of trying to climb the bell tower but it is forbidden. It calmed me, being there, and I managed better when I came out but I was glad to meet Mr Russo and Kenneth as arranged and return home at sunset. Mr Russo looked worried. I asked if his eyes were worse, but he said no, he was merely tired, and concerned about someone he knew, a lawyer, who had disappeared. Giorgio said something then and I understood the gist, which was that people, *good* people, were disappearing all the time now. I don't know what he means.

Kenneth had a headache and retired early, thank goodness. Mr Russo has sensed the enmity between us and is, I think, amused. He asked tonight if I had any brothers and I told him about George and the twins and Michael. He was interested in what I told him about George and said that one of the reasons he had bought this house was that living here made the whole idea of war seem absurd. I asked him if he would feel the same in America and he said alas, no, and sighed. I marked particularly what he said next. In America, he said, I will rejoin life, just as you will back in

164

England. Rejoin life, I echoed, and I thought of *A Tale of Two Cities*, but did not say so. Yes, he said, we are withdrawn from people here and the chance of relationships is very small. If we stay withdrawn, we stultify. It was dark and I could not see his face, only the glow of his cigarette. Don't think me impertinent, he went on, but I feel you have not yet been in love? His voice did go up at the end, the questioning tone was unmistakenly there. I said no, I had not, that I had only felt a fleeting attraction for a time to a man who had soon gone out of my life. Well, said Mr Russo, all that is to come, for the first time for you and, God willing, again for me. But it won't come here. We sat a while longer on the terrace. I felt I wanted to say something without knowing what. I wanted to tell him how I admired him and liked him but thought it would sound unctuous. Do I mean unctuous? Yes, I think so. We stood up together soon after and wished each other goodnight. I suspect I will never sleep. I feel alert even though an hour or so ago I was so very tired.


## 28 July

My last day here. Farewells to Mr Russo and the obnoxious Kenneth have already been made because they are staying in Rome for the next few days. Mr Russo has arranged all the details of my departure and I have nothing to worry about. I thanked him effusively for his kindnesses to me and his generosity and he said that on the contrary he was in my debt because I had done so much for his daughter, and he only wished he could have persuaded me to accompany her to America. I did not tell him how tempted I have been to do just that, tempted and tormented also, by the thought that I may be making another wrong choice and turning aside from an opportunity which I will not get again. Will I look back in future years and wish I had gone to America? It would be too terrible. But there is Mother to think of, and Tilda's need, and America is a very long way away and going there quite different from coming here. Well, the die is cast.

*     *     *

*It was a good time to get out of Italy. As Mr Russo doubtless knew, Mussolini's contempt for democracy and belief in violent action were making the country a dangerous place to live in unless the fascist creed was accepted and obeyed. Elections were by then a fraud, torture was used in prisons, and people disappeared suddenly, 'enemies of the State', to be buried in unmarked graves. Most of this had passed Millicent by, but by the time she leaves she has at least picked up hints of what is going on and is concerned for those she is leaving behind. Mr Russo assures her that, in so far as he is able, he will try to protect them. When he departs, the villa will be shut up but places found for the servants.*

*After a surprisingly emotional goodbye from Francesca, which touches her greatly, Millicent travels back to England, by train, and goes first to Brighton where she spends an unsatisfactory month becoming increasingly irritated by her sister-in-law Esther (already pregnant) and increasingly concerned about her own, yet again, uncertain future. It is hard to gauge, from her diary, just what Millicent expected from Italy, but I think her expectations of some kind of adventure were quite high and that she is therefore disappointed nothing exciting has happened. She's spent seven very quiet months teaching a rather uncommunicative child in a beautiful but isolated villa and that was all—there have been no dramatic developments and her life has not been changed for ever. She is back where she started and the romantic in her feels cheated. There is no mention in her diary, however, of applying for jobs. She spends her days helping her mother with the younger children, developing some degree of closeness to 9-year-old Grace, and walking the dog that Michael (who is said to be a very solitary child) has just been given. Then, at the end of August, comes the summons from Tilda, whose baby is due. Florence is born on 1st September.*

## 6 September 1925

Why Tilda could not keep on the maternity nurse for longer I do not know. Florence cried all last night, I swear. I could hear her clearly, and lay gritting my teeth and willing Tilda to attend to her, but the crying, the *screaming*, went on and shattered my nerves. At two in the morning, I could stand it no longer and got up only to find Tilda was up already and walking up and down with Florence, and crying herself. Why can't Charles do something about this, what is the point of being married to a children's doctor if he cannot find out what is wrong with his own baby? But Charles was not here, he was at his hospital attending to other women's babies. And Tilda a *nurse*, surely she should be able to quieten Florence. I took her from Tilda's arms and for a moment she stopped yelling, only to start again. But it gave Tilda the chance to make her up a bottle, though she was not due another for an hour. The relief when the milk silenced her! I went back to bed, unable to imagine how Mother had coped and with twins. Tilda and I discuss it, and agree that though Mother had a nursemaid it is still impossible to believe how well she managed. Neither of us can recall Michael or Grace screaming the night away, but then the house was bigger, much, than this one and we were younger and sound sleepers. But I can't go on living here. I will stay only a month. I don't want to return to Brighton but it is preferable to here. Why am I so hopeless that I cannot find a job and a place of my own to live?

## 7 September

A letter from, of all people, Mrs Harris, forwarded from Brighton. I never thought to hear from that unfriendly lady ever again nor did I ever want to, though I expect, and want, to keep in touch with Mr Russo. Mr Russo provided her with my address and she hopes I will not think her letter an intrusion but she believes she can put me in touch with what she calls 'a great opportunity'. This opportunity is the offer of the post of companion to the bereaved daughter of friends of hers, a Miss Daphne Willes who lives in Yorkshire. Miss Willes is 17 years of age and has recently lost both her parents and been very ill herself. She needs someone to be with her, though not to look after her, she has servants to do that, but to read with her and take walks as her strength returns. Mrs Harris remembers how good I was with Francesca and, though Miss Willes is much older and the situation different, she thinks I would be ideal and has suggested Miss Willes could write to me herself if I am agreeable. This letter, the tone of it, annoys me intensely. It is condescending. I fail to see where any 'great opportunity' lies. Teaching Francesca, and having the opportunity to live in Italy for a while, was one thing, but going to Yorkshire, with winter not that far off, merely to keep a young woman company is in my opinion quite demeaning. On the other hand, it would get me away from here. It is weak of me, but I have replied saying Mrs Harris can give Miss Willes my address. Nothing to be lost in that.

## 11 September

A letter from Miss Willes. I am quite taken with it. Her approach is not at all like Mrs Harris's. She sounds diffident and is very self-deprecating though also has a touch of wit, describing herself as, at the moment, a bit like a wilted stalk of asparagus because she is all floppy and green around the gills. She says she needs stimulation more than anything or she will drown in self-pity. She encloses a photograph of a solid-looking house, which is on the outskirts of Leeds, and of herself 'before the accident'. She looks a cheerful, happy girl. There was a separate note included, telling me how much I would be paid and for how long the agreement would be after an initial trial period. It was typed, whereas the letter was handwritten. I thought that showed a certain delicacy and a business-like mind, unusual, surely, in one so young. I am going to think about it.


## 12 September

I am still thinking. Florence cried all day as well as all night, or so it seemed. Charles says it is 'just' colic, and will cease soon. How soon? It grows more attractive hourly to be far away in Leeds, though when I mentioned the prospect to Tilda she was horrified, not just at the thought of my leaving but of Leeds. She is sure it is a ghastly place and I would hate it. She may be right.

170

## 13 September

I have written to Miss Willes agreeing to come and see how we suit each other and offering to arrive next week, if that is convenient. Tilda made a scene, claiming only to be concerned for me. What was I thinking of, she asked, banishing myself to Leeds, and not even as a teacher but as a companion, a complete waste of my abilities and training. She said she couldn't understand me, but then, as I said to her, that is hardly surprising when I do not understand myself. Tilda says I need a man in my life to settle me down. I resented this, and said so. I do not need a man. I do not wish to settle down either. It is the very thing I do not want to do. If I'd wanted a settled life I'd have stayed teaching in Surrey.

## 14 September

A telegram from Miss Willes, expressing her delight that I am willing to join her. Her enthusiasm cheered me up and made me think this venture is not as absurd as Tilda has tried to convince me it is. I have started to prepare for going to Leeds, which is a bit different from getting ready to go to Italy. At least there is no need for new clothes, though I have bought a new warm coat. It is lined with a fleece-like material and has a big collar which can be pulled up to keep the wind out. I bought a book, too, thinking that as my role is to be stimulating it would be sensible to have something to stimulate with. I spent a good hour in Foyles choosing it. Not knowing Miss Willes's taste, it proved quite a problem to decide on a book but in the end I selected a novel I felt she could not possibly have read because it is only just published and I have not read it and I like the sound of it. It is called *Mrs Dalloway* and is said to be the story of a woman who is having a party and is shopping for it and remembering her life up to then. I am hoping it will be jolly. But Father used to say that the only books worth buying were those sure to enhance one's own library and that nobody could be sure about anything new when it came to literature. I am taking a volume of Katherine Mansfield's stories too because they are not new and I am sure of them at least.

## 15 September

Went to Brighton to see Mother before going to Leeds. She is as horrified as Tilda at the thought of Leeds, claiming it will surely be all nasty smoke and dirt. I showed her the photograph of the house where Miss Willes lives and this reassured her somewhat. No sign of smoke, or blackened buildings. Mother said it was a pity that if I had to go north it could not be to the other side of the country, to Westmorland, which is so beautiful and where we spent holidays in the past. She has never known anyone from Leeds. But it consoles her that at least I am not going abroad again and that Leeds, for all its faults (mostly imagined) is only a train ride away. I can telephone her each week, and promised to do so. She seems well, and thrilled about Esther's approaching confinement. Esther is vast. It makes me feel faint to look at her.

## 20 September

What a curious thing it is to be going off to meet a perfect stranger with whom one has said one will try to live. I felt excited but apprehensive setting off from Tilda's house in the cab. It was quite different from the feelings I recall having when I was waiting for Mr Russo to arrive. Then, I had met him, and it was thrilling besides to be going to Italy. It was not thrilling to be going to Leeds. Yet, at the same time, it *was* rather thrilling to be making such a gamble and following my own instinct about Miss Willes. At any rate, I boarded the train feeling glad to be going. The journey seemed short. Daphne— she is Daphne already—had arranged for me to be collected by a Mr Barker, whom she had described as a friend. He was there waiting, carrying a bunch of yellow chrysanthemums. Daphne had told me about the identifying flowers, saying she could not resist this touch even though Mr Barker would be terribly embarrassed. He was, unless his rather fat face is naturally scarlet. I'd thought he would be old, or at least middle-aged, but he was young, probably my own age. I don't know yet the connection between him and Daphne. We did not talk much on the way to her house. I was busy looking out of the window, and frankly not too impressed with what I saw. There was none of the smoke Mother feared, but all the buildings did seem black, or at least dark and dingy. However, we were soon out of the city and then the countryside became quite pleasant, though nothing like Italy. Daphne does not live far out. Her house is one of about a dozen large houses about a couple of miles from the outskirts of Leeds going, I think, in a north-eastern direction. The house is built of stone and is double-fronted with a short circular driveway. It is on two storeys, a ground floor and an upstairs. Daphne's rooms are all on the ground floor, her bedroom and bathroom and sitting-room conveniently arranged together on one side. I am upstairs, at the back, in a very pleasant room overlooking the garden and beyond are what I take to be the moors. I am too tired to write about Daphne tonight.

## 21 September

I was up at seven, but then at a bit of a loss until ten o'clock when Daphne was ready for me. It seems she sleeps badly and falls into a deep sleep at last around four in the morning and consequently does not waken until late. I will get used to this, but today I did not quite know what to do. The night before, Daphne had said I was to make myself at home and treat the house in what she called a familiar way but of course since it is not familiar that was impossible. I drifted about examining the layout but not feeling comfortable about doing more than peeping round doors that were open. Upstairs is all bedrooms. I gather the housekeeper has her own quarters in an addition to the back of the house somewhere. I found the kitchen downstairs but there was no sign of Mrs Postlethwaite, nor of Molly, the girl who comes in daily. I made myself some tea but didn't feel like anything to eat. Then I prowled about and finally, because it seemed so terribly quiet and I worried I was disturbing Daphne, I went back up to my room until I heard signs of activity below. It was a relief to hear Daphne call my name and shouting a cheerful good morning. She is a most cheerful girl in spite of her infirmity. She smiles all the time, and her eyes, very large greenish eyes, are full of curiosity. She asks questions, one after the other, apologising for being cheeky if I think them so (I don't) and gives the impression of great energy. But what is a little frightening is the way she suddenly fades and turns pale and seems to catch her breath. It happens at regular intervals, this partial collapse, and when it does she has to sit still and compose herself and wait. Her walking is poor. She has a stick but mostly scorns it. Unlike in Mr Russo's house, there are no mysteries here to ponder. The first thing Daphne did was tell me what is wrong with her and why. It was a terrible car accident. She and her brother and her parents were driving in Switzerland up a steep, winding road and a lorry coming down skidded on a bend and crashed straight into them. Her parents were killed instantly and her brother died in hospital. She survived, but with all kinds of injuries. This was eight months ago but she has only been home a few weeks and is still not completely recovered. She has inherited the house and describes herself as having no financial worries but she doesn't intend to stay here. When she is better, she will sell the house and move to London and she'll buy somewhere smaller. She doesn't yet know what she wants to do with her life. When she had finished telling me all this, which I could see had exhausted her, she closed her eyes and invited me to tell her about myself.

I felt embarrassed to do so. It is a fairly feeble account. I have no excuse for not having managed to have a more creditable existence. After all, I haven't been in an accident, or ill.

## 27 September

Daphne is clever. I should have guessed it. She likes to discuss everything and relishes an argument. We have now read *Mrs Dalloway*, which was not so very jolly though quite interesting, and all of the Katherine Mansfield stories, and she sees things in them that I do not. We read 'The Wind Blows' this morning, each reading to herself, silently, and when I got to the end I said, well, what on earth is that all about?—it is all a puzzle, this girl and the wind and her music lesson. No, Daphne said, it is not a puzzle; read it again, it is about adolescence and how disturbed and confused and excited one can feel for no reason; it is about all the inner turmoil, the hormones, everything. I read it again and saw she was right. Haven't you ever felt like that, Daphne asked, and I have, of course I have. But I had not realised that was what this little story was about. Daphne is perceptive and also anxious to educate herself in every way whereas I see that my interests are narrow. Every day, she reads *The Times* and then wants to discuss with me what is being said in its leaders and I find this difficult. When Father was alive, I used to take an interest and loved to try to discuss things with him but I have lost the habit. Daphne's knowledge of political affairs is extraordinary. Father would have been amazed at a young woman being so very well informed. She told me her father was going to stand for parliament at the next election and that he had educated her and her brother to understand the issues of the day. I asked if this had not bored her and she was quite shocked. Her mother was involved in the suffrage cause and at one point was briefly in prison. Daphne shares her beliefs and wants to do something to further the cause. Stupidly, I asked, hadn't what her mother fought for been won now that some women had the vote. Daphne was appalled at my ignorance and said that only those over 30 could now vote, and that *all* women should be able to. I feel *she* is going to stimulate me, not the other way round.

**4 October**

I have been here two weeks and both Daphne and I had no need to wonder if, the trial period being over, I will stay. Of course I will. I will stay as long as she wants me to. We are both doing a correspondence course, just for fun, in English Literature. Daphne says that if she decides to go to university she will read English and so this course serves as an introduction and even if it is not of a very high standard it will do no harm and keep her brain fresh. Her brain is very fresh compared to mine. We have begun on Shakespeare, *King Lear*, and whereas Daphne has no difficulty with the language, I do. We are reading the play aloud in the mornings, and then after lunch, when Daphne retires to rest, I ponder over the passages I have not really grasped. In the afternoon, if the weather is fine, we take a turn round the garden or along the road. Daphne wishes I could drive. So do I. If I could drive, we could go into Leeds and visit other places. As it is, Mr Barker takes us, but by arrangement, and often the arrangement has to be cancelled for one reason or another and it is all a bother. Daphne has suggested that Mr Barker should teach me. There is a car in the garage here which was her brother's and I could learn to drive that. I am game. She is going to consult with Edward (Mr Barker).

## 6 October

Mr Barker (Edward) is happy to teach me to drive but it will have to be at the weekends, on Saturday and Sunday afternoons, so long as I have no objections to having lessons on a Sunday. We are to start tomorrow.

## 7 October

My first driving lesson. It did not go well. Edward says I am too tense and that my co-ordination is not good. He is the sort of man who loves to be superior and was quite in his element teaching me. I hope I have never been that kind of teacher. I am determined to do better tomorrow.

## 8 October

I thought I did better today but Edward groaned and said I was murdering the gears and probably ruining the car. I gritted my teeth and said nothing. But he grudgingly allowed, after an hour, that I had got the hang of the clutch. It is lucky this road is so quiet, but he says it is not safe enough and that next week he will drive me up on to the moors road where I can get some real practice.

## 12 October

Disastrous driving lesson, though not because of the driving. I have dreaded Edward making any kind of advances and hoped and prayed I had been stand-offish enough to make sure that he would not. But today he put his hand over mine when I changed into reverse gear, saying I was not being firm enough. He kept his hand there far too long. Then I found him sitting sideways and staring at me. He said I had a beautiful profile, quite the most beautiful he had ever seen. I laughed and said, For heaven's sake; and he was upset and blushed one of his ferocious blushes. What can I do, I am stuck with him until I learn to drive. Later, I amused Daphne by telling her about Edward, exaggerating the pass he made, to entertain her. She teased me, saying he would be a good catch, certain as he is to inherit his father's meat-packing business. I retaliated by suggesting *she* was his real target and that he was only making do temporarily with me until she is fully recovered. But it is not funny, this kind of thing. It is not funny for Edward either, I know.

## 20 October

Decided to invent a boyfriend for myself to solve

the Edward problem. To make the lie convincing, I used Tom, making much of my devotion to him as a wounded hero. It worked like a charm. I did not even really have to lie, there was no need to go so far as to say Tom was a fiancé, which I was glad about. Edward is an honourable man. It is just a pity he is so very unattractive and dull.

* * *

*Millicent masters the art of driving by Christmas (there was, of course, no test to take). Once she has done so, the routine of her days changes. She is able to drive Daphne around, and they begin a series of trips to places of interest within a twenty- or thirty-mile radius of Leeds. She so enjoys the driving, even in poor weather, that she begins to think of buying herself a car once being a companion to Daphne comes to an end. When that will be, she doesn't know but assumes not for a year or so since her employer is still obviously weak and nothing like ready to apply to a university. When Millicent goes to Brighton for Christmas and New Year—grateful to miss the birth of Esther's baby by two days (Stephen King was born on 4th January)—Daphne misses her dreadfully.*

* * *

**2 January 1926**

It was the nicest thing to have Daphne so excited to see me return. I think, poor love, that she has had a dreary time of it on her own here over the festive season. Heaven knows, I was not exactly having a

180

gay time of it in Brighton but at least I had my family about me and there was plenty of noise and laughter with so many children and that is what Christmas is supposed to be about. But Daphne had no one, though plenty of neighbours, feeling sorry for her no doubt, invited her for Christmas dinner and to parties on New Year's Eve. She did go to Edward's parents for Christmas dinner but declined New Year festivities which she is not strong enough to take part in anyway. I do wonder sometimes about the absence of family and friends in Daphne's life. Mrs Harris referred to herself as a friend of the Willeses, but Daphne hardly knows of her. She says her parents were both only children of elderly parents who in turn had been only children and so there is a terrible dearth of relations. She has no guardian, even, and has had to manage everything herself. As to friends, she was at boarding-school in Switzerland and, though she did make friends there, has not managed to keep in touch since the accident. Yet she is such a friendly person, it still seems odd that she is so solitary. She loves to hear about my family and cannot believe I find them a trial and that I have concentrated so hard on getting away from them. She hints at how much she would enjoy meeting them and told me that one day she hopes to be matriarch of a large family herself. I said I had no such ambitions and she pressed me to reveal what ambitions I do have. I wish I knew. It is a question I always dread. It is awful not to have fixed goals in life. I came out with weak mutterings about wanting to travel. Daphne asked me if I wished I were a man. I said no, though I had often envied the greater freedom of men to do things.

181

## 11 February

Daphne spends longer than ever these days reading *The Times*. I don't know how she can be bothered, it is so dull, but I am too ashamed of my lack of interest in current affairs to say so. Daphne is worried about the miners. She doesn't know a single miner, I am sure, but she worries because she says some report has been published recommending their wages should be reduced. She says there will be a strike and the miners will lose and suffer terribly. Well, I don't want anyone to suffer any more than Daphne wants them to, but I cannot get worked up about the fate of people I do not know.

## 20 February

Took Daphne to London to see her specialist, Sir John somebody, in Welbeck Street. We went by train and took a cab to the consulting-rooms. The waiting-room was like a mausoleum, a vast place with uncomfortable chairs. It was deathly silent and very unnerving. I sat there for almost a full hour waiting for Daphne, thinking how I should hate to be ill and have the need to come to a place like this. Because we had tried not to burden ourselves with heavy bags I had not a book with me and the only magazines in the waiting-room did not appeal. They all seemed to be about antiques, full of pictures of hideous furniture. I stared at an ugly object, said to be a William IV four-division canterbury, and wondered what a 'canterbury' was. There was also a painting of a bull, said to belong to Queen Victoria's Jersey herd. It looked exactly like Edward, or rather he looked like the bull. I walked up and down the horrid brown carpet and stood at the window staring through the muslin drapes. They were not very clean. After half an hour a woman with a young boy was shown in. The boy looked awful, a ghastly white colour, and his face was so thin the bones showed through. The woman whispered to him and seemed to want him to sit on her knee but he would not. I said, good morning, and she said, good morning, but showed no inclination to talk. The silence was oppressive. When she gave the boy a barley sugar it was a relief to hear the unwrapping of the paper and his crunching of the sweet. I heard Daphne come out of the doctor's room and gathered our things and bolted out to meet her before she could come back in, not wanting to delay our departure by even a minute. She introduced me to Sir John but he hardly looked at me. He was very abrupt and I did not like him. Neither does Daphne, but he is a colleague of the doctor who treated her in Switzerland and she was referred to him. The news was good. He thinks she is recovering well and will now make rapid strides. Her bones have mended satisfactorily, and her lungs are clear. It is just a question of gaining more strength. He has given her a diet sheet to follow. She hardly eats or drinks anything and will have a struggle following it. It is full of eggs and cream and beef to fatten her up. We went straight from Welbeck Street for lunch at a restaurant called Isola Bella in Frith Street, Soho, which Edward Barker's mother had recommended, and had a delicious lunch, reminding me of the lovely food I enjoyed every day in Italy. I amused

Daphne by telling her about how I used to be a vegetarian, not out of principle but because I wanted to be different, and then I went to Italy and it became impossible to resist the food. My favourite dish was *scaloppine alvino bianco e aroncio*, and I had it today. It was bliss.

Daphne was tired afterwards so we took a cab to the station and came home. She slept most of the way, looking very vulnerable hunched in the corner of our carriage. I do like looking after her, far more than I ever liked looking after my brothers and sister. My feelings of tenderness towards her quite surprise me. I feel a little uneasy about how much I want to mother her, not ever having suspected I might have such maternal feelings. I never felt them for my younger brothers and sister and never for Francesca. Daphne makes me feel much older than her yet there are only seven years between us, older and more experienced. She seems to me so very fragile and open and I worry that she will be hurt. I want to protect her. I feel needed by her and it pleases me. I have never wanted to feel needed before, quite the reverse, I know I have always evaded responsibility. I suddenly thought last night of Aunt J. and how she seemed to draw such satisfaction, even pleasure, from being needed. God forbid I am becoming like her.


**21 February**


Daphne stayed in bed most of today, recovering. She is disappointed that she did not manage to do anything in London but have lunch. It was a strange feeling to be in London again and I must confess I liked it. Something in the air, a sense of bustle and importance. I don't know. It is a pity we did not have time to visit Tilda. Daphne would have loved that. And yet there would have been something awkward about taking her to visit my sister. They each belong to different lives and I realise I want to keep it that way. It is not that I am embarrassed by either of them but perhaps I am embarrassed at the thought of what Tilda might make of my being with Daphne, seeing me as her employee, her servant. Or maybe even suspecting something else.

## 15 March

Daphne walked a mile today, without her stick, and was not at all tired. It was I who insisted that she should rest and made her sit down while I went back for the car. It was a lovely, warm day and we were up on the moors, on the top road, with not a soul in sight. When I came back with the car, we sat and had our picnic, not talking, just basking in the sun and listening to the peewits. Well, Daphne said they were peewits, but I know nothing about birds. It seemed a shame to go home, but eventually a stiff, cool breeze sprang up and I thought we should move. I realise I have become a little bossy and that I'm treating Daphne like a child, which is wrong. No wonder she grows a little irritated with me and has started to refuse to do what I suggest, even when it is clearly for her own good.

## 20 March

An estate agent came to the house today. Daphne had not told me he was coming so I was rather taken aback. She wants the house valued with a view to selling it soon. I think she is being a little premature, but I didn't say so. She has no affection for this house, I must say, even though it seems she was born here. She always wanted to live in London.

## 24 March

A big post today. Daphne has sent for information about the colleges she fancies and the brochures, but that isn't the right word—prospectuses, I mean—have begun to arrive. She would like to go to Cambridge, to Girton, and has suggested that we should both go and look round. We are going to stay a night there and as it is an awkward journey by rail I will drive. I love long drives and so does Daphne. She thinks she is now strong enough to learn to drive herself and is going to ask Edward to teach her. I offered, and don't see why I can't teach her, but she seems to prefer a man, which is rather insulting and, I should have thought, against her principles.

## 26 March

To Cambridge. We stayed at the Bull Hotel, in Trumpington Street, which was very busy with parents of students, come to visit them. They all

186

seemed so smug, terribly pleased to have their darling sons at the university and making constant loud references to the superiority of one college over another. We went off to Girton, which is a good way out of the town I thought, and looked round. It is a very gothic building, rather ugly. I don't think I should like to be there. Goldsmiths' was much more attractive. Then we came back to the town and walked along the backs. Now, that *is* beautiful, and one could not help but be impressed. I told Daphne it was more beautiful than the river in Oxford and when she asked how I came to know this, I had to tell her about Tom. She leapt on this and cross-questioned me about him until I became quite irritated. She pressed me to admit I'd cared for him and would not believe I had not felt anything stronger than friendship. Daphne can be very childish sometimes. She is going to apply to Girton.

**3 May**

A General Strike has been called, much to Daphne's excitement. She is on the side of the miners, of course, and has donated money to the strike fund. She would not tell me how much so I suspect it is a shockingly large amount. She reads *The Times* avidly, and listens to the wireless she has bought, and wishes she were in London. We are not much affected by it here, or not that we have yet had reason to notice.

## 6 May

A letter from Tilda, full of what is happening in the Strike. Daphne couldn't get enough of it. Tilda says that for the first two days everything seemed to stop and there was complete silence in the streets with no buses running and few cars. She wheeled Florence to Regent's Park and was amazed to find the army camped there and the park full of tents. But she writes that already, on day four, when she wrote this, there are signs of things starting to move again. Some underground stations are open, and a few buses are running, and supplies of milk and other essentials are plentiful. Here in Leeds, or rather on the outskirts of Leeds, we are still not affected at all. I think Daphne is sorry. She had a row with Edward Barker about the Strike when he came to give her a driving lesson. He said if he were in London he would volunteer to drive a bus, and she raged at him, saying strike-breakers were a disgrace and that everyone should support the miners. She says Edward looked astonished but said nothing. Daphne said afterwards that they went on to spend the whole lesson in silence, except for his instructions to her. I do admire Daphne's outspokenness. She has such confidence.

## 26 May

The Strike is over. The miners have lost and will be worse off than ever. Daphne was near to weeping at the news, and even I felt sad. She is making me politically conscious, which I never was nor wanted to be. I have always thought only of myself and how things affect *me* and Daphne makes me see that this is not good enough. But I still find politics dull, which she can't understand.


## 6 June

Mother wrote, reminding me that Albert and Alfred are 18 in August, and asking if I will be able to come home for a celebration. I can recollect no party for George's or Tilda's or my 18th birthday. However, to please Mother I have said I will go. I hardly know these brothers of mine. I suppose that is my fault. I think I am unfairly prejudiced against them because of what pests they were when young. We have never written to each other and don't know what to say when we meet. All I know is that Alfred is lazy but cleverer than Albert, though not clever enough to go on to university. He is better-looking too. Daphne asked what they did and I was ashamed to have only the faintest notion and may have been mistaken in telling her that Alfred is some sort of salesman, to Mother's disappointment, and Albert is a clerk in the post office. I must check that I am right.


## 15 July

I could not help feeling depressed today. I am not tired, but feel listless. I think it is the usual thing, to do with birthdays coming round, and that awful inner panic which rises in me when I wonder what I am doing with my life. Every birthday it overwhelms me, this realisation that I am doing

189

little more than drift. I never seem to have plans. Where has my ambition gone? But then it was a formless ambition at best, just to *be* someone and *do* something. An empty sort of yearning after I know not what. I wait for things to happen but all that happens is ordinary and I long for the extraordinary. I try to be sensible and think about this. The fact is that I am qualified to teach in an elementary school and that is all. I am qualified to do what I do not do and do not want to do. This is ridiculous.

## 16 July

Daphne noticed my mood. I suppose it would have been difficult for her not to do so. I know I have been very quiet and unlike myself since my birthday. She asked if I was worried about anything and I was silly enough to say yes, about myself and my future, and that gave her the opening to invite confidences. It was embarrassing to give voice to the kind of thoughts I write in this diary and I made a stumbling job of it. But Daphne was very understanding though *what* she understood was not quite what I'd meant her to. I think she thinks I am merely like her, and burn with some kind of nameless desire *to do good*. But I don't. Doing good does not appeal to me. It isn't that I want to be doing something worthwhile, as she does. Oh, I don't know what it is that I do want. Just, as ever, something to happen.

\*    \*    \*

*Almost at once, several things do happen. For a start, Daphne finds a buyer for her house and accepts the offer, with a completion date in mid-August. She and Millicent then begin hunting for a house or flat in London which entails frequent trips there before they find a small house in Edis Street, Primrose Hill, not far from where Tilda lives. But this place is only to be a base for Daphne while she is an undergraduate: she has been accepted at Girton and is to take up her place in October. Obviously, this will mean the end of her need of Millicent, who is surprisingly upset about this. It seems, from her diary entries throughout this period, that Daphne's success in obtaining a Girton place underlines her own sense of having failed ever to go to university. Daphne suggests to her, as Tom had once done, that she should apply as a mature student, but she will not hear of this. Meanwhile, in the middle of all this upheaval, she at last takes Daphne to Brighton to meet her family, choosing the twins' 18th birthday celebration as an opportunity to do so. Daphne is at once attracted to Alfred, to Millicent's consternation (and bafflement).*

*   *   *

**20 August**

Well, here we are, in Daphne's new home, and everything in a state of chaos but she doesn't seem to care whereas I hate this mess. We have beds and that is about all in the way of furniture. I cannot imagine why Daphne did not select items from the Leeds house to furnish this place but she says everything there was too big in scale to fit into

191

these small rooms and too old-fashioned in taste to suit her ideas. Maybe so, but it dooms us to discomfort until she has bought chairs and sofas and tables and I don't know when she will get round to doing that. She is much too preoccupied with thinking about Alfred. Twice already he has been up to see her and she proposes to go to Brighton next weekend, and all that with so much sorting out to do here. I feel more and more like a mere housekeeper every day and I do not like it. She expects me to go on living here whatever I decide to do but, although it is generous of her to offer her house to me, I have no intention of accepting it. I must move on.

## 21 August

Alfred is here. He is sleeping on the floor downstairs, wrapped in a quilt. Daphne seems to think him endlessly amusing but he does not amuse me. He reminds me of George before he went off to the war, very sure of himself and full of smart remarks. I suppose he is attractive to look at, tall, with a good head of hair, and an easy way with him. He took Daphne dancing last night. I don't know where they went and I don't care. They announced that they danced until they dropped. Alfred is apparently a good dancer. I wonder where he learned, in Brighton. Daphne has never had a beau before and all this attention is going to her head. Since she has no mother or aunt or sister I feel I have to take on those roles and warn her to be careful, but with Alfred being my brother I should perhaps warn *him* to be careful. I will be glad when he goes home.

## 26 August

I have done it. I have applied for a teaching job at an elementary school in Brighton. It is not the one Grace goes to, which I think is a good thing. I may not even be given an interview since the authority will not look kindly on my lack of real teaching experience since I left my one and only post. But I have to apply for something, and somewhere in Brighton would make sense. It is not that I wish to be near my family, but I do for the time being need a place to live and to go back to Tilda's would seem too much of a backward step. If I live in London, I must live on my own and though I have saved a good deal these past months it is not enough, without the security of a salary after October, even to rent, never mind buy, somewhere pleasant. I must live with Mother and make the best of it for a while. I refuse to live on Daphne's charity. She would be very angry at my referring to it as that. She is so happy now. I wonder how she will bring herself to go to Girton at all now that Alfred is the light of her life. He is quite overawed by her intellect, and so he should be.

## 1 September

The strangest thing happened today. I was alone in this comfortless house and had warned Daphne I was determined to put at least the sitting-room into some sort of order. She said I was welcome to do whatever I liked but really it was beyond her why I fussed so, like an old mother hen. I knew she said this affectionately but it upset me. I feel like an old mother hen whenever she and Alfred are clinging to each other and being silly. Once they had gone off to Brighton, I set to and started dealing with the packing cases covering the whole floor. Daphne had wanted to burn the entire contents of her father's desk without even looking at them which was pretty shocking but in the end she simply shovelled all the papers into packing cases and said she'd go through them later. I knew she never would. She said there would be nothing of value there, that everything to do with money and insurance and all that kind of thing was with his solicitor or in the bank and that these piles of papers would just be old letters and paid bills and she couldn't be bothered with them. She has no reverence for the past. At any rate, I set to and began emptying the cases, though I did not feel comfortable doing it. I felt like a spy. There are letters there too personal for me to read, from Daphne's mother to her father during their courtship. She should treasure them, and I will tell her so. But she was right about the bulk of the stuff, there are packets and packets of bills, all ticked and with 'paid' written on them, and old policies of one sort or another. I tied them all up in bundles, labelled them accordingly. Daphne will never look at them but I did not feel I had the right to burn them. The love letters I put beside her bed. But then, at the bottom of the third and last packing case, I came across a few sheets of yellowed paper, brittle with age, covered in fine, spidery writing, the ink faded to a faint grey. The

194

writing began in what was obviously the middle of a sentence and I saw, turning the sheets over carefully, that it ended in the same way, so whatever this was, it was incomplete. I read it, and read it again, and for some reason wanted to copy it out for myself. Here is what it said:

'—was a headless skeleton lying on the beach, the bones of a child in an abandoned hut, and a slate buried in the sand with scratched upon it the barely legible words I am proceeding to a river shown on my map some 60 miles north. Should anyone find this . . . There were more scratches, but they were indecipherable. All around were the bleached bones of countless whales, beautiful structures, great curving arcs of strong white bone. Seals crowded the line of the shore, barking and baying at the crashing waves. The wind was merciless, steady and stinging, lifting the fine white sand in handfuls and driving it forward in clouds. I was cold, so cold, though the sun blazed from a blue sky and I had just come from the heat of the desert behind me. Sixty miles north. I knew there was no river there, whatever this map had seemed to indicate. He would have walked to his certain death, or did he return, was this his skeleton? The child, left behind, would have died sooner, if not already dead when he left. A shipwreck, without a doubt. The coast is littered with them. Ships over the centuries smashed to smithereens and the survivors left with the choice of floating on any raft they could fashion and being attacked and eaten by sharks, or of walking into the desert stretching a thousand miles behind, or of walking the beach. A safe beach, wide and flat, with no sharp coral to negotiate or inlets to cross, but, like the desert, offering no sustenance for hundreds of miles. I stood beside the skeleton wondering which fate was the worse, death at sea, death in the desert. I wondered how he could have thought anyone would see his wavering scratches on the slate. Did he hope others had survived the shipwreck and that they would appear soon, with water and food, and go in search of him? Sailors, perhaps, who knew this treacherous coast and would know how best to survive. The pity of it filled me. I stood and prayed over the remains. A life unknown, come to this, bones, a slate, the memory of desperation still whispering in the air. A life unknown which—'

That was all. I don't know why it makes such an impression upon me, why it makes me shiver. It is something to do with those last words, 'a life unknown'. I don't want my life to be unknown. I don't want to die having done nothing. I feel time is passing me by and nothing matters and *I want to matter*. It is all a muddle, as usual, what I feel.

**4 September**

I showed Daphne the sheet of paper I found and made her read it. She had no idea who had written it or what it was about, but at least she was intrigued, which I had thought she might not be. She said her father had an explorer friend who wrote to him about his travels and that this must be from him, part of a long letter which had become separated from the rest. She thought this man spent his time in Africa and we speculated as to where this coast and desert might be. Damaraland, maybe. But unlike me, Daphne did not seem struck by the words 'a life unknown'. She said briskly that surely the vast majority of lives are unknown in the sense of most folk not being famous, yet thoroughly well-known to family and friends at the time of being lived. Isn't that what matters? Daphne asked. She doesn't understand what I feel and I cannot express myself adequately. It is not that I wish to be famous but that I don't want to be unknown. Oh, it is no use.

**5 September**

I had given up all hope of hearing from the education authority in Brighton and was not altogether sorry because I don't truly wish to go there even though I am desperate to be doing something, but today I got a telegram, of all things, asking me to go for interview tomorrow. I imagine they have been let down and that I am the only applicant not yet tried. I will have to go for the interview, heart sinking. I wonder if I should have my hair cut short again. It has grown so long and I'm obliged to pin it up if I want it to look tidy.

*Millicent goes to Brighton, is offered the teaching post there at once and accepts it. She starts work three days later, at a salary of £5 12s a week. There then begin the four unhappiest years of her life (which is how she refers to them when she is 80). The work is hard, much harder than it had been in her first and only teaching job. The classes are large and the children unruly. She hates the staff, particularly the headmaster who is a vicious disciplinarian. The plight of many of her pupils distresses her, coming to school as they do with inadequate clothing, and clearly in need of nourishment. She had never imagined such poverty existed in Brighton which she had always thought of as an affluent town. She is exhausted at the end of each day and too tired at the weekend to do more than rest. Her only comfort is finding a flat to rent three months after starting her job. It is in Hove, the ground floor of a Victorian house, and she takes pleasure in decorating and furnishing it. It is the first real home of her own, of course. But on the whole her diaries during this period are repetitious and full of complaints and become tedious in their detailing of school routines. There are frequent protestations of being unsuited to teaching, and more lamentations that she ever trained as a teacher at all. There is a great deal of railing against the headmaster and a couple of the other teachers. But her personal life improves.*

*Two new people of real significance enter the diaries. Both are men, and it is one of these men who finally helps her change her career and find satisfaction in her new work. Percy Webb is a doctor, a colleague of her brother-in-law Charles, and she*

*meets him at her sister Tilda's house in the summer of*
*1930 (Tilda and Charles have by this time had*
*another child, Jack, born in 1929). Millicent is*
*supremely conscious of being almost thirty years of*
*age and of Tilda constantly trying to matchmake.*
*Daphne, with whom she keeps in touch (though the*
*romance with brother Alfred soon fizzles out), does*
*the same, but in a less obvious way.*

*It is through Daphne that she meets a young*
*lawyer, Frank Johnson, with whom Daphne has been*
*at Cambridge. Since both Frank and Percy are in*
*London, she does not see much of them and begins*
*to wish that she could. Daphne, who has graduated*
*from Cambridge (though not with the double first to*
*which she had been aspiring) is trying, in 1930, to*
*embark on a political career and to that end is going*
*to attend an International Socialist Conference in*
*Brussels and then intends to travel to Germany and*
*Italy. She invites Millicent to live in her house while*
*she is away, for the whole of the school summer*
*holidays.*

\*　　　　\*　　　　\*

### 31 July 1930

Percy came for the day. It is the first whole
weekend he has had off for weeks and weeks, and
he said he felt giddy at the prospect. We walked the
full length of the promenade and on past the
Grand Pier, and then back again, before settling on
the beach where we sat on a rug with our backs to
the wall and our eyes closed. Percy is so pale I
feared the sun would burn him but he said he did

not care, it felt so jolly good having it on his face and made him feel better already. He talks such a lot about his work. I envy him his absolute dedication and the satisfaction it brings him to know he is doing something so important and worthwhile. But anyone can see how worn out he is. He looks much older than his 31 years, and not at all strong. I do like him. What I like best about him is that for all his absorption in his work he is interested in others. Well, he shows interest in me and what I do and tries to persuade me that my teaching is as important as his doctoring, which is ridiculous. He won't accept that I spend half my time trying to keep order and watching pupils falling asleep through lack of adequate nourishment. I can hardly bear to witness the beatings these children receive for the most trivial misdemeanors. I told Percy it makes my blood boil but that I cannot stand up against the headmaster who is such a brute: I am too afraid and too weak. Percy said he could not believe I was too weak. He asked if I had been to any of my pupils' homes and I said I had, to two or three, and how shocked I'd been to find mothers younger than I looking like old women and trying to care for children in rooms little better than hovels, with no running water and no comfort of any sort. Percy said it was far worse in London. In his hospital he sees children dying not of disease but malnutrition. They need changes in society not any medicine that he can prescribe. He is a member of the Labour Party, as Daphne is, and hopes in his life to see radical changes in the distribution of wealth in this country, and things made altogether fairer, he says. He asked if I belonged to a political party and I had to say no. I was relieved that he did not press the point.

## 1 August

Today felt empty without Percy's company. It costs
me something to admit that, even here. I know
Mother is wondering if at long last her elderly
spinster daughter has a beau, and Grace, whom
unfortunately we met while out walking yesterday,
is bound to report back that she saw me hand-in-
hand with a young man. There will be an
inquisition when next I go for Sunday dinner. I
thought about indicating to Grace that I would
appreciate it if she said nothing to Mother but that
would have made matters worse. I really do not
know if I am attracted to Percy *in that way* or not. I
like him. We get on well. Heaven knows, I have not
much experience to judge him by. All these years
and only mild involvements with Tom and Matthew
to look back on. I have hardly been kissed, whereas
Daphne has already done a great deal more than
that, if she is to be believed, and I do believe her. If
it were not for Frank, I might think I am made of
stone. I would like to feel within me when Percy
touches me what I feel for Frank—oh, that is
clumsy and badly put but *I* know what I mean. But
I don't like Frank as much as I like Percy and I am
not nearly as comfortable with him. Frank is a bit
like Matthew in that he takes a great deal for
granted and by no means regards me as an equal.
He is very masculine, and takes charge, and has no
hesitation at all about embracing me. I always have
to struggle to keep my composure and it is a strain.
Frank tells me he loves me, which I hate to hear

201

because his lack of sincerity is evident. He buys me flowers and gives me presents all the time and I am not stupid, I know he wants something in return. It is lucky that he is in London and I am in Brighton, but if I take up Daphne's offer I will see much more of him and that may become dangerous.

## 4 August

I have decided to live in Daphne's house for a month. I told Mother today, and she said she could not understand why anyone would wish to leave the seaside for London in the height of summer and what, pray, was the attraction of that dirty, noisy city. I said there were plays I wished to see and libraries I wished to use but even to my own ears this sounded feeble. It did not help that Grace, who at 13 is far too pert, said she expected there were gentlemen to meet too. I slapped her down sharply, but not before Mother had changed from being anti my going to London to suddenly being in favour. If I had *friends* there I wished to spend more time with, then of course she understood.

## 6 August

Moved into Daphne's house. It is hardly more comfortable than when I left it four years ago. That is an exaggeration of course but not much of one. She treats her home as a dumping ground for her things and a place to sleep and that is all. While she was at Cambridge there was some justification for her neglect but now she lives here all the time it seems inexplicable. There is not a cushion in the house. Her curtains are bedsheets strung up on bits of cane. When I think of my own home and how cheerful and comfortable it is, and all done on so little money whereas Daphne has plenty, I see the enormous difference in us. It is no good saying anything to her. She will only call me an old woman and say I fuss over the unimportant things in life, like most women. It hurts when she says that because I suspect it is true.

## 8 August

Went with Frank to see *The Importance of Being Earnest* at the Lyric Theatre. It was great fun. Frank and I both laughed a lot. He liked the actress playing Lady Bracknell, but I thought the young actor, John Gielgud, in the part of John Worthing, was the best. Afterwards, Frank took me for a late supper. It was quite the smartest restaurant I have ever been to, but then it was not exactly a restaurant, or not what I think of as one. It was more like a club. We went down some stairs into a basement which was rather dark and smoky and sat at a small, round iron table, very close to others. There was a band playing jazz and a woman in a tight red dress singing, and the atmosphere was hectic. I thought we would never get any food, but finally some smoked fish and bread arrived and the wine Frank had ordered. I had one glass. The noise was so terrific after the singing stopped that I couldn't hear a word Frank said, so I just smiled and nodded.

He drove me home in his new car, in which he

wants to take me for a spin on Sunday. I fretted all the way back about how he would say goodnight and whether he would try to come in with me, but he merely kissed me in a friendly way. I thought that odd, when twice before he has kissed me very passionately. Maybe he is going off me. Maybe he is tired of attempting and failing to seduce me. I am struggling to be honest, trying to decide if this would upset me, I mean if he is cooling towards me and will soon not call any more. Yes, it would. But if that is so, what am I going to do about it? I wish I did not always analyse everything so much. I wish I was able to be spontaneous.

## 10 August

I am not sure why I agreed to come and live in Daphne's house here. It is so hot, and I could be beside the sea. And I am not so poor that I could not have a real holiday. I could go back to Italy, I could visit places to which I have never been, or I could even accept Mr Russo's invitation to Long Island. But here I am, in this small, rather airless house. In fact, I know why I came. It is all to do with Frank and Percy. I am making myself available, that is what it is. To see what happens.

## 11 August

Percy came by, looking dreadfully haggard and full of the awful news of how one of his favourite patients, a little boy of 5 with leukaemia, died. Doctors are not supposed to take things personally but Percy does. We walked in the park, then he came back for a cold supper. I know a little about him now. He is one of four boys and seems devoted to his parents. He is going to visit them next weekend and wonders if I would fancy a day in the country. It is not so very far, they live near Reading, and he goes by train. But if I go, it will look as though we are courting and I do not want to give that impression. Taking a girl home is a big step for Percy. Being taken is a big step for me. I have said I will think about it.

## 12 August

Frank drove up this evening and peeped his horn. I wish he would not do that. It makes the neighbours stare. I did not immediately fly to the door. Instead, I stood at the window and raised my hand in what I intended to be a mere acknowledgement of his presence. He had to get out of his car and come to the door, which did not please him. He said it was too lovely an evening to be indoors and that he had come to take me on the river. I was told to fetch a jacket and a scarf in case it turned cool later and I was so thrilled at the thought of going on the river that I could not conceal my childish delight, which of course gratified him. We drove to Charing Cross Pier and boarded a boat for the evening cruise to Greenwich. Frank had brought a hamper and we sat at the front and he produced champagne and smoked salmon and brown bread and lemon wedges and then strawberries and cream. I laughed and when he asked why—though he was laughing himself—I said because it was all so *romantic.* He looked quizzical and pretended to be grave and said romance was nothing to laugh at. But it *was* so very romantic, the river rippling in the sunset, and the skyline of London slowly slipping by, and the stars and moon on the way back when we sat close together because by then it was a little chilly. Frank was quiet, not at all his boisterous self, and when he did speak it was to make what I thought were very perceptive observations.

I was prepared for what came next. We drove back to Daphne's house and he turned the engine off and looked at me in the dim light of the street lamp and said he loved me. He said it very steadily and quietly. I felt strangled with emotion and could do nothing but put my hand over his. He leaned forward, I thought to kiss me, but it was to whisper, Shall we go inside? He knew the house was empty. He knew I was living here alone. I felt that if I refused he would be angry, and that it would be ungrateful of me after he had gone to such trouble to give me such a wonderful evening. But I was afraid to say yes, knowing that if we went inside there would be far more dangerous requests. Finally I found my voice, and still holding his hand I managed to say how much I cared for him too, but that if he came in I knew what would happen and I was not ready for it to happen yet, and if I had misled him I was sorry. He drew back and sighed but didn't seem angry. Then he asked me what I wanted, did I want a ring, was that it. I was the one then who was angry. I tried to get out of the car, but he stopped me, saying, I am serious about you, Millicent, but are you serious about me? Because if not, let's stop this now. I said I was serious but at the same time unsure. He asked of what and I said the future, our future, what a future together would turn out to be like. He said I exasperated him but that as he loved me he would excuse me. Then he started the car engine and told me to go and enjoy my beauty sleep and he would see me on Saturday.

## 12 August

No sleep last night. I lay awake fretting over what to do about Frank. Do I want him to propose? No, because then I would have to decide. Do I want to make love with him? Yes. My body tells me yes and has been telling me for a long time and I am tired of ignoring it. So why do I hold back? Well, it is obvious. I am not that sort of girl. Making love with a man has to mean something more than, I hope, satisfaction and pleasure. I do not want to be dragged deeper into an affair with Frank only to find we are not really made for each other. Then there is the worry of it all. I could not bear to become pregnant. I am sure Frank knows how to guard against this but accidents can happen. I must talk to Tilda. She is the only person I can consult who knows about such things, except for Daphne and I would never ask her. She would enjoy my embarrassment too much, and plague me ever after to know what happened.

## 13 August

Went to see Tilda. We walked in the park with Florence and Jack, and when they were happy playing I brought up the subject of Frank. When I had finished she asked what was wrong with me that I dithered so. She pointed out, which she had no need to do, that I am 30 next year and surely must be thinking about settling down. I said she sounded like Mother and that I hadn't confided in her for her to sound like Mother. She apologised then and said it was just that she had thought that I was happy at last and had found a man I could love. I said I was attracted strongly to him, but was that love? The children had started to fight by then and Tilda had to pull them apart and this gave me the opportunity to say that I wished I knew how to be able to prevent having a baby because then I might be able to take things further with Frank. Tilda frowned and said did I mean sleep with him without marrying him, and I said yes. She appeared shocked. I reminded her of what she had said on her wedding-day about knowing how to prevent becoming pregnant and asked her to tell me about it. She hesitated, and then said she had been fitted with a 'cap' which was the safest method of contraception known. She said there was a clinic now where women could go. I said I wanted to go to this clinic and asked where it was and what I should do. Tilda gave me the address very reluctantly, when we got back to her house. She said it was a poor area, near the Holloway Road, and that I should dress as dowdily as possible or I would stand out and be uncomfortable. She said I would have to pretend to be married, and added that she hoped I would not go: she did not approve.

## 14 August

Have bought a cheap brass ring and put it on my ring finger. I thought I would have to wait ages for an appointment at the clinic but I was told just to come along and was given directions on how to find it and the hours it is open. I felt so nervous, more nervous than I have ever been in my life. It was not hard to dress the part of a badly off young married woman. My navy teaching skirt is well worn and my shoes down-at-heel and I have a jumper with darns in the elbows and an old coat I wear when it rains and which Mother says makes me look like a tramp and not a respectable schoolteacher. The clinic is in North London, in Marlborough Road in an ordinary house. My heart thudded as I neared it, but once inside I felt calm. It is not like a clinic at all. The walls are painted white and there are blue curtains, pretty curtains, at the windows, and a big jar of roses on a wooden table as you go in. Really, it is a very surprising place, and so was the reception given to me. I was not even asked *if* I was married, only how long I had been. I lied and said three weeks, and then panicked because as I said this I realised that when I was examined the doctor would know I was a virgin and so I hurriedly said my husband had been obliged to go away immediately after our wedding and he was returning tomorrow—oh, the rigmarole I came out with! Lie after lie tumbled out and I knew I was blushing furiously but in a way this helped because I expect she assumed the blushes were about confessing my marriage had not been consummated. At any rate, I was then taken into another room and told to take my knickers and stockings off and climb up onto the bed and relax on my side. The doctor chatted away all the time she was examining me and I must say, uncomfortable though this was, it was not painful. She said everything was in order and that I was easy to fit. Then she produced a small rubber cap and put some ointment on it and slipped it in. Once inside me, I could not feel it. Then she made me practise how to do this, which was embarrassing. Twice the cap slipped out of my fingers and went whizzing across the room and she laughed but I did not. Eventually, I acquired the knack and she was pleased. She put the cap into a tin box and gave me a tube of the spermicide and said to come back if there were any difficulties. I left feeling exhausted but elated. I felt clever too, and proud, to be looking after myself, and also a little wicked.

## 15 August

Percy came by, to see if I have made my mind up about tomorrow. I felt so guilty saying I could not go with him because I had forgotten about a prior engagement. He took the news well, and asked how I was, and whether I would like to go to an open-air concert with him on his next night off and I said that I would love to. I never worry about Percy being alone with me in this house. He is so trustworthy and polite, and would never try to force his attentions on me. I feel so at ease with him, and I keep wondering if this is not a sign that he is far better for me than Frank, with whom I never feel at ease, I am always wary with him and suspicious and I suppose excited. Percy talked politics tonight. He explained to me that the Labour Government is not at all secure and that it will be in danger of defeat at the next election and all its plans to create a more just society will come to nothing. Frank never talks politics, and never seems to care what the government is doing. I did not tell Percy I would be with Frank tomorrow, and felt deceitful.

\* \* \*

*It seems very surprising that Millicent went to the Marie Stopes clinic, but she has all the details right and obviously did. There are hints throughout her diaries in the years before this that she feels she is suppressing sexual feelings which arise quite independently of any attraction to a man and that this worries and confuses her. Tom and Matthew were attracted to her but she could not respond as they wished and she has begun to think, before meeting Frank, that she will never match her desires with any man's for her. The relief of finding herself responsive to Frank's advances is therefore great but it is still, considering the times, and considering her upbringing, surprising that Millicent is prepared to be so daring. Clearly, it excites her, though the fact that she says she isn't going to tell Daphne, or seek her advice about birth control, shows she is not entirely free of concern for her reputation. She mentions again and again, once she and Frank have slept together, that 'no one guessed' and this pleases her. She relishes knowing of her own irreproachable respectability in the eyes of the world and behind it her new passionate love life. Not much, though, is written about this love life. There are no details about the sex. Indeed, the entries for the weekend she spent with Frank at this time, at a hotel*

211

*in Suffolk, are quite brief, and prim in tone. She describes the hotel as seeming like a country house and writes that it was beside a river and that the view from the bedroom was over an orchard. She also mentions having bought a peach-coloured satin nightdress which she worries is too 'slinky'. She says she doesn't want to write about making love because 'it will sound sordid written down and it was not, it was simply wonderful'. What confuses her is that, in spite of her passion for Frank, she is more drawn than ever to Percy as a friend. With colossal understatement she comments that this is 'awkward'. I have perhaps included too many of the entries to do with her agonising but she herself thought of this Frank/Percy dilemma as so crucial she could hardly stop writing about it and seemed to have no idea how it made her appear.*

\* \* \*

### 31 August

Spent the day tidying and cleaning the house thoroughly, ready to leave it tomorrow. Daphne will not even notice how immaculate it is, how different from the appalling mess in which she left it, but it pleases me to make this transformation. I resisted the temptation to list all the things I have done, from scrubbing the oven (it was thick with grease) to washing and ironing the material pretending to be curtains. Why being a political activist, which is what dear Daphne calls herself, has to mean living like a slut I do not know. Percy's rooms are as neat as a pin and he is a hard-working

212

doctor and just as politically active. He only has two rooms, which he showed me with some embarrassment I felt, but they are made very pleasant by lots of little touches of a type not usually associated with young men, or none of the young men I have known. He has a beautiful cloth, which he brought back from Spain, on the round table in his sitting-room and some pretty bowls of pottery on his shelves, also from Spain. He is such a gentle man as well as a gentleman. I will be sorry not to see him as often as I have been doing these last few weeks. He has had a big influence on me, making me see that I cannot go on complaining that I hate teaching and dread returning to it and yet do nothing about changing this state of affairs. Others have said the same thing but Percy is constructive about it. He has made me sit down and think, really think, about my future. Percy doesn't laugh when I say I want to *do* something with my life, I want to make it mean something. He is only surprised that everyone does not feel the same need to make some kind of contribution to society. Well, Frank doesn't, but I could hardly tell him that—Frank says life is for living and enjoying yourself while you can, and I do enjoy myself with him, but the trouble is that for me enjoyment is not enough. I am in my thirtieth year and still in a muddle.

## 1 September

Back to Brighton, on a beautiful day. My home most welcoming, though with the windows closed for so long the whole place felt stuffy. I am not at

213

all sure that Grace really did come and air the place as promised but she says she did. She is becoming very pretty, prettier than Tilda or I ever were, but she is ever so pert and full of herself. Mother says she is like I was at 13 but I have no recollection of being so cheeky and would certainly never have asked any adult the kind of questions Grace asks me. She is quite disturbingly inquisitive about one's personal life. I must ask Tilda if Grace subjects her to the inquisition to which she subjects me, but then I suppose living in Brighton I have become closer to Grace. She does not like Esther and wishes she and George and their baby lived somewhere else. I try not to pass comment though comment is exactly what Grace wants, to use as ammunition, I suspect.

## 2 September

Last day of freedom. Frank wanted to come down but I would not let him. I don't want him in my home. That is a terrible thing to say but it is how I feel. I would rather meet him in London, or go with him to an hotel, as we did in Suffolk. Having Frank stay here would seem sordid to me. I don't think Frank minds. He likes the excitement of hotels. I don't think he has quite got over my boldness. I don't think I have quite got over it myself. I will never tell anyone, though of course Tilda must suspect. She never asks if I went to the clinic and I never mentioned going. I look at other young women all the time now and speculate about them in the crudest fashion. I will not confide in Daphne. To her, it would seem unexceptional

214

because she has been having affairs for so long. She would want to know the details and I have no intention of divulging them.

## 6 September

Today, Mr Brennan beat Tommy Dixon in front of the whole school, for spitting at Miss Watkins. He beat him so hard that his cane broke, but not before he had drawn blood, which we could all see running down Tommy's legs. He is such a tiny, fragile little boy with hardly any flesh on him and the cane had cut straight through the seat of his threadbare pants. The child collapsed in a heap and had to be carried off the platform. Mr Brennan then threatened all the children with the same fate if they ever did anything as disgusting as Tommy had done. Miss Watkins looked pale, though she is nearly as big a bully as Mr Brennan is, but the sight of this savage punishment had affected even her. I was shaking and despised myself for not having leapt onto the platform and rescued poor Tommy. He should not have spat at Miss Watkins but she is a tyrant and no one knows what she had done to him. I am sure he was provoked beyond endurance. Nobody said anything in the staff room. We were all very quiet. I could hardly get through the rest of the day. The children in every standard were cowed and docile so it hardly mattered that I found it difficult to concentrate.

But by the end of the afternoon I had made up my mind. I went to see Mr Brennan and gave in my notice. He laughed and lolled back in his chair and told me not to be so foolish. He said I was too soft-

215

hearted and that children like Tommy Dixon needed to be taught a lesson they would never forget. I managed to say that I would never forget it either and that it had made me sick. Mr Brennan snorted and said if I resigned he would not give me a reference and I would never teach again. I said he had made me never want to teach again. He snatched a piece of paper from his desk then and told me to put my resignation in writing for the education authority. I said I would do that from home. I turned to go out, shaking, and he sprang up and put his hand on my shoulder to detain me and I was so alarmed I cried out but all he wanted to do was make me stand still and listen to his denunciation of my entire character. Eventually, he let me go and I took my things from the staff room and left. For ever.

## 7 September

It was silly to write that. I have not left that awful place 'for ever'. I cannot leave for a whole half-term: those are the rules. I don't know what would happen if I disobeyed them but I am not going to do so. It would not, after all, be fair to the children in my class. Leaving them at half-term will be hard enough on them and if a replacement for me is not found they may have to have Mr Brennan himself which would terrify them. He is going to make these weeks as horrible for me as he can, I can tell. My class is overcrowded as it is but today he sent extra children to join in without any explanation as to why this was necessary. They are all very unruly and disrupted my teaching with throwing pieces of chalk at the blackboard and other petty kinds of misbehaviour. I could not bring myself to send them to Mr Brennan for punishment, knowing what he would inflict upon them, as he well realised. One of these boys is nearly as tall as I am and I cannot physically handle him. He is a well-known troublemaker but one for whom Mr Brennan has some kind of peculiar fondness. At any rate, he is never beaten as little Tommy Dixon was. Tommy is not at school.

**10 September**

I went for Sunday dinner to Mother's, Esther being away visiting her mother, which Grace had helpfully told me she would be. Mother looks tired, but then she is nearly 60 and one must expect to notice a difference. Life ought to be easier for her, with the twins no longer living at home and both Michael and Grace being of a more independent and useful age, but she is worn out with looking after Stephen. Grace tells me he is a very boisterous little boy and spoiled by his mother who dotes on him and does nothing to restrain his energetic escapades. Grace, of course, is prejudiced. I heard her declare today that she is never going to have children—my own voice, coming back to me. Well, I meant it and I have kept to my word, but all the same I would not say those words again. It is not that I have changed my mind and now wish to have children. Not in the least. I take great care to prevent such a disaster, but the idea of some day perhaps having a child is not so repugnant. Mother worries about my spinster state and lack of offspring of course, but apart from wistful glances in my direction when any conversation turns that way she says nothing, merely hopes. She is most upset that I have handed in my resignation from teaching at that school even though I graphically described the reasons for it. She pities poor Tommy but wonders if I am helping him by resigning. I said, quite sharply I am afraid, that I knew I was not helping him but that was not the point, nothing I could do could help him, but at least I could disassociate myself from being, by implication, part of the institution that condones his beating. By resigning, I had said I would not stand for it. Mother asked, very mildly, but will the child know that, dear? Well, of course she is right, he won't. Unless I tell him, and how could I do that?

## 18 September

Went up to London for the weekend and stayed with Tilda on Friday night. Saw Frank on Saturday. Went to the theatre and then dined at a restaurant in Soho and stayed the night at his place. Not a success. I feel so worried about what I am going to do now I have resigned, and Frank is not really interested in my troubles. He is not a sympathetic person. He wants me to be fun and lively and cannot bear it if I mope. It is not, I'm sure, well, fairly sure, that he does not care about my state of mind but that he thinks I ought not to let myself get dragged down. He is impatient with me. He has a lawyer's way of analysing things and I don't want to be analysed by him. I can analyse myself, thank

you. Everything is so simple to Frank. He sums up
what he calls the Tommy Dixon Incident by saying
one, the headmaster is a brute / two, you were
obliged to witness an act of brutality / three,
because of it you made your protest by resigning.
Excellent, he concludes. You dislike teaching
therefore the fact that you are without a reference
and unlikely to be appointed to another post is of
no consequence. You are clever, smart, attractive
and can easily get any job you choose and
meanwhile you have a roof over your head, a little
money in the bank, a loving family, and my own
good self at your service. That is Frank's appraisal
of my situation and he sees no cause for anxiety.
But I am anxious, and I spoiled the weekend.


**21 September**


I am ill. It is only flu, but Mother sent for the
doctor. She is naturally terrified of the very word
influenza. It was so unfortunate that she happened
to call in, which she hardly ever does, when I had
had to come home after school and go to bed. I had
a fever and hardly knew what I was doing, and she
was alarmed. I did not tell her that I had fainted in
class during the last lesson, which I am told led to
screams of fright from the children and the cry that
Miss was dead, bringing Mr Brennan running full
of hope, I am sure, that I was. Even he could not
deny that I was ill. He declared I had been
thoughtless and had in all probability infected the
entire school by coming in at all. I had not the
energy to make any sort of reply. He asked me if I
had money for a cab. I said I did, and one was

219

called, and I came home as Mother happened to call. I lay on my bed fully clothed, glad simply to lie down. She went for her own doctor, whom I have never seen in my life, and he prescribed what I could have told her he would, which is to take plenty of fluids, and aspirin, and bed rest. Mother said she would stay with me and I could not dissuade her so she has been here the last three days, fussing over me. I am much better, but so weak and listless. I lie here thinking of the last time I had flu, and how I resented the lack of attention and *wanted* to be fussed over. One good thing, I am now released from school for at least the next two weeks and have a doctor's note to sanction my absence. That will then only leave a few more weeks before I am completely free.

## 5 October

I was ready to return to teach today but was miraculously reprieved. A note arrived from Mr Brennan saying that a replacement for me had been found and his appointment confirmed by the local authority and since fortuitously he could start at once my services were no longer required and I need not work out the remaining weeks of my contract, though pay would be deducted of course from my salary. Good. As if I cared about the money. It is not as if I am rich but I have a nest-egg to see me through, as Frank pointed out. It will not last long though. I have already had enough experience of unemployment, if only mild compared to others, to know that it does not suit me. I want to do something connected with trying to make things better for the Tommy Dixons of this country, but it is the old question: how? It is all very well confronting Mr Brennan as I did, though that was not so brave after all. I was shaking with fury and didn't say half what I wanted to say. But now I feel so passionate about trying to right the wrongs I saw every day in that school and I *must* find an outlet for it. Percy told me once that hospitals have lady almoners, who deal with the home problems of patients. I wonder if education authorities have a similar category of employee to help pupils with problems. There is no harm in asking.

## 6 October

Today I went to London to ask Percy's advice. I did not tell Frank I would be coming, though he has been most solicitous during my illness, sending flowers and telephoning and in general showing he cares rather more than I thought he might do. The truth is I am not up to Frank. Percy was on duty, but I went to the hospital and he was able to spare half an hour to meet me in a little café round the corner. It was embarrassing telling him why I had come and I felt schoolgirlish having no clear idea of what I wanted from him. But he was, as ever, very sympathetic and helpful. He said he had talked to someone who had suggested I could perhaps become a social worker, but I'd have to retrain. I am perfectly willing to retrain, I expected to have to, and will gladly start at the beginning again. Percy is going to ask the lady almoner at his hospital if she knows how I should proceed. I left him with quite a spring in my step, or so I felt, and walked to Tilda's. She said I was looking very pale and that I had lost a lot of weight. We met Florence out of school. She has just gone into the infants' class. Waiting with Tilda and Jack in the playground and watching the children come out I was struck by how well they all looked, so well cared for, not a Tommy Dixon in sight. Florence is now very sweet and solemn and full of the importance of being a scholar. I was surprised actually to feel something for her. Tilda says she looks more like me than like her or Charles, but I cannot see it. I think families always tell unmarried aunts this. I wonder if Tilda is happy. She has every reason to be, but I thought I detected a slight restlessness. She said twice that I was so lucky to be independent and free of responsibilities. I wonder about that. Am I free of responsibilities? I suppose so. I suppose I have made sure that I am. Mother is not exactly my responsibility, though I do acknowledge she has a claim on me and I will always honour it. But the truth is that while Esther and George live with her I do not need to and, frankly, I am glad.


## 7 October

Stayed with Tilda overnight, hoping that I might hear something from Percy today, which was really asking far too much of him. I heard nothing, and cannot bother him again so soon. I should return to Brighton but I am reluctant to. I want to be in London. It was such a mistake to settle in Brighton, but in London I would never be able to afford a

222

lovely flat like the one I have and would be obliged to live in a much less pleasant area. Tilda says I can lodge with them but I could not bear the noise and mess and lack of privacy. I am sure Daphne will say the same, and sharing her house would be a better proposition, but we would clash all the time over all kinds of things on the domestic front.

## 9 October

I am still at Tilda's and ought not to be, but tomorrow I am to see someone who knows about a course to train people to do 'social work'. I like the name social *worker*. Work is what I want to do, not any kind of do-gooding. I had no idea such a job existed. Tonight I am seeing Frank. I could not go on being in London without letting him know and indeed have concealed from him how long I have already been here. Like Tilda, he said the last time I saw him, that I was looking very pale and thin, and what I need is a holiday. He wants me to go with him to the South of France for a week. He swears the weather will still be good there, and that I could lie in the sun and relax and it will perk me up. But I can't afford it, and don't want to be a kept woman. I may have given Frank the wrong idea by appearing to surrender my virtue, I'm sure he thought easily, but I will not be paid for. If he cannot see the difference that is too bad. He was very quiet for a while after I'd said this and then he looked me straight in the eye and said, You know how we could solve this? and I knew he was going to propose marriage and I put my hand over his and said, Don't.

*It is not surprising that Millicent knew nothing about the existence of social workers because in the 1930s the profession was still in its infancy. It was not until the disappearance of the old Poor Law administration that 'social workers' came into being, and by 1931 social rehabilitation was becoming the task of local councils, though when Millicent enrolled at the London School of Economics to do her course, few councils yet employed social workers to assess needs and fewer still were giving grants. Unfortunately, Millicent does not write in any detail of what it cost her, or how exactly she was trained. She finds going back to studying hard, and her diary for the period is one of the briefest, with entries very often giving no more than 'at college 9 a.m.—6 p.m., too tired to write'. She is also moving from Brighton to London during this time and found flat-hunting exhausting. Eventually, she finds a flat to rent on the borders of Notting Hill/Bayswater but it is in a poor decorative state and not very clean and the little spare energy she has goes into trying to get it into better shape. Her practical training begins in Paddington.*

## 30 April 1931

No one, except Percy, would believe the sights I've seen today, poverty of a sort and degree I never believed existed in this country, but then as Mr Messenger, my supervisor, points out, with something of a sneer—or so I interpret it—I have led a sheltered life. It offended me when he said this, since I think my life has been far from sheltered, but of course he thinks I am quite refined, I dare say. But today when we visited a family in a block of flats off Praed Street I knew he was right, I have been sheltered from this kind of hardship. When we were poor we were not *poor* like the McPatricks. Mrs McPatrick is only 26 but looks 46, worn out with giving birth every year since she was 16. Three of her babies died, but she still has seven, all of them crammed into two rooms and sleeping end to end in what looked like a big wooden box. They share a privy with four other families, all as large as their own, and there is no bath, just a tin tub brought out from under the kitchen table once a week—though I suspect not that often, but then who can blame her when it is all such a bother. The place was not clean, I saw cockroaches on the walls, and absolutely comfortless without an easy chair in the room and only a wooden table with a broken leg in the way of furniture. On the table was a loaf of bread, already cut into, which Mrs McPatrick said was all they had to eat for today. Two of the children cried all the time, and the others hung about listlessly staring at us. The father is out of work, of course, and Mrs

McPatrick supports the family by cleaning offices at night. But now she is pregnant again and too sick to work, and so they have no income at all and have applied for relief. They are Irish and Catholic, and get some contribution from the church—Mr Messenger questioned them closely on this, too humiliatingly closely for my taste—but not nearly enough to provide for even their basic needs. Their rooms are not heated and it seemed colder in them than outside though it was raining and a miserably chilly day.

I am going to have to learn so much about how to handle my feelings. I felt like weeping and I'm sure it showed and that my distress and pity were noted and not welcomed by Mrs McPatrick. I could see she both hated and despised me, and had me down for a Lady Muck. Even my clothes must have seemed an affront. My costume is my old teaching costume and by no means smart but in her kitchen it looked glaringly new and expensive and I saw her eyeing it. I felt like taking the jacket off and handing it to her. She looked so cold and ill and her thin, patched blouse gave her no warmth. But Mr Messenger was brisk and business-like. He helped her fill in a claims form and told her where to take it and assured her she would be given some money. She asked when that would be and he said he thought very soon, within a week, and she burst into tears, setting off all the children not already crying and said that was not soon when all she had in the larder was the bread we could see and nothing to put on it, no margarine, no syrup, no dripping. Mr Messenger said he was sorry but there was nothing he could do, and we left. I was shaking on the way out, and crimson with shame. I said could we not have given the poor woman a few shillings in advance to tide her over and he smiled and said nothing would ever tide her over, she was a hopeless case and I would have to harden myself to all the Mrs McPatricks. I hope I never do.

## 1 May

We saw a different side to the face of poverty today. Mr Messenger took me to another street, full of small houses which have been condemned as unfit for habitation but which are still lived in, and we visited a Mrs Riley, also Irish and Catholic but, my goodness, the difference. She, too, had lots of children, five of them, and looked older than me though she was younger, but her rooms were clean and an attempt had been made to make them cheerful. God knows, her resources were small, but from somewhere she, or her husband, had got some distemper and the walls were freshly done, and out of orange crates some crude furniture had been fashioned, seats for the children and a cradle for the baby. There were some colourful religious texts on the walls and a rag rug in front of the fireplace, a cloth on the table. There was even a clock, a rather handsome clock which Mrs Riley said had belonged to her father and had stood her in good stead because it could be reliably pawned, as it had been many times. Her husband is ill but is normally in work. He is a labourer and fell from some scaffolding and broke his leg, hence their application for temporary relief. Mrs Riley was so polite and humble and made the whole transaction painless, managing to fill in the form without help, and understanding completely that there will be a delay. She even said thank you. I said to Mr Messenger how I admired her, and he smiled another of his contemptuous smiles without saying anything. I wonder what sort of background he is from. He seems so knowing. But he has shown no curiosity about me, therefore I hold back from showing any about him. They say he is very experienced at his job and I am fortunate to have him as my supervisor, but I do not feel lucky at all. His manner is so cold and formal.

**5 May**

A glorious day. Picnicked in the park with Percy. We were both so tired, it was bliss simply to lie on a rug on the grass and feel the sun on our faces. I was thinking all the time about Mrs McPatrick's children, knowing they would certainly not be out in any park having picnics, and Percy was thinking about his patients, who are unable to get out into the sunshine at all. Percy says that, as he expected, the Labour Government is in trouble and will probably be defeated at the next election. I asked what that would mean and he said it would mean no far-reaching social change would take place. The Labour people need the security of a large majority and they will not get it. I have known Percy a long time now, nearly two years. He has never again asked me to go to visit his parents with him and I hope this means he has accepted that our friendship is just that, a true, platonic friendship. People say—well, Daphne says—that such a friendship between a man and a woman is not

228

possible. I have proved her wrong.

**6 May**

Drove with Frank to Southwold, but we did not spend the night. He wanted to book into an hotel there, but I have work tomorrow morning and must be prompt. I can imagine what Mr Messenger's face would be like if I rolled up at Frank's side in his car in the morning. My fate as a hussy would be sealed. I've known Frank nearly as long as I've known Percy and of course I *know* him in the biblical sense too, which ought to make him seem even closer and more important to me than Percy. But he isn't. He is just different. I like to be with him, he is clever and a good conversationalist, but it is his physical attractiveness which is the pull. Frank isn't particularly tall, so he doesn't tower over me, but he is strong-looking, and I like that, strong and athletic in build. He has a Cambridge blue for sprinting and plays rugby and is altogether sporty. It surprises me that I should be attracted to a sporty man—when I was young I used to imagine my ideal man as poetic in looks, not that I would ever admit I thought about such things. I'm not sure if it is the same for him. Is it how I look which attracts Frank? He tells me often enough that he finds me irresistible, but I would hate to think that is all. He says that I seem quite the Ice Queen, and he feels in possession of a delicious secret, knowing that I'm not. Perhaps I ought to be pleased, but I can't say I am. He asked me if I never wanted to settle down and have children, was I going always to be one of these new career women. I said probably. He seemed perturbed.

**7 May**

Arrived home to find Daphne literally sitting on the steps of the house waiting for me. My heart sank. She was the last person I wanted to see after a hard day, devoted though I am to her. She is so tiring these days, never listens to anything I say, interrupts all the time, never finishes sentences, it drives me to distraction. She *claims* to want to hear about my work but then when I begin to describe it she switches off. She comes to talk about herself and what *she* is doing, and to ask my advice, but without any intention of heeding it. In fact, she does not value my opinion, or so it would seem. It is all politics with Daphne. She would like to be a Member of Parliament. Well, I am impressed, but I know nothing about it. Percy would know more about the process of becoming one, but when I said so she made a face and said Percy was boring even if he had the right ideas. I suppose that is true. Percy is rather staid and dull though I don't find him boring. But he cares about the Labour Party and its advancement just as much as Daphne and far more selflessly. Daphne says there will be an election soon. She wishes she could stand for a seat somewhere, but has no hope even though she says she has worked tirelessly for the local Labour Party and attended all the meetings and paid her own expenses to go to conferences. On and on she went until I was quite sick of her and wished she would leave. When she did, I was so tired I have come straight to bed.

## 8 May

Slept so badly last night and have been exhausted all day as a consequence. All Daphne's fault. She made me start wondering about Percy, and then about Frank, and the difference between them, and what each of them meant to me. With Frank I am what people would call wicked, wanton, and other offensive words. Frank means pleasure to me, and pleasure of a secret sort. I was trying to calculate how often I see him and for how long and came to the conclusion that over the eighteen months or so that I have known him I have not spent as much time in his company as I have in Percy's, which seems strange given the nature of our relationship. I realise that I see Percy for whole days at a time, and that when we spend these days together we simply walk and talk and that is all. Whereas when I am with Frank we are going to the theatre or the pictures, or eating in restaurants, or dancing, or, of course, being lovers. It is as if I am two people, or rather need to be with two different people to satisfy conflicting sides of myself. I am never keyed-up with Percy. He is so comfortable to be with. Even when all his talk is of politics he is not like Daphne, he makes it all interesting and understandable. So I slept dreadfully badly, and today felt ashamed that I had wasted so much time on introspection, especially when during my working day I witnessed scenes of such misery, enough to make my tossing and turning over petty problems seem so trivial. Mr Messenger asked me this morning, in a most sarcastic manner, if I was in any way aware of the problem of unemployment. I was furious and said of course I was, but when he asked me if I knew how many people were currently unemployed, and how much dole money was, I knew the answer to neither question. He took pleasure in informing me that the unemployment figure touched three million, and that the Labour Party had failed to do much about it; and that unemployment pay stood at 17 shillings per man with an allowance of 9 shillings for his wife and 2 shillings for each child. He told me all this because I had speculated, after one visit we made, as to why the woman of the family did not manage her husband's money better, and suggested she needed lessons on how to do so. He obviously thought I needed a lesson on the realities of finance for a family where the wage earner is unemployed. I was silent after he'd finished. He said nothing more, but at the end of today said, quite kindly for him, that I would never make a social worker until I learned to be objective. He said a social worker had to be like a doctor and distance himself or herself from the person they were dealing with so that they could deal with the problem. I thought about arguing that surely he was mistaken to compare social work with medicine, because for a social worker the person is, quite often, part, and a big part, of the problem, whereas for the doctor the disease is mostly nothing to do with what the person is like. But I knew I would get in a muddle, so I said nothing. I will practise on Percy first.

*       *       *

*By the autumn of this year, 1931, Millicent is well into her new career and out from under Mr Messenger's supervision. She acquires a heavy case-load and becomes an expert on rules pertaining to grants and allowances but is not inured to the distress she feels about the plight of some of the families she visits. Sometimes she is so depressed she hasn't the heart, she comments, to write much in her diary and it begins to read a bit like a list, a mere timetable of her day. She is so worn out she has no energy for good times with Frank and sex with him begins to lose its attraction. Frank, perhaps realising this, tries to do something about it just as the New Year begins.*

\* \* \*

## 6 January 1932

Frank had planned to take me to a Twelfth Night party, but I was much too tired to want to go, and said so. I thought he might be annoyed, or very disappointed and show it, but he accepted my decision calmly and was sympathetic. Instead we went for a quiet supper, and he was attentive and considerate. He saw me home, and though I had told him I was not in the mood for him to stay, he came in and had a night-cap. I should have known what was coming. In that manner of his which I find so off-putting, he began with his one, two and three, analysing what he called 'our predicament'. At the bottom of it all, he said, was my constant exhaustion which was not just physical but emotional, too, because I was always fretting about my clients. My job had taken over my life in a way teaching had never done, and there was no longer much room in it for us as a couple. He said he

233

worked hard too, and was devoted to his career, but he wasn't drained by it. I interrupted to comment that I hoped he was not going to suggest I give up my job, because however tired it makes me I love it.

No, he said, he was not. What he was going to suggest was that we marry. I wish he hadn't said that. I wish I had managed to stop him before that point, as I have done before. I think I even groaned aloud. I asked how being married would change anything even had I wanted to marry. He said he could look after me, and that I would be more secure. Since security isn't the problem, this did not make sense, and I said so. But then he changed tack and, instead of being sensible and analytical, became sentimental and told me how much he loved me and how he wanted to be with me all the time. There was a lot more, about what an unusual girl I was and so on. I know it cost him a lot to say all this, and he was very tender and I do love him, in a way, and feel upset that I don't love him enough to do what he wants and marry him.

We ended up kissing, and he would have liked to end up in bed but I wouldn't. I said I couldn't, it would be wrong and not fair to him when I had just declined his proposal. And then he became exasperated and jumped up and paced about and almost shouted, Why don't you want to marry me? How could I explain when I do not know the answer myself? Frank would be most girls' dream. He is attractive, has a good career, is well off, a good lover, kind, generous, fun to be with, cultured, the right age. And I have already slept with him and some might think therefore pledged myself to him. I don't know what it is. But I know I

234

don't want to marry him. He asked me, very abruptly, if there was anyone else. I said of course not, he was, is, my one and only lover, which is true. That seemed to help. He sighed and said very well, he would leave, and he supposed we would just go on as before. I dared to say perhaps that would not be such a good idea when I was not much fun to be with and always tired and maybe we shouldn't see each other for a while and he should see other girls. That seemed to frighten him. He looked stricken, and said was I giving him the boot, and I stupidly said no when I should have said I didn't know, maybe I was. He said I was driving him mad and he didn't know if he could stand it and I said that was why I thought we both needed a rest. He looked very sad, and shrugged, and said very well. I'll leave you to call me when you're ready. He trailed off, looking utterly dejected and unlike himself, and I felt awful—but also relieved. I still feel relieved now.

\* \* \*

*During the next six months she sees Frank only four times and says very little in her diary about how these meetings go, except to describe outings to the theatre, with no mention of his coming back to spend the night. There is an intriguing mention, in May, of Frank having written a letter to her which impressed her, but intimacy does not appear to have been restored. Frank fades out of her life, though not entirely. She writes at one point that she is glad he and she can remain good friends.*

*Her diary then concentrates on her work, with very many descriptions of the state of the families she is*

235

*concerned with. She feels she does so little to make any real difference and has to struggle not to become depressed by her failure. Percy, who continues to be her closest male friend though never a lover, urges her to see that it is the system which is failing the poor, not any fault of hers. Society must be reformed, Percy is quoted as telling her, and with the Labour Party ousted in the October election the previous year, he can't see where the necessary reform is going to come from. He is worried about the rise of Mosley's party, and about the rise of Fascism in Europe in general and warns a sceptical Millicent that another war might be on the way.*

\*    \*    \*

## 22 January 1933

Percy called this evening, unexpectedly. I made him a sandwich and cocoa because as usual he hadn't had time to eat. Poor Percy. Now he is worried because Adolf Hitler has been made Chancellor of Germany and Percy says this is ominous. I have heard about Hitler of course, but I don't really know why his rise to power is such a bad thing. Sometimes when Percy is so pessimistic and gloomy he makes me long for Frank again. I don't think there could possibly be another war. It is only fifteen years since the last one and those who had to fight then would not allow it to happen again, surely. I asked Percy if he would join up if war did come and he surprised me by saying, of course. I cannot imagine Percy as a soldier. He is much too gentle, but then I suppose there were lots of men

236

like Percy who fought and were killed in the last war. I couldn't bear Percy to be killed. He has got me feeling as fearful as himself.

## 4 February

Esther has had another baby, another boy, to be called Harry. I expect she wanted a girl but it is so long since Stephen was born that perhaps she was just glad to have another baby at all. Mother wants me to go and visit to see the new baby. She says it is ages since I visited, and she is right. If Esther and George were not in the same house with Mother I convince myself I would go to visit her more often.

## 20 February

Just back from a weekend in Brighton. The new baby, Harry, has red hair, which has pleased Mother because of course Father was a red-head when he was young and I am auburn too, and she likes family resemblance. Esther is vast and looking even more unattractive than usual. I know she has just had a baby but even so she is grossly fat. Grace can't bear her. It must be hard for Esther to have her in the house. Grace really is beautiful now, quite the best-looking in our family. Father would have been so proud of her. I can see him in my mind's eye walking the promenade with Grace on his arm and everyone admiring her. I keep forgetting she is 16 and not a child any more. She leaves school this year and wants to train to be a dressmaker. It seems a lowly calling to me for such an intelligent girl, though who am I to talk, but Mother says all she thinks about is clothes and that she loves to make her own and is good at it, so I suppose it is all right. Grace was certainly very critical of my dress. She looked me up and down, and told me to turn round, so I gave her a little twirl to show how beautifully my skirt swirled, but she sighed and looked as solemn as a judge and pronounced the skirt of my dress *impossible*, because it is not cut on the bias! I burst out laughing to see her so serious about such a nothing. She also informed me that my dress was too long and that today the mid-calf length is more fashionable. She even got out a tape measure and measured the distance between my hem and the ground and declared eight inches shocking! There should, she declared, be a ten-inch gap. I let her do it to amuse Mother. She offered to make me a dress for the summer if I paid for the material, and I agreed. She went off to sketch what she thought my dress should look like, muttering some nonsense about butterfly sleeves, whatever they are. Before I left, George cornered me. He said Esther wondered if I had realised it is Mother's 60th birthday in April. Well, of course, I had. I do not need Esther to remind me. The point was, Esther thinks we should give her a party with all the family present. I was so annoyed this suggestion had to come from her when I, or Tilda, should have made it. I just managed to murmur that it was a good idea but then George capped it all by saying that as Esther had just had a baby she would not be able to organise the party and hoped I would. The cheek! I said, naturally I would, and would speak to Tilda, and he could tell his wife she had nothing to worry about. The truth is, I was angry with myself for not having thought ahead and pre-empted Esther's insufferable virtue.

## 1 March

I am distracted with trying to fix a date to celebrate Mother's birthday. It cannot be on the day itself because that is midweek and we are all at work and dare not ask for time off. Then it is so difficult getting Alfred to agree to anything. He is vague about his movements. I don't understand why, or indeed what he actually does these days beside 'travel', but where, and for what company? He seems to fancy himself as some kind of Scarlet Pimpernel instead of a low-class commercial traveller. I wonder what he tries to sell. Hair oil, maybe. He uses plenty himself. But we seem finally to have fixed on a family luncheon on the Sunday before the actual birthday. I think before is better than after. George will take Mother out for a drive in the morning and when they return we will all be there to surprise her, including Alfred, I hope. I am going to engage caterers. How else can it be done? I expect Esther will think I should go down and spend a week somehow secretly cooking, but I am not going to. Caterers are costly, especially on a Sunday, but there is no choice. Tilda says she will share the cost and perhaps the twins will contribute a little something. The meal will be simple. Salmon, Mother's favourite, and lots of puddings, which she loves.

## 15 March

Phone call from Esther. She wonders if she is expected to lay and decorate the table before the caterers come. I told her, very coolly, that she is not expected to do anything, but that if she had the energy and time—and I knew she was a very busy wife and mother—it would be kind of her to look out the big white linen table-cloth Mother used for special occasions and the napkins that go with it. She sighed and said she supposed she would manage to make time, and then asked if she was *expected* to do the flowers. I took pleasure in saying certainly not. I dread to think what Esther's idea of floral arrangements would be like. She once told me her favourite flower was the dahlia.

## 20 March

A cake. I have forgotten to order a cake. It was Florence who asked if Grandma's cake would be iced. How Esther would've crowed if there had been *no cake*. I will order a sponge cake, not a fruit one. Mother finds fruit cake too heavy, and besides the children will enjoy sponge more. Sponge, and pink icing, with sugar roses all round, and sixty candles. I am quite getting into the swing of this.

## 27 March

Oh Lord, only a week to go and I haven't bought Mother a present yet or myself something to wear. Tilda has bought Florence the prettiest of dresses and Jack has a sailor suit. He looks so adorable in it, and is very proud of his hat. Tilda herself has a dress she got only last month for a wedding and very smart it is. I am sure Grace will find the shoulders very fashionable. I *must* go shopping.

## 30 March

I must be crazy. I have spent far too much on a dress and bolero I am never likely to wear again and now I am not even sure I care for it. It is white, or rather off-white. Perfectly stupid. Esther will ask if I am thinking of getting married. It was the only outfit I liked and without being vain, I think it is very flattering. It gives me curves I have not got, and the colour—or rather lack of it—makes my hair look gorgeously flamelike and my eyes strikingly blue. I can't help but feel satisfied. I wish all the same that women could wear trousers. Some do, but not many and never as formal attire. Even Daphne only wears her slacks at home, though she constantly threatens to be bold and wear them all the time. At least this dress indicates that I have made an effort. My family will never have seen me so dressed up and I will have to put up with a great deal of teasing. It suddenly occurs to me that Mother will not be dressed up as she would wish for a party, with it being a surprise. I don't know what can be done about that.

## 8 April

I am trying to remember when we were all last

together and think it must be as long ago as Tilda's wedding—I missed Esther's and George's, and Tilda could not come to Alfred's and Albert's 18th birthday party. I think today's gathering was more of a family reunion to cherish because there was only family present. How splendid the big table looked with us all around it and Mother at the head, beaming. I had thought she might be overcome, and weep, but not a bit of it, she was happy and delighted and looked better than I have ever seen her for years, positively radiant. She even managed a little speech, in praise of her family, and it was we who shed a tear, or at least Tilda and I did. But coming home afterwards was a dismal business. I could not stay the night, with so much work to do tomorrow, and now, sitting up in bed here, I feel not only desperately tired but a trifle depressed. Mother's age depresses me and makes me feel old too, though I am only 31. It is something to do with that, I expect.

## 10 May

Mr Messenger has been replaced by Mr Robert Rigg. He is younger, and quite different. He is from somewhere in the north of England and has worked on a settlement in Liverpool. His lack of knowledge of our area will surely be a handicap, but then he can learn as I had to and in no time at all the streets will become all too familiar. Mavis is rather taken with him. She whispered to me, when she brought the tea round, that she thought him handsome and asked if I agreed. I said I supposed so, to please her, since she so likes people to agree

242

with her, but I can't say I truly care for his kind of looks. He is quite foreign-looking, with black hair and a dark moustache, and is rather slim, though not weedy. I noticed he has lovely hands, unusual for a man, with long fingers. I wonder if he plays the piano.

**12 May**

Mr Rigg asked me to go with him today on his visit to the Roper family. I was not surprised to be asked. Mrs Roper is well known to assault social workers, especially men, and then she accuses them of interfering with her, which is quite ludicrous but has to be treated as serious. Robert, he says I am to call him Robert not Mr Rigg, seemed rather nervous at first. Mr Messenger was confidence itself, so Robert's manner seems all the more striking. Doris and Gloria wonder how he came to be a social worker at all, and one senior to us. But he is good at his job, I realised today. He is kindly, unlike Mr Messenger, and sympathetic, but ultimately quite firm. When Mrs Roper began on her usual long list of insults about every authority she could think of, he stopped her and gently told her that abuse would get her nowhere, and that she'd be much better off letting him help her fill in the forms instead of tearing them up as she has done up to now. He was quite unbothered by all her children milling about and roaring, and even lifted the 2-year-old on to his knee which, considering the child clearly has impetigo, was hardly wise. Mr Messenger would never have let her near him, especially as she was not wearing any

243

knickers and Mrs Roper doesn't know the meaning of toilet training. Robert was lucky not to get drenched. The forms took an age to complete, but Mrs Roper was pleased with herself for co-operating, and even more pleased when Robert assured her she would get some money to clothe the children and that he would try to get the damp which runs down her walls seen to and the infestation of cockroaches dealt with. I only hope he can manage it.

## 14 May

Robert asked me today if I liked walking. I said I did. He said he didn't know London and wondered where there was somewhere to walk that was pleasant and green and easy to get to. I laughed and rattled off a list of all the parks in which he could walk; and he rather shyly wondered if perhaps I would show him my favourite park to walk in. I could hardly refuse. So tomorrow I am to take him to Richmond. I am not sure it is my favourite park, I haven't been there often, but it has the best and longest walks.

## 15 May

A long day out with Robert. The weather was lovely and the park looked beautiful, all green and lush, and we saw lots of deer. Robert was impressed; he said he couldn't believe a city like London had such countryside on its outskirts. He walks quickly, with long strides, and looks about him keenly, spotting birds and knowing their names, and admiring the trees. He says he loves the country, so I felt I could ask him why in that case he had come to London. He said the post was offered to him, but he didn't say how, and that he thought he needed the experience of trying to deal with the very worst problems. There was nothing preachy about how he said it, though.

We went to a café after walking for nearly two hours and had tea and scones. He asked me a bit about myself but didn't press me too much and I got away with telling him the bare minimum. I don't know why I wanted to be fairly reserved, but I did. I did admit I had once been a teacher, though, and it turned out so had he, briefly, and that he'd come into social work for the same reasons. I didn't tell him where I live. He lives in a bed-sitting-room in Vauxhall. He says it is all he can afford, and that moving from Lancashire was expensive. I wonder how old he is. He might be a little younger than I am.

**2 June**

Percy wants me to go on holiday with him, a walking holiday in Cornwall, following cliff paths right round the southern coast and staying in bed-and-breakfast places. I felt awful saying I would think about it. I have no holiday plans and I have never been to Cornwall, and Percy is my dearest friend and I love his company and we get on so well and there is no need to fear he would get ideas. He has known for ages now that, though I like him so much, love him even, in a sort of way, I am not attracted to him and nothing romantic can come of our friendship. There has never been any need to spell this out. But I hesitated, and still do.

## 4 June

I have accepted Percy's invitation. His pale face flushed with pleasure and I couldn't help being touched—to mean so much to someone! We go in a week's time. There is no problem about taking my holiday so suddenly since no one else is going away then. Robert showed some curiosity about where I was going and with whom but I gave nothing away, except to say my destination was Cornwall. He said he is not taking any holiday till next year, which seems odd. We had a bit of chat about Hyde Park, which he has been exploring, and Regent's Park, which is next on his list. He asked if I would fancy walking with him there on Sunday but I said I was busy. I am not busy, but I do not want to encourage him to believe I am always available.

## 9 June

Spent the day with Tilda and the children. I told her I was going on a walking holiday with Percy and she annoyed me by saying she felt sorry for him because I have kept him dangling all this time. I denied it angrily. Being angry was a mistake. It made Tilda think I was embarrassed and that she had hit the nail on the head. She asked why I didn't just marry the poor man and get it over with and I had to say again that marriage with him was out of the question, I was not attracted to him. Tilda said, rather suggestively, you mean not like you were to Frank, and I said *exactly*. She stopped laughing and was quiet for a bit and then said attraction wasn't everything and it might not last and I shouldn't regard it as so important. I said I hadn't. If I had, I would never have let Frank go. She nodded. I wonder if she is talking about herself and Charles. I never, or hardly ever, see them together, he is always at the hospital, so I cannot judge, but I have always thought they are devoted to each other. I would hate to find this is no longer true.

**10 June**

Packed today for the holiday. I have bought a proper knapsack, of the type Percy told me to get. It seems horribly heavy, though I have tried to keep the contents to a minimum. I have only put in one book—I must have one—which is *Brook Evans*. Maybe I will not need two thick sweaters or a spare pair of shoes, but I do not trust the weather. I am going to wear slacks. I asked Percy if he would be ashamed to be seen with a woman in trousers and he said not at all, in fact he thought it very sensible of me. I have packed a skirt for evenings, and one dress, in case we eat anywhere smart, though that is unlikely. Percy never thinks about food. He doesn't care what he eats and never, as far as I know, goes to restaurants.

## 14 June

I am not the excellent walker I thought I was. So mortifying. I have to pretend to want to look at the view to make Percy stop, he tears along at such a great rate. Most of the time the paths are narrow and very near the edge of the cliff and so we walk in single file and it is like walking on one's own much of the way. It is only when we have our packed lunch that we are together, which does make me wonder why Percy wanted a companion at all. In the places we have stayed overnight so far he has hardly needed my company either. They are quite humble bed-and-breakfasts, where everyone sits round the table together. Percy is not good at small talk and takes no part in general chat. And we go to bed so very early, being tired, especially me, too tired to read *Brook Evans*, and with him wanting to make early starts. I don't know if I am enjoying this holiday or not. At least the weather is good.

## 18 June

Rain. Heavy rain, all day. I thought we might stay inside, but we had to leave the B & B by 10 a.m. We could have taken a bus to Truro and looked round whatever it has to offer in the way of museums or such like, and even treated ourselves to a decent lunch. I did dare to suggest this but Percy looked astonished and asked where would the fun be in that. I wondered where the fun was in plodding through the rain and getting soaked. Percy said I'd find it *exhilarating*, a quite different experience. So I had to don waterproofs and follow him, or else make a scene and I did not want to do that. In no time at all the rain had found its way down my neck in spite of my hood. Ahead of me I could see Percy with no head covering at all, his hair plastered to his head and apparently enjoying it. We walked three miles in the first hour or so and I could not see a thing. As well as the rain there was a mist which did not lift until the afternoon. We had our lunch in an abandoned hut and though at first I was glad of the shelter I soon felt cold. I shivered and Percy put his arm round me and said he'd keep me warm. How could he when he was soaking wet himself? I suppose I sulked, and he became anxious and said he felt guilty and that if I wanted we could make our way onto the road and hitch a lift to our next stop. But pride made me refuse to give in. I said no, we would walk on, as had been planned.

**20 June**

Better weather, though still no real sun, and I have a cold. Percy says it is nothing, that by feeling my forehead he can tell I have not got a temperature and he has looked down my throat and announces it is not inflamed. I don't care, I feel bunged up and seedy. I wonder if I should get the train home. But we have only four days to go and I will not give in.

**23 June**

Last day, and wonderful sun. Felt well and cheerful

for the first time in a week. The route today was easy, and so pretty, and for once Percy did not stride ahead but positively slowed to an amble and we had lunch outside at a pub and sat there for ages with a beautiful view of the bay before us. I suppose this is how I had thought it would be, sauntering along and spending time sitting in the sun eating and drinking and admiring the view. Who would've thought Percy would be so tough. He was very thoughtful today, and I said, a penny for your thoughts, as we sat there. He said he could not believe all this could ever be threatened. I asked what he meant by 'this' and he said the English way of life, the peace and serenity of areas like this. I was puzzled, and a little slow on the uptake, and said I couldn't see how it could be. This bay, this pub, this little village had been like this for centuries and surely always would be, and the people here, I was sure, didn't feel threatened at all. Percy said then they should because with Hitler's rise to power in Germany everything could change. I don't know why he had to mention Hitler on such a beautiful day. It made me cross. I think I have had enough of Percy for the moment. I realise I am looking forward to going home. I wonder if he is. I am sure I have been a terrible disappointment to him.

## 24 June

Home to London. The train was almost empty for half the journey and then it filled up. We were alone in our carriage for the first two hours and I was settling down to read, thinking how wonderful to have such peace, when Percy began to talk. He asked if I had enjoyed the holiday and there didn't seem much point in lying, considering I had been asked a direct question, so I lowered my book and said I thought he knew the answer to that, which was that I'd enjoyed only some of it. How could I have enjoyed those days of rain, and having a cold, surely he didn't expect me to? He stared at me and I had a dreadful premonition of what he was going to say . . . Did I realise, he said, we had been friends, quite close friends, for over two years and that some people might think that significant. I said, Don't, Percy, you know how I feel, but he shook his head and said, I have to say it, I can't put it off any longer: I love you Millicent and I want you to be my wife. I closed my eyes and I know a sigh, or something like it, escaped my lips. It was not like refusing Frank because I've never felt for Percy what I felt for Frank. This should have made a refusal easier but it didn't, it made it worse. How could I say to Percy that I wasn't in the least attracted to him, or even that these last two weeks had shown me I'd been deluded to think we got on so well. Feebly, I said I didn't want to marry anyone. I said, I do like you, Percy, you know that, and I admire you, but there has to be more than that to a marriage. Does there? he said. I was speechless. I echoed him, repeating, Does there? incredulous. He said, I think liking and admiring and getting on with someone is a good basis for marriage. What about love? I asked, faintly.

He laughed then and said, did I mean *sex*, very abruptly, almost spitting out the word. And I grew bolder and said yes, I did, I meant sex and love and passion. But he said how could anyone know about all that until they were married and tried it; that we might be very passionate together and that on his part, if desire was anything to go by, we would be. There didn't seem any point then in holding back. I looked him straight in the eye and said I had experienced passion and knew I would not find it with him. At that moment, our carriage door into the corridor opened and a woman with two children came in. The relief for me was overwhelming. There was such a bustle with the mother settling her children it was impossible for Percy to speak, and I took up my book pointedly. The words swam before my eyes but I kept it in place for a good ten minutes and at the end of that time, when I looked up, Percy had left the carriage. I felt anxious about him and was glad when he returned, looking very pale and tense but composed.

There was no further opportunity to speak until we had arrived at Paddington. As we walked down the platform I said I was sorry but he stopped me. He asked if I was going to get a taxi and when I nodded, he said in that case he'd say goodbye, and he held out his hand very formally. I couldn't bear it and moved to embrace him but he shrugged me off and walked away very quickly. Oh God. I will have to write to him and apologise and ask him to forgive me, but for what, for being honest? I never wanted to hurt him, and never would have done if he had not forced my hand. Surely he cannot argue that I led him on. I suppose that what will really hurt is that he knows now that I have been with someone else. I never concealed Frank from him, it was just that he never knew about him, and why should he? Perhaps if he also knew I had broken with Frank it would help. He could label me a complete hussy then and be done with it. What an awful holiday. I must have been insane ever to agree to go on it, and yet I did that out of a sort of pity, without self-interest, but no one, least of all Percy, would believe that now. Thank heaven I was never put in Naomi's situation or I am sure Percy would have acted like Caleb Evans.

\*   \*   \*

*The book Millicent was reading on the train, and which she'd chosen as her one book to take on holiday with Percy, was* Brook Evans, *a novel by Susan Glaspell, published five years previously in 1928, by Victor Gollancz. Millicent was probably attracted to it despite herself, because it was hailed as a wonderful love story, with a heroine, Naomi, who tries to stay true to her own passionate nature even though her lover is killed and, pregnant with his child, she is forced by her shocked parents to marry the kind but dull Caleb Evans whom she finds physically repugnant.*

*After this, she mentions writing once to Percy but doesn't reveal what she wrote and doesn't mention whether he replied. He seems to have gone out of her life even more suddenly and completely than Frank did. Robert Rigg, on the other hand, starts to become a major factor in her life but all the entries about him are very guarded. This, it is clear, is not the sort of relationship she has had before. Despite her first impression, and her feeling that she was not attracted to him, she confesses he has grown on her and that she does now find him physically attractive, but there appears to be no intimacy between them. The link is*

253

*their joint work. Robert is her immediate superior and she grows to admire his direction. He is not political, as Percy was, but on the other hand is knowledgeable about politics. It is through Robert that she becomes mildly involved in the Peace Pledge Union (a movement begun in 1934 when war in Europe was thought imminent after Hitler became Dictator). They go together to several demonstrations and she mentions that they read* Peace News *as well as pamphlets such as Aldous Huxley's case for pacifism: 'What Are We Going To Do About It?' All this time, Millicent gets no nearer knowing much about Robert's background, or why such an attractive man is unattached. Then, towards the end of 1935, she makes a startling discovery.*

## 10 November 1935

Stayed late at the office with Robert, trying to work out what to do about the Thompson family. Mavis positively leered at me as she left and I said I was staying to have a meeting with Robert—Staying late with Dreamboat again, are you? she said. I wish she wouldn't. She knows perfectly well that there is nothing between Robert and me. Nothing romantic. She makes me cross, and then I become flushed with irritation, and she interprets this as a guilty blush. It is infuriating. Robert has never even held my hand let alone tried to kiss me. That is another puzzle to Mavis, of course. She puts it in her usual crude way: is he a Nancy-boy? All because he shows no interest in any woman in the whole building and this, declares Mavis, is *unnatural*, especially as so many women show a great interest in him. I am sure he is not what she thinks but, in her maddening way, she has a point. He does seem very detached. He never flirts, and turns any attempt to flirt with him away. I go over in my mind all the time I have spent in his company and realise I have never seen him notice a girl, his eyes have never wandered after anyone however beautiful. It is as though he has trained himself not to notice. I think that is the key to him: restraint. I wonder what he would be like if he let himself go. I expect Mavis wonders too. I am as bad as she is.

## 15 November

Another late night with Robert. We took the Thompson children into care and had Mrs Thompson committed. It was horrible. Mrs Potter could not take the younger two and I had to place them with Mrs Preston and she is not nearly as good. It is all such a mess and I can't help blaming Mr Thompson's absence. Until he disappeared this was not a problem family. I ranted on to Robert about how murderous I felt towards the man and Robert as usual showed equanimity, saying we'd never met the man and didn't know the circumstances and there was no point being judgemental.

We went afterwards for a drink. Robert has never, at least in my company, touched alcohol, but tonight he ordered a brandy and so did I. We both felt in need of something to buck us up. It was warm in the pub, a nice fire going, and it wasn't too crowded so the corner we parked ourselves in was peaceful. I don't know if it was the brandy, I suppose it must have been, but Robert was different, much less distant. He suddenly asked me if I had a steady boyfriend, and then immediately apologised for having asked. I said I didn't mind a bit. I told him that no, I hadn't a boyfriend, and hadn't had one for some time. He said he was sure it was through choice. Flatterer, I thought, but found myself hastening to reply that, yes, as a matter of fact it was. Then he said, you're very attractive, if I may say so. I felt the way I used to feel with Frank and tried not to show it. I would so have liked to reach out and take hold of his hand and tell him how I was feeling, but of course I did no such thing. Instead, I asked him if *he* had a steady girlfriend, and then he took my breath away. No, he said, looking straight at me, I am married. The shock made me start and I spilt my drink a little, and then was furious with myself because there was nothing very shocking about what he'd said and I'd made myself look like a silly goose reacting like that. He talked quite rapidly then, telling me he had married at 18 to a childhood sweetheart. When he was 16, he'd lied about his age and joined up, and when he came home from the war he was so shaken by what he'd been through that he had more or less fallen into her comforting arms and married her. Almost from the beginning the marriage hadn't been a success and, when they had a baby a year later and it died, things got worse and worse. But his wife, Doreen, wouldn't admit it and wouldn't agree to a divorce, and so, after ten years of this, he left her, and came to London. He said only Doreen had grounds for divorce but since she wouldn't start proceedings there was nothing he could do. He wasn't a free man and couldn't act like one, and that was that. I didn't know what to say. It was all too much to take in. But all the time he was talking I felt more and more attracted to him and horrified myself by wishing he would kiss me. In the end, I managed to murmur a few strangled words, of sympathy I suppose, can't remember what they were. Then we left the pub and as he walked me to the tube he put his arm round me to share his umbrella. I let him keep it there and he tightened his grip a little. He said goodnight very seriously and sadly, and I said it too, and that was all.

## 8 December

Promised Mother I would come to her for Christmas and stay at least a week but now that the time has almost arrived I wish I hadn't done any such thing. I can't take Robert with me and I don't want to be without him: it is as simple, and as awkward, as that. I don't know how I got into this state so quickly and I worry that the speed of it all means I will regret it, but then I remind myself that I have actually *known* Robert for over two years and it is only recently that things seemed to happen so quickly, since he confessed that he is married. He says now that he thought telling me this, speaking the truth, would mean the end to any chance of our becoming more than friends. He doesn't know, I tell him now, how long and hard I thought about what I should do, how afraid I was that he would think me forward and the wrong kind of girl. It cost me a great deal in pride to make an overture and if he had hesitated for even a second in accepting the invitation to tea and a walk before, I would never have asked him again. It was so hard to take the initiative and I will never tell anyone that I did.

## 12 December

How changed I feel. A great quiet has come over me and I dream my way through half the hours in the day. I feel as if something raw in me has been soothed and for the first time I know the meaning of the word relaxed. All of me is relaxed and it feels delicious. I never felt this with Frank. With Frank, there was an excitement, a physical thrill, but it scared me sometimes and left me exhausted when the exhilaration was over. Now, lying in Robert's arms, I feel as though I might melt entirely into him. It makes me weep. I want him with me all the time, I am distraught when he leaves and find myself returned to my old tense state. He is necessary to me, to my well-being, and I have dared to tell him so.

## 19 December

I go to Brighton tomorrow, leaving Robert alone in London for the whole Christmas period. I wanted him to stay tonight but he has just left, saying he thinks it wiser. He does not have Frank's attitude to love-making. To Robert, it is all very serious and he goes on and on about being a married man unable to get a divorce and how it is not right for him to compromise me. It is such an old-fashioned word but it is the one he uses: 'compromise' indeed. I think he might be shocked at how little I care about such things as my reputation. If I worried over that I would never have slept with Frank, but then Robert does not know about that. There is no need for him to.

## 20 December

Mother says I look very well indeed, with what she calls a sparkle in my eye. Grace immediately piped up that I must be in love, which made me blush, and of course this was taken as proof. Mother

259

asked so eagerly if I did have a new young man that I could not deny her the small pleasure of knowing that I did but warned her not to start imagining anything would come of it. She asked why ever not and I hadn't the heart to say because he is already married. It would have hurt her so much. Poor Mother, always having hopes and plans for her unmarried older daughter and the most important of these being marriage. What a holy grail that is for her, ever to be sought. In her eyes respectability is all.

**22 December**

Alfred arrived with the news that he is getting married, with what Mother calls 'unseemly haste' which in her opinion can only mean one thing and she daren't think about that, so is all in favour of the haste. Alfred is, after all, 27. Surely she wants him married, considering he is such a worry to her with his unsettled life; but no, it is me she really wants to see married. She has even started to add 'before I die'! It is my *great* age, of course. I am on the shelf. She is even a little ashamed of me, though she won't admit it. I don't know how I am going to get through this week without Robert.

**29 December**

One more day to go. I think I would go mad if it had to be longer. Esther is so irritating in every way, fussing about the most trivial things and wanting to control everyone. She pretends to be interested in my work but I can tell that she thinks it no different from the voluntary work she does, which consists merely of taking a tea trolley round the hospital wards. Then she quizzes me all the time about how I spend my leisure time and with whom. It is worse than Mother and her endless inquiries about romances, or Grace with her teasing about what she calls lover-boys. Albert does not have to put up with all this. He seems never to have had a girlfriend and is the very opposite of his twin. I think Father would've been pleased with how Albert has turned out: he is so sensible and dependable even if his job is not very grand.

## 1 January 1936

That was the happiest New Year I have ever seen in. It is rash to say so, but I feel it is going to be a good year for me even though there are no actual omens for such optimism. Robert will still be married, unless his wife relents, which is unlikely, but I am not going to let that ruin our lives. We can be together in all the ways that matter. I am lucky: I rent my own flat and I do not see why he cannot share it with me. He is the one who thinks this would be wrong and will not agree, but I am determined to persuade him.

But it was a wonderful night, and he did stay, and I don't think regretted it. I still haven't told him about Frank and now I don't think I will. It is not as if I had been married to him. I do feel a little guilty about this, it isn't quite honest, and honesty between lovers is important. I will *not* make comparisons with Frank. That would be despicable.

**6 January**

Hard to be at work with Robert and obliged to keep up the pretence that we are just colleagues, especially with Mavis ever alert and beady-eyed. Robert manages better than I do. He is his usual distant, cool but kindly self, taking no more notice of me than of Mavis or Doris or Gloria. He says he had grown so used to having to deny his attraction to me that it is quite easy to keep it up. But I find it difficult. I long to touch him, and have to resist smiling at him in a meaningful way. When we go out on visits together it is such a relief to wait until we are clear of the building and then hide in a doorway and kiss.

**14 January**

Robert stayed the night again, but still will not move in. It is awful to think of him going back to his bed-sitting-room. I have seen it, though he did not want me to, and it is a horrid, dark little room without any comfort at all. He has lived there like a monk all this time and there is no need for him to go on doing so. He is so moral, and worries so about my reputation in a sweet but old-fashioned way. Frank never worried in the least. It is not as though Robert is a clergyman and it is not as though I cared two hoots about reputations. Except, I suppose, for Mother's sake. She would be appalled to know I want a married man to live with me, and shocked beyond words that I am already sleeping with him. I wouldn't like her to know, that's all. Stupidly, I said so to Robert—adding that since she lives in Brighton she never would get to hear of it—and he pounced on this and said these things always leaked out and my mother would hear, which was exactly why he would not agree to living openly together. But we do not have to live *openly*. We could be ever so discreet. It could be managed somehow but Robert won't even discuss how.

## 20 January

The King died today. I can't say this means much to me. Mother telephoned, wanting to talk about it and full of royalist distress. I was surprised that Robert turned out to be quite a royalist too. He says he is for King and Country, it's just an instinctive feeling. He says the new King will be a good one. As Prince of Wales, Robert says, he has shown concern for the poor. I didn't know that.

## 24 January

It is extraordinary how many women I've visited in their homes these last few days have expressed royalist opinions. What has the King been to them, or done for them? Nothing, I would have thought, and yet they act as though he had been a much loved relative. One woman, Mrs Carruthers, was actually red-eyed with weeping over the poor King. She likes the Prince of Wales but wishes he were married because she's heard—who from, in the circles she moves in?—he's 'a bit of a lad'. Well, it brightened up what is usually a pretty grim visit.

## 1 February

Alfred got married today, but thankfully my presence was not required with it being not much of an occasion and taking place in Skegness where his bride hails from. Mother went all that way, with Grace, and Albert too, quite enough to represent the family. My new sister-in-law is called Ethel and she is only 18. Heaven knows how Alfred is going to look after her and the infant when it arrives.

## 5 February

Most entertaining letter from Grace about Alfred's wedding. She says Ethel is rather fun, much preferable to Esther, and very pretty indeed. Her family own a fish and chip shop, much to Mother's chagrin, and are all big and fat and talk in broad Yorkshire and are impossible to understand. Ethel was a waitress in a hotel where Alfred stayed and that is how it all began. Grace says Mother kept muttering to her that at least Alfred had behaved honourably, but she was clearly smouldering with resentment that her precious son had been, she was sure, taken in and hooked by a trollop. The baby is due in June. The bride wore white all the same. No one knows where the happy couple are going to live but apparently Mother has a dreadful suspicion they will turn up in Brighton. I was enjoying all this gossip until I got to the end of the page and found a second sheet with some alarming news: Grace is coming to London. She has been offered a job at an establishment in Bond Street, making dresses, and is thrilled. She wonders if she could stay with me rather than Tilda, though Mother thinks it would be better if she went to Tilda. I must reply carefully, not seeming to reject her as a guest but siding with Mother. I will point out, though it is not really true, that Tilda lives much nearer to Bond Street and that it will be so much easier for her to get to work and back. But Grace is smart. She will be suspicious.

**2 March**

Grace arrives tomorrow. I am meeting her at Victoria and taking her home with me for the first weekend and then to Tilda's. Spent the day removing all trace of Robert from the flat. It seems so silly to be hiding the truth from my own sister but she is young and impressionable and I don't really know her intimately. But then I conceal Robert's existence even from Tilda. I don't know why I haven't told Tilda. Partly, a big part, this is Robert's fault. He doesn't want my family to know. He says he would feel ashamed in front of them, and knows all too well what they would think of him.

**6 March**

Grace has moved to Tilda's though made it plain she would much rather have stayed here. I tried to give her a good time. We did the sights, all the obvious ones, and walked for miles and went to the cinema and had tea at Gunter's. Grace is a pleasure to be with, but I do feel more like a mother to her than a sister. She was asking me last night about Father and what he was really like and it was hard trying to describe him and how much I loved him. She has no memory of him at all, of course. Those years after Father's death fascinate her and she wanted to know all about my being a shop girl and said she could not imagine it. Neither can I sometimes: it seems unreal.

## 21 March

Spring, at last. All week it has been warm and sunny, and even in the dismal streets I visit the blue sky above makes a difference. I want to go on holiday with Robert, somewhere abroad, Spain or France or Italy, somewhere foreign where no one knows us and we need not be furtive. Mr Russo included an invitation to his Long Island home with his Christmas card. I would love to go to America and introduce Robert to him and I could meet his new wife. Robert says America is out of the question, it would be too expensive, but he will think about somewhere on the Continent. But why does he have to, why does he hesitate? I cannot see a single thing against it. He says he has not much money yet he is paid more than I am. I don't understand this. It hurts me to think he is just making excuses. He says he isn't, but in that case why not go away with me?

\*  \*  \*

*Quite why Robert was so reluctant to go on holiday with Millicent is never clear, but after some pressure and persuasion (exhaustively detailed in the diary) he agrees, though insists that everything should be done as cheaply as possible. They go to Spain, travelling through France by train. Millicent keeps quiet, or says that she does, about memories of her previous luxurious ride through another part of France. The train is uncomfortable (they are in third class and the seats are wooden) and because Robert is watching the francs they make only one overnight stop, staying in a not very clean pension.*

*But once they reach Cadaqués, a fishing village some eighty miles north of Barcelona, she is happier. They find lodgings in one of the white-arcaded houses which line the main street hugging the shoreline. The two of them swim, walk, have long wine-drinking meals and make passionate love. At least, Millicent is passionate, or judges that she is, but there are one or two entries which seem to suggest Robert may be rather overwhelmed by her. There is just a hint of smugness about the way she records his astonishment at her sexual energy and she even goes so far as to deduce that since his only experience has been with his wife then she, Doreen, must have been frigid. The sun shines the whole time and Millicent wishes they could stay for ever. She never comments on the political situation in Spain, though there must surely have been plenty of signs of unrest, even in the quiet region where they were staying. But she does record that Robert describes how, in the elections of February that year, the Popular Front had gained a majority over all opponents, and that as a consequence many socialists and radicals had been released from prison. Millicent imagines that this pleased him, but he says the right-wing generals will never tolerate the new government and that trouble*

267

*will soon result. He assures her that there is going to be a struggle between good and evil, it is as simple as that. Millicent reckons that he is being pessimistic and refuses to entertain the idea that there will be a war in Spain or anywhere else.*

*Not long after their return to London the Spanish Civil War begins in mid-July, with the generals' revolt, and to her surprise and alarm, Robert considers going to fight for the government forces against the rebel fascists. Millicent has never thought of him as likely to do such a thing (and he doesn't do it) in spite of knowing that as a young man he volunteered in the Great War. She concludes that she does not know him as well as she thought she did, but she is rather proud that he is turning out to be a man of such principle.*

\*     \*     \*

**4 June**

Robert follows events in Spain so closely, but I am afraid they bore me. I know it is wrong to admit this but I can't help it. Daphne is as bad (or good) as Robert. She is sure a European war is going to break out and Robert agrees. They both become so excited and worked up talking about the probability of Hitler overrunning some little country and of us having to declare war. They both say they would join up at once. I asked Daphne what she would join. I didn't even know women could join the armed forces. She and Robert then argued about whether women could or could not be sent on active service. I don't think either of

268

them knows half as much as they pretend to. I say nothing, just listen. I expect they consider me unpatriotic and maybe I am, and selfish. I do see things only from my own personal point of view. It is what affects *me* that counts. Is that so very wrong? Robert thinks so. But I am *happy*, and I don't want to think of anything spoiling my happiness.

## 16 July

Such lovely summer days, but I can't take more time off to enjoy them. Robert doesn't seem to mind being cooped up in London but I do and yet my flat is quite airy with big sash windows, and he has only that dreadful stuffy room which he goes on refusing to give up, though for all the time he actually spends in it these days he might as well. He is so stubborn. He says he is quite content to continue as he is but would not blame me if I were not. This made me angry, and we quarrelled, about what he meant. It is our first real quarrel and it upset me. I said it sounded as if he was encouraging me to part with him and that he can only be doing that because *he* wants to part with me. He said that was nonsense, and that all he meant was that he would understand if I wanted a more settled future with someone else because he cannot give it to me. In a temper, I asked how recently he had requested a divorce from Doreen; not, I insisted, that I cared about marrying, but being still married to her seemed to be his excuse for not moving in with me. He went quite white and asked, was I insinuating that he was a liar? It

269

was very upsetting. I am afraid I wept a little.

**17 July**

Hardly slept. Robert went back to his dingy room and I tossed and turned all night. I hate to think of us quarrelling. I thought and thought about the start of it, and that made me go over and over what he'd said about whether I was happy the way things are. He didn't exactly say that, but near enough. I suppose the answer is that however much I try to be, I am not. I want Robert to live with me. I would be willing to face the consequences, even hurting and shocking Mother, if he would live with me. He has asked many times if I do not want children and seems puzzled when I tell him that though I like children, some children that is, it does not distress me to think I may never have any. At 35 I am probably almost too old already anyway, and I've grown used to preventing them. I would never have a child without being sure of its father's support, and I told Robert that. It is too hard and awful to be an unmarried mother, as he knows from the pitiful cases we have seen. I wouldn't wish that fate on a child, or on myself. Robert worries constantly about accidents and my becoming pregnant. I tell him I know what I am doing and have taken care of myself from the beginning, but he can never quite believe me even after all this time. He presses and presses me to say what I would do if I did become pregnant and I don't like him doing this. I don't know what I *could* do. I would be too afraid to have the kind of abortion I have heard about and I would not know how to have the safe kind, if such a thing exists. Maybe Daphne would know, or Tilda. I suppose I would have to have the baby, and that is what Robert is getting at. It is odd that this never bothered Frank.

## 1 August

Weekend in Brighton. Mother is missing Grace dreadfully, though she is of course pleased she is doing so well. She wonders if I think Grace will come home or settle in London and I had to say I had no idea though really it is obvious that Grace will never go home. Tilda says she has loads of admirers and is never in. Mother does not look well. She has lost weight and seems to have no energy. I think she should see a doctor but she refuses, claiming only to be tired, and reminding me she is 63. Alfred's wife has had her baby some time ago but has only just had him christened. Mother is scandalised by the name: Julian. She says it is not a family name and to her sounds unmanly and affected. I hope she has not passed on this opinion to Ethel. Had a long, long walk before I left, and couldn't help recalling the walks I had here with Percy. It seems such a long time ago, and so sad that our friendship ended as it did. I wonder if Percy ever found the woman he needed. Certainly I was not the right one, and I never thought I was, not for one minute. I wished Robert was with me. When I am not with him I talk to him all the time in my head.

## 5 August

Lunch at Tilda's. Charles was at home for once, looking horribly tired and older than when I last saw him, but then I suppose that is ages ago. He seemed vague and abstracted and got irritable with the children who really are sweet, especially Florence. Florence asked me very solemnly if I minded being a spinster and was I very sad not to have a husband. She was sharply reprimanded by Charles, but I laughed (I hope it didn't sound forced) and said I wasn't in the least sad and that being a spinster had its advantages. Tilda said, Yes, I'm sure, and banged the dishes around a bit unnecessarily as she cleared the table. Before I left, she took me aside and said she had something to tell me. She is expecting again. I was so surprised. Florence is nearly 11 and Jack nearly 7 and I'd imagined her family complete. She doesn't know how it happened: she took every precaution and made no mistakes, she says. She is three months gone and, even in spite of her religious beliefs, admitted to having tried every reasonable means to dislodge this baby, but nothing worked. Charles knows of a doctor in Holland who could abort the baby but it would be very difficult and expensive to arrange and besides she could not bring herself to go through with it. So I am lumbered, she said, tears in her eyes. She hasn't told the children yet, or indeed anyone, but is hoping Grace will help out when the time comes. I immediately said I would arrange time off and come to help as well, and really my heart did not sink as much as it would once have done at the thought. Poor Tilda. She is not young either and that worries her. She knows

272

too much about the dangers of a woman nearly 40 having a baby.

**7 August**

Robert said I was very quiet and subdued today. He asked if I was feeling ill and I saw the dread in his face which for a moment made me wish to be cruel and pretend that I might be pregnant. I don't know why such evil thoughts come into my head. But I put him out of his misery by telling him about Tilda. But it was a mistake, because he at once took her fate as a dreadful warning to us, saying if this could happen to a woman who is a nurse and whose husband is a doctor it could happen to the most careful of people and that he had been saying this all along and I never seemed to heed him. What do you want me to do, then, I asked him, stop making love, is that the solution? Maybe we should use other methods as well as the one we already do, to be doubly sure, he suggested. It is all so sordid. For the first time, I thought maybe I did not want Robert to stay the night. I felt tired of his fretting and his *worthiness*.

**8 August**

Just as I was going to bed there was a telephone call from Esther. Mother has had a heart attack and is in hospital. I must go first thing in the morning.

273

## 11 August

The doctor says Mother is out of danger, but her blood pressure is higher than he would wish and she must rest and take things very easy from now on. Esther sighed and said she supposed that would mean more work for her, but it couldn't be helped. I felt furious with her, but the truth is that were it not for Esther, I would have to give up my own work, and Robert, and come home to look after Mother. Esther's boys are so noisy and not nearly as well brought up as Tilda's children. They racket around the house roaring and banging and I'm sure make Mother's head ache. I shushed them at one point today and Esther was annoyed and said this was their home and it was natural for boys to be lively, and if I had children of my own I might understand. George doesn't seem to have any influence at all. When I think of how Father's 'stop that at once' was instantly obeyed by all of us, I cannot believe how lacking in authority my brother is.

## 12 August

I am going back to London tomorrow but will come down again at the weekend. Mother quite understands. She looked so sweet today, propped up in bed and wearing her best bed-jacket and with some colour in her poor cheeks at last. She protests against being kept in bed and says she feels a fraud and wishes to be up and helping Esther. I was pleased and relieved when Esther herself said she was managing perfectly and needed no help and

Mother was to stay put. She is not so bad really. I am grateful to her, and said so, and she seemed satisfied and said she would see Mother stayed in bed a while yet.

## 14 August

At least Robert seems to have missed me. I had told him which train I intended to catch but since never in a million years did I expect him to meet me I thought it of no consequence when I decided to get a later train. By the time I arrived he had been in Victoria Station three hours, meeting two previous trains, and had begun to imagine something had happened. I got off the train in something of a trance, still thinking about Mother, and feeling low about her, and I almost didn't see Robert walking towards me with his arms open. It was the most lovely shock and resolved quite a few doubts in my mind. He was very sympathetic about Mother, prompting me to ask him about his own. I'd asked before about his family but had got little out of him beyond the fact that both his parents were dead and he was an only child, or rather that he had had a younger brother who had died as a baby. But he spoke tonight a bit about his mother, saying they had never got on. She had great hopes for him and he hadn't realised them, and she had been against his marriage and never spoke to Doreen or made her welcome. He said his mother had been a snob and that what she mainly had against Doreen was that she was a shop assistant. I laughed, and told him about my own spell in a shop, which somehow I never had done. It struck

275

me as so sad that Robert hadn't got on with his mother and had felt almost no affection for her. If I had a son and he confessed such a thing I would be distraught. I can't bear it when children don't love their parents.

**15 August**

Telephoned Esther. Mother is doing well. The doctor called today and says she may get up for a little while tomorrow.

*     *     *

*But two days later, Mrs King has another heart attack and dies before Millicent (or Tilda) can get there. It grieves Millicent greatly that it was Esther who was there at the end. She notes this death tersely, but there is no gap in her diary as there was when her father died. She does say how much she loved her mother but her love is loaded with guilt because she feels she has not been a good daughter—'I have always thought too much of myself.' She goes on to record matter-of-fact details about her mother's will, but there is no account of the funeral (except to note that it occurred on 20 August).*

*George is left the Brighton house, as expected, and everything else is divided among his siblings. Because of her second husband's wealth, Mrs King (though she ought properly to be referred to as Mrs Marshall) has left a good deal of money, mostly in stocks and shares. Millicent now finds herself in possession of £5,000 in cash plus some investments. In 1936, this was a small fortune. She decides to buy a house, and*

276

*does so in October, choosing to move nearer to Tilda in Primrose Hill. The most significant part of the move is that Robert is now persuaded to come and live on the top floor of her house. The fact that he has what amounts to a self-contained flat within Millicent's house seems to satisfy his qualms. But colleagues at work, when they discover his new address—which he has tried to conceal but isn't able to for long—quickly put two and two together. So does Millicent's sister Tilda.*

\*       \*       \*

## 2 November

Tilda has disappointed me. I know she is not well, and I should make allowances, but I never expected her to be so mealy-mouthed. I had been looking forward to her meeting Robert and thought she would be glad for me and it was going to be such a relief not having to hide him from her or anyone now that poor Mother cannot be hurt and I needn't pretend not to have a lover. But Tilda was shocked when I told her about him and looked so cold and unloving when she asked how long this affair had been going on. Well, I suppose it *is* an affair, that is the correct term, but the way she said it made it sound disgusting. She softened a little when she saw I was upset and said it was just that she couldn't bear to think I was entangled with a married man who couldn't get a divorce. She said a divorced man would've been bad enough but at least then we could have married. Then she said something I couldn't believe. She doesn't think

277

Charles would want Florence and Jack to know, or to meet 'this Robert'. She said they might get the wrong idea. They go to Sunday School, and Florence goes to church, and Charles and she do too, if not often, and she claims they try to be good *Christians*. When I said it was the first I had heard of it, things got nasty and we argued over how Christian she and Charles really are. I felt maddened, but the sight of Tilda's huge stomach calmed me down. I knew I had to be calm for her sake. She hasn't even met Robert. This is what he has always warned me would happen, of course.

## 15 November

Went round to visit Tilda, wondering if I would be allowed in her house now that she regards me as a Scarlet Woman, but she was welcoming and we had a nice chat, at first. Then after tea, she asked if I had told Grace what I had told her. I said did she mean about Robert and she flinched at his name and said yes. I said I hadn't seen Grace lately, but that I would tell her the moment we met again which I expected would be soon. Tilda said I should think about protecting Grace, who was very impressionable and only 19. I stared at her in astonishment. Really, all this was going too far. Then Tilda was a little apologetic but she said she was sure Mother wouldn't want Grace to know I was living with a married man who couldn't divorce. I resented her bringing Mother into it and was going to say so, but she rushed on to express anxiety about how Grace was living anyway, and wishing she hadn't bought a flat of her own with

Mother's money, because she wasn't old enough and seemed to be in with a fast crowd. I said I was sure that Grace could look after herself, just as I had done, but Tilda shook her head and said Grace was quite giddy and not at all how I had been. Somehow we had got off the subject of my scandalous liaison and I made sure we stayed off it.

## 10 December

No one can quite believe it. This evening the King broadcast to the nation to say he was giving up the throne to his brother because he wasn't allowed to marry the woman he loved, a divorcée, an American called Mrs Simpson. I only heard it by accident. It was so sad, hearing him say 'the woman I love'. I felt such rage against whoever it is who will not let him marry her. What is so awful about being a divorcée? It all comes down to the fact that our King is head of the Church, and the Church can't condone it. Robert was not as affected by the broadcast as I was. He just shrugged, and said it did not surprise him: the establishment always wins.

## 11 December

Am I the only one who feels sorry for the King and is angry about him being forced to abdicate? I cannot believe the opinions I have heard all day. Mavis declares Mrs Simpson is a trollop who just wanted to be Queen, and even Doris, who is usually so quiet, said we couldn't have had our King taking *used goods*. I was incredulous, and spoke up for both the King and Mrs Simpson, and Mavis sniggered and said that of course I'd be prejudiced in her favour: it was only natural in my circumstances. I had to leave the office. I did not dare ask her what she meant and then have everything come out, which is what she wants. I wonder how she has found out. Even though I left the room, and felt agitated, half of me was glad.

# 4 January 1937

Glad to be back at work. Such a sad Christmas and New Year, the first without Mother. Tilda tried to rally the family but it didn't work. I wish she had managed to find some real Christmas, Christian spirit and invite Robert to Christmas dinner. I still wonder how she could have imagined I would come without him. But we didn't have a very happy Christmas either which is why I have hardly written in this diary. We both had flu, myself worse than Robert, and everything seemed dismal. Then Robert had a letter from Doreen which upset him. He wouldn't let me read it. I don't know that I wanted to, but all the same I think he should have offered to show it to me. Keeping it to himself created an atmosphere. Well, we are over that now, and it is a new year.

# 1 February

Tilda gave birth today—to twins! How Mother would have loved it. She was always hoping twins would pop up again in the next generation. They are a boy and a girl. How clever of Tilda, doubling her family and keeping it even at the same time. But it was a shock. Nobody had known there were two of them. Charles seemed more shocked than anyone and a little dismayed. Both babies are very healthy and for twins a good weight, each just under 5 lbs. I stayed the night with Florence and Jack, and took them to see their mother and the twins very briefly, only five minutes. Jack was delighted with his new brother and sister but Florence was rather quiet, I thought. She wanted to know how Tilda would manage two babies. I said she would have help and manage very well and that she herself could be a great help. I knew as soon as I'd said it, that this was the wrong thing to say. In a flash I recalled how I myself resented helping Mother when Michael was born and even more so when Grace arrived.

## 5 February

Grace came today to relieve me and I must say seemed rather grudging about it. She has lived here long enough to be thoroughly acquainted with how the household runs, but affected not to know where things are kept though it is barely three months since she moved out. Florence is not happy about my departure. We get on well and she trusts me more than she does Grace, I think. Grace is very distracted and obsessed with her own appearance, forever looking in mirrors and twiddling her golden locks. She says she can't get time off work so can only cover this weekend. Charles's mother is coming on Monday, as well as the help he has hired.

## 12 February

Tilda has asked me to be godmother to the girl twin, who as yet has no name, though the boy is to be Toby. I can hardly refuse, though I long ago lost any religious faith as she perfectly well knows. I was very surprised she asked me, in view of her opinion, and that of Charles, of my relationship with Robert. Surely I am not suitable, from every point of view. But she has asked me and maybe this is a sort of olive branch and so I feel I should agree. After all, being a godmother doesn't mean much when I am already the child's aunt and always would look out for her.

**21 February**

I really, truly feel I would not be Tilda for anything. Her babies have never been easy, and these twins are the worst of the lot. What with their incessant crying and Jack choosing this time to have chickenpox, and Florence sulky and difficult, Tilda's life is hell. I've never been so glad to get out of that house and back to my quiet home and Robert and the pleasures of just being two adults.

**2 March**

The girl twin is to be named after Mother. She is so sweet. She was mercifully quiet today at her christening, whereas Toby cried, while she looked up at me so very gravely as I held her in my arms. I wonder if Constance will turn out to look like Mother as well as bearing her name. It is too early to tell, but I fancy her eyes are shaped like Mother's, very large for such a tiny baby, whereas Toby's are mere pinpricks. Robert observed when I came home that I seemed dreamy. That was the word he used, dreamy. I said it was because I was feeling sentimental, thinking about Constance and Toby.

## 8 March

I did something odd today. I'd read in the *News Chronicle* about an organisation called Mass-Observation which has been set up by three men, to record how ordinary people live. People are invited to record their day in detail for one day in a month, every month, and send in their account. The point is to build up a picture of our society. It appeals to me so much. There is no money involved, no payment, and no one need know where you live if you don't want to reveal it. After all, what are my diaries but a record of the life of an ordinary woman. So I wrote off to the address and I am to send my first report next week. I have fixed on a Wednesday to do it. Robert is very amused by it. He says he can't imagine of what use such reports could ever be, and that everyone will just make things up to make their report interesting. I said they won't, or anyway I won't. I love to know about people's routines and habits and when I am on a bus or train I am always speculating about the other passengers and how their days go. Robert said such speculation never enters his head. Well, I said, that is the difference between us, and we left it at that. But I am looking forward to being a Mass Observer whatever he thinks.

\*       \*       \*

*It is true that Millicent is intensely curious about strangers and that her diaries are full of sometimes quite minutely detailed observations and speculations. She is particularly interested in people she sits beside in buses, and often describes them right down to the condition of their fingernails or the design on a tie. Whether all this went into the stories she wrote at the period when she was working for Matthew Taylor is impossible to say, since none of them have survived, but I suspect she tried to make use of these vignettes in a creative way.*

\*　　　　\*　　　　\*

## 15 March

My first report as a Mass Observer. It was so much more difficult to do than I had imagined, not at all like writing in this diary. Here, I can put what I like, and I don't need to write down exactly what I have done or explain things. This was the problem with my MO report, what to put in and what to leave out. No real guidelines have been given. But it was quite exciting too, to think that what is so ordinary to me might seem significant to someone else, and that without knowing it I might fit into a bigger picture. I made notes all day so that I would not forget. I didn't know how to refer to Robert, or whether to explain about him, but decided explanations, which would be so complicated, were not necessary, so I've just called him my friend, and whoever reads the report can put two and two together. I stuck mainly to what I *did* rather than

285

how I felt. It was a busy day too, with three house calls to make and a meeting with a Child Protection Officer at the Town Hall. I finished writing it all up in bed, with Robert watching and making fun of me, but I didn't care. He says now, just as I've finished, that I must have been a very serious student. So I was, I said, and he must have been, too. He says he got by on brains alone.

**30 April**

All London's busmen are on strike, for more pay. I had to walk miles and was late for every appointment, and I had a great many of them today as luck would have it. I think I will buy a car. I have always wanted a car. Robert says I don't need one, that his does for both of us, but his is a clapped-out old Hillman and I rarely get the chance to drive it. He says cars are not necessary in London and that he only has one because he had it in Liverpool and was not going to leave it with Doreen who couldn't drive anyway. But I would like a neat little car of my own and I can afford it. Robert says he forgets I am a rich woman. Not true, but I suppose, thanks to Mother, or rather to Harold, compared to him I am rich (especially when some of his money goes every month to Doreen). I think Robert thinks it is rather awful for me not to have earned my house. I should feel guilty, especially in the light of the poverty I see every day, but I don't. I am just glad of it, and thankful.

## 14 May

Grace called. Haven't seen her in ages. She was looking very sophisticated, wearing the most beautiful dress, a gauze-like thing, floral, with a tie neck, and it swirled around her delightfully as she moved. Just an old thing she'd made herself, she said. I suspected she must have come for some reason and I was right. She has been offered a place in a fashion house in Paris and can't decide whether to take it and wanted to discuss it. She says Tilda is adamantly against her accepting, pointing out that she knows not a word of French and that she is so nicely settled in London and has friends and family around her and will know no one in Paris. But Grace thinks that there is a little bit of self-interest in Tilda's discouragement because Grace has been helping a lot with the children at the weekends. I said, if I were her, I would take the job. She will soon pick up French, and Paris is *the* place for fashion and she would be a fool to turn it down. After all, if she doesn't like it she can come back and her Parisian experience will stand her in good stead.

A friend has warned her that the political situation in Europe is dangerous and she asked me what I thought. Surely France is safe enough. Pessimists have been moaning for ages now that another war is coming, but it never does, thank goodness, and I for one don't believe it will. Mother would be so proud of what a success Grace is, and in the fashion business, which she could understand, but if Mother were alive she wouldn't want her little darling going to Paris, and would side with Tilda. I wish Grace could meet Robert

287

and know about him. I still haven't told her. She thinks I am a lonely spinster. It is strange that I never see my brothers, or even hear from them much. Esther does all the communicating for George, and Alfred sometimes turns up like a bad penny, but as for Albert and Michael I hardly know them. Grace is quite close to Michael. She says he is very shy and has a sweet girlfriend but he misses Mother dreadfully.

**15 May**

Robert alarmed me this evening by saying that for Grace to go to work in Paris would be a very bad idea because Europe is going to erupt. Those were his words, *Europe will erupt*. I became cross and asked him how he could be so sure. He reads the newspapers and says it is obvious. I suppose I don't read them properly, not since I lived with Daphne, when I tried to. I skip the long political articles, it is true. Should I pass this prediction on to Grace?

*       *       *

*Whether she did or not she doesn't say, but the question of what might be about to happen in Europe comes up again during discussions with Robert as to where they should go on holiday. To Millicent's annoyance, he insists they must stay in Britain, and suggests touring in Scotland, saying he would like to visit Arran, where his mother's family (she was a Mackay) came from. This Scottish holiday takes place in September and to Millicent's surprise is a great success. It doesn't rain at all and she loves*

288

*Arran and writes long diary entries describing the landscape. Robert is well up on Scottish history and gives her entertaining lectures as they drive round the north-west coast, going across first to Arran and then Skye, and then back down the north-east. They register as Mr and Mrs Rigg in hotels and bed-and-breakfast places, and she wears a ring in order to look authentic. She admits to her diary that she enjoys the pretence and finds it extremely satisfying. Robert recognises this and says he knows she's deluding herself when she vows she doesn't care about being married. This leads to a great row on the last night of their holiday—the diary entry goes on for pages and is very repetitious—but once it is over, and they are back in London, Robert proposes a scheme to persuade Doreen to divorce him.*

\*　　　\*　　　\*

## 2 October

I still have not written to Robert's wife, as he wants me to. I keep turning the idea over and over in my mind and it doesn't seem right. I am not the sort of person who begs: I am too proud. And though I have told white lies, as everyone has, I have never told a big, serious lie. I am superstitious about it too. If I pretend to be pregnant I might fall pregnant, it is tempting fate. But I do want Robert to be divorced. He is right, it felt so much better to be married when we pretended to be. I wouldn't mind in the least being cited in a divorce. I expect to be. It would be very easy and straightforward for Doreen to divorce Robert. I suppose I will write

289

what Robert suggests, but I am fearful about it.

*      *      *

*Her fears were justified. She writes to Doreen later that month (on a Mass-Observation report day, but she says she doesn't mention the letter in her report) and, after a wait of nearly a month, receives a reply not from Doreen herself but from a solicitor. Mrs Rigg, he writes, will never agree to a divorce, it being against her religious convictions, and she is outraged to have been written to by a woman who is, in her opinion, little better than a whore. If she chooses to indulge in carnal sin with a married man and become pregnant that is her own fault and Mrs Rigg pities the bastard she will give birth to. The letter leaves Millicent trembling.*

*      *      *

## 1 December

So that is that. Unless Doreen dies, and I wish she would, however dreadful it is to wish that, Robert and I can never marry and, if I did have a baby, it would be born a bastard. Sometimes I think of seeking Doreen out and confronting her but it would only, most probably, lead to an ugly scene. I would like to see what she is like, though, what she looks like. I expect she is pretty. I asked Robert once and he frowned crossly, and said prettiness had had very little to do with it. The point was Doreen had been *there*, he hardly knew any other girls and when he came back from France the idea

290

of marrying and having a home of his own and settling into domesticity was very attractive. I suppose I can understand that. I have no choice. I have to.

## 8 December

Snapped out of my low spirits by the arrival of an almost illiterate letter from Ethel, my sister-in-law, Alfred's wife. Alfred has left her and she wonders if I know where he is. Heavens, I have rarely known where Alfred is, and haven't the least idea now. I don't know why Ethel wrote to me of all people, or even how she found my address. Since we've never met I only know what I do know about her, and that's precious little, from Grace and poor Mother. Went round to Tilda's after work and it turned out that she had had the same letter. She's disgusted with Alfred, says he always was irresponsible and that Father would be turning in his grave. Next thing, Tilda said, is that Ethel, whom of course she has not met either, will turn up with her child (neither of us could remember his name, which is awful) on her doorstep. Neither of us can decide what to write back, but we must, if just to make it clear that, though Alfred may be our brother, we have no sort of contact with him. Poor Ethel, though. At least she has her family, but I expect they are feeling quite vengeful towards Alfred. What can he be thinking of, deserting his wife and child?

## 14 December

Grace has definitely made up her mind to accept that offer in Paris and goes to start there immediately New Year is over. Robert and Charles and almost all the men of her acquaintance say she is foolish but I think it is a great opportunity and I am delighted for her. Paris is not far, Grace could easily come home. She is going for Christmas to Esther's and George's, feeling that she should, and then she will spend New Year with Tilda, and I will see her to say *bon voyage*. I think of myself at 20 and cannot help admiring Grace, who has such a clear idea of what she wants to do and has known how to set about it and has stuck to her last job and done well.

## 18 December

Last day at work, and a wretched one. We have a little money to give to our poorest families, an allowance made by the council in what Robert sarcastically calls their munificence, and today we spent it on small luxuries for the children— chocolate and jars of honey and bottles of pop and biscuits. We made up parcels in the office, wrapping each one in coloured paper, and then we took them round the Buildings. I felt uncomfortable about it from the beginning—it was so like playing some kind of hateful Lady Bountiful—and my feelings of distaste for the task grew stronger once we were delivering what were really rather pathetic gifts. It was painful to see the excitement of the children, especially the O'Briens, eight of them tearing at the paper and snatching the few chocolates and fighting over the biscuits. We'd said to Mrs O'Brien it was a little Christmas parcel to keep for the day so that the children would have something to open. Something to open? she echoed and started to laugh and then grew angry and positively threw the parcel onto the floor. And of course the children pounced. She said nothing more, but once they had eaten everything, even the honey, just straight out of the jar on their filthy fingers, sucking them, she started to cry. She didn't need to say why—Christmas is such an insult to families like the O'Briens, living in those dreadful rooms with no hope for the future. Mrs O'Brien isn't even one of the feckless ones. She tries hard but she has too much to cope with. While we were there the priest came and I must say that if nothing else his arrival had a magical effect on the children who were in awe of him and quietened down at once. As we left, he was getting them to say a prayer of thanks for their good fortune in being given a present and they were actually kneeling among the tattered remnants of the paper and the empty pop bottles and scrunched-up biscuit wrappers.

**4 January 1938**

Said goodbye to Grace. She promised to keep in close touch, but I wonder if she will have time never mind the desire when her life will be so different, and I don't expect to hear from her for a while. It's been good seeing her these last few days and I made the big decision to disobey Tilda and introduce her to Robert. Well, she is going to Paris, and is a sophisticated woman of the world now and not a child who could be influenced, and I thought why on earth should I let her go abroad not knowing the man her sister loves and with whom she has been living for more than two whole years, and whom she will be with for the rest of her life? I felt defiant about it, and so I invited Grace to tea and told her everything. Then she met Robert and liked him very much, or so she said. Robert liked her too. He says she has an air of me about her, which I cannot see at all, though others have said the same, but he added that she does not look like me. Of course she doesn't, I replied, she is so elegant, for a start, and I am not. Robert said I could be if I chose, which for some reason irritated me and I snapped back at him, Oh, you like elegant women, do you? He just nodded. I said elegance was not important beside integrity, and Robert laughed and said I was growing pompous in my old age. I was so furious I slammed out of the room, not really knowing which insult had hurt more. Compared to Grace, of course, I am old. It can't be denied. Robert's jibe reminded me of what Jack had asked me at Christmas dinner: Are you very old, Aunt Millicent? And I'd replied I was only nearly middling old, which confused him and made everyone laugh. But to Jack everyone over the age of 12 or so is old. He turned immediately to Charles's mother, his grandmother, and said to her that she was *old* old, wasn't she, and Mrs Routledge, who is about 70, nodded and said that soon she would be the very oldest of old, and Jack was satisfied. The twins started screaming for their bottles at that stage and Tilda sighed and said she felt the oldest of old already. I am not surprised. She has been aged terribly by their birth. Beside Tilda, I feel young.

## 30 January

Such drama! Alfred appeared on our doorstep last night. It was a filthy night, raining hard and bitterly cold, and Robert and I were sitting over the fire reading and sipping hot toddies for our colds when the bell went. We looked at each other in surprise. It was after ten and we were not expecting any caller and rarely would anyone we know come round at such an hour. Then the bell went again, accompanied by a banging on the door. I began to think something terrible had happened and we were needed urgently somewhere. When Robert opened the door a man almost fell into the hall. Robert attempted to stop him and then I heard my own name called. It was Alfred. He was absolutely soaked and shivering with cold and the first job was to get him dry and warm. I had to introduce Robert of course, as 'my friend', for how else can I describe him to those who do not know, and I saw his eyes flicker as he worked out what this might mean, and how it might be used to his advantage. I was quite sharp with him. He may be my brother but he is also a man who has left his wife and child. I said, Well, Alfred, what is all this, what have you been doing? He then began on the hard luck story of all hard luck stories and I did not believe a word of it. When he had finished his sob-story I asked, What about your wife? She wrote to me, and to Tilda. He coloured a little, obviously taken by surprise, but launched into another saga. Robert and I exchanged glances and had no need to say anything. Then Robert went to bed, in his own flat, which I could see did not fool Alfred. I don't know how we will get rid of him.

*       *       *

*It takes weeks and drives Millicent to distraction. Alfred is ill at first with what turns out to be pneumonia. It suits him to make a slow convalescence and it is a month before he is up and dressed. Millicent is obliged, at the beginning, to take time off work to look after him, which she resents, but there is no alternative. Robert dislikes Alfred so much that he can hardly bear to be in the same house never mind the same room, and things become fraught between him and Millicent. It doesn't help matters that in March Hitler annexes Austria and even Millicent cannot go on being so sure that there will not be a war. Eventually, in May, she gives her brother an ultimatum: either he leaves by 1st June or she will write to Ethel and tell her where he is.*

*       *       *

**2 June**

Bliss to come home and find Alfred at last gone. Last night, he asked if he could 'borrow' £20 to send to Ethel. I let him have it, though it is a great deal of money and all I had in the house. I don't care where he's gone, I don't want to know, it is enough that he has. There was no note of thanks, no token of appreciation for all the weeks he has been an uninvited and unwanted guest. And I am quite sure my £20 has *not* gone to his poor wife. What on earth has made him turn out as he has done? I cannot understand it and am not going to waste any more time trying. He is convinced luck is always running against him but that is simply untrue. I don't feel in the least sorry for him. Instead, I despise him. If ever he turns up again I will refuse to take him in. I was even contemplating moving house at one point, though I love this house, so that he would never know my new address. He would then only have George or Tilda to go to and they—well, in George's case, Esther—would know how to deal with him.

**1 July**

Robert was called to a meeting today about plans for evacuating London's children in the event of war, which he says is now seriously expected. At any rate, the authorities must think we are next on Hitler's list. The logistics of such an evacuation are enormous and I don't need Robert to point that out. I thought about all the poor children on our case-load and wondered how on earth they would survive being taken to the country, and who would cope with them and the state most of them would be in when they got there. Then I thought of Tilda's children and wondered what she will do. Surely she can make private plans and will not need to rely on government schemes to get her children to safety. I must talk to her about it.

## 18 July

Finally got round to mentioning evacuation to Tilda. She says she dreads it, but if war comes her brood must be got out of London. And since the twins are so very young she will have to go with them, though her nursing experience might be needed, and she would want to offer it. She wondered about going to Brighton, where Esther and George have plenty of room to take her in, but we both realised the south coast would be a dangerous place to be. In any case, George and Esther are thinking of moving to her parents' farm which, since her father's death, has been managed by a cousin who has himself just died. It felt dreadful to be having this kind of conversation, quite unreal, but I know now it is all too real. Tilda asked what I will do, and I was so surprised that she thought I would do anything but what I am already doing that I couldn't think. I expect there will be plenty to do. Robert, of course, will join up immediately. He has always said he would. I can't understand why, after his experience at the end of the last war. I don't think men who fought in the last war should have to fight in this one. Robert laughed when I said it was not fair, but I meant it. What about George, what will happen to him? Surely he is too old to be conscripted and would never volunteer. What about Charles, though? What about Albert and Alfred and Michael?

**1 August 1938**

For once, Robert has been the one to suggest a holiday. I can hardly believe it but am very glad. He says it may be our last chance before war is declared and that we should seize it and enjoy it. What a gloomy reason for a holiday, but I shall ignore it and simply be happy about the opportunity. I don't care where we go but would like it to be somewhere warm.

\*     \*     \*

*They do not, however, go somewhere warm. Instead, they go to Norfolk and hire a sailing-boat for the first week. Robert turns out to be a good sailor, but Millicent doesn't take to sailing, and the weather is poor. The second week is better. They stay in a cottage at Wells-next-the-Sea and the sun shines and they swim and take long walks along the coast. But Robert is 'moody' and given to morbid thoughts which he wants to share with her but which she does not want to hear. He also insists on listening to news bulletins on the wireless and all the news is bad until the end of September.*

\*     \*     \*

**29 September**

*Why* will Robert not smile? It is such wonderful, happy news, but when we heard it he just shrugged

299

and stared out of the window at the sea. I told him they might as well have broadcast the news that war *had* been declared for all the pleasure he seemed to be taking in Mr Chamberlain's peace guarantee. Why can't he rejoice like everyone else? I said, rather meanly I know, that maybe it was because he cannot bear to have been proved wrong and me to be right. He groaned at that, and told me not to be so *silly*. Hitler, he says, will never keep his word and all we have gained is a breathing space. It is almost as if Robert *wants* a war. We packed up in silence and when the car was loaded went for a last walk along the shore. It was so quiet and beautiful, the sun just setting and the whole sea turned pink. I wanted to stay in Norfolk because there we were properly a couple in a way we still can never be in London. We have been together so long now: we are an old married couple who just happen not to be married.

## 15 October

It has happened. For years, I've expected it, while taking every care, and now it has, though I can't yet be sure. But my Visitor is never late, or never more than a day or two, and now it is a week overdue. And there are other signs—a soreness in my breasts—though no sickness. I have said nothing to Robert, but he is very watchful and aware and keeps an eye on my cycle, which I have never quite liked, because he worries so. I ought to confess my fears and discuss with him what should be done. It is deceitful to keep my suspicions from him.

## 21 October

Still no Visitor. Why am I not frightened? I should be, if I am going to have an abortion. The very word has always chilled me and of course I don't know how to procure one safely. I've always thought Daphne would know, but I haven't seen her for ages and now that we are no longer as close as we once were it will be embarrassing to ask her. Tilda would be no use. She didn't arrange one for herself and with her newly strong Christian beliefs, she would be horrified. What will I do? The strange thing is that I am *not* frightened and I know that is because I am not really contemplating getting rid of this baby, if baby it is. I want it. I feel excited, even thrilled, as though I have a delicious not a dreadful secret. I will be an unmarried mother with all that this means, and I do not care. Am I mad, or brave?

## 20 November

A second period missed and I feel so, so different. I ought to see a doctor but I can't do that without telling Robert, so I will tell him tomorrow, Friday night, then we will have the weekend to discuss this momentous news. However foolish of me, I hope and pray he will not be horrified.

## 22 November

We are still hardly speaking. Never before have we gone so long after an argument without making up

301

our differences in some way or another. I don't think Robert slept last night after I had told him and I certainly didn't. I suppose I thought that after the initial shock he would become as excited and thrilled as I am and, like me, say he didn't give a damn what people would think. But no. He went immediately into a panic about how to get rid of it, assuming I, too, would be thinking only that. Then he wondered aloud how this mistake, this accident, could have happened and went near to implying that I had been careless! He even chided me for not going back to the Marie Stopes clinic to check that the cap still fitted—and that made me cry, it was so cruel. He was sorry then, and said it was only anxiety making him talk like that. But still he began again on how could we get rid of 'it', and who did we know who might help. He even got a pencil and a piece of paper and said let's think hard who might know where to go. When I said he could put his pencil and paper away because I wanted to have this baby, he was thunderstruck. He asked me if I was joking. I said no, and that was when we began quarrelling in earnest. He said he couldn't let me ruin my life. Then he tried to persuade me that because I am pregnant I am not in my right mind, not capable of being rational, and I exploded. How we both will resolve this I do not know.

**1 December**

I went to see a doctor today, without informing Robert. I have never been to him before, indeed I have never been to any doctor in London, which surely must show how healthy I am. I chose the nearest surgery to our house, not having any other reason for selecting a doctor. I have passed his consulting rooms every day for two years, his brass plate is always shining and there is a window-box always full of geraniums in the summer and it is an altogether bright and cheerful-looking house. The doctor is quite cheerful too, a small rather portly man, middle-aged and brisk. I was cowardly and said my name was Mrs Rigg and that I thought I was pregnant. He examined me and said yes, about three months, and congratulated me. My eyes filled with tears but I managed to smile and I think he put my emotion down to joy. He said I was fairly old for a first-time mother but that I seemed exceptionally healthy and fit and he was sure all would be well if I looked after myself and took care. Then he wanted to discuss where I would have the baby, and recommended a particular nursing home. I am to go back to him in a month and he will book me in. He charged 10s. I don't know if that is expensive or not. The baby is due in May.

## 2 December

Robert saw me taking one of the iron tablets the doctor prescribed. He looked hopeful for a minute, as though I might be taking something to get rid of my baby, or so I imagined, and I despised him. Before he could ask, I volunteered the information, in a contemptuous tone, that I was taking an iron tablet to enrich my blood during pregnancy and that I had been to a doctor and had it confirmed.

303

He looked aghast, and then sighed, and said we couldn't go on like this and I said no, we certainly could not—what did he want to do, leave me and go back to Doreen? And he said, and he was right, that this was a stupid thing to say and that I should know he would never desert me. Then I cried. I seem to be crying an awful lot. But Robert was his old kind self this time and held me close and calmed me down and then we talked in a different way. He said he had a plan. It had just come to him in the night that what I could do was take his name by changing my own surname by deed poll and then the child could have our joint name perfectly legitimately. I cannot think straight.

## 6 December

Robert has another plan. He has applied for a job in Manchester. It is not such a good job, but if he gets it, we can move there and start afresh, pretending to be married. There are difficulties, but we have thought everything through. We will both give in our notice as soon as he hears that he can have the Manchester job and then everything will move fast. I will sell this house and we will go to Manchester at the very first opportunity, while I am still mobile. I have hardly put any weight on and don't yet look the least pregnant and haven't been sick. People at work comment that I look blooming and even Mavis, though she is always suspicious about everyone's looks, constantly suspecting people are ill or hiding some secret, even Mavis has guessed nothing. Once we give our notices in of course the rumours will begin, and the interrogation.

**12 December**

No definite confirmation from Manchester yet. With the Christmas holidays coming up it may be the New Year before we hear, which is a pity. Meanwhile, Robert has inquired about how deed poll works, and it looks as if it will be surprisingly easy for me to become Rigg. I wish it was not such a horrid name. I don't like the sound of Rigg in the least and have always liked King. I wish it was usual for men to change their name on marrying and not women. I would have thought Robert should be jolly pleased to become a King.

**1 January 1939**

What a year this is going to be! I seem to smile all the time and I feel wonderful. Tilda says she has never seen me look so well and happy, and I was tempted to tell her the reason which I will have to tell her sometime anyway, and soon, but I held back, wanting to be able to present to her with a *fait accompli* as far as Manchester is concerned.

**7 January**

Robert came home very preoccupied tonight. He says he knows I hate him talking about such things and he tries not to, especially of late, but there is no doubt there *is* going to be a war. All kinds of preparations are in hand, as they have been for some time. Air-raid Precautions have been organised, and the evacuation plans are near to being finalised. He says I would have to leave London anyway, but that Manchester will not be a very clever choice of city because the industrial north will be bombed as much as London. What a terrible time to bring a child into the world, he said, and was all gloom. He wonders where I should go when war does come and he did what he always does in such situations, get out his dratted pencil and paper to make a list of possibilities. One of them is that I should go to the Russos in America. He pointed out I'd been invited often enough, and in his last letter Mr Russo said if war came and I needed what he called 'a haven' he would welcome me. Then he said something so shocking I couldn't believe it. He said it wouldn't much matter about what the job in Manchester turned out to be like, if he gets it, because of course he'd be joining up and would be in the army. But I'm having our baby, I said, you can't join up. His reply was that lots of women would be having babies, so this couldn't be an excuse or we'd have no fighting force. I stared at him.

How can I not be upset? How will I manage on my own, about to have a baby, or just having had it, if war is declared and Robert goes off at once *when he does not have to*. He can at least wait until he is conscripted. I accused him of showing off by wanting to play soldiers, but he said I was forgetting he'd seen war and knew the horror of it. Hitler, he says, is a madman who has to be stopped, and he isn't going to wait to be *told* to do his duty. I don't care. His duty is to me and his baby. He says I am utterly self-centred. Well, in this respect, I am. He will hear about Manchester tomorrow.

## 8 January

Still no word about Manchester.

## 12 January

Robert has got the Manchester job. I don't know whether I am glad or sorry. I must give in my notice. Mavis will want to know why I am leaving. She will express astonishment, saying she thought I was very happy in my job, which I am, and will ferret about for reasons. What shall I say?

## 15 January

Mavis expressed astonishment, as I expected, but then said, Oh, I might leave myself, get out of London. How odd. At any rate, I have given my notice in. Things are moving!

\*     \*     \*

*And there, on this happy-sounding note, the diary entries stop for the longest period in the whole eighty years, a matter of just over three months. As usual when something devastating happens in her life, Millicent does not choose to tell her diary, but in this case it may be because she was ill for a time and incapable of writing. Few clues are given, when on*

307

*30 April she does resume her diary-writing, as to exactly what has happened, but from the entry on 15 May—'Sad day. Could not help but think of my son and how I would have welcomed the darling into the world'—it is obvious she had a late miscarriage, or late enough for the sex of the baby to be clear. Since she'd made such a point of being proud of her own health, and since there had been not a sign of any other trouble, perhaps she had an accident of some sort. Many years later, she does mention her terror of crossing icy roads and adds 'It is not surprising I have this fear, considering what once happened and how I nearly died', so maybe she slipped on some icy road, or was knocked down by a car that skidded. At any rate, she lost the baby, and she stayed in London, so presumably the move to Manchester was never made.*

*The diary entries for May, June, July and August 1939 are minimal and concerned only with what Millicent is doing, not what she is thinking or feeling. She doesn't seem to be doing much, but maybe she was convalescing and not allowed to. There is no holiday that year, though she says the doctor thinks it would do her good to get away, and Robert agrees, but she writes that she has no energy and just wants to stay at home. It is sad to read her listless little notes— 'Managed to walk to the park. Sat and watched the ducks.' She reads a lot, but then she always has done. A. J. Cronin's* The Citadel *(published 1937) makes an impression on her, which may be further proof that she herself had an accident (the doctor's wife in this novel has a fall on a rotten bridge, loses her baby, and as a consequence cannot have any more children). There is no mention of any important events that year—Hitler's invasion of Czechoslovakia,*

308

*for example—and no apparent awareness that the war Robert had constantly predicted was now very near. Millicent is locked in her own unhappy, restricted world, until September 1939.*

\*     \*     \*

**1 September**

Tilda came round with the twins. She is in such a state, worried to death about what to do, and berating herself for not having decided earlier. Florence's and Jack's schools have both been requisitioned for other uses in the event of war being declared and not even I can bury my head in the sand now that Poland has been invaded. War will be declared any minute and the children must be got out of London. I think Tilda has left it too late to make private arrangements and will have to go with her children wherever they are sent. Robert has already told me that there will be chaos in spite of attempts at preparation. He says no one is co-ordinating the coming evacuation and that the government will be forced to depend on voluntary organisations who are not used to planning and coping on this scale.

**2 September**

Spent the day making blackout blinds for our windows, then went to Tilda's to help her make hers. She has so many windows and had not nearly enough material and the best we could do today

309

was the children's bedrooms and the kitchen. Luckily, most of her windows also have wooden shutters, though when we tested them it was to find they are not nearly tight-fitting enough and chinks of light will definitely show through. But if Tilda and the children are to leave, as they must, and Charles expects to have to be on duty at the hospital on twenty-four-hour call, it will not matter because the house will be dark anyway. After we'd done our best with the windows we collected the last of the children's gas masks. Florence and Jack have had theirs for some time, but the twins, being so small, have had to be specially fitted. It was so pathetic watching their darling little chubby faces disappear behind that horrible rubber, even though the masks were Mickey and Minnie Mouse ones. Connie was good about it but the boy howled.

**3 September**

Oh God, it has happened, war declared and no hope any more, and yet I still cannot believe it. *Why* has it happened again, so soon after all that nightmare which went before? If only women were in charge, such a disaster would never have been allowed. There is no good news at all. Already a liner bound for Canada has been torpedoed by the Germans and sunk somewhere off the Hebrides with more than a hundred people drowned. Tilda had thought of sending Florence and Jack to cousins of Charles's in Canada, but now she will not dare let them try to cross the Atlantic.

310

## 4 September

Tilda is leaving tomorrow, without knowing her precise destination. Children under 5 are supposed to be accompanied by their mother, but Florence and Jack are going with their respective schools which means of course that the whole family will be split up at this worst of times. I think she should try her mother-in-law again, but she says there is no use. Mrs Routledge only has a small cottage in Blockley, in the Cotswolds, and Charles's sister Joan and her children have already moved in. She wept, and says she feels so responsible for the mess they are in and that she ought to have thought ahead. She must pull herself together and pack for the children. I helped her, she was in such a muddle. She said how efficient I was, and capable, and then asked me if I would go with her, but I had to point out that I was not entitled. Then I suddenly thought how well qualified I was to be a helper for the WVS. Robert said only last night that they are desperate for experienced people to help with all the unaccompanied children.

I left Tilda and went straight round to their head office and enrolled, and the minute my status (unmarried, childless) and my occupation were noted, I was welcomed with open arms and given a uniform, etc. I am to report tomorrow to an assembly point at Liverpool Street Station to go with a party of forty East End children to I know not where. I raced home to pack a bag for myself, and then back to Tilda's to tell her and to wish her luck, and we both agreed to write to Charles at the hospital because he will always be there. Then I went out and stocked up with some tinned food, just basics, to leave for Robert. When he came home he was more relieved than anything to hear what I had done, since leaving me in my present state was something he had been dreading. He had been going to urge me to go with Tilda if possible before he reports for duty in three days' time. We had a very solemn last meal, I mean last for who knows how long, together. Strangely, I don't now resent his joining up. It seems right, or if not exactly right I don't care about it. It isn't that I don't care for *him*, but I don't seem to care about anything. I will be glad to have a purpose again even if it has come about through such a terrible event. Robert, I think, feels differently. He said there were a great many things he wanted to say but he didn't know how to say them. We were both very quiet.

## 7 September

There is so much I want to put down here, so much to write, especially when for months there has been so little, but I hardly know where to begin. The chaos has been indescribable in spite of everyone's best efforts. Liverpool Street Station was pandemonium when I arrived there, as instructed, on the 4th. Hordes of people, most of them children with mothers, and no one knowing quite what to do. They were all from zones selected as essential for evacuation, so of course these were the poorest areas near the docks and gasworks, and most of the children in a pitiful state. It was my job, together with three other WVS volunteers, to check that every child had a label attached somewhere to its clothing with its name and age and London address on. Some of the mothers had done a good job and sewn labels onto their children's jackets—and these were the children with bags or little suitcases packed with their essential belongings, also labelled—but there were far more with no marks of identification and no possessions. It wasn't that I was surprised, knowing how these families lived and the panic they were all in, but still it was a shock to come across tiny mites literally *sewn* into their shabby clothes. I only discovered this when I gently asked one little girl if she had any clothes with her and she said, bright as anything, I've got them all on, Miss, and she showed me the bottom of her jacket where underneath a jumper appeared, and, underneath that, the edge of some undergarment, and then she demonstrated with pride how it was all sewn together. She was called Amy and was 6, and there was no sign of any mother. This was a blessing, because the mothers slowed everything down and many of them were naturally very emotional and set the children off crying. The noise was appalling, what with the crying and the trains coming and going and the loudspeaker announcements all of which were incomprehensible. There were no clear rules about adults travelling with children. Children under 5 were the only ones meant to be accompanied by an adult, preferably their mother, but this wasn't strictly enforced because, in those conditions, it couldn't be. The trains were bursting with children, and every time one drew out of the station, there was a great wail from the remaining throng and frantic wavings and shouts of goodbye. A siren went off about midday and though it was a

313

false alarm it terrified everyone and made the war feel real, and, in an awful way, once the siren had stopped, the boarding of trains was more orderly, because fear quietened everyone in the end. I don't know how many hundreds of children and mothers we sent off that day, but it seemed like millions.

Then the next day I was asked to go with one of the groups to East Anglia (I was told our destination but the evacuees were not) to help with settling them into foster homes. The train went so slowly, stopping and starting all the time, and to my horror I realised even as we were drawing out of the station that because it had no corridor, we had no access to any lavatory. The inevitable happened within the first hour. The small children wet themselves and the older ones had to be persuaded to use a hastily improvised po, which was a biscuit tin one of the two mothers in the carriage had packed sandwiches in. If any of we three adults had needed to relieve ourselves, I don't know what we would have done. What a scandalous lack of foresight on someone's part, but then I suppose far worse indignities are to come.

It was a hot day and though we had the window let right down (and *that* was dangerous, with all the children wanting to hang out of it) it was stifling and of course smelly and all the children were thirsty and we hadn't enough water with us. It was a nightmare journey, and no amount of singing and clapping games could make it anything else. We were so very glad to arrive in the country and everyone brightened up and looked eagerly for a reception committee who would welcome us and take us to homes where we could wash and be fed. There wasn't one. There had been some mix-up and the WVS had not been told in time, so we arrived to find not a soul there. I and the other WVS members on the train had a quick conference and agreed that while one of us should go into the station-master's office and telephone HQ the rest of us would line the children up and start walking in the direction of the village (we could see a church steeple). There was always the chance that our hosts would be waiting in the village. The children quite liked the walk and made no fuss. The hedgerows were a mystery to most of them and they kept stopping to pick the bright red hips, which they promptly tried to eat, in spite of warnings, and discovered tasted horrid. It was only a walk of about twenty minutes and when we got to the village we parked ourselves on the green and waited. We'd been there about ten more minutes when there was a sudden flurry of activity. Two cars arrived bringing local WVS women and at the same time doors opened all around us and the inhabitants came to inspect us. After fulsome apologies, we were led to the village hall where a trestle table was set up and lists produced and the process of settling our charges in began. What a business. The WVS woman in charge, a Miss Mallinson, called out names and the village women came forward and she checked her list and then children were chosen. It was a painful system. The better dressed and cleaner-looking children were of course picked first, leaving the real ragamuffins, especially the boys, standing exposed as undesirable, which I'm sure they perfectly well realised. Two little boys, who I swear were under 5, though they said they were 6, and who had no mother with them, stood for ages. No one would have them. One farmer's wife said maybe she could use them on the farm—were they strong? But to my relief Miss Mallinson said no, they were not, couldn't she see that, and the farmer's wife lost interest. I ached for them. They were so stoical, standing there being stared at and rejected. Neither of them cried. One of them yawned repeatedly and the other whistled, to show, I suppose, that he didn't care. Eventually, rather ashen-faced at the prospect, the vicar's wife swallowed hard and took them. I came back to London late that evening, wretchedly aware of how unhappy some, maybe most, of the children would be, and thinking about Tilda and wondering how she had fared.

## 8 September

At WVS HQ today, helping with the paperwork. Phone call from Daphne before I left home—she has joined the WAAF and is loving it. She is going to be trained to plot planes, or so she says. She sounds delighted, as though she was enjoying the prospect of a party not of enduring a war. I suppose there will be plenty of young women like Daphne, who will see this war as exciting and a chance to do something different. She asked if I am going to join up. I said I'd never thought of it, believing I'd be more useful in the WVS. I don't know what has happened to Daphne. She used to have such a sense of purpose. Well, this war will certainly restore it, in an awful way.

## 9 September

It is strange being in London when so many people have left. No bombs have been dropped so far, but there is an atmosphere of apprehension. The streets seem quiet, though buses still run. All the theatres and cinemas are closed, but most shops are open, though many of them have boards across their big plate-glass windows. No word as yet from Robert, but Charles phoned an hour ago, just as I got home, to say that Tilda and the twins have gone to his mother's, after all. His sister insisted there was room for them all. I feel so happy about this. Blockley is as safe as anywhere can be, and however crowded the domestic arrangements, Tilda will be out of harm's way. Perhaps she doesn't know how lucky she is but, having been on that train, I do. Charles says nothing much is happening at his hospital yet, and in fact his work-load is lighter for the time being, with all the patients able to be moved already evacuated and no new ones admitted, so that the wards can be prepared for casualties. Not much news on the wireless. Only the Home Service seems to be broadcasting. I read all evening, a novel by Elizabeth Bowen, but I couldn't get into it—their lives seemed so irrelevant, my mind kept wandering to the evacuees and those two last little boys. I thought of the vicar's wife taking them home and trying to do something simple and obvious, like giving them a bath, not appreciating that they'd almost certainly never seen a bath never mind got into one. They'd be horrified by her wanting to undress them, and she'd be horrified to discover they had nits in their hair and all kinds of skin

317

infections. Will all this be good for them? I suppose that's the way to look at it, but it is hard to believe.

*     *     *

*Millicent works with the WVS until June the following year, mainly concerning herself with the evacuees and their placements. She doesn't say where Robert has been posted, only that his regiment is the Manchesters and that at the moment he is safe and comfortable but bored by his administrative job. By January 1940 two fifths of the children and nine tenths of the mothers have returned home, convinced that London is safe after all because there has been no bombing. But what was called 'the phoney war' ended in the spring. Food rationing begins in earnest, and Churchill forms a National Government. Then, after the evacuation of troops from Dunkirk at the beginning of June, the war really hits Londoners.*

**26 June 1940**

The first air-raid last night. It was such a lovely
night. The moon was full and everything seemed so
peaceful and harmless that the shock was all the
greater. I was asleep when it began, at about one in
the morning, and I could not at first imagine what
the noise was and thought I was dreaming. But
then the thundering grew louder and the screech of
the sirens nearer and the house seemed to shake,
and I realised, my God, we are being bombed. I got
up, pulled on my clothes and lit the candle I have
had ready for months for just such an emergency,
in case the electricity was cut—not that it was but I
didn't dare press the switch until later to find out. I
went down the stairs, with my heart thumping,
convinced that the walls were shuddering, and then
I didn't know what it would be best to do. I opened
the door into the garden and saw the whole sky
blazing with flashes of brilliant white light and
further over to the east hung a great smoke cloud
ringed with red. I thought I might make a dash for
it, to the Armstrongs' shelter next door, which they
had invited me to share, but the noise of the bombs
seemed to fade and I thought I would look foolish
going there if the raid was now over, which in fact it
was. I learned this afternoon that the bombs
dropped were nowhere near us, so I don't know
how I can have felt my house shake, but I swear I
did. When I went back to bed, I saw I had left my
gas mask on the dressing-table—how careless.
There is a Gas lecture at the Town Hall tomorrow
and though I was not going to bother to go to it,

319

now I will, and I will even stay for the respirator drill practice following it.

## 27 June

Very busy all day helping with the bombed-out families. Nobody was killed, but the impact of the bombs brought down the roofs, and in some cases the back walls of the adjacent houses, and the families had to be rehoused. They had already been evacuated last September but they'd hated the country and most came home at Christmas and now they don't want to leave. I would have thought being bombed would make them want to hurry back to the safety of the country but no, they all had tales of not being welcome there and the food being 'funny'. They had nothing to do and were looked down upon and their accents were mocked. We gave them sandwiches and tea, and those who had fled without clothes were kitted out, probably in better garments than they'd left behind. The atmosphere wasn't at all as anyone might have anticipated, there were no tears or signs of distress, but an air of excitement and even of congratulation, that the Jerries hadn't got them and never would. I don't think many of them realise how grave the situation is and if I hadn't started to listen to the wireless regularly I don't think I would either. London has seemed so quiet: it has been impossible to think there is a war on.

## 6 July

Met Charles today, at his house. It is the first day he has been home since Dunkirk. He looked exhausted and it was easy to believe he hadn't had a proper sleep for weeks. His hospital has taken some of the wounded and, though it is not his field, he helped attend to them because there is a shortage of surgeons. He said it was frightening being plunged into such work and he'd been desperately trying to remember what he'd learned as a student but never practised. He had never done an amputation in his life but had to do two within the first day. The men arrived in a pitiful state with their uniforms soaked in blood as well as sea water and the nurses had to cut them out and had a tough job doing it. He has been doing a course on burns, as well as everything else, to be ready when the real bombing starts. He said I'd better get myself out of London before it does. But the usual arguments still hold: I am of use here, if not as much use as Charles, and I am single and childless and have no real justification for fleeing. In fact, I have been given the opportunity to go to America at the end of this month, accompanying the first batch of children to be sent there, but I have said no. I find growing in me, to my surprise, a real sense of patriotism and of duty. If Robert were here, he would be incredulous. It is so strong, this feeling that I want to do something *more* meaningful than WVS work. Driving, maybe. I hear ambulance drivers will be needed. Or should I join one of the forces, like Daphne?

**10 July**

I am so worried about Grace. There has been no word from her since Paris was occupied last month and, though she has always been a poor correspondent, this is the longest gap there has ever been. I wish I knew what has happened to her. Charles says postal communication with London is non-existent, of course. But he thinks Grace will be perfectly safe. He has heard that about 3,000 Britons have been put into a camp at St Denis but he thinks Grace will not have been among them. He's been told that the Germans are encouraging normal life in Paris and she will, he says, probably be working as usual, protected by her employers from harm. I wish I could be so optimistic.

**14 July**

Letter from Robert, at last, after such a long gap. If I'd allowed myself to be, I would have been frightened by his silence. I might have guessed the reason: he has been ill, with flu, but says he is perfectly well now. He says he is a rotten soldier so it's lucky that his job, at the moment anyway, still consists mainly of admin. and not exactly front-line soldiering. He is not suffering much privation at all, and is well fed and not in as much danger, he says, as I am in, and he wishes I would leave London. The more everyone wants me to leave London, the more stubborn I become about staying.

\*　　\*　　\*

322

*Millicent begins to feel less stubborn once the Blitz starts at the beginning of September. Twice she is nearly killed by a bomb, once when she is walking down Oxford Street, thinking she has time, when the sirens go, to get down into the Underground but instead is caught by a bomb blast which takes the glass out of every shop window in the street; and once when she is with some children in a school and the roof falls in and two children are badly injured. From September to November, London is bombed every night—fifty-seven consecutive nights—and she is becoming almost immune to the devastation all round her. There is plenty of work for the WVS, but in October she takes the decision she'd been thinking about.*

\*   \*   \*

## 5 October

When I asked about driving ambulances I was told to apply in writing to the HQ in Haverstock Hill, Hampstead—really, as if anyone has time to write letters with all this hell going on. But anyway, I wrote, saying I'd been driving since I was 25 and was very experienced and knew London well, not absolutely truthful, but never mind, a little fudging is permissible, surely. I have not had a reply, and so I rang up and got a very bad-tempered woman who had no knowledge of any letter from me and cared less. But she said they were very short of drivers and that I could come for a test if I thought I had a realistic chance of passing it. I asked how could I judge that and she snapped that it was a most stringent test and that the vans and cars used were often heavy vehicles with difficult gears, and I mustn't imagine anything dinky. I was so outraged at the insinuation that I was some sort of flibbertigibbet that I lied and said I'd driven a lorry. Well, I did once, for about a hundred yards on a school outing when a lorry driver delivering something had left his cab, with the keys still in it, and the lorry needed to be moved from in front of the school gate so that our coach could get by. I remember feeling very pleased with myself. So I am going for this 'stringent test' tomorrow.

## 6 October

Why do people testing others have to be so very unpleasant about it? There is no excuse at all, especially in the present situation. But I think I coped well, refusing to be made nervous, and putting up with the endless criticisms of my examiner, a woman who didn't even have the manners to tell me her name. It was 'Get in' and 'Start' and 'Drive forward', all of which I did, coolly, taking my time, and not for one minute betraying my dismay at the state of the vehicle I was meant to drive. The car itself was not old, maybe two or three years only, but it was in a poor state and must have been driven many miles because everything about it seemed so worn. I had no problem with the gears, but the handbrake was hellish to operate, a real sweat, and my examiner kept saying 'Handbrake!' whenever she ordered me to stop, as though she couldn't see I was struggling to use it. We drove about for half an hour, and luckily I knew my way because of living around the area, and so no instruction really took me by surprise. The brakes were poor and needed the full thrust of my foot to work, which was difficult because my legs are so short, but I managed well. There was no conversation at all. At the end, I was asked to come for another test on another vehicle tomorrow but I said I couldn't, I had work to do. So, I suppose, that is that and they won't have me.

## 11 October

Miraculously, had a letter from the ambulance HQ telling me to report for duty next Monday. I like the way they assume that the job I'm doing now can just be dropped and I can be at their disposal. I told Miss Arkwright today, and she said she would be sorry to lose my services but she quite understood and wished me luck. I will need it. I have seen these ambulances tearing around the bomb sites and the drivers are fully tested by all the debris and have to discover ingenious ways to get round it. I'll only be driving an ambulance, or what has to serve as one, not attending to the wounded who are going to travel in it, but all the same I am nervous. I know the drivers do help if they are needed. Nobody asked me how I would cope with gruesome sights, and I don't know myself.

## 2 November

Rain all day and all night and one of the worst nights for bombing, though every night is bad and

325

has been for weeks and weeks. Haven't been home for three days. Slept a little at HQ between sorties and ate here, pretty disgusting food but after what we'd seen there wasn't much of an appetite. As everyone says, it is seeing the dead and injured children which tears one up. I don't really think I want to write much about it. We took three little bodies out of the rubble in Euston Road today, all covered in grey dust but with no obvious lacerations and when we got them into the ambulance Irene said, I want to wash their poor faces, and she did, so tenderly, washed the grime away until their white skin was flawless. They should never have been in London, all the children should have been got out and not allowed to return.

**9 December**

Victoria Station hit last night. Not our area but there were so many fires throughout the City and so many ambulances needed that we were ordered to go to Victoria. I thought I knew the way and headed off at full speed but then had to twist and turn because of obstructions due to bomb damage and thought I would never get there. When we did, we were instructed to take several people with horrific-looking leg injuries to Westminster Hospital and I had the same difficulty finding my way and worried terribly about how I was throwing the wounded around. I could hear their groans, and one woman was keening in a high-pitched hysterical way and I was sweating with anxiety. It was a long night. Today has been quiet. I am to have forty-eight hours off, at home.

## 10 December

The house is so cold even though I've lit fires in the living-room and my bedroom. It looked forlorn and neglected when I came in, but then it has been, it hasn't been cleaned for weeks, and the blackout being left up and the windows boarded for most of the time hasn't helped. It was like coming home to a tomb and I had to be strict with myself and repeat over and over how fortunate I am to have a house in one piece. Being truly homeless would make me wretched, I care about my house so much, too much given that it is only bricks. Again and again I've seen women standing outside the ruins of their homes wailing, My house, my house, and people soothing them by saying, Never mind your house, love, you're alive and that's all that matters, but I know how they feel. Still, not much joy in my home today. All I've done is sleep. When I woke up I couldn't credit I'd slept ten whole hours without interruption, though it occurs to me that a siren may have gone off and I simply didn't hear it.

## 11 December

Horrible night in the Underground. Left home about eight to go and visit Charles and the sirens went as I was near Goodge Street, so I went down into the Underground to shelter and got trapped there until dawn. How lucky I've been not to have to use Underground stations as shelters up to now.

327

They are terrible places, stink to high heaven, and the dirt is appalling. So many people were packed down there I couldn't believe I would be able to find a square inch of space, and when a woman whose legs I'd stepped over said I could sit beside her, she'd put her bag on her knee to make room, I could hardly bring myself to squat on the filthy gap she made vacant. But I did. I closed my eyes and clutched my knees and tried to shut everything out but it was impossible. There was so much crying of one sort or another going on, and then someone tried to start up singing, there were yells of 'Shut your face', and every time a bomb was heard there were screams. A man near me was praying out loud, over and over, and at the end of every rendition of the Lord's Prayer paused only to have a fag. The smoke was thick in the foul air, poisoning it further. I didn't have a book with me, and cursed my lack of foresight, I should always keep one with me, but unless I'd also remembered a torch I wouldn't have been able to read, with the light being so dim. Most people, I noted, were doing nothing at all, either just sitting, enduring, or sleeping. A few women were knitting, a few playing cards with their children, but mostly we all just sat.

## 15 December

Tilda wants me to go to her for Christmas. She has moved into a vacant cottage near her mother-in-law and says there is plenty of room. I think I will go. There is no Robert to leave behind, unless he gets leave, and he hasn't mentioned that he is due any. Sometimes, images of him pop into my head and I long for him so much, but then I become so upset I've had to train myself to banish them the moment they appear. It is the only way I can manage. It will be good to get out of London to a place where there are no bombs, though it's hard to credit such a place does exist.

## 24 December

Hellish journey, took nine hours and three changes of train to make such a simple journey. Tilda met me, driving her sister-in-law's car, terrified that the little bit of petrol in the tank would run out before she got home, so the last bit was easy. She hadn't brought any of the children because she said she wanted a few minutes alone with me. I thought at first that she meant just to enjoy the peace and catch up on what I'd been doing but it was something worse. Alfred has been killed, shot down over Hamburg ten days ago. I just sat beside her in the car trying to absorb the news. People always say this, but this sort of death *is* unreal. I saw Father die and, though I didn't actually see Mother die, I saw her dead, but Alfred's death is unbelievable. All day since I heard, even when there was so much noise, happy noise, in this pretty cottage, I have been hearing silence in my head. Alfred just seems a blank. I can't feel grief, and certainly haven't shed tears yet. I remember how glad I was when he left my house and how fervently I hoped never to see him again. I wonder how Albert feels. They were not close, the way twins are supposed to be, but they each used to say they could sense when the other was ill. Albert is in the navy, on a destroyer,

329

and he may not know about his brother's death. George, of course, will tell him, he keeps in touch with the twins. How lucky that George is too old to be in this war, or at least at the moment he is, though if things go on getting worse even he might not be safe. Tilda says that Esther and the children have left Brighton as planned and moved in with Esther's mother, and George is to manage the farm.


## 25 December

A lovely Christmas Day, far removed from war except for the absence of some luxuries, though we did have a large chicken and an excellent Christmas pudding with real fruit in it. Charles managed to get here late last night, after the children had finally gone to bed, and so we were a very happy family. I say 'we', including myself, but that is what has happened, Tilda's family has become mine. I am the maiden aunt, taken in and made one of them, and I had better get used to the role. But about one thing I am determined: after this war is over, Robert must be accepted. Even spinster aunts can have friends, special friends. When I had the accident, and Tilda was forced into meeting Robert at the hospital, he said she was perfectly civil to him and kind and that she didn't seem at all the sort of person to be as narrow-minded as I'd said she was. Well, we will put that to the test after the war.

## 29 December

Home again, another wearying journey, and pretty dreary trundling the last few miles into the station. The train stopped and started and we all stared out at the devastation we were passing through and a sort of eerie silence settled on us all. The train was packed to capacity, with the corridors as crowded as the carriages and full of men in uniform. Women too, actually. How smart the WRNSs look, but I think if I were in the services I'd rather be in the WAAF like Daphne. The war in the air seems more important somehow and I'd feel I was helping it. I wonder if I am now too old to join up if I wanted to. I think 40 is likely to be the cut-off point and I am not yet quite 40 and certainly don't look it. That is not vanity talking either. When I enrolled with the WVS, and again when I reported to the ambulance people, they all thought I was much younger than I'd said. So if there was any problem, I could lie quite convincingly and lop five years off. At last, some advantage to always having looked young for my age through being small and slight.

## 2 January 1941

Thick snow, almost impossible to drive down some streets, but thank God there were no emergencies last night. My house is so cold, each room a little igloo, and I sleep with two hot-water bottles (one of which is nearly perished and I will never be able to get another) and all the blankets I've got and then my big overcoat across the bottom of the bed.

I lie there cuddled up to the bottles, thinking how the only real warmth comes from another body, and then I think of Robert, though I try not to, and wonder where he is and remember how he clasped me to him so that we fitted together like spoons, his front to my back, and that way fell asleep.

**5 February**

More snow. God, what a winter. We might as well be at the North Pole. I try to train myself to remember what sun feels like and struggle to be back in Italy all those years ago, barely able to walk in the garden for the heat. I wonder what Francesca looks like now. But thinking of Italy doesn't work, my imagination can't make enough effort to convince me that I am back there. We're not supposed to have proper baths but last night when I came home so weary after a long day trundling round bomb sites, I thought to hell with this and I filled my bath to the absolute brim and used the last of the bath salts Tilda gave me for Christmas, and I soaked myself in the deliciously hot, scented water and never wanted to get out. Just as well I indulged because today the Ascot heater will not function and there is no hot water at all. Here am I, moaning about hot water and there is a war on, and I haven't the foggiest idea what is happening. I don't even seem to listen to the news any more. When I am not thinking about wanting hot baths I am craving fruit. There is *no* fruit anywhere. The last apple I had was at Tilda's. I fantasise an orchard of apples and myself picking a Worcester and sinking my teeth into its gorgeous red skin.

## 14 March

Robert comes home tomorrow, for forty-eight hours. The telegram arrived when I was at the ambulance station and was already eight hours old so, by the time I got home and read it, I knew he would be on his way. I feel nervous more than excited. Of course I must get time off, so I rang HQ and they were not pleased and not very understanding but then they never are. It was Miss Buchanan on duty and she said if there was an emergency she hoped I wouldn't put my own pleasure first. I was furious. Then she grudgingly added I was one of their best drivers, but I wasn't going to be taken in by that sort of soft-soaping. I will do my shift tonight and then I am determined to claim a full forty-eight hours off. I wish I had time to have my hair cut. It has grown so long and ragged, and shampoo is so hard to get I don't wash it as often as it needs and keeping it under my uniform cap most of the day makes it greasy too. There is a hairdresser's still open near our HQ but I don't think I have time to go there. No chance of finding a lipstick either.

## 17 March

Well, that's it. He's gone. Classic scene at the station, me clinging to him and he kissing me with a passion he certainly didn't show over his leave. I looked at all the other couples on that crowded

333

platform and wondered if any of them would have similar tales to tell. I don't know what went wrong. God knows, I tried to be loving and to look attractive. I dug out that blue dress he used to love me in and though it is far too cold for it I wore it and pinned up my hair and thought I looked quite beguiling and, in fact, it cheered me up to have made such an effort and find myself looking not half bad. I'd made the best meal I could, too, for his arrival. He can't have known what a struggle it was to get the meat even if it was only brisket, and how much of an effort to find proper cheese and some celery for afterwards. He didn't seem to appreciate anything. All he said was that he was exhausted and it is true he looked it, very gaunt and grey. On his arrival he slept for a solid twelve hours which out of forty-eight is a lot. Then he said what he most wanted was some fresh air and so we went to Kensington Gardens and walked in the park. The weather is lovely, so sunny and warm, and all the crocuses were out and I felt suddenly happy and hopeful and we had lunch in the cafeteria near the Albert Memorial, not a very good lunch, the fish was peculiar-tasting, but it felt quite festive. Afterwards we went and sat by the Round Pond where children were sailing boats just as they always have done. But Robert spoiled this tranquillity by talking about the progress of the war and the battle going on in the Atlantic, and I really didn't want to hear about it and said so. Blinkered as ever, he said, and I snapped back that I drove an ambulance and was certainly not blinkered, but that this was a lovely afternoon and for once I wanted to forget all the horror. He apologised. But the mood was altered and when we went home he took up a book almost immediately and started reading. It was *Pilgrimage*, one of my books, and I know he wasn't the least bit interested in it, but he pretended to be. And now I am in bed and he has gone and we only made love once and it was awkward and he felt strange and behaved roughly, and I felt used afterwards. I think he was ashamed. He says he is depressed and hates the army. Then, on that station platform, when it was no good at all, he suddenly kissed me how he used to, and his eyes filled with tears and he said he loved me and he was sorry to have been so useless and of course I said it didn't matter and that I loved him too. But his gloom and lack of interest in me had mattered. It's left me feeling resentful and wondering if in fact I spoke the truth. *Do* I love him?

**27 March**

Such quiet nights lately. I wondered aloud today at HQ if maybe the bombing of London is over and there was a bark of contempt from Miss Buchanan. She says of course it isn't, am I a simpleton, this is just a lull. It is amazing the way everyone except me seems so confident that they know best. I am so tired of Miss Buchanan. Someone told me that in real life she is a prison warder at Holloway and I can well believe it.

**30 June**

Awful dreams about Robert, can't bear to record them, but as a consequence woke up determined to involve myself more in this hateful war. I want to try to be more *active*, to share in the fighting. So I went to the Recruiting Office today, feeling very self-conscious. There were several others already waiting, none looking all that much younger than me, though I'm not good at guessing ages. Filled in a form (lied, said I was 35) of basic information. I enjoyed putting social worker as my pre-war job and even more writing down ambulance driver as current employment, pure swank of course. And then went into another room for a physical examination. Was weighed (8 stone), measured (5 feet 2 inches) had my eyes tested (20/20 vision) and teeth looked at. Then questions about illnesses I had had—none. I kept quiet about the other thing, feeling not quite comfortable about doing so, but it was not an illness and is none of their business and makes no difference to my fitness and general health. They said I was a model recruit. Because of my qualifications they said I was suitable for Admin., which sounds boring but is apparently a high grade, but that rules required me to go before a psychologist. What fun, Daphne will like this. Was then officially enrolled, and another form was filled out which asked for next of kin. I hesitated over that. I wanted to put Robert, and I know he has put me, but it would have led to so many questions and I'd already put that I wasn't married, and I don't know exactly where he is now, and so I put Tilda. Poor Tilda, being next of kin to so many of the family and always bound to get any bad news first and be obliged to pass it on. After all this, told to report to Gloucester in two days' time.

*      *      *

*In fact, Millicent would still have been accepted if she'd revealed her true age (40 the following month). Daphne, who is having a great time stationed at Grimsby, sends her a list of what to take when she reports for duty: '2 pairs of pyjamas; 1 dressing-gown; 1 pair of slippers; toilet things;* natural *nail varnish; 1 large tin of Silvo (for cleaning buttons); large tin Cherry Blossom shoe polish; some fine hair nets (to keep your hair off your collar); soap and towel'. She warns Millicent not to wear her hat on one side, not to take anything of value ('it will be swiped') and not to get down-hearted at first 'because take my word for it, it will soon be fun'. Millicent's comments on what Daphne considered 'fun' were sarcastic. She writes that she could not see any fun in tearing around in a Triumph Herald car packed with six airmen (as well as Daphne) and then spending the night in the Airways Club getting drunk on gin, nor did she think it amusing to be told that her friend had slept with one of the men afterwards but couldn't remember his name. He'd cooked her eggs in butter for breakfast and given her two whole packs of Senior Service cigarettes to take back to camp—'to be thrilled, by that!' writes Millicent.*

\* \* \*

**2 July**

Arrived at the Depot near Gloucester, after the usual roundabout and long drawn-out journey all travelling now involves. It felt as if it would've been quicker walking. In a hut with eleven others, like

337

arriving at boarding-school, I imagine, except none of us are children. Beds awful, with appallingly thin mattresses. Slept badly. Woken at 6 a.m. with a bugle sounding through a loudspeaker and lights going on. It was funny watching the different ways women got dressed, some so embarrassed and modest, struggling to put clothes on under the blankets and others stripping their pyjamas off boldly and standing stark naked before the wash basins (and not always the ones with bodies to be proud of). I like to think I fell somewhere in the middle, not flaunting it but not ashamed. Breakfast was revolting but seemed to please most people and there was lots of it, I was amazed, lots of fried eggs and even bacon and baked beans and fried bread. I've never liked fried anything. I stuck to toast and tea (strong, ugh). Boring day after that, seemed to hang about in queues, waiting to be photographed, then to collect pay books, then to be interviewed by the psychologist, tedious. Meanwhile, we got to know each other, or had the chance to while all this was going on. Remarkable how eager some women, or 'girls' as we are all called, are to tell their entire life history. I revealed very little. Only said I was a Londoner and had been driving an ambulance. Someone asked me if I had 'a bloke'. I said yes, smiling to think of Robert hearing himself described as a bloke. The interview was pretty pathetic, with all the questions obvious—or rather the answers which would please were obvious, e.g. if someone shouted 'Fire!' while you were at your desk, what would you do: (a) immediately run from the building, (b) collect anything important you were working on, then leave the building as quickly as possible, (c) stay

338

put till the actual fire alarm went off. I mean, really! Only someone who has never been in a bombed city could hesitate over that.

## 3 July

I have been accepted for Admin., though no one has asked me if I want to be, but eight of the twelve of us who were put in for it failed. I can't say I'm thrilled, it was never my idea to be in Admin., surely I am better qualified to be a driver. Our uniforms arrived today, complete with regulation underwear, ghastly coarse knickers and all. A lot of swopping went on since hardly anything fitted. One girl immediately got out needle and thread and began adapting her skirt to fit her. She proved good with her needle because she alone looked stylish when we were all dressed. She looked a little like Grace and of course because she was so good at sewing she made me think of Grace, which on the whole I try not to do: it is too distressing wondering what is happening to her in occupied France. Haven't heard from her for months, and neither has Tilda.

\*     \*     \*

*All that is known about Grace is that before the war she was living and working in Paris for one of the big fashion houses (possibly Coco Chanel's, since there is one reference in early 1939 to her wearing a Chanel suit) and they certainly went on flourishing during the occupation. Millicent often writes in her diary that she is proud of her little sister doing so well and that she*

339

*intends to visit her. When war was declared, she
somehow expected Grace to return immediately to
England and when that didn't happen she was
surprised but not too worried because she received a
reassuring letter from Grace saying she was perfectly
safe, life was going on as normal. But then the
German army occupied Paris on 14 June 1940 and
Millicent's worries were justified when Grace proved
not to be one of the two million or so who made a
hasty exit. But, as her brother-in-law Charles had
once told her, the Germans at first were anxious to
make the occupation as bearable as possible for the
French and life in Paris did indeed go on much as
usual. Hitler himself had chosen not to enter Paris at
the head of a victorious army because he said he
didn't want to destroy French pride entirely, and he
gave orders that the troops were to behave correctly
and maintain strict discipline. In fact, the German
soldiers were said to have behaved like tourists,
spending their time taking photographs of themselves
in front of landmarks, and were so much on their best
behaviour that they astonished the Parisians with
their good manners. So the likelihood is that, though
English, Grace was in some way protected and not
sent to the St Denis camp but allowed to continue
working.*

\*          \*          \*

**8 July**

Still dark when we left this morning for our training
depot. The camp seemed so forlorn when we
arrived, very cold in the huts and, at first, no sign of

340

any food or even tea to welcome us. Mud everywhere. Getting from hut to hut a filthy business. A lecture in the evening, pretty pointless stuff about Egypt, except I think that is where Robert may now be, so I listened carefully. I wish I could start working properly and justify having joined up. At the moment I know I was far more useful driving ambulances.

## 12 July

Saturday, and some of the girls went to a dance at the army camp, a bus helpfully coming for them. I didn't go. What a state of excitement they were in, spending hours titivating themselves and pooling all our hut's resources. I contributed what is left of my last lipstick, never liked the colour anyway, it clashes with my hair, but kept to myself the scent Robert bought me. The rest of us, left behind, pretended we were happy to stay and read. A surprising amount of reading goes on, especially of detective stories which have never interested me—plenty of Agatha Christies around—but a lot of girls stick to magazines. A lot of letter-writing too. I wrote to Tilda, and to Daphne, because I owe her one. I said that as yet the 'fun' she'd promised hadn't materialised and that everything was dreary and I feel like an overgrown schoolgirl in detention. She will say it is my own fault and that I never have known how to join in and that I should have gone to the dance. Those who did came back in the early hours terribly drunk, and making a dreadful noise as they fell over things and tried to put themselves to bed.

341

## 15 July

What a birthday! Did not mention it to anyone. On the move again, posted to a satellite station. The worst journey yet, via Birmingham. Lucky it is July because there are holes in the roof of the hut I am in and the rain trickles through. I asked why they hadn't been mended and was told everyone had more important things to attend to. Not much sign of anything important being done that I can see.

## 17 July

Real work at last, though not the type I want. Am being taught how to track planes. I don't know how that fits into Admin., but here it does. I'm going to complain that I would be of more use driving. The shifts we work are eight hours long, on our feet, and at the end we are ready to collapse. There is a lot to learn and it is all very much more complicated than it looks. It needs a certain kind of mind, more Daphne's sort than mine. I don't like working underground. The room is enormous, it feels a mile long though it can't be. There's a huge centre table covered with a map of Southern England and we are being taught how to wield long croupier-like sticks so that they move little arrows showing the direction and numbers of aircraft. I am not yet adept at it. One girl is brilliant, took to it straightaway, but then it turns out she plays snooker with her boyfriend.

## 20 July

Heavens knows why, well I suppose I do know why, but we are given lectures on VD. They are always at 11.30 a.m., such an unsuitable time when lunch follows them. The visual aids are disgusting, pictures of women with half their noses eaten away and syphilitic sores on their lips. But instead of everyone being horrified and falling silent so many girls giggled without, I'm sure, being able to explain why. I didn't, but felt on the edge of doing so just because others were. I was ashamed of myself. Afterwards, there was a lot of talk about French letters and Johnnies and other names for condoms. I kept quiet. I expect the others would think that meant I know nothing about sex. I wonder if the men get the same lectures only with the visual aids showing male noses and lips. Well, I don't have to concern myself with any of this. I hope Daphne has paid attention.

\*     \*     \*

*The diary for the rest of 1941, and for the first six months of 1942, shows how much Millicent begins to relish the feeling that she was doing something worthwhile and satisfying at last. She feels guilty that she actually enjoys being in the WAAF, and is reluctant (unlike Daphne) to admit this or to acknowledge that her part in a war which has already killed one brother, and might go on to kill the others on active service, is giving her a real sense of fulfilment, especially after she is transferred to a bomber squadron in Yorkshire. Here at first she plots planes but then is switched to being a driver.*

343

*This was something of a demotion, because drivers were the lowest paid class (12s 6d a fortnight), but Millicent didn't care. She not only loved to drive but felt that having been an ambulance driver she had valuable experience which was not being put to good use and she had petitioned to change jobs.*

*She drives lorries on the airfield, learning to drive the RAF way (double-de-clutching when changing gear, changing down before a corner, and using hand signals). She collects and delivers crews to planes, and helps lay the flarepath when planes signal for landing. Early in 1942, she is put up for a commission. She goes to the Air Ministry in London for an interview but is not given a commission, claiming in her diary to have sabotaged her own chances by not being respectful enough to the 'Brass' interviewing her.*

\* \* \*

## 30 March 1942

On leave. Decided to come home even though the difficulties of the journey mean I'll only have a full twenty-four hours here. It is so long since I've been in London and I wanted to walk in a park and go to a cinema and just feel like a Londoner again. Felt lonely when I woke up in my own lovely bed, remembering Robert's last leave here, I suppose, not that that was exactly blissful and worth recalling, but then relished the comfort and privacy. Met Daphne in the afternoon. She's here to see if her house has survived, and also for the same reason as me, just to stop feeling like a country bumpkin for a few hours.

We decided to go to Kenwood and walk there. The house is closed and the pictures stored somewhere safe. We walked all round the grounds in beautiful sunshine and then carried on to Highgate where most of the houses seemed empty. We walked back on to the Heath and sat by one of the ponds under a tree and talked. Daphne is determined that I should admit I have wasted time being with Robert and that I don't love him any more, but it isn't true, though sometimes in low moments I have wondered if it might be. She can be quite cruel when she wants, though she likes to think she is just being 'honest'. Funny kind of honesty. She's never liked Robert, though has always admired his looks, looks being so important to her. Tell me, she said, *why* you love him, convince me, do. I sat and thought about why for a long time, long enough only to convince Daphne that I had no answer, but in fact because the answer was so hard to put into words. I am not glib about such things as she is, I can't joke about being in love. Finally, I said I had to admit that I was very physically attracted to him but I hadn't equated that with love. I knew it wasn't. There is just something about Robert which responds to something in me, an ease with him, a feeling of belonging and of being understood by him. That was the best I could do, and it was a poor, stumbling best but, surprisingly, Daphne appeared impressed. I have never felt that with any man, she said, and she patted my hand and said, Lucky old you. Daphne's not really the ideal friend to have a heart-to-heart with, she is too abrasive and lacks real sympathy, but then I've never really had the

345

sort of friend I could confide in properly, or maybe it is that I am not the sort of person who can do the confiding. I am not well off for friends whereas Daphne has heaps, or says she has. She's met an American, a GI, and is sleeping with him, that's when she's not sleeping with a Dutch airman called Kees. She insisted on showing me one of the Dutchman's letters, which I didn't at all want to read so she read it aloud, roaring with laughter. It was all about her kisses and how he'd never had kisses like them, and how he could feel her communicating her true self to him and other tosh. But thinking of any man trying to write so intimately and obviously struggling to find the right words, *and* in a foreign language, I couldn't see anything funny about it. I thought it was mean of Daphne to mock him, and said so. It is odd, but listening to Daphne I sometimes feel, in spite of what I've just told her, as though I have never loved or been loved, as if I've returned to a virginal state. Stupid.

**31 March**

Robert's regiment has been captured. He is almost certainly in Changi Prison. Everyone was talking of the fall of Singapore last month but I paid little attention, because the Manchesters were supposed to be in Palestine. His last letter was from a hospital where he was being treated for some strange stomach infection and was on a diet of milk only. I don't understand how he can then have been sent to the Far East. Why wasn't he invalided home? The Japanese have not yet given out a list of prisoners but the information, such as it is, suggests he will be among those in Changi. I wish it was not a Japanese camp. There are so many stories leaking out already about how prisoners are treated. And he is not strong, especially with having been so ill recently. I thought of him, more frail than ever after his milk diet, and suddenly feared he would not survive. He hasn't the physical resources and he may not even have the spirit.

## 15 April

Sent a parcel to Robert, though God knows if anything ever gets to him. I can't be sure he is definitely in Changi, but I don't care. I wanted to send it. I bartered everything I had in the way of stockings, jewellery and cosmetics, even the last of that L'Aimant scent he gave me, to buy some chocolate bars from a girl who has a GI boyfriend. Added some dried fruit, apricots and raisins, which cost me about three times what they cost before the war, and a tin of pineapple chunks, same source as the chocolate. I saved my tea ration for two weeks, got it decanted into a packet every day, and sent that, and a tin of condensed milk. It didn't amount to much. I wrapped it all in an inner lining of *The Times*, thinking it would give him something to read. Maybe I shouldn't have done that, maybe the parcel will be censored and no news allowed. At the last minute I slipped in some cream for the treatment of sores, and some Elastoplast. I'm not sure why, I suppose because I have dreams about him being bitten by mosquitoes. He will probably never get the parcel anyway.

*The prisoner-of-war camp Robert was in had been the Changi Garrison in peacetime, holding about four or five thousand soldiers but, once Singapore fell, it was made to accommodate forty thousand. Millicent's parcel, and indeed any letters she sent, had virtually no chance of getting to him. The Singapore Post Office ceased to function on Friday 13 February 1942 and it took until August for the Swiss Red Cross to establish a link with the Japanese through which mail could flow. It took two years for a list to be supplied of all those captured, by which time half of the men had died or been moved from Changi. In 1944, the Japanese allowed each prisoner to send one postcard to a relative. It resembled the card George King sent home, during the First World War, that is, it was preprinted and only required the prisoner to tick whichever applied (with very little choice of comment). The first letters received by any prisoners arrived at the camp in November 1943, together with a few, very few, parcels. It is just possible Millicent's was among them, but very unlikely.*

\*     \*     \*

**19 April**

Such lovely weather, wonderfully warm and springlike. At the end of our shift this afternoon we all sat outside the hut with our backs against it and our faces lifted to the sun and our eyes closed. Someone pointed out the daffodils growing on the

348

bit of a hill near the gate, and I spouted the Wordsworth poem. Avril said, You are clever, Millicent, but sarcastically. I don't usually give anything away about my educational background but I didn't think that was giving away anything when everyone knows 'Daffodils'. Avril's the sort of girl I'd never meet in normal life. She's clever and quick but left school at 15 and works in a tyre factory. I'm surprised they didn't make her stay there since manufacturing tyres is so important, but it turns out she lied and said she was a secretary. Well, I lied too, so I shouldn't be shocked. She never stops talking and asking questions, all of them of a rather personal nature. She was behind me, unfortunately, when I was posting my parcel to Robert and very rudely peered over my shoulder and said, Ooh, so you do have a fella, then. I didn't reply, and as I was in front she didn't see me flush with irritation. In fact, it would be a relief to talk to someone about Robert but definitely not to Miss Nosy Avril.

**15 May**

Weekend leave, but didn't go home. Decided to go up to the Roman Wall and walk along it. Stayed the night in Acomb Youth Hostel, only 1 shilling, even though I am no youth. I was surprised it was open, but it was and there were six other walkers, all service people doing the same as me. Today was even better than yesterday, the route along the wall was quite exhilarating, soaring up and down as it did. The scenery is wild and barren and I suppose some would find it forbidding, but I don't and I

349

find the sheer fact that the wall has survived comforting. I think I walked about twelve miles in all, stopping only once to eat my sandwich and drink some lemonade. I was remembering the walking holiday I once had with Percy. Poor Percy. I don't suppose he ever forgave me. I did really *like* him but was never physically attracted to him, and that matters so much. The odd thing is, that I liked Robert before I was attracted to him, much the best way round. But I was determined not to let anything spoil the day, so every time any thoughts whatsoever of Robert popped into my head I squashed them. It's maddening when my head becomes busy with pointless worries and vexations, everything buzzing about in my brain as I jump from one aggravation to another. The only thing to do is recite a poem to quieten myself, so that is what I did, out loud, poems and songs and hymns. Anyone hearing me would have thought me mad, but there was no one, only sheep. Towards the end of the walk, I found myself wondering if this is how I am going to spend the rest of my life, on my own. I was pleased that the thought didn't terrify me, or make me utterly miserable. I'd rather not be on my own, I'd rather be with Robert, the Robert he was before the war, but if I have to manage I can, which is more than a lot of women can say. In our hut at night, the talk is endlessly about men and marriage, it's absolutely incessant, their desperation to have a man, and I rather despise it, which I know is not kind of me. The girl in the next bed to me is at this moment describing how she will have dark red roses at her wedding and the bridesmaids will be in blue and silver, yet she hasn't even a boyfriend.

350

## 6 June

Letter from Tilda. She writes such a good letter and is so affectionate, far more so than she is when we are together, and it warms me to think she cares about me as much as she seems to. She is going home for the weekend next Friday, taking Florence and Jack to see their father but leaving the twins with her sister-in-law Joan. It's months since Charles has been able to get away to come to them and when he's so exhausted she doesn't want him to do the travelling and tire himself more, and besides she longs to be in her own home just for a short while. Charles has apparently got tickets for the theatre, *Dear Brutus*, on his birthday and she is so looking forward to it. She says she will save me the programme.

*     *     *

*But Millicent never got the programme. On the night of 13 June 1942 her life was changed for ever. No other previous tragedy, not even her miscarriage or her father's death, or her mother's, had such a dramatic and long-lasting effect on the course of her life. Tilda and Charles Routledge and their two children Florence and Jack were all killed by a bomb which fell on central London that night. There are no entries in Millicent's diary for the next six weeks—a black line is slashed through empty page after empty page, though each page is nevertheless headed with a date—and when they do begin again, in early August, no details are given of precisely where and how the Routledge family died, or how the news reached Millicent, or what she did in the immediate aftermath of hearing it. This kind of silence after a terrible event is, of course, characteristic, as she herself realises. Later on in this traumatic year, she reflects on what keeping a diary can mean if it becomes blank at times of great shock and grief. She realises that her reaction at such periods is to become catatonic, 'words freeze in my mind', and she literally cannot write. But she also says that there is to her something distasteful, 'a kind of wallowing', about describing death. But, when she takes up her diary again, what is unusual is that she does record the reason for not having written in it for so long, if only simply to state the facts before beginning again.*

\* \* \*

## 2 August

Tilda and all her little family except the twins killed by a bomb in central London on 13 June. RIP.

## 3 August 1942

Slept properly last night for the first time since 14 June. Woke feeling optimistic, though there is no reason for such strange optimism. I think it was physical, merely the result of a good night's sleep without nightmares or weeping or being clung to by the poor children. It soon faded, the lovely cheerfulness. I started to worry about telling Robert, what to tell him and how to do it. It is not because I fear he will fail to understand how my life, and therefore his, is irrevocably changed and set in an entirely different direction, I am sure he will indeed understand, and maybe even be glad that we now have two lovely children to care for as our own, but he may not grasp how this tragedy has changed me. I feel it in every fibre of my being. I feel as though suddenly I have put on two stone in weight (though in fact I have lost weight) and am now a solid, rooted, bovine person whose function is to cook and clean and be housewife and mother and never look up from all that means. He can never be the centre of my life again. He will find himself an intruder. I should write to him but what puts me off is not so much knowing that the letter has little chance of reaching him in Changi, if he is still there, if he is still alive, but the impossibility of describing to him what becoming the guardian and mother of two 5-year-old children means. I can tell him about this cottage, I can tell him about Blockley, I can list the pubs and shops, I can say there are only about 1,700 inhabitants of whom I know about a dozen. I can even give him a time-

353

table of my day from dawn to dusk, because it is already set in stone, but all of this would tell him nothing. It would be meaningless. So I have not written.

**4 August**

This country is full of orphaned children but few have been so completely robbed of their family as the twins. I fear I've done more damage by the way I broke the news to them, but there was no one to tell me how to do it, what the best and kindest way would be, and they are only 5 years old, too young to understand properly but too old to be unaware. They keep expecting Tilda to come home. This kind of death has no reality for them, they simply can't envisage it. And Connie is jealous because Florence and Jack are with her mummy and daddy, and she wants to be wherever they have gone. Their grandmother and Aunt Joan talk of angels and heaven and make it all sound so desirable and, naturally, the twins want to go there too. But I've learned that for small children this religious talk is a blessing and I fall into it myself, holding out hope of a future in which the little family is reunited. It is shameful, when I don't believe a word of it and have no religious faith, but it is comforting to the twins and easy to do.

**5 August**

Mrs Routledge has died. Joan says it was the shock of Charles's death, that she simply couldn't get

354

over it and didn't want to live if her brilliant, precious son was dead. She had a heart attack and it was all over in a matter of hours. She was 78, older than I thought. Another death for the twins to absorb. Joan came and told them that Granny had gone to heaven to be with Daddy and that started Connie off again, wanting to go too. This heaven is such an attractive-sounding place to the child. Joan thought it might help if the twins were taken to see their Granny in her coffin, She looks so sweet and peaceful, said Joan, but I am not going to allow it. I have seen Mrs Routledge and she looks neither sweet nor peaceful. Her dead body would terrify Connie who still thinks of her mother alive somewhere above her, floating on a pink cloud surrounded by angels. I am not going to let the twins go to the funeral either, though this will annoy and maybe even anger Joan. Her own children are going, even Helen, who is only a little older than the twins. But if I am now their mother I must start acting like one and making decisions for them according to what I think is right. So I will. No viewing of corpses, no attending funerals.

## 6 August

I have to decide whether to renew the lease on this cottage. Tilda and Charles would have done, I know, for the duration of the war, with Blockley as safe a place as any, I suppose. The twins are used to it, and in fact have little memory of their real home in London, and they have their Aunt Joan and their cousins living here with them, just round the corner in Brook Lane. Yet in spite of all these advantages I somehow feel reluctant to stay. It will mean the twins starting at the village school in September and, once they do, it will be unwise to disrupt them. I wish we were in London. I feel strange here, not comfortable, and would face the future more cheerfully in London, or even Brighton, but of course it would not be sensible to go to either place. It would be dangerous, pure folly.

## 7 September

The twins started school today and I started having some time to myself. The shock was considerable. I never appreciated what relief mothers feel when the house is empty. All those years of seeing Tilda harassed and desperate for peace and quiet and I could never understand the craving, because I'd never experienced the intensity of the mothering. I used to wonder why she didn't just go to her bedroom and read a book if she so much wanted to. That was what I did today, went home and lay on my bed, though it still doesn't feel like 'my' bed, and read. Nothing challenging or particularly satisfying, just *How Green Was My Valley*, because there's a film of it now—not that I'll have a chance to see it, we're nowhere near a cinema—and I'd never read it. I could hardly concentrate for the silence, and for this nagging worry that I should be doing something else. Well, so I should. There are the children's clothes to mend and the cottage needs a good cleaning, especially the kitchen floor. All these household tasks which I once did so effortlessly and now feel too tired to do properly.

## 18 September

School is going well for both twins, which is a bit of a surprise and a very lucky thing for me. They are both so bright and keen, Connie even more so than Toby. Tilda would be so proud of them. Quite a few of the children cry each morning when they have to leave their mothers, but not the twins, they can't wait to get into the school and when the teacher emerges and rings her hand-bell they are first in line. I think everyone is amazed at how settled they seem. Certainly their Aunt Joan is. She congratulates me on how I've 'handled' what she calls 'the whole tragic business' but in a sort of oddly suspicious tone. My devotion to my nephew and niece is widely commented on in the village. When I go into the post office or the shop I receive admiring glances, though no one actually says anything to me, it is all reported by other people afterwards—'that Miss King, she's a marvel'. I must say I like being a marvel, though of course I'm not.

## 2 October

There was a piece in the paper yesterday saying that the fashion collections had gone ahead as usual in Paris. This must surely mean that the Germans are not interfering with the people who produce them, so Grace might still be working. I need have no fantasies of her being hauled off to some prisoner-of-war camp. But surely, if this is the case, she could have somehow got a message through to me. Except, of course, she doesn't know where I am, and who knows if arrangements for

357

forwarding mail work properly all the time.

**4 October**

Daphne came for the day, on a motor-bike, if you please, a great snarling machine and she in leather jacket and goggles. I'd told the twins about her in some detail to prepare them in case she was as off-hand as she can sometimes be, and they were impressed she was a WAAF, but she exceeded their expectations by arriving as she did. She let them sit on the motor-bike and was all for giving them a little ride, but I wouldn't let her. She teased me, saying I was becoming a proper tartar of a mother who ruled her children with a rod of iron. When the twins had gone to the bottom of the garden to play in the sand-pit she asked if I thought I had found my true vocation at last. She didn't mean it unkindly, but for some reason it annoyed me and I snapped back that no, I did not, and that I hadn't chosen to become a guardian who in turn had to become a mother and never would have done, and then she apologised and said all she'd meant was that as I seemed so happy in my new role and the twins happy too she just thought maybe I felt that in this roundabout way, if through a terrible tragedy, I'd found a niche I'd never found before. I asked what made her think I hadn't found this niche, as she called it, what made her think I hadn't loved my work and already had been happy. Daphne said she didn't know why I was being so grumpy and taking offence when all she'd intended was a compliment, for heaven's sake. But she doesn't realise, she can't realise, partly because I

358

take pains to hide it, that however content and fulfilled I seem I cannot bear to think that the future for at least the next twelve years will be devoted to Connie and Toby. I love them dearly, more sincerely than I ever thought I would be able to, and I want to do my duty and do the very best I can for them, but still I feel dismayed because I no longer have the freedom of choice. I know the effects of this war have meant very many people have had that freedom taken away, and God knows I didn't do much with my freedom when I had it, but I didn't want to be one of them. I couldn't tell Daphne any of this. She wouldn't have understood.

## 31 October

A letter from Robert, miraculously forwarded from my London address (so the service is working in spite of the war), or rather a scrap of paper which was in a packet of such scraps delivered to the wife of one of the officers. There was a covering note explaining that she'd no idea how it had reached her but that it must have been smuggled out of Changi Prison somehow. This scrap is a half sheet of rice paper which has some tiny holes in it and is stained with faint pale brown marks. The writing is microscopic, not at all like his usual bold hand, for obvious reasons. All he has room to say is that he is well and that he loves me very much and thinks of me all the time. I smoothed the fragile paper out and read the message over and over, changing my mind each time about what I thought. I can't credit that he is well. Naturally he would say that. But at least he was well enough to write. I put the letter in

Tilda's Bible.

**8 November**

Astonished to have a visit from Esther and George, completely unannounced. They just turned up on my doorstep and what was awful was that for a full minute I didn't recognise either of them. Esther was always plump, not to say fat, and now she is quite gaunt, and George, who was always painfully thin and weedy after the war, is now so muscular looking, really strong and fit. They were in a car, a pretty clapped-out old car, but still a car, and one for which they'd got petrol somehow. They say they sent Christmas cards giving their new address to Tilda and Grace and me, but if so I never got mine and if Tilda and Grace got theirs they never mentioned them, so I am not sure I believe them. At any rate, they'd found out about what happened only last week through an old copy of *The Times* in which Mrs Routledge had put a death notice, a long saga about how they came across it, told in excruciatingly boring detail by Esther, and had come to say they will give the twins a home. I had to take a deep breath not to say something I would regret. I made tea, glad the twins were at school, and said they already had a home and that Tilda and Charles had appointed me their guardian and I was only too happy to be a mother to Connie and Toby. And I apologised for not trying to find them and let them know what happened. I felt guilty about that, I should have made the effort. Then Esther said she just wondered if the twins wouldn't be better off in a proper family with two big brothers to take the place of Florence and Jack. Luckily I had my back to her when she said it, refilling the teapot, so I was able to close my eyes and count to ten, and then turn and say, More tea?, ignoring what she'd said. She might have repeated it, but George coughed and shot her a look and instead she launched into an account of her recent illness, something to do with her thyroid. The only thing George asked me was whether I was all right for money, and of course I am, that has never been a problem. They stayed about two hours, wanting to meet the twins, and came with me to the school. I must say it was of great satisfaction to me that Connie and Toby raced out and flung their arms round my legs, taking one leg each as usual so that I couldn't move. They were shy with their aunt and uncle, but then they've never met them since they were babies. Esther thinks Connie looks like me and Toby like Alfred. I said I presumed they'd heard about Alfred and they said yes, and had I heard from Albert, which I haven't, not recently, and neither had they, though they are in touch with Michael who is flying Spitfires.

They gave me their address before they left and seemed sincere in their encouragement to visit. The twins would enjoy going to a farm so maybe we will one day. Before she left, Esther asked if I had a 'sweetheart' in the Forces. I nearly said no, but that I had one in Changi Jail, but I held back. I don't want Esther feeling sorry for me, but of course my saying I had *no* sweetheart makes her feel even more sorry. You never had any luck with men, did you, Millicent? she said, mock-regretful. Her final remark was, You've got two lovely children, so you've turned out lucky in the end, every cloud has its silver lining. She *maddens* me.

\* \* \*

## 31 December

Glad to get rid of 1942. Surely the new year cannot be so bad. Mr Waring, the old man who gardens for Joan, says the tide has turned in the war and that now the Americans are in we will win, if not next year then the year after. I hope he is right. Christmas was a strain. Not so much the difficulty of getting food, with shortages of everything worse than ever, but the sadness of the first without Tilda and Charles and Florence and Jack, but I think I felt it far more than the children who were much more taken up with their presents, and as Joan had invited us for the day itself there was enough of a crowd to make everything seem festive. It would have been too pathetic if we three had had to manage on our own. The twins don't really remember last Christmas, thank God, though Connie did say, when Joan's husband arrived home, Daddy came last Christmas Eve, didn't he, in the snow. I said yes, and she nodded, and let it go. No snow this year. It was mild and wet.

\* \* \*

*The whole of 1943 passes so slowly for Millicent that she comments often that she is in a 'dream', a 'haze', a 'stupor' and that she carries out all her maternal and domestic duties automatically without really knowing how she does them. There is a great deal about the problems caused by rationing, which as a single woman was never a real problem for her before. The twins grow out of their clothes and she can't find new ones to buy in spite of having the coupons and feels embarrassed at dressing them in cast-offs, which don't fit properly, given to her by their Aunt Joan. She has never grown close to Joan, but when Joan leaves Blockley to go back to her own home (location not mentioned) she misses her and begins to wonder all over again if it would be safe for her also to return to her own house in London. A fierce raid at the beginning of October, in which 30 tons of bombs were said to have fallen on the City, dissuades her.*

*In November, she hears from Esther that Albert has been killed and Michael has been reported missing believed killed. She is appalled at how she accepts this awful news, with resignation and without real, agonising grief. Daphne comes for a weekend leave just before Christmas and is full of the wild times she continues to enjoy with her Dutch airman. In the whole year there has been no letter from Robert.*

\*　　　\*　　　\*

## 1 January 1944

What a dismal New Year. Dreary weather, the twins ill with measles, and a feeling of utter listlessness. Connie is worse than Toby who, though the spots are out, hasn't a fever and is quite lively. Connie's spots all run into each other and she burns with a temperature of 101°. Dr Grant came and said she was to be bathed with cold water

363

at regular intervals and kept in bed. There is no problem about that, she just lies there, very obedient. Last night she cried for Tilda, it was heart-breaking. She has never mentioned what she calls her 'gone' Mummy for months but last night I would not do. She feels the difference somehow, I suppose in how I hug her and hold her, which must be different from how Tilda did. Buried in Connie's memory must be a recollection of Tilda's arms round her and in her fever it rises to the forefront of her brain. And of course Tilda was a nurse and expert at nursing, and I am hopeless and do not know what I should be doing beyond the obvious things. I try so hard to stifle the awful boredom which comes over me and, even worse, that edge of resentment of which I am so ashamed about being in this situation. If I have to play Snakes and Ladders with Toby one more time I shall scream.

**1 February**

The twins' 7th birthday. What was it some Jesuit is supposed to have said, give me a child until he is seven and he is mine for life, something like that, meaning, I suppose, that the first seven years are the crucially formative ones. I look at Connie and Toby and speculate endlessly as to the effect of their parents' and their siblings' deaths and feel afraid of the consequences for them later. They both seem so content, both good-natured and bright, neither of them given to the sulks and tantrums I have seen other children indulge in. Their teacher said to me last week that they were a credit to me and for a moment I felt a pinprick of pride and pleasure until I caught myself preening and said to her no credit was due to me. All I've given them is stability, better than nothing but hardly compensation for what they have lost. This teacher, Miss Haddow, said to remember how young the twins are, and how children so young can adapt better than we realise so long as they have that very thing, stability. She asked if, after the war, we would stay in Blockley. I said no, that I had to think of myself too, and that there was too much about London that I missed, and besides I had a fiancé who would be coming home and his work was in London. She nodded and smiled, and said she was glad to hear I had a fiancé and that he was safe. I thought, as I came home, that she is of an age to have lost some man in the First World War and wished I had talked to her longer and more openly. So many women like Miss Haddow, and I could have been one of them, a spinster schoolteacher teaching in a village school, except I could never have stood it. Well, whatever happens, whether Robert comes back or not, whether we are ever able to marry or not, I will never have Miss Haddow's life. For some reason this cheers me up, though, considering Miss Haddow is the very picture of a happy woman, I don't know why.

**6 February**

I have to make Toby into a tree. He is very proud of being chosen to act the tree in a play they are to perform, written, I believe, by Miss Haddow. How I am to do this when getting hold of any kind of materials is impossible, I don't know but I must try.

Connie is to be a wood nymph—much easier.

## 7 February

Found some thick brown corrugated cardboard lying on the floor of the attic, as a sort of insulation I suppose. Dragged it down in one piece and by the time Toby had come home from school had cleaned the dust off. Wrapped it round him, making holes for arms and breathing spaces for his mouth and nose, and then wound ivy from the garden from top to bottom. He is thrilled.

\*     \*     \*

*Lots of entries of this kind follow, with Millicent rising to the occasion and clearly getting a great deal of fun out of this side of mothering. But there are some anxious moments too. Toby, whom she has thought of as sociable (as is Connie) and popular, writes a story, which Millicent clips into her diary: 'Once upon a time there was a boy called Roy. He wanted a girl to live with him but she died. He wanted someone to play with and he went out and met a boy and said will you play with me and the boy said no I have to go to Sunday School so he went on and met another boy and said will you play with me and he said no I have to go to my aunt's so he went on and met a baby boy and said will you play with me but the baby could not speak and then he died and the boy never got anyone to play with and he was sad. THE END.' This alarms Millicent so much that she goes to see Miss Haddow to ask if it means Toby is suffering from some kind of ostracism. The teacher*

366

*reassures her but she is still worried and watches Toby carefully. This kind of intensity runs through the diary for this period—she's always terrified she is failing the twins and is not the good mother Tilda was. She tries so hard, exerting herself to play every kind of game with them, from ludo and snakes-and-ladders inside to cricket and rounders in the garden. She takes them brambling and they all struggle to make jam (it doesn't set); she collects wild flowers with them, teaching them the proper as well as the common names; she helps them draw and paint and does all manner of educational as well as recreational things with them. All the time she wonders what sort of father Robert will make when he returns.*

\*　　　\*　　　\*

## 20 March

The most extraordinary thing: Doreen, Robert's wife, is dead. A letter from Robert's solicitor, the one who handled his attempt to get a divorce, arrived, saying he had had a communication from Mrs Rigg's solicitor informing him that she had died and that he would be obliged if Mr Rigg could be told, in agreement with an instruction in Mrs Rigg's will, made in 1938. That was of course the year Robert persuaded me to pretend I was pregnant. But it caused such fury to his wife that I cannot believe she arranged for him to be informed if she should die. It seems too kind and thoughtful. But maybe she imagined a child really had been born to us and this was consideration for its illegitimate state. It was the strangest feeling,

367

elation and excitement and having no one to tell except Robert and he is so far away and no letter will reach him for weeks, if at all. He is the one who cared so much about my reputation, as he called it, and he will be thrilled to be able to marry me. If I want to marry him. Why did I write that, how shocking, of course I do, especially with the twins to think of. I sat down and wrote to him before I went to collect the children from school and posted the letter on the way.

## 23 April

There was a raid the night before last on Montmartre, the church of Sacré Coeur was damaged, and I worry about Grace, whose new apartment was near there the last time she wrote. But that was nearly four years ago. Dear God, four years.

## 7 June

The allies have landed in Normandy. I gather this really is the beginning of the end of this war. If I were in London, I expect I would be more aware of its significance, this landing I mean, but we are so remote from everything here. We hear bombers going over sometimes, on their way to the Midlands and the industrial cities, and there is an American base somewhere near, but there are no bombs dropped here, everything is still green and lovely, and if it were not for rationing and news on the wireless and in the papers, and the lack of men around, we would not know there was a terrible war being fought. Sometimes I think the people here believe the Blitz is all exaggerated and I wish I could have taken them on just one of my ambulance runs to see for themselves the horrific devastation and the fires and injured people. They are so sheltered from what I know to be the reality.

**14 June**

Reports of flying bombs hitting London. I feel so anxious, in a selfish way, about my house. These 'doodlebugs' are random and could fall anywhere. I count so much on my house being there for me when the war ends. I think about it all the time, wandering in my mind from room to room and feeling relieved to be back in my own place. I think about how I can alter it to accommodate the twins, how I can give them each a room and let them decorate these rooms as they want. In fact, I've begun talking to them about it, preparing the way. I thought they might have a faint memory of being there but no, they don't, it was silly to think they would and brought up an unfortunate discussion about what had happened to their family home which Connie swore she did remember; and since she announced the kitchen lino was in black and white squares like a chess-board, I am bound to admit she may indeed be right. Anyway, I talk about us going back to London and both of them seem quite happy about this, though Toby worries about leaving his friends and whether he can take his rabbit.

## 26 August

Paris has been liberated. It was a shock to hear this not because of what it means about the war being closer to an end, but for what it means about Grace. I have tried so hard not to think about what has happened to her because it is too worrying and unbearable, but I have never understood how she could disappear so completely when Robert, much further away, got news to me. Where has she been? So long as Paris was occupied there was always an excuse for not having heard from her, not much of an excuse but still, but now there is none. If I don't hear within a week or so I will have to start some kind of investigation into her whereabouts. I've written to her last address over and over, but not recently. I do not think she can be there or somehow she would have contacted me. She doesn't know about Tilda, or our brothers. She doesn't know I am here, and why. So much that is awful she doesn't know.

## 28 August

The ban on visiting coastal towns has been lifted. In Blockley, this doesn't mean much, since we are so far from the sea in any direction but, the moment I heard of this, I thought of Brighton and how wonderful it would be to take the twins there some day and watch them paddle and how I'd love to feel the sea breezes, even the wild winds, and how exhilarating it would be. It was reported tonight on the wireless that all the trains had been packed with families rushing to other seaside places, where the beaches are open, and I so wished we had been with them. The twins think they have never seen the sea, though they have— they just don't remember, because they were too young—and they speculate very seriously about what it must be like and whether they will be brave enough to swim in it. But then it emerged that they *can't* swim and have never even been in a swimming-pool never mind the sea. I must put that right. I will teach them myself just as soon as I can find a public bath we can go to. There are so many treats like that which we can look forward to when the war is over. It is like a fairy tale, When The War Is Over, full of magical surprises, and I love telling it to them and promising them visits to the zoo and the cinema, and telling them how we will have chocolate and bananas and oranges. Perhaps I overdo it, but it bucks me up as well as them.

**4 September**

Twins back at school. I wish someone would give us an estimate as to how long it will be before a cease-fire. Daphne says the war is won and it is just a matter of time. But how much time, that is the point. I don't know if I should have let the twins begin a new term or not, was it wise when we will move to London the minute there is an official announcement? Daphne asks why I am in such a hurry, what's wrong with staying tucked up in the country? But that's what's wrong: the being tucked up when I don't want to be.

371

# 1 October

I don't know that my hand is steady enough to write clearly, but I want to order my thoughts and writing calms me. Today I was in the garden, lifting the last of the rhubarb, my mind running on whether I had enough sugar to make it palatable to the twins and at the same time fretting about shoes for both of them, and other mundane things. My mind, these days, is so dull, cluttered up with trivia, no spark of intelligent thought in it. It was cold and I had two jumpers on and a scarf, and was in Tilda's old wellington boots which are much too big for me so I slop about in them. I heard the dog next door bark, but it often barks for no reason—it's a silly yappy terrier, and I paid no attention. Then I heard a banging and thought it might be on my door but, if so, I wondered why whoever it was hadn't entered, because it is never locked. I listened and there was silence and I couldn't be bothered to go and check until I'd finished collecting the rhubarb and hacking off the big leaves and putting them on the compost heap. So I carried on, and then, with several thick sticks of rhubarb in my arms, I turned to go in. There was a woman and a child standing hand-in-hand watching me. I called out, Hello, and walked down the garden towards them, puzzled as to who they were. About a couple of yards from them, while they still stood there motionless, my skin began to tingle, all over me, a sort of alarm whipping round the surface of my body, and my mouth went perfectly dry, but still the stranger said nothing and neither did I, not being able to. Then the woman smiled and I saw tears running down her cheeks, such pale

372

cheeks, and I dropped the ridiculous rhubarb and held out my arms and she moved into them without speaking, lifting the child so that she too was embraced, so clumsily, so awkwardly. What I couldn't understand was the absence of *joy*. This was a reunion, longed for, looked for, and yet all I felt was first alarm and then a funny kind of dread. It was how Grace looked that did it. It *was* Grace, but not her, and the difference was shocking and dreadful. She looked so wretched, not just worn and thin and desperately aged, but cowed and defeated. Then there was the child, so unexpected, and her presence added to the unreality of the whole arrival. Well, we went inside and I put the kettle on, though felt more like a strong drink, and we sat down and stared at each other, both of us with questions in our eyes which neither of us wished to give words to. I said, Grace, you're safe, thank God, and she nodded and tried to smile, and put the child on her knee. This is my daughter Claudia, she said, she's nearly 4. I got up and found a biscuit and gave it to Claudia and said hello to her. She is very small and fragile with black, black hair in two little bunches either side of her narrow little, solemn face. I was thinking idiot thoughts, like her father must be dark-haired and brown-eyed, because Grace is blonde and blue-eyed. I got to London yesterday, Grace said, I went to Tilda's first. Her eyes filled with tears again, and she trembled so violently I had to put my arms round her again, and Claudia felt excluded and began to cry too and I had to pull myself together sharply before all three of us dissolved into howling. I went to Charles's hospital, Grace gasped, they told me there, they gave me this address. I forced some tea into her, and some bread, and at that moment the twins burst in, full of beans, noisy and laughing and shoving each other and brandishing models of ships they'd made out of boxes at school. Claudia was frightened and hid her face in her mother's coat, and they stood in front of Grace, frankly curious, waiting to be told who she was, but she stared at them, unable to speak, and I said, This is your Aunt Grace, my little sister, and your cousin Claudia, and they've just come from France, say hello. They said hello in unison, and waited again. Grace finally managed to find words, said how they'd grown, how big and strong they were, how lovely it was to see them, how she'd longed to see them. Things got a little easier after that, with Connie exerting herself to win over Claudia, and Toby going in search of his rabbit to amuse her.

We all ate together, just mince and potatoes and a great many onions and carrots to eke the meat out. Claudia ate none of it, and Grace very little. She said she was too excited and too exhausted to eat. So she has gone to bed with Claudia, and is at this minute sound asleep, because I have just checked, and I know nothing yet about where she has been all this time or what has happened to her. I dread hearing what I am sure will be the saddest of stories. I won't ask her. I will wait, I will be patient, and she can tell me in her own good time, when she is rested and recovered. She has only a small bag with her and it seems to have only things for Claudia in it. Her own clothes are shabby, the biggest give-away of all. Never, never has the elegant Grace been shabby.

## 2 October

Hard to get the twins to go to school but I insisted. Grace, and Claudia too, need peace and quiet. They slept twelve solid hours and looked when they woke as if they could do with another twelve. I had some fresh eggs, a great prize, just got them yesterday morning, and I scrambled them, four of them, and Grace ate nearly all of it, to my immense satisfaction. Good girl, I said, and she smiled and said I sounded like Mother and I said I felt like her. Claudia couldn't be persuaded to have any, though. She ate only some of the twins' Weetabix and a little bit of toast, but she drank quite a lot of milk so I didn't fuss. It was a nice morning so we had a short walk, not far, just along the brook and back. Grace said how pretty and peaceful everything was, as if there was no war and never had been, and I told her about my ambulance career and being a WAAF. She asked after the family and I had to tell her about Alfred and Albert and Michael, and this took a long time, with so much background to fill in.

Claudia slept again when we got back and I thought Grace might start to enlighten me as I made soup for lunch, but she just went on asking more questions and we got on to Robert and I had to fill her in about the camp and then about Doreen dying, and then we ate and she yawned and said she thought she would have a nap and by the time she woke up the twins were home and there was no privacy to talk even if she had wanted to. As soon as supper was over, she went to bed again with Claudia and the twins. How long will this go on? Ought I to prompt her? Is what she has to tell

375

me so awful or so painful that she needs encouragement to confess it? I thought at first Claudia's father must be French, but now it begins to enter my head that this may not be the case. He may be German.

## 3 October

Connie came into my room this morning and whispered that Aunt Grace was crying. I got up and followed her into the tiny room where Grace and Claudia were sleeping and saw that she was right, Grace was lying there weeping, the bed shaking with the force of her sobs. I said, Grace, Grace, darling, what is it, sssh, sssh, while Connie stood by me watching. I sat down on the edge of the bed and held her face in my hands but the dreadful sobs continued and the tears flowed so thick and fast that the neck of her nightdress was soaked. I was so aware of Connie watching and what this sight would do to her, and even more aware of Claudia, lying next to her mother, still, mercifully, half asleep but her eyes beginning to open. I told Connie to go and get a glass of water and she trotted away, and then I found a handkerchief in my dressing-gown pocket and began wiping Grace's face, all the time telling her that she was safe, she was home, there was nothing to fear. The sobbing began to quieten though the tears still came, and when Connie returned, carrying a glass so full of water it was slopping everywhere, I raised Grace's head and put the glass to her lips and got her to swallow a little though most of it spilled onto the bedcover so that really, what with her own tears and the water she was practically lying in a swamp. I went on trying to dry her face and eventually the tears dried to a trickle and though she opened her eyes once and stared at me, she then went back to sleep. I was weak with relief. Claudia snuggled up against her mother, thumb in mouth, and slept on. I took Connie's hand and we tip-toed out and she came into bed with me. She wanted to know, of course, why Grace was crying and I told her she was having a nightmare, probably accurate enough, and Connie said she had nightmares too and seemed satisfied. She dozed off, but by this time it was half past six and there was no point in my trying to go back to sleep, and I didn't want to, so I got up and made tea and tried to think what to do. All the time I was listening for Grace, but there was no sound till well after the twins were off to school. Then she emerged, wrapped in a blanket, shivering and saying she was so cold and thirsty. She drank some tea and I asked if she felt ill and would she like some aspirin and she said yes, and that she would take two aspirin and if I had a hot water bottle she'd like it filled and she'd go back to bed. When I pointed out that her nightdress was wet round the neck, she felt it and seemed surprised. I told her she'd been crying, that it was wet with her own tears. Then I waited, giving her the opportunity to tell me why she'd been weeping, or to say it was because she was having a bad dream, but all she said was sorry, sorry. Then she took the hot-water bottle and went back to bed and stayed there till lunch-time. I pottered about, making yet more soup, listening for movement all the time and thinking that Claudia couldn't possibly still be asleep. I crept up the stairs at midday and peeped into Grace's room. She was asleep but Claudia was not. Her little eyes were wide open and she lay on her back, her right hand holding her mother's left hand on top of the bedcover. I smiled at her but she didn't move a muscle of her face, just tightened her grip and Grace moved in her sleep in response to it. So I left them. An hour or so later, when I'd been in the garden getting a cabbage, Grace came down, dressed, carrying Claudia, still in pyjamas. We had the soup. I wondered about a walk, when Claudia was dressed, maybe to meet the twins out of school, but Grace shook her head and said she hadn't the energy. I'd sorted out some of the twins' old toys and showed them to Claudia, tempting her to play with them but, though she allowed me to put a teddy bear into her arms and cuddled it in a half-hearted sort of way, she wouldn't examine the contents of the open toy box. The afternoon passed, the twins came home, we ate, I read stories aloud to the children, they went to bed, and I waited again for Grace to begin her story. But she didn't, she hasn't.

**10 October**

A whole week of these terrible crying fits, always in the early hours of the morning, about four o'clock or so, and the same pattern of violent sobbing fading away into an exhausted sleep. I make sure Connie's and Toby's door is firmly shut and so is Grace's and when I get up to go in to her I check Connie has not been disturbed. It can't go on. I said so to Grace this morning, I said that if perhaps she talked to me about what had happened maybe

378

she would feel better and the nightmares would stop. She shook her head and because I was feeling tired myself and worried I said that at least if she talked to me I'd understand more. She just shuddered and said what she always says, sorry, sorry. Today I tried another tack. I said if she wouldn't talk about the past we had to talk about the future and what she was going to do. She looked stricken and said, You mean I have to leave? and I said no, of course not but, if she was going to stay, there were things to do, necessary things, like getting her and Claudia ration books, and thinking about clothes because neither she nor her daughter were equipped to face winter. Practical things like that. In fact, I'm not sure how I will get her registered with a ration book, or where we will find a warm coat and boots for each of them. She seems to be expecting me to take charge, and I will, and I am desperately sorry for her, but she must co-operate a little or I can't do it.

**11 October**

This is new. Tears now during the day, sometimes most of the day. I will have to get the doctor to come. I said that to her today and then regretted it because the sobbing became worse. But I will have to. God knows what this wordless distress is doing to her own little girl, who is the saddest child I have ever seen. And the effect on the twins, especially Connie, is serious. They don't rush in from school as they used to but instead peer round the door anxiously, afraid they'll see this strange aunt of theirs crying. Toby asked today when Aunt Grace

379

was going home. I said I didn't know, not daring to admit this was probably her home now.

## 12 October

I wish the doctor was a woman, and young. Dr Grant is very nice, and has always been good with the twins, but somehow I feel Grace needs a woman doctor. Still, a doctor is a doctor and there is no choice. I have to have a medical opinion, some help with this crying. I keep thinking of George and what he was like when he came back from the war and how long it was before ever he got proper treatment. Grace at least needs something to calm her, to settle her nerves.

## 13 October

Dr Grant came today. I'd been to see him and explained the problem and he was very kind and understanding and said he'd just pop in, as if he were a friend, and run his eye over my sister. By great good fortune, or at least that's what I thought, he came while Grace was in the middle of one of her crying fits, sitting at the kitchen table supposedly peeling potatoes for me, her tears blinding her and making her careless with the knife so that she was cutting great thick wodges of skin off them wasting half of each potato. She hardly heard or saw Dr Grant sit opposite her though he said good morning and asked how she was feeling. She made no objection when he felt her pulse. After a few minutes of looking at her, he got out his prescription pad and wrote something down and then took some tablets out of his bag and asked for a glass of water and gave them to her. Claudia was watching him all the time, clinging to her mother's leg, half under the table. Dr Grant tried to play peekaboo with her, but she wouldn't respond. I went with him to the gate, and he looked worried and said Grace was undoubtedly in the middle of a breakdown and that he wasn't sure it could be managed at home even with medication and that she really needed to be hospitalised, but that in the present circumstances he wasn't at all sure he would be able to find a suitable place for her. He said it was a lot for me to cope with and did I have a relative I could call on to help and I said not really, though I have a brother and sister-in-law who have a farm and he said a farm would be a good place for Grace to be if nursing care there could be arranged, but he repeated that it might come to hospitalisation. My sister, he said, had clearly suffered terribly and the fact that she was unwilling or unable to talk about it, even to me, meant she had not begun to recover. It's not just the soldiers who have suffered injury in this war, he said, as he left.

## 21 October

Daphne arrived, quite without warning, and I have never been so glad to see her in my life. She took one look at Grace and said, Good God, whatever has happened to you? and it was so direct and honest it seemed to startle Grace, who actually said, Everything, everything has happened, every

381

terrible thing you can name. And I held my breath, hoping she was about to start talking but instead, as usual, she began weeping and then rushed upstairs, followed by Claudia, who never lets her mother out of her sight. Daphne raised her eyebrows at me, but I shrugged, and shook my head, and sighed and told her this had been going on ever since Grace arrived nearly three weeks ago. I told her I'd called the doctor and he'd prescribed tranquillisers and that the night-time sobbing had stopped but there are still outbursts in the day and that I am no nearer knowing what has happened. Daphne smoked and looked thoughtful and asked if I wanted to know what her guess would be. It was the same as mine. Daphne said only time and tender loving care would help poor Grace recover and I said I knew that but didn't know if I was up to providing it. I have to look after Grace and Claudia but it isn't the same as having to look after the twins, the obligation isn't the same, and I have to think about the consequences for them too.

\*       \*       \*

*Life is tough for Millicent for the next eight months and there is a great deal of tension displayed in the diary. She reflects often that she hadn't known how lucky she was in the previous year when she had had nothing more serious than feeling detached and bored to complain about, nothing more trying than the domestic and maternal duties she was bound by. Now, at the end of 1944 and until the end of the war in 1945, she is driven frantic coping with Grace who goes from those desperate bouts of sobbing to total inertia. She won't get up, won't wash, won't eat and won't attend to her child. Dr Grant finds a place for her in a mental hospital which is fifty miles away, near Oxford, but when Millicent goes to arrange for Grace's transfer she is so appalled by the conditions there she cancels it and keeps her sister at home. The doctor helps by finding a nurse who will come daily, and gradually Grace improves. But that still leaves the problem of Claudia who, copying her mother, and wanting always to be with her, comes near to starving herself and is entirely mute. Millicent records that the twins, from being happy delightful children, are becoming aggressive and discontented. They say they hate Grace and hate Claudia. Millicent is bitter that having helped the twins survive their own tragedy she can now do little to protect them from the effects of someone else's trauma. But she hangs on grimly, her sights set firmly on the ending of the war, her return to London and the return of Robert (from whom, in August, she does receive an official postcard saying his health is 'usual'), when she convinces herself everything will sort itself out.*

*The frustrating thing is that never, in all these months, is it revealed what happened to Grace or who Claudia's father was. Grace, when on the way to recovering at last, doesn't explain and Millicent stops expecting her to. It seems extraordinary that she didn't insist on an explanation, but if she did, and if she was given one, it is not in her diary.*

*But I think it is almost certain that Grace did have a German protector, who fathered Claudia, though whether this was a liaison of choice or whether she was coerced into it, is impossible to tell. A few clues to what happened emerge long afterwards, but at this point Millicent knows nothing, except that her sister has obviously suffered terribly and is greatly changed in appearance. It was not surprising, though, that Grace was so thin and worn because ever since 1943 food had been very scarce in Paris. Half to three quarters of all French produce was reckoned by then to have been siphoned off to Germany, and malnutrition among the population in Paris was inevitable. Rationing was strictly applied, but even the miserable rations were difficult to obtain. Not even bread could be relied upon, and though having Claudia would have entitled Grace to more generous amounts of staples like milk and eggs it is difficult to see how, being English, she could obtain a ration card—making it even more likely, of course, that at least at first she very probably had a German protector.*

\* \* \*

**23 April 1945**

The blackout has ended, not that it was taken very seriously here. All the same, removing the thick black linings Tilda had fixed to the back of the shutters felt very significant. Became quite carried away, turning it into a metaphor for the removal of all that is black in my own life. Didn't throw the cloth away though. The wartime habit of thinking every little thing may come in useful will not leave me easily.

**7 May**

The war is over. I wept. Grace, who has cried

enough tears over the last few months to fill an ocean did not. She looked at me, as I stood transfixed in front of the wireless, tears streaming down my cheeks, and asked why I was crying. I felt so angry with her, and said sarcastically that I couldn't think why but I wondered, I just wondered, if perhaps it might be because a war that had turned my life upside down and caused the death of a sister and two brothers, probably three, and the imprisonment of a lover, might possibly, just possibly be the reason for my distress, a natural reaction to news that was joyful but loaded with memories of deaths. She stared at me, astonished. My outburst over, I said we must start making plans. Plans? said Grace, alarmed. I repeated plans, very firmly. I said I would let the twins finish their last term with Miss Haddow and then, at the end of July, I would return to London with them and settle in before the school year began again. So, Grace, I said, you have a choice. You can come with us, or you can stay here, you can have this cottage, the rent isn't much and you can afford it, I'm sure. There was silence, but then there often is when I suggest things that have never occurred to her. I don't, of course, know anything about Grace's financial situation but I do know what Mother left her and I don't think she can have spent it all, and she inherited as many shares as the rest of us did. Then there is the flat she lived in, but whether she bought or rented it I can't remember. Tilda would know. Oh, I miss Tilda so very much. It is when she won't discuss practical issues that Grace exasperates me most. She will *have* to apply herself to these matters, I can't make these decisions for her. I wonder if she even knows how much she has in the bank. I've never asked her for a penny and she's never offered one, seeming to imagine food costs nothing and is hers by right. Not that I begrudge her it, I can afford it, but it is the assumption that I can and will that offends me. This war has made me a selfish person, counting the cost of everything all the time.

**8 May**

There was a party in the village today. I had no inclination to go, but the twins were desperate to join in the fun and so I went and really it was more enjoyable than I could have imagined. All very makeshift and humble, with tables the length of the street, all higgledy-piggledy, and flags strewn from house to house, and an impromptu band consisting of nothing more than an accordion, a drum and some cymbals but what a noise. Everyone contributed food for the children (and by the look of the icing on the buns and cakes a lot of sugar had been mysteriously hoarded) and there was lemonade and big urns of tea, and someone had donated Christmas crackers and hats. Only the weather let us down, a bit grey and drizzly, though it brightened up later. Grace and Claudia came too, which surprised me, and I hadn't tried to push them. Claudia even ate a bun, attracted, no doubt, by the violent pink of its icing. Miss Haddow was there, and asked if I would be going back to London soon, and I said yes, in July. It is odd and a bit sad that with the exception of Miss Haddow there is no one in this village with whom I have made even a tentative friendship. I had more friends the short time I was in the WAAF. Well, what I mean is I chatted to more people and got to know them. I feel as if I've been living down a mine here.

## 9 May

Perhaps predictably I felt utterly depressed today. So much to see to and a lack of energy to act. I really need to go to London and look at my house before returning, but it can't be managed. I can't leave the twins or Grace, and taking them with me would be too exhausting and defeat the purpose. But it is not just feeling daunted by thoughts of the move, it's more the realisation that the war in Europe may be over but the war in the Far East isn't, and Robert is still there. No scrap of communication from him for so long now except for that official postcard with its hideous Imperial Japanese Army stamp. I've repressed all anxiety for ages because of struggling to keep my head over Grace: I knew I couldn't afford to think about why I hadn't heard from Robert. It needn't be significant, this lack of any news. I know it was a miracle anything ever reached here from that camp, and things will be much worse now. But I am full of forebodings, which I try to tell myself are merely the result of weariness and the draining effect of having Grace and Claudia round my neck. It's become so impossible to believe myself in love any more, never mind what I told Daphne, and yet I so desperately want to be. I strain and strain to remember how it was before the war. It is like looking at a photograph which is proof in a way of happiness having existed but it is flat and has no life and has to be taken on trust. Oh, that is badly put. I mean, I can't project what I know to have existed in the past into the future. Not much better put, but nearer. All faith has gone. And I've changed, as he will have done, especially as he will have done.

## 1 June

How old and worn I look. Today was a beautiful sunny day and I felt more optimistic and cheerful than I have done recently, and thought I would get out of these dreary clothes I've been living in for months and make an effort. So I dug out what used to be my favourite blue dress, or rather Robert's favourite, and I put it on, after I'd had a bath and washed my hair, and I looked awful. My neck has gone scrawny. There's no denying it, the mirror tells all. My neck is scrawny and I won't be able to wear a dress with a deep v-neckline like the blue one, and my complexion pasty and I've lost so much weight I look like a stick. My hair used to be my crowning glory indeed, but it has grown long and become dull and lost its spring and hangs lank and hideous and I want to shave it all off, which I would, but I'd look even worse bald. I got back into my old WAAF skirt and pulled on a jumper and decided not to look in any more mirrors.

## 18 June

Big surprise. Today, the subject not having been

mentioned again, Grace informed me that she and Claudia would like to stay in this cottage. I could have cheered, but instead asked if she was sure, wouldn't she be lonely, would she be able to manage, was she well enough, and so on. She said she felt safe here, and the village people were kind, and she liked Dr Grant, and most of all she didn't want to uproot Claudia again, not so soon. She has money in the bank, I was right about that, she's going to buy a sewing machine if she can find one and start sewing. This is all such good news, but I felt I had to conceal my relief that she would not be coming to London, or not yet. I am not sure how fit or strong she really is. She *looks* better, no longer cries, or at least doesn't have crying fits, but she is still nowhere near being the Grace of before the war. I will have to get Dr Grant to promise to alert me if anything goes wrong after I've returned to London. I can't think, though, that this village is the place for a fully recovered Grace any more than it is for me.

**15 July**

The twins' last week at school. We've begun packing. It helps to have Grace and Claudia staying on because we can leave some things and collect them later. I'm leaving the car too. Well, it was Tilda's and Charles's car, and, once Grace learns how to drive, she can use it. We will go to London by train and I will buy a car, but not immediately. Better to wait for Robert and let him choose, and meanwhile I can drive his old thing if it is still there and working. So many things to check up on. I

389

wonder about work, about whether I could go back
to my old job part-time, but I'll have to have the
twins settled first. They are wildly excited, too
excited, but then so am I. England will be full of
people returning home and expecting so much, but
at least I know what has happened to London, what
it looks like, how hard it will be to adapt to all the
devastation. Daphne is there already, she was in
Piccadilly on VE night having a riotous time and
now she's almost sorry the war is over and her fun
at an end. No two experiences could be more
different than hers and mine.

**19 July**

Twins' last day at school. Many tears saying
goodbye to Miss Haddow. She had a present for
them both, a book each, and she made them
promise to write and said all the children they
know will write back together. Claudia starts in the
first standard in September which will keep the
connection going. It was a surprise when Grace
said she was going to be 5 in October. She doesn't
look 5, or even 4. Thank God she's begun talking at
last, not much but enough to prove she isn't a
mute. Rather late in the day, Connie is becoming
quite fond of her. She reads to her and Claudia
listens very carefully and seems to enjoy the stories.

**20 July**

Last day in Blockley. Couldn't sleep last night, not
so much with thinking about going to London as

because I was remembering coming here and going over the bleak years since, only just over two but they feel like a century, they feel as if they will dominate my whole life. What I most want is to forget them and yet nothing could be less likely. We had a picnic, went to where the children can splash about in the brook and spent most of the day there, Grace and I lolling on the grass watching them. It was idyllic, the sky blue, the sun hot, the breeze just faint enough to keep us cool in spite of it. Grace looked pretty for the first time since she came here, her hair catching the sun and bringing out all the gold in it. She had a dress on, a floral dress which she'd sewed by hand herself, made out of a length of curtain material she got at the jumble sale, and I saw she'd filled out a little, that her arms and legs are not so sticklike. But I also saw something else. The dress has cap sleeves and just under the cap bit on her left arm there are some scars, quite deep-looking ugly holes, like burns, but hollow, little pitted craters where the skin looks rough. I thought about asking what they were, it would have been natural to, but something held me back. She seemed so content, lying stretched out beside me, her arms behind her head, her eyes half closed, watching Claudia as she let the twins take her, each holding a hand, into the water where it is shallow. She kept giving little murmurs of contentment and pleasure, said what a perfect spot it was, and commenting on how peaceful and lovely everything seemed. It was true, the scene was delightful, the children playing, the river glittering, the scent from honeysuckle in the hedge behind us intoxicating, a few swifts swooping over our head, and yet I couldn't enjoy it as much as Grace did, I

391

couldn't block out the wider world and what had gone on there, what is still going on. I feel everything is spoiled for ever, which is a very pessimistic outlook and I try to overcome it. Grace asked me if I ever thought of Mother, and I said of course I did, and of Father and Tilda and Alfred and Albert, and Michael. I just think of Mother, Grace said, and her voice was so choked I looked over at her and saw the tears and was afraid of them, but they were contained quickly, and she just said, I miss her but in a way I'm glad she died before the war, think of how she would have suffered. I took her hand and squeezed it. Grace is not even 30 yet, Mother's baby. A curlew began crying, far away, so mournful, so beautiful, and then the children ran up the bank, laughing and shrieking and demanding food, and even Claudia joined in the merriment. For a moment, I wondered why I was leaving this and going to dirty, bomb-damaged, tired old London.

## 21 July

Mr Waring took us to the station. We made our farewells to Grace and Claudia at the cottage, both Grace and I thinking it would be too emotional having to wave goodbye at the station and the train might frighten Claudia. Of course we made much of this not being goodbye but merely *au revoir*—the twins like saying that—and made plans to meet in a few weeks' time before the schools start. Then we were off, laden with cases, though I'd tried so hard to keep everything to a minimum but, with Mr Waring to help us onto the train at this end and

Daphne promising to meet us at the other, we managed. The journey felt quite short, but that was because I was comparing it with wartime travelling. The twins loved it, especially Toby, sitting bolt upright and fascinated by everything they could see out of the windows, but as we approached London they began to look anxious. It was not that we passed any terrible sights, but that everything looked so grey and grim with those dreary rows of houses backing onto the railway line, and in the background vistas of roofs and chimneys and that numbing sense of anonymity. They are used to green fields and pretty individual cottages and space and knowing exactly where they are and where everything belongs. Paddington scared them. The excitement vanished and was replaced by apprehension, clearly visible in their little faces, and I had to keep reassuring them that soon we would be out of all this noise. Thank God Daphne was there, she'd kept her word, even though she is off to Paris with her GI tomorrow, and they brightened as they saw her running down the platform, arms wide open, ready for a big hug. The real test, though, was arriving home, my home so meaningful to me but not to them. They walked through the door very hesitantly, then peered into the rooms nervously, and seemed reluctant to go upstairs whereas I was rushing around thrilled to recognise my furniture and belongings. When they hadn't come down after a good while, I went up to them and found them sitting hand-in-hand at the top of the stairs, pale-faced and on the edge of tears. We don't know where to go, Connie said. I laughed and said they could each choose a room, there were three bedrooms and they'd know which one was mine because it had a bigger bed than the others. What I hadn't taken into consideration was that because the cottage had been so small my house now seemed vast and they were intimidated by it and felt lost. I took them round the bedrooms and they asked to be together and we moved a bed into the back top room where they could see the garden and in the distance, over the rooftops, the trees of the park. It was for them, though, a disappointing arrival. They are asleep now, and tomorrow I can start winning them over, I hope.

## 2 August

So much to do, even if so much already done. At least keeping the twins busy has stopped them feeling displaced, or I think it has. They've picked up the charge London gives and responded to it and enjoy best being out and about, eager to see what they've never seen before. They love the buses, of course, especially riding on the top and, though frightened of the Underground at first, now it thrills them to be rushing under all the traffic. I reminded them that they *were* Londoners and had been in the Underground before. I don't know if it's a good idea to remind them of a previous life and so, I suppose, make them remember how it ended. Should I take them to see where they once lived? It is not as though Tilda and Charles and their sister and brother died there, and the house, from the outside anyway, will be exactly the same. It hasn't even been sold yet, though it's been on the market long enough. Suddenly it occurs to me that we could go and live there if I wanted to. I own the house, or rather I do until the twins are 21, I think. I must go and discuss this with the solicitor when I can find the time, but only to get things straight, not that I really want to live there. I much prefer my house. But it's true that when Robert returns the Edis Street house would be better because it is a little bigger than mine. I give thanks daily that I have no money worries and that I have my own house.

## 7 August

A bomb has been dropped somewhere on Japan, an enormously powerful atomic bomb which has wiped out a city and its population. This is being justified on the grounds of forcing Japan to surrender. Well, I want them to surrender and the war to be over and Robert to come home, but I don't want a city annihilated. I wonder how the city was chosen for this awful fate?

## 9 August

Another atomic bomb dropped on Japan today. Was there really no other way? I wish I had someone to discuss it with, I wish Daphne was back, but I haven't talked to another adult since we left Blockley, not properly. Toby asked if the animals would have been killed too, even the puppies and kittens, and I said yes, I imagined so. He'd heard the wireless giving the details and was fascinated, wanting to know all kinds of things I couldn't answer. Who can I ask? Maybe *The Times*

395

will have the answers. I must buy *The Times* and read it carefully and equip myself to educate Toby and in the process educate myself.

## 14 August

Japan has surrendered. No victory parties here, none of the euphoria of VE Day. I feel strange, excited but slightly sick, with I don't know what, some feeling of apprehension. I wonder how long it will take for the prisoners to be brought home. I know there are thousands of them, and most of them probably in a pitiful state physically. What will the authorities do, try to improve their condition first before the long voyage back or get them here as soon as possible? Will they be given the means to contact relatives immediately, to say they have survived? I could contact the Red Cross, or Robert's regimental HQ, I suppose.

\*       \*       \*

*This is what Millicent does, and is informed that not all the camps have had their PoWs listed thoroughly and there is a great deal of confusion as yet. She is told to call back in three days, by which time the names of all survivors should be available. But Robert's name is not on any list for Changi Prison. She is told not to give up hope, because he would probably have been moved between camps and, until all the camp lists are available, nothing was certain. It is also reassuring that his name is not on any list of the known dead either. So she waits, her days occupied with the twins, and still, after three more weeks, there is no news of Robert. By then, a complete list of survivors has been collated and hope is fading. His regiment is sympathetic and says that when the remnants of it have returned home, information will be sought and Robert's fate discovered. One day, in the middle of the twins' second week at their new school, when Millicent returns at 9.30 a.m. from taking them there, there is a man standing on her doorstep.*

## 10 September 1945

Hard, as it always is when something dreadful has happened, to know where to start, or whether to start at all. What's the point? This could be the last time I ever write my diary: it has gone on long enough cataloguing my very humdrum existence and is not the comfort it once was. But I have thought that before and held on for some odd reason and it has helped somehow, so for the time being I am turning to these pages, if just from force of habit.

So, a man was standing on my doorstep this morning, a man who from the back and from a distance was roughly the same build as Robert, or how I remembered him. My heart started to race, my mouth to go dry, but before I'd made a fool of myself the man turned and I saw it was a stranger. Are you looking for me? I said, and he asked if I was Millicent, and I said yes, come inside. I knew of course what he was bound to tell me and did not want to hear it on the doorstep. He followed me in very unhappily and when I invited him to make himself comfortable and offered him tea, he declined to do either. He was so thin, his shabby blue suit hanging on him to the point of the trousers looking almost as though there were no legs in them, and his skin was a dull sepia colour with sores across his forehead and on his neck. I felt so sorry for him. You've been in Changi Prison, haven't you? I said, to help him out. He nodded. Well, I said, you must have been sent to tell me about Robert, so if you don't mind I'd like you to get it over quickly. His silence was beginning to get on my nerves, but still he hesitated and kept swallowing and didn't seem to be able to get any words out. I'm sure he thought I was a cold bitch, standing there waiting, how could he possibly know what I was feeling. Tears might have made it easier for him, my tears. When he began to tell me the whole story he sort of slumped onto a chair and shaded his eyes with his hand and spoke in a monotone, as though he'd rehearsed what he had to say over and over, which he probably had. Robert hadn't died of dysentery or cholera, or malaria. *He'd been executed. Beheaded.* For insulting the Emperor. He was made an example of, when he refused to applaud the beheading of a Chinese woman who was being executed for stealing food. He had tried to wrestle the sword from the Japanese soldier's hands. The man telling me this was shaking as he relived it and I was shaking myself as I heard and visualised it. I thought you should know the truth, he croaked, whatever the pain. I'm sorry. He said he hadn't had it in him to be a hero like Robert, survival was all— he had a wife and family and wanted to return to them at any cost. I got up, my legs feeling so weak I hardly trusted them to get across the room, but they did, and I found some whisky and poured the man a glass; but he hardly touched it, saying his stomach couldn't take much at the moment. I wanted him to go, that was all I wanted, for him to disappear, but he was so weak and sat on as though he hadn't the energy to move and he seemed to want some response from me which hadn't been forthcoming. He rambled on—I only heard bits of it, my thoughts far away—all about Robert and how strong he had been and how the others had looked up to him and he'd been a cut above them and how furious he was that the army had been trapped in Singapore. He said Robert swore that the leaders had miscalculated and it was all the fault of Churchill and higher command that the city fell, but, surely, Robert could never have said that, never have blamed Churchill. The man said he wasn't clever like Robert and didn't know if what he said was true or not. He asked if there was anything I wanted to know. There wasn't, but I felt I had to give him the chance to be helpful, so I asked the date Robert died. He told me, and the time, and already I've forgotten it. Then at last he struggled out of the chair and said again he was sorry and held out his hand. I took it. It was a claw, all bone. He told me his name, and I've forgotten that too, something beginning with D. I thought he seemed such an unlikely friend for Robert, but then the army makes unlikely men into friends. I wonder what kind of life he's come back to. How can I wonder such a thing when I have just been told my lover, my husband-to-be, doesn't exist any more. My head is full of odd, unconnected musings swirling around, and behind them this image of what the messenger saw, all quite vivid but without sound or feeling, like a silent film. The twins are asleep. I've just looked in on them. Sweetly asleep. How lucky I haven't told them much about Robert at all. I keep wondering if this man is trustworthy, was Robert really beheaded, but no one would make that up. It is just that I cannot credit it.

\*　　　\*　　　\*

*The story Millicent was told was so horrific that it was only natural that she should half-doubt its truth, but she does later receive a full account of what the messenger had described. The Japanese did indeed execute prisoners of war in this barbaric manner and there are even photographs of such beheadings. The crime Robert was killed for, insulting the Emperor, was given as the justification in almost all cases even when the alleged insult was impossible to prove. As for Robert's reported fury with Churchill—whom Millicent, like most of the British population, revered—this was shared by many of those trapped in Singapore. It was widely believed by the army there that Churchill had known the time of the Japanese attack and had withheld this information. The official records will not be available until 2025, but Millicent had little interest, in any case, in knowing the true facts. Robert had died in a hideous way and she struggled to suppress the terrible images which haunted her. Yet at the same time, because it had taken so long for her to hear what had happened, and because it had happened so far away, the feeling of disbelief persisted and, she afterwards concluded, acted as a barrier to overwhelming distress. And, of course, she had to remain strong for the sake of the twins. Her determination to do so runs through her diary for the rest of that year and shows her at her most admirable.*

*The entries after this exceptionally long one become very short and matter-of-fact, right up to New Year's Day 1946, so Millicent may well have been seriously considering, as she said, discontinuing her diary for good, but, as ever, she keeps going, mentioning once that she now has a new reason for doing so: a duty to record things for the twins. This changes what she chooses to write more than might have been expected, and perhaps more than she ever realised. Her subject-matter becomes what the twins say and do and she is entirely taken up with worrying about them. This results in lots of anecdotes which at the time they were written down may have seemed amusing to her but which now don't survive the telling. Toby longs for a toy gun, which she refuses to give him, but he swaps a pile of comics for an old imitation revolver from which he shoots tiny pebbles, breaking a window on one occasion—that kind of thing takes a lot of space in the diary. There are descriptions of walks (she learns to call them 'hikes', to make them sound more exciting) and visits to the zoo and attempts at brass-rubbing and all the other pastimes she tries to arouse the children's interest in. When they are 8, she manages to procure second-hand bikes for them, which she cleans and paints herself, and then there are accounts of bike rides in Regent's Park. They yearn for a pet and she agonises over whether to allow them the dog they really want, but settles for a hamster and a guinea pig. Camps are made in the garden, sales held at the garden gate, fancy dress costumes made for parties. Millicent wears herself out straining to be both mother and father and in doing so the focus upon herself is lost. Daphne points this out to her—that she is losing her own identity—but she denies it. Though gradually, in 1946, she begins to fret about herself.*

## 1 January 1946

The twins slept late today, result of course of letting them stay up to see the New Year in. We went to Trafalgar Square, against my better judgement, but persuaded by Daphne and their passionate pleadings. I was worried that we might get separated in the crush, but Daphne said, as she so often has said, that I sounded like an old woman and had no sense of adventure and made me ashamed of myself, so we went and it was fun and nothing untoward happened except Connie lost one of her new gloves. Daphne left us on the stroke of midnight, with kisses first all round, and then off to join her fellow, her GI, who wants her to marry him. He is so much younger than her, but then, as she tells me, she is 'young at heart'. Infantile sometimes, in my opinion. He's off to Panama soon and she is supposed to be going to join him. We will see. I've told her that she knows nothing about this man really, to which in true Daphne fashion she said she didn't need to know anything except that he is a wonderful lover and when I said that is not the most important thing in the world there were more accusations of my being an old woman. Well, I am. There is no denying it. Forty-five this year and feeling every year of it in spirits. Today, when I caught sight of myself reflected in a shop window, I was surprised and relieved that I didn't look as dreary as I feel. The costume Daphne gave me is flattering, this belted style suits me, and so does the soft perm she persuaded me to have—it's given some body to my hair without crimping it, and I like the way the hairdresser has pulled it up above each ear with combs. I must keep it like this and find some prettier combs, perhaps tortoiseshell. I can't hope to match Daphne's glamour—she looks like a film star in her silver fox fur coat and that hat with the dotted veil—but at least I can try to look neat and fresh, and not dowdy, as I'd grown to look in Blockley. I don't want the twins to be ashamed of me and for my appearance to be an embarrassment. My skin, I'm pleased to realise, is better than Daphne's, always was. There, a bit of pride! Robert always used to say that my skin was as smooth and flawless as the most perfect of pearls. I don't know about that, but I am healthy and physically young, which even Daphne admits, and the twins keep me young in mind. There is a lot to be thankful for. How prim that sounds. Later today, Connie asked if I was sad and I quickly replied no, just tired, and she accepted that. Connie watches me carefully, I realise, and worries if I seem downcast. I don't want her to have to do that, she's too young to take on the burden of worrying about an adult, so I must make more of an effort to smile and be brisk, and I must not go off into daydreams about times that will never come again. And I must interest myself in the world around me and not let myself get so withdrawn. I do love Connie, and Toby, and don't want them to suffer from my feeling that an important part of life is over for me.

404

## 3 January

Grace and Claudia arrive tomorrow for the last weekend of the holidays. I'm surprised Grace has found the energy never mind the desire to come, braving the travelling and the confusion of London with Claudia, but I take it as a sign that she is much better. The twins don't seem particularly interested in this visit, Toby going so far as to ask who Claudia was, which earned him a scornful kick from Connie. It's odd the way Toby seems determined to remember nothing about Blockley, pretending ignorance at the most unforgettable things. It annoys his sister, who remembers in minute detail, right down to the names of various cats and dogs in the village.

## 8 January

Twins back at school, Grace and Claudia back to Blockley, and myself back to an empty house and deeply grateful for it. Place a shambles, but tidying and cleaning can wait. Sat most of the schoolday reading an Evelyn Waugh novel, *Brideshead Revisited*—heaven to be removed from the actual world I live in. And yet the weekend was enjoyable, a great success, and it was wonderful to see Grace so restored and Claudia smiling and talking, if still shy. The pantomime treat was the highlight, but it was more the general air of contentment which warmed me. When I think of those months in that cottage, the strain, the tension—it was dreadful. Grace has put on weight and her lovely hair has regained its shine and the dark hollows in her face

405

have gone and so have the shadows under her eyes. She has been making clothes for local people and performing what I am sure are held to be miracles with old curtains and sheets, dyeing them herself and reconstructing them using her own patterns. She says it is the sewing that has made her feel better every bit as much as the peace and quiet of the village. She wants to stay there at least a year. I've promised to visit with the twins in the Easter holidays. There were no tears the whole weekend, nor even a sign of them.

## 15 January

I wish rationing was over. It doesn't seem fair that, though the war is over, food is harder than ever to get and with two ever hungry growing children to feed it is exhausting finding enough food. I swear it was easier in Blockley, with my own vegetables from the garden and a butcher who seemed to have more meat than the one I am registered with here ever does. With the twins' birthday coming up I've been trying to save luxuries like sugar and eggs to make a cake, but that means having to deprive them in the meantime.

## 12 February

Twins' party over, I'd made my mind up to go and see the solicitor about their affairs. I should have done it ages ago, but there were always more pressing matters to attend to. I knew there were no problems, Charles's will was straightforward, and all the necessary things, like the sale of the house, were being done by the solicitor. I'd signed whatever he'd sent me and there was nothing to worry me. But he had always said I should come to see him sometime and today I did. I suppose I was thinking that it was my duty to understand the financial standing of the twins, and to know what was being done with their money until they come of age. Both of them are bound to ask questions later on and I want to be prepared. The firm of solicitors has its premises near Gray's Inn, easy to get to, quite an imposing place and with an atmosphere busier than I'd imagined. I saw the man who'd handled everything from the beginning, a Mr Purcell, about my age, a quiet, sensitive-looking man, more like my idea of a poet than a lawyer. He'd been a friend of Charles's and we talked a bit about him, with Mr Purcell—Peter, his name is—reminiscing about Charles and how brilliant he was. He has four children of his own, all girls, and showed great interest in the twins, saying how fortunate they were to have me to take care of them. He then went on to tell me that money could be released to help me bring the children up, enough if I wished to buy another perhaps bigger house, or a car. Unusually, provision for that kind of flexibility had been made in Charles's and Tilda's wills, but then they had been made, as so many wills were, in the shadow of war and what might happen. I said I didn't need any money, or not yet, that I am fortunate and own my own house. Mr Purcell asked about my income and I told him it was adequate, and came from the investments my mother left me, but that I might soon return to work. He said that the money held in trust for the twins consisted of what would come from the sale of the house, and some stocks and shares Charles inherited, plus a few thousand from their paternal grandmother's will, and another few from what Tilda and Charles had in the bank. There was enough available to buy clothes for them and take holidays and so forth while they were growing up. I thanked him, but said I wanted their money to remain intact, if I could possibly manage it. We chatted a bit more and then, as he shook hands with me at his door, a man came out of the room opposite. Mr Purcell stopped and said to me, Ah, let me introduce our senior partner, Mr Johnson. Mr Johnson, Miss King. It was Frank! I recognised him straight away, but he seemed not to realise who I was for all of a minute or so. Frank, I said, Good heavens. You! An embarrassed Mr Purcell stood perplexed between us, watching Frank take my arm, as if to test I was really there and hearing him say, My God, Millicent, after all this time, how are you? What are you doing here, how marvellous to see you. He was nervous. That was my first thought. How peculiar, I thought, Frank is *nervous*. I wonder why. He didn't know how to handle our unexpected encounter. We walked down the stairs together, Mr Purcell having discreetly disappeared, and stood in the hall. How has life treated you? Frank asked. I started to tell him about Tilda—and then I stopped, remembering that I'd met Frank through Daphne, who was at Cambridge with him, and she might have told him what had happened. Yes, he said, hurriedly, I thought when I heard what a terrible business, very bad luck. And you're looking after the children, I believe. I meant to write, but I was

408

in Egypt when Daphne wrote and then, with so much to do . . . His voice trailed off. I despised him for making excuses. I asked him how his life had gone, and he launched into an account of his war which I hardly listened to. He is married, of course, and has three children. He got that in. He said we must get together and talk about old times, and I said that would be nice, and we parted. He didn't ask for my address or phone number. I don't, of course, wish to see him again. All the way home, I was wondering how a man who had meant so much to me could now mean nothing. Nothing.

## 27 February

Felt so angry and restless all day and had hardly slept the night before which didn't help. No need to wonder why. Frank can't have meant nothing or I wouldn't still be feeling irritated by him yet I can't quite decide exactly why I was, and am, so annoyed. It is something to do with that nervousness of his which I sensed, as though I embarrassed him and he was afraid I might want something from him. Why am I embarrassing to him? Why should he suspect I want something? It is ridiculous. Perhaps he has forgotten that it was I who broke off with him. He was acting as though *he* had jilted *me*. But maybe his awkwardness was more to do with seeing me and wondering how on earth he could ever have made love to this dried-up old spinster—a different kind of embarrassment. I find myself wanting to let him know that I had a lover far superior to him and whom I truly loved. Not true, though, not all of it. I did love Robert in a way I

409

never loved Frank, but he was not as passionate as Frank. Thought this afternoon as I went to meet the twins, to take them to try to find new shoes, that nobody seeing me stand at the school gate could possibly guess I was thinking of and comparing old lovers. No, I am poor little Miss King, demure and chaste, a noble aunt looking after her niece and nephew with no life of her own. I rage at my own image, but do nothing to correct it. Connie, on the way home, asked why I was angry, though I had said nothing at all to indicate anger. She picks up moods dangerously quickly.

## 28 February

I am mortified to find I am still disturbed by thoughts of Frank. I wish I could decide exactly why. I wish I had been wearing my green suit with the tie-neck cream blouse and that pretty hat Daphne made me buy, but I thought I ought to look sensible, visiting a solicitor, and trustworthy, and I wore that dowdy grey thing with flat shoes and my black velour hat. What can I have looked like? So, it is vanity which makes me so cross, feeling that I looked dull and worn out, and this must mean that I wanted to be thought desirable still. But I am not, not in the least desirable, and must face up to it. If Robert had survived, would he have found me desirable? Would I have desired him? I can blame the war for this sad state of affairs but I am more inclined to blame myself. I dreamed about Frank last night. He was as I saw him two weeks ago but I was young again. It was a sexual dream. I woke to find myself wet and

410

*throbbing*, as though a heart was beating between my legs, and I had to calm it. I lay willing myself to be still and eventually it was over, that terrible ache of desire. Felt shaky all day, and dread tonight. I don't want to have anything more to do with such longings and yet it is stupid to ignore them. They will fade of their own accord, I suppose, as I age, and it will be a relief. How sad it makes me feel, though.

**1 March**

Daphne came, looking mischievous. She said she'd had a drink with Frank last night and he told her he'd met me. I was furious to find myself blushing. Daphne loved that. She enjoyed telling me that he'd said I was as lovely as ever, a lie of course. I said nothing and busied myself with making tea. Daphne wouldn't leave the subject alone, insisted on telling me that Frank was not very happy with his wife, as if I would be interested in such news. Daphne went on teasing me, saying she hadn't known until ages after it ended that I had had an affair with Frank, how sly I'd been, how daring when I always looked as though butter wouldn't melt in my prim little mouth. Then she said I'd made a wise choice, that Frank was good in bed, *she'd* enjoyed her fling with him. Well, if she thinks I care that he was her lover too she is mistaken. She says he is going to ring me, so I pointed out that I hadn't given him my number, but she laughed and said he'd got it from her. I was so upset I couldn't hide my distress and then she stopped tormenting me, and said she was sorry. She grew quiet and thoughtful, and went on to say how she worried about me and how wrong she thought I was to shut myself away with the twins and have no friends of my own age with whom I could enjoy some social life. She refuses to believe I am quite content. I cannot confide in Daphne, I never could.

## 6 March

I must do something. Spring in the air, I suppose, making me agitated, wanting to be off somewhere. Daphne said the other day that she wondered why I didn't get someone to be here for the twins so that I could go back to my job. She says there are loads of women, refugees from Germany and other countries, who would jump at the chance and not cost much to employ. She's right. I could engage someone to clean the house and shop and be here when the twins got home and stay with them till I arrived back. But I hesitate, and not just because I worry that it would not be good for the children, which is silly, since they are 9 and very mature for their age, and it is more likely it would be good rather than bad for them. No, it's the thought of asking for my old job back, and whether I want it. I could write to the department but I don't know who is in charge now and there is probably no one of the old team still there. Doris, maybe, but none of the others, I suspect. It will all have changed anyway, the whole organisation. I need Robert to talk it over with but I haven't got him and must make do with myself. I think the trouble is that, though I do yearn to be something other than housewife and proxy mother, I don't particularly

412

want to be a social worker. The alternative, I suppose, is to go back to teaching. The government is said to be looking for more teachers and encouraging those who have left the profession to return to it.

## 7 March

Discussed returning to teaching with the twins. Very amusing. They were both amazed that I had ever been a teacher, which was a bit insulting. I asked them what they thought I had done and they said help the aeroplanes find their way, which I suppose is how Tilda described my valiant early days in the WAAF. When I pointed out that was in the war and I'd had a job before that they looked blank. To them, there *is* no 'before the war'. Their memories start with the war, except for a few vague, hazy recollections. So I gave them a little résumé of my life up to 1939 and they were incredulous. What, I had lived in Italy, I had been a teacher in Brighton, I had been a social worker? (Though that took some explaining.) They were doubtful that all this was true, to say the least. To them I am just an aunt who appeared from nowhere to take the place of their mother and do what mothers do. Then Connie said, Were you married, Aunt Millicent, before you came to us? She seemed disappointed when I said no. She is too young for me to launch into an account of my personal life but one day I will tell her about Robert, though maybe not about Frank. Did no one ever propose to you? Connie went on, her little face already settling into an expression of the

413

greatest pity and sympathy. Oh, I was asked, I said, I was proposed to by three men at different times. She loved that, and begged me to tell her who they were and why I refused their offers of marriage, but I shook my head and said I'd tell her when she's old enough to understand. But then we got back to the main business in hand: did they think I should go back to teaching? Not in our school, said Toby. Apart from that proviso they both thought I should, but were not keen on having a stranger here when they got home to make their tea. Connie thinks they are old enough to let themselves in and look after themselves. She even recited off a whole list of classmates who do that. But I said I couldn't allow that, not yet.

**15 March**

Have finally sent off an application to the education authority, or rather a letter inquiring if my services as a teacher might be of use. We will see. No harm in taking that first step and it makes me feel I am trying. I've kept all my Goldsmiths' lecture notes and my lesson plans which surprises me, that I didn't throw them out, I mean. I looked through them today and thought they seemed quite good, but then I remembered the difference between planning the lessons and delivering them. How tough that Brighton school was: Lord, how I hated it. Surely any other school would be better. The twins' is excellent, it seems to me, though the classes are very big, and the Blockley school was a model of its kind.

## 1 April

Daphne has decided to marry her American and is in the process of trying to get a passage. It seems it is very difficult, with all the ships overbooked. The American, Jimmy, is doing what he can from his end, in Panama City, where he is a radio operator working for a Radio Telegraph company. As usual, Daphne flaunts his letters, laughing over them, though they are not in the least funny. She read out a passage—I refused to read it for myself—in which this Jimmy tells her he thinks she will be his perfect lifetime partner. I wonder if he knows her at all. Then another letter had her in stitches as he told her his idea of what a wife should be. It was rather fine, I thought, full of quite noble sentiments about a wife as an enthusiastic partner and not some kind of excess baggage, and ending with the firmly expressed conviction that they will be very happy together because they are not going into marriage with any 'head-in-the-clouds' idea or because of what he called 'infatuation or impulsiveness'. Daphne thinks he's 'a hoot', but I don't think so at all. Really, how can he not have realised that she is the most impulsive woman in the world, her head always in the clouds? I can't help predicting disaster.

## 2 April

Letter from Grace, saying she is expecting us at the end of the week, 'as agreed at Christmas'. Don't recall actually fixing a date. Trouble is, the twins don't want to go, especially Toby, even though

415

Christmas was such a success. He doesn't give reasons, just says he hates the country, which is not true, and I had to point out all the things he'd loved about being in Blockley and how when he first came back to London he was forever wishing himself back in our cottage there. He says he's changed and now he doesn't want to leave London: he'd be bored and miss his friends and Saturday morning cinema and the zoo, and a whole host of other hastily cobbled together reasons. Connie is more reflective. She says she's afraid of how she will feel, because of 'you know'. No amount of encouragement would get her to enlarge on this 'you know', but I presume it is memories of Tilda there. Not exactly logical, but then feelings don't have to be, indeed rarely are. I feel I should respect their reluctance, but on the other hand what about Grace? She has feelings too, and needs us, needs her family. Very carefully, I tried to explain this to the children, reminding them of Grace's distress when she arrived and how she got better but still needed support. It was all a bit over their heads, a bit wasted on them. Connie looked concerned, and said couldn't Grace and Claudia come again to us, but agreed that taking turns mattered. I said we must go, but not for long, only a weekend. Toby grudgingly agreed that might be bearable. Now I have to concoct an excuse for Grace, a reason why we can't stay the whole week which is what she wants. Interviews, I think. It will have to be that I am to be interviewed for a teaching post. True, but not next week. Must make sure the twins don't realise I'm lying. Very bad example.

## 10 April

The weekend was a strain. Difficult to decide why. Maybe if it hadn't rained so hard all the time everything would've been different, but cooped up in that cottage—I'd forgotten quite how small it is, how cramped the rooms—or else plodding through the rain on endless walks was not enjoyable. Don't think Grace enjoyed having us either, though nothing was said. Toby behaved badly, refusing to put wellingtons on and ruining his precious school shoes, and complaining frequently there was no one to play with. He tried to find his old friends but none of them were at home. Grace got near to saying he needs a man's hand, as if I wasn't aware of that. There is no man in his life at all, not just no father but no grandfather or brother, and the uncles he has are mere names to him. I worry about this, though God knows it must be a worry shared by thousands of women now, managing to bring up boys without any masculine influence. Grace said she was glad Claudia was a girl, it made everything bearable, she never stops giving thanks for it. I took the opportunity to ask if Claudia's father was dead, and regretted it. Grace flushed crimson, and her whole face tightened and she didn't reply. Now that Grace is better, I would have thought she could confide in me a little. After all, this is a question others, including Claudia, are going to ask her in the future and she will have to come up with some sort of answer. Still, we parted friends, each blaming the weather for a less than rapturous weekend, and made plans for her to come to us again. On now to George's.

## 15 April

Couldn't actually write anything at George's. Thought we'd never find his farm in spite of Esther's detailed directions. So many signposts still are not replaced, and those that were point in wrong directions. We got there eventually and it was a pleasant surprise: lovely farmhouse, all on its own in beautiful rolling countryside. We were given a great welcome too, both Esther and George seeming really pleased to see us, and it made me feel warm towards Esther for the first time. But best of all was that Toby had Harry to look up to and went off with him at once to be shown all the animals and especially the horses. Harry is the dead spit of Father, same eyes, same chin, same build. I have photographs of Father at 13, Harry's age now, which I've promised to look out and send Esther. Stephen, the older one, was not there, but Esther says he takes after her side. We ate an enormous meal, no signs of rationing, and Toby tucked into the roast beef as though he had never tasted it before—well, he hardly ever has, and he's certainly never seen a roast such as that one. The weather was as good as it had been bad at Grace's, and since Toby was out with Harry from dawn to dusk, everything was peaceful. Connie loved the kittens and wasn't at a loose end at all, seeming quite happy to wander about feeding the chickens and doing other jobs Esther gave her. Who would have thought that Esther would become such a good farmer's wife, or George a farmer, and yet they seem so happy in this new life. Esther says leaving Brighton was the best thing they ever did and that they have the war to thank for that. We

418

sat, the three of us, drinking port of all things, talking until after midnight, mostly reminiscing about old times, and going over the tragedies that have hit the family. It was odd to feel so companionable with this brother of mine, and with my sister-in-law, when I have never felt we had a single thing in common. Only the blood tie has bound me to George until now. Mother used to say 'You always have your family', to console me if I was friendless, but somehow it never comforted me as much as she thought it should do. Of course, I don't know George at all, I don't know what he thinks, what he likes. To me, he's been the brother wrecked by the first war and this older man is a stranger to me. He made Esther laugh, remembering my wildness as a very young girl, giving examples of my rages, but I don't recall them at all. He said Mother despaired of me, and Esther backed him up, saying she had heard Mother say so. But look at you now, George said, look at how you've taken the twins on and become dependable and sensible. He meant it, I know, as a compliment but it depressed me to hear it said. Dependable and sensible instead of wild. Oh dear. Esther cautioned George, saying I might still have a wild side. She was teasing, but I chose to take her seriously and said yes, I thought I had, I hoped I had, and one day it might surface again, when the twins are grown up. Esther said, Don't let them hold you back, we would always take them. It was kind of her. Toby would love it here, and maybe would've been better off, but it is too late now, and Tilda and Charles made me their guardian. The strange thing is what a start of alarm I felt inside me at the mere thought of not having Toby and

419

Connie with me. They have become my life, dangerously so. I don't say that in any spirit of martyrdom either. Oh, I may have begun by feeling sorry that this burden was thrust on me by fate, by the war, but that passed very quickly.

Esther asked me, before we went to bed, if I had never wanted to marry and have children. Normally, I would have been furious at her insensitivity, I'd have seen it as smugness but, whether because of the port or the good food, or simply the company of other adults to which I am not used, I didn't resent her inquiry. I told them about Robert, the whole story. I hope I don't regret it.

*　　　*　　　*

*Once back in London, Millicent goes for an interview for a teaching job. She hadn't really expected to be offered one, because of her limited experience and her long absence from teaching, but in this immediate postwar period there was an urgent need for qualified people and her qualifications were undoubtedly good. She accepts a part-time post in a primary school in Primrose Hill (though not the one the twins go to). She works four mornings a week, teaching a class of forty children (7-year-olds). At first, she finds this a strain, nearly as exhausting as her Brighton experience, and wonders if she can continue, but gradually she adjusts and even begins to enjoy the teaching. Her main problem becomes not so much the constant struggle to impose discipline—she admits she is now good at this—as her failure to fit in with the rest of the staff. As a part-time teacher, she doesn't spend much time in the staff room, but when she is there, having her tea during break, she feels out of place. No new friends are made, and she never progresses beyond the exchange of pleasantries.*

*This disappoints her, and she has to make an effort to disguise her feelings of slight depression from the twins, especially from Connie. What adds to her depression is that she is going through what she thinks of as an unfairly early menopause (which begins when she is 46). It is not, she writes, that she ever expected to have children of her own now—she has had no relationship with a man since Robert left for the war—but nevertheless she hates to have this proved impossible. She is very much alone during these years, starved of adult company in her leisure time, with Daphne, her only real friend, in America (and a poor correspondent), Tilda dead, and Grace (till 1950) still in the country. She does an enormous amount of reading and her most regular outing is to* The Times *Book Club and circulating library in Wigmore Street. She is what was called a 'guaranteed' customer, paying £3 7s 6d a year for the privilege of being able to take out a book the day it is published. Millicent is often there first thing on the day she doesn't teach, eager to get a novel she has seen reviewed in* The Sunday Times, *and returning home quite triumphant with it. (Two such triumphs she mentions are C. P. Snow's* The Masters *and Anthony Powell's* A Question of Upbringing, *both published in 1951.) She regards the library subscription as her one luxury and treasures it. Her other great pleasure, gardening, also absorbs her, though the modest size of her garden doesn't give her much scope. She develops a passion for climbing roses, especially Albertine, which she successfully trains to cover the back wall of her house. She feels that she is marking time and,*

421

*though she knows she doesn't look middle-aged—she is always, of course, proud of looking much younger than her years—she feels it. What adds to her despondency is a new worry, about money. She has lived all this time on the income from the investments left to her by her mother and on her savings and has managed very well by being frugal. But the twins are growing alarmingly and by 1950, when they are on the brink of adolescence, she is having a struggle to keep pace with what they need. She can't afford extras such as hockey sticks, and dance shoes (and lessons), and football boots, as well as essential clothes, for the twins. In the end, she accepts the offer to release money from their trust fund which the solicitor had made years before. This makes her feel guilty and inadequate, though her sister Grace (who returns to London in 1950, to the Bond Street couturier's she had worked for before the war) tells her she has no need to be—quite the opposite.*

*It is in these years that Millicent does seem at her most ordinary, very much the average early middle-aged woman of her times and her diaries reflect this. But what is far from average is her obvious financial independence and security. Money is not mentioned often in her diary and when it is, always in a veiled sort of way. She never reveals what these investments are which provide her income, nor does she state what that income amounted to. She seems to push aside all inquiries as to her financial position (as she did when the solicitor, Mr Purcell, asked) and fobs people off with vague references to having 'enough' money, or not needing to worry about money. Since she is such a careful woman, I suspect she had a separate account book in which she recorded everything to do with it and felt her diary was not the appropriate place to do so. But there is one entry, made when she bought her house, which would seem to indicate that she had inherited shares in the National Provincial Bank. I am told these shares were an excellent buy in the 1930s and went on increasing in value right up to the 1960s. How many Millicent had of them, of course, we are never told. Like many of her generation, she clearly believed talking (even, in her case, to her diary) about money was somehow not quite nice.*

*Again and again, she writes during the postwar period that she has nothing of interest to record, nothing to say. Even the doings of the twins no longer seem to her worthy of relating in detail, and there is very little mention of her teaching. The weather, to which she once scorned to give space, gets a lot of attention (especially in the hard winter of 1946/7 when the Thames froze over, and for a while water had to be got from a standpipe in the street). She thinks, by 1950, that her diaries for the previous three years have hardly been worth keeping, and she is not so wrong. Their function, she observes with some bitterness, is to reassure her that the days and weeks have not just vanished into a hole. In spite of her part-time job, and in spite of looking after the twins, she has an oppressive sense of marking time.*

*But then, in the spring of 1951, there is the first indication that Millicent may lift herself out of the rut she has fallen into. In April, her nephew Harry, the younger son of George and Esther, now aged 18, is sent to Korea, as one of the Gloucestershire Regiment, to do his National Service. Millicent has been only vaguely aware that there is a war going on in Korea, but has not really taken in the involvement of British troops and is horrified when she realises that Harry will be fighting not in a minor skirmish but in a war which could escalate into a Third World War. When he is taken prisoner by the North Koreans this naturally brings back painful memories of Robert's fate. Rage bursts forth to enliven once more her diary.*

\*     \*     \*

## 30 April 1951

Esther rang to say that Harry is alive but taken prisoner, and God knows what hellish torments he is enduring, but at least he survived this awful battle on some remote hill out there. His regiment was completely surrounded by the Chinese army north of Seoul and fought heroically. Esther, in the midst of her tears, seemed proud of this but it makes me rage, because *what* were they fighting so heroically for? Why were they killing and being killed? I don't understand it though I have struggled to do so, reading *The Times* with close attention and becoming none the wiser. It is like the two world wars all over again, and women like me bewildered and appalled and unable, it seems, to have any influence whatsoever. Why do we allow it? Why do we let men lead us into this nightmare again and again? I feel like screaming. I think of poor Harry, only 18, that lovely boy packed off to a distant country he knows nothing of and forced to fight people with whom he has no quarrel. It is insane. I cannot, cannot bear it. All day since Esther rang I have gone around in a state of savagery, wanting to murder those in charge who

424

are murdering the likes of Harry. My hands shake, my head thumps, I am beside myself. And when Toby came in from school, caked in mud from football, I looked at him and had a sudden vision of him in a mere *four years* being sent off like Harry to fight in some god-forsaken corner of this earth. It was horrible, looking at his young body, so handsome and healthy, and seeing in my mind's eye his whole torso covered in blood and his beautiful limbs shattered. I won't let it happen. But writing that here I know how feeble it is to say so. It happened to Alfred and Albert and to Michael, and to Robert, and there was nothing I could do to stop it. But for Toby I will find a way, I swear I will. I may not be able to stop wars but I can surely find a means to make sure he is exempt from being forced to take part in them, by means foul if not fair. I will scheme and trick, I will do anything to make sure he is spared. I had to tell him about Harry. I thought he would be terribly upset but, on the contrary, he seemed excited and wanted every detail of the battle Harry had fought in, which I could not give him. I heard him later on the telephone almost boasting about his cousin to a friend of his and I had to speak sharply to him and point out this is not a game and that Harry's plight now is pitiful. In reply, Toby asked if he would get a medal when he came home, and I was so disgusted that I said *if* he comes home, which I hadn't meant to say, it was cruel, and Toby then grew anxious and wanted to know what I meant and I had to back-pedal and say all I'd meant was that being a prisoner of war was no soft option.

## 1 May

Lay awake all night, thinking of poor Harry, trying to imagine the conditions in which he is being kept. It will be hot there, as it was in Singapore for Robert, and it will be rife with all kinds of tropical diseases. They'll feed him on rice, I should think, rice and what else? Are the North Koreans as cruel as or even more cruel than the Japanese? Or is he a prisoner of the Chinese? I forget what Esther said. Harry is a strong young man, stronger than Robert, a lot stronger. He will lose weight but unlike Robert he will not quickly become emaciated: he has reserves of fat and muscle. But I don't know about his mental and emotional strength, I don't know how he will survive imprisonment. It is all so far away and, though Singapore was too, it is not the same because there's no war on here as there was ten years ago, and so it is much more unreal. I thought we had done with war forever, or at least for this century. There we are, surviving it and all set to celebrate this very summer with our Festival of Britain, while over in a country whose location few of us could identify on a map, we are at war again, though hardly anyone seems to realise it. Yesterday, I was in such a state, I said to the postman, that my nephew had been taken prisoner in Korea. I just blurted it out as he handed me a parcel, and he said, Where's that, then? and I couldn't reply, just stood there stupidly staring at him, when he added, Funny to think of our lads being in a foreign war, ain't it? Then he said he was sorry about my lad and went back to his van whistling. I know he wasn't being heartless. He doesn't know me, he

426

doesn't know Harry, he doesn't know Korea. But in the last war, we all knew what was happening and who the enemy was and even what we were fighting for.

## 6 May

More sleepless nights. Last night I was thinking about that friend I had at school, can't even remember her name, but the girl I longed to go to a Peace Rally with in the First World War. We were going to be pacifists. What happened to that Peace Pledge Union, and their newspaper which Robert and I read? I wonder. Maybe it's still in existence, but if so I haven't read about it. What has it done about Korea? Nothing, nothing that I know of.

## 13 May

News today that America has tested a hydrogen bomb. Will it be used in Korea? Surely not, but if it is being tested then this must be because it is intended for use somewhere. How wicked, how monstrous.

## 15 May

Spent most of yesterday writing a letter to *The Times* expressing my horror about the testing of the H-bomb by Americans or Russians, or anyone, and urging our government to have nothing to do with the manufacture or possession of this hideous instrument of war. I tried so hard not to be emotional or hysterical, but simply to be matter-of-fact and succinct, stressing that I wrote as an ordinary woman who had had to live through two world wars in which members of my family had been killed and injured and that my nephew was at this moment imprisoned in Korea. I drafted it six times and wrote the final version out twice. It is nothing, writing to *The Times*, but it made me feel I was doing something, making the only kind of protest I seem capable of.

## 20 May

Five days, and *The Times* has not printed my letter. I was so sure they would, but I now see I was deluded, thinking I'd written such an important and impressive letter when on the contrary it was run-of-the-mill and from nobody. I did get a polite printed slip saying my letter had been received and was being considered for publication. But it hasn't been thought worthy of publication and I am a fool to think it would be.

## 26 May

The newspapers are full of the defection of two diplomats, Guy Burgess and Donald Maclean, to Russia. It seems they can betray our secrets and cause great harm. What secrets are these? It's strange that Russia is our enemy now, when in the war they helped save us from Hitler. All to do with communism and our fear of it. Toby asked me what communism is and I had a struggle defining it. He thought it sounded a good thing, everyone being equal and sharing everything, and of course put like that it does. He is fascinated at the moment by spies and reads everything about Burgess and Maclean.

## 1 June

Daphne is back from America. Turned up this morning, straight from Heathrow, her marriage over, or so she says. She seems not a fraction upset—on the contrary, she is in excellent spirits and delighted to be home. She says she hated America, which surprised me. I reminded her that in the few letters she'd written to me in the last five years she had boasted about how wonderful everything over there was and had had me drooling over her descriptions of food and sighing over her images of sunny Californian skies when over here everything was grey and cold and miserable. Had she been lying? No, she says, the food was wonderful and plentiful, and once they'd moved to Santa Monica from Panama City the weather was sublime. The trouble was Jimmy. He was boring. She can't think why she liked him, except for the sex, and because he provided a way out of dismal Britain. And in civvies he wasn't even good-looking, not the way he was in uniform in the war. So she's ditched him and isn't a bit ashamed. No children, luckily. Jimmy wanted children, another bone of contention between them but, though she wants them 'some day' not yet, and not with him. I pointed out that she hasn't much time left (if any),

429

considering she's about to be forty-three, but biological facts don't seem to worry her. She asked if she could stay with me till she gets sorted and I've said of course, though it will mean her sleeping in the sitting-room, not that that will worry her, though it worries me, thinking how messy she is. Connie and Toby both remembered her—shrieks from her when they came home from school and she saw how they've grown. When they'd gone to bed and we were sitting drinking whisky—not that I have it in the house these days, but Daphne arrived with a bottle, together with all kinds of other luxuries—she said how gorgeous Toby is, so handsome and sexy, just like his father. I said I'd never thought Charles either handsome or sexy, and she laughed and said my idea of an attractive man had always been weird. She smokes, all the time. This house is going to smell like a public bar before she goes.

## 8 June

A week of Daphne and I long for things to be back to normal. She has bought a gramophone, much to the twins' delight, and she plays noisy records—jazz and what she calls boogie music—which make my head ache. Yesterday she asked me how I could stand doing nothing but housework and gardening in my leisure time. She asked where my friends are and my own life, and I said this was my life, the very life she found so dreary, and that I am quite happy with it. She told me if that was true, I was abnormal. It didn't develop into an argument, but she does annoy me when she becomes so patronising. What, after all, is *she* doing with her life? She hasn't achieved any of her ambitions, political or otherwise, or made good use of her superior education and now she has a failed marriage behind her and she is at a loose end. One day this week, she even said that she wished the war was still on, and I was furious. Just because she had such a good time she never thinks of all the suffering and killing that went on, never takes into consideration the wrecked lives. Oh don't be so stuffy, she said, You enjoyed the WAAF too, and yawned.

**20 June**

Daphne is leaving us tomorrow, just in time for us still to be civil to each other. Even the twins have got over their infatuation with her, though they still relish the treats she provides. Connie wondered aloud what kind of life she and Toby would have had, if Daphne had been their aunt and guardian. It made us laugh, to imagine it. Connie wanted to know all about Daphne's background and listened very closely while I outlined it. The fact that Daphne was orphaned as she herself was struck her forcibly and she gave me the strangest look when I said there had been no relatives and that at 16 Daphne had been left entirely alone. If Daphne hadn't come in at that moment I think Connie might have said something significant, though I don't know what.

## 21 June

I am now the proud but nervous possessor of a washing machine, present from the departing and ever generous Daphne. She says my kitchen makes her quite ill, it is so primitive, so devoid of all the appliances she had in California, and a washing machine is the most needed. It is entirely automatic and I am scared I will wreck it, but Daphne says I am not to be so stupid, all I need do is press buttons. She wanted to buy me what she calls a 'proper' refrigerator but I refused to have it—there is nothing wrong with what I have got, and I'm very lucky to have one at all. I am assuming, from all this largess, that Daphne is still well off. She *looks* well off, what with her fur coat and expensive clothes and shoes and her jewellery, but looks can be deceiving, though not in her case, I think. She questioned me quite sharply about my financial affairs but I refused to reveal quite how careful I have to be and swore I had no money problems. Then why don't you buy yourself a new dress, she asked, why don't you buy a new car? That Hillman is a museum piece. I just shrugged. She has bought a flat in Frognal, a large flat. Says she doesn't want a house. She even says she might open a shop. That does make me laugh—Daphne, running a shop: how mundane, how unlikely. She thinks it might be a bookshop, but she hasn't decided yet. It will never come to pass.

## 5 July

Toby and Connie have both been invited to go on

holiday with friends. Connie's friend Barbara's family are going to the Isle of Wight for three weeks the moment school breaks up and have invited her for the first two. Toby's chum Graham Maxwell has asked him to join him and his father on a sailing holiday off the north-west coast of Scotland. Toby is wildly excited and it is perfect for him, especially the all-male companionship. The dates are the same as Connie's which means I will be on my own. Connie realised this and worried I might be lonely and have no one to go on holiday with, but she believed me easily enough when I said I had plans already. But I don't. I have no plans. It will be the first time for nine years that I will be entirely free to do what I want. But what do I want? There's the rub. I long for sun and foreign travel but lack the funds to indulge myself. I don't want a companion, that's for sure. I am quite content to holiday on my own if I could just decide how and where. I keep thinking I ought to spend more time with Grace and feel guilty that I don't want to use my precious free time to do this. And I could visit George and Esther who are so sad because Harry is still a POW and would, I'm sure, appreciate company. But I'm not going to. I am going to be selfish and think only of myself for once. Maybe I could manage a week in Italy. I've no idea what it would cost. I will go to a travel agent and ask advice. All I want is a modest pensione sort of place and I don't mind travelling third class by train.

Little sparks of excitement keep jumping inside me at the mere thought of going abroad. Whatever happens I am determined not to stay here at home. It will do me good to get away and I may not have

433

the chance again for a long time; though, on the other hand, this may be the beginning of my having a great deal of time on my own. Toby and Connie are nearly of an age to want to be off on their own, and then how my life will change again. It makes me feel queer, thinking of it.

\* \* \*

*Millicent, in fact, doesn't go on holiday that summer. She is ill, and spends most of the two weeks the twins were away—'mercifully', she comments—flat on her back with a slipped disc. It is the first time, apart from the accident when she lost her baby, that she has ever been ill, except for occasional bouts of flu. Her general health throughout the diaries is excellent, with barely a mention of any aches and pains. She slips the disc, in the lumbar region at the base of her spine, moving a statue in her garden. It is only a small statue, of a lion, but it is heavy and she blames herself for being foolish enough to attempt it. She has no one to look after her, of course, and the doctor she is obliged to call is concerned about how she will manage, but she is determined to do so. Lying on her back most of each day for the first week gives her plenty of time for introspection and she doesn't enjoy it.*

\* \* \*

**26 July**

Am I to be a crock? The mere thought of not being well and active appals me, but then it would appal

434

anyone. I can't be an invalid, I just can't. Is this what old age will be like? Then I don't want to be old. Every movement is agony and the days interminable. Reading is uncomfortable because I can't seem to get into a position where I can hold a book without having to squint at the words, and the wireless has so little on that I want to hear. *Mrs Dale's Diary* is the ultimate in boredom and the programme Toby finds so hysterically funny, with those men talking rubbish in silly voices, doesn't raise a smile.

## 27 July

Daphne turned up. She still has a key so there was nothing I could do to stop her barging in and finding me lying prone in bed. She flopped down on my bed not seeming to realise that the slightest thing causes me pain. You poor old love, she said, and asked if I wanted a cigarette, though she knows I haven't smoked for years. But when she'd finished telling me about the furnishing of her new flat she did ask if there was anything she could do and I got her to go and buy some provisions, otherwise I'll starve. She bought all the wrong things, taking no notice of my list, but it doesn't matter, it's food, it will do. And she did kindly buy some extra things she thought I should have, such as whisky and wine. The awful thing is that a slug of whisky does help. Maybe I will end up an alcoholic. What a pair we are, she said before she left, all alone in the world and no one to nurse us. I resented that, but said nothing. I am not all alone. But I don't want the twins to have to look after me, ever. I won't allow

435

it. Fine words, but I mean them.

## 31 July

Postcard from Connie. She's having a lovely time. Nothing from Toby. Managed to get out into the garden today, with great difficulty, but I made it and lay there, in the sun. It felt better than lying inside in bed. I lay and looked at the sky, blue all day, with tiny fluffy clouds scuttering across it, and thought how I *do* have time to stand and stare in this life so full of care. Well, lie and stare. My life isn't full of care either. What is it full of? Housework. Shopping. A little teaching in term time. A pleasant enough life. If it ended, would it matter? It would, for the twins. Not a morbid train of thought, however it sounds. I'm not thinking about dying. I'm thinking, in all this enforced leisure, of the future, funnily enough, of when the twins won't need me. I suddenly realised I ought to prepare myself and work out what I am going to do or else I will end up truly pathetic. Rightly or wrongly, I gave up my career when Tilda was killed and didn't go back to it when I could have done. In four years' time, when the twins reach 18 and go to college, I *must* do more than teach part-time. My brain hasn't quite rotted away. I think for a long time I've been deluding myself that I'm quite happy, and also there has been a touch of martyrdom, making care of the twins the excuse to avoid facing up to the fact that I am going to have to motivate myself and find more meaningful work. Yet I doubt if I could return to being a social worker, and I don't want to teach full-time.

*Millicent is fully recovered and mobile by the middle of August, and able to go to the Festival of Britain on the South Bank. The preparations for it had fascinated her in the spring—just seeing all the rubble left after the wartime bombing cleared away cheered her—and she thoroughly approves of the whole idea of this celebration, copying into her diary the words of the Archbishop of Canterbury that 'the chief and governing purpose of the Festival is to declare our belief and trust in the British way of life, not with any boastful self-confidence nor with any aggressive self-advertisement, but with sober and humble trust that by holding fast to that which is good and rejecting from our midst that which is evil we may continue to be a nation at unity in itself and of service to the world'. Millicent comments 'My sentiments entirely.' The Skylon impresses her, and she enjoys looking round the various pavilions, going twice, once on her own and once with Connie.*

*Over the next few years, 1951–5, the twins grow more and more independent and provide much entertainment, though Connie causes Millicent some anxiety by staying out late on Saturday nights, secretly smoking and indulging in other mild forms of teenage rebellion. Toby is not so close to Millicent now, though his interest in current affairs makes Millicent once more try harder to pay attention to what is happening in the world in order to be able to talk with him. Harry returns from Korea in early August 1953 and visits them. Millicent is shocked by his appearance—he is gaunt and thin—and inevitably she suffers again for a while from nightmares about*

437

Robert. Toby is disappointed because Harry won't talk about what happened to him, and Millicent hopes this will teach him that war is too terrible to describe.

She shares Toby's excitement when Everest is conquered by Hillary and Tensing (though curiously there is no mention whatsoever in the diary of either George VI's death or of the coronation of Elizabeth II), and again when, in 1954, Roger Bannister runs a four-minute mile. She is anxious that the twins should both go to university and delighted when they both do very well in their O-levels. Toby gets five distinctions, passing ten subjects altogether, and Connie, who passes nine (but fails Latin) gets two. Just as, in 1955, both of them are preparing to go to university (Toby to Cambridge, Connie to Manchester) Millicent's settled routine is disturbed by a family crisis.

In 1952, Grace marries Will Baron, a fabric designer, in a quiet ceremony with Millicent as witness. A son, Sam, is born early in 1955. Grace and Millicent seem to see a good deal of each other, meeting regularly for lunch, and it gives Millicent real satisfaction to see how happy her sister is at last. Millicent likes Will, whom she considers ideal for Grace because he is so serious and dependable and quite a bit older than her. She thinks she need never again worry about Grace, and there are several entries on the lines of 'all's well that ends well'. Whatever happened to her sister during the war has long since been accepted as something she will never know. But then, just before the end of the school holidays in 1955, she gets a phone call from her brother-in-law Will.

438

## 28 August 1955

Grace has disappeared. Will, when he telephoned, obviously expected to find her here, but I have not seen her since we all had lunch two weeks ago on Sunday and I haven't spoken to her since last Thursday. It is most peculiar. She has left Sam behind. Claudia is on holiday with a schoolfriend's family. She has simply vanished, leaving no note or any kind of message. She left the house to go to work at 9.30 a.m. as normal. Will came over soon after he'd called and I tried to calm him down. He says Grace has not been herself for some weeks, she's been having nightmares and waking up screaming. He's tried to get her to go to the doctor's but she has refused, telling him these bad dreams happen from time to time and she gets over them. He asked if I knew about them. I had to say I did, and told him about Grace coming back from France and the state she was in then. I'd always assumed she'd told him about whatever happened there, but it seems he is no wiser than I am. You would have thought she would confide in her husband. She must surely have had to explain the existence of Claudia. I asked him if he hadn't been curious about Claudia and he said no, not really, he'd just accepted that she belonged to Grace's past and if Grace didn't want to talk about it, that was her affair. He loves Claudia, he says, and adopted her officially soon after he and Grace married. He seemed frightened, I thought, more frightened than Grace's absence yet warrants— she's only been missing twenty-four hours and there may well be some simple explanation. She would never desert her children. I tried to comfort him by assuring him of this, but he wouldn't accept that there was no need for alarm. I kept wondering, and still do wonder, if he has told me everything. When I asked what she had taken with her, he said that, so far as he knew, hardly anything: all her clothes seem to be in the wardrobes and no suitcase is missing. He hasn't even thought to look for her passport and, as for money, he doesn't know how much cash she might have.

But my mention of her passport had him rushing back to look. He sounded relieved when he phoned later to say that it was still there, in the drawer in his desk where he keeps it. He has also rung all the hospitals in North London and there is no record of any admission of a woman answering to her description, and the police have no record of an accident. He has given her car number to the police, but I don't know if that means they will make a search. He asked for George's number, which I gave him, though quite sure she wouldn't have gone there, and I promised faithfully to ring him if Grace contacted me, whatever time of night. I told him I was absolutely sure Grace would have done nothing foolish. I told him simply to await events.

## 29 August

Still no news of Grace. Now *I* am beginning to worry. Will says Sam is crying for her and the nanny is finding him difficult to comfort. How lucky they have Eileen at all, and that she is so devoted to Sam. Went over to Will's today, though there is nothing I could do. He asked me to look around the house for anything that might explain Grace's absence. It felt embarrassing somehow, especially going into their bedroom, which I did not really want to do, and also into their bathroom, but Will insisted. Neither room revealed a thing. I looked at her clothes, such lovely clothes, and as Will had said they all seemed to be there, or at least all the garments I've ever seen her in. They are all so tidily arranged, each dress on a padded, scented hanger, the sort Mother used to make for sales of work, and everything arranged according to colour. She loves green, so many shades of green from the palest moss to a strident lime. On her bedside table she has a photograph of Mother, just a tiny snapshot in a silver frame, and another of the children, taken soon after Sam's birth. There is a book, too, a novel, *Bonjour Tristesse* by Françoise Sagan. There is a bookmark in it, half-way through. Is that significant? Tempting to wonder, but I didn't say anything to Will, who was following me around dementedly. The bathroom cabinet was full of her toiletries, talcum powder and scent and other things, all expensive and prettily packaged. I wonder where she manages to get them. There were aspirins, and veganin tablets, but otherwise no drugs or medication. Then I went to her little workroom, right at the top of the house, thankful that Eileen was calling for Will to take a phone call and he didn't immediately follow me. I felt Grace more in that room than anywhere in the house, simply, I suppose, because it is a room entirely hers. She has her electric sewing machine set up on a small table in front of the window and a wicker basket beside it full of reels of coloured threads. Another table, at right angles to the sewing table, is obviously used for cutting out patterns. There is a pattern laid out on it, a Vogue pattern for a dress. It is pinned onto the material, a length of rich, ruby red wool. On the walls are black and white photographs of models in various poses. I peered at them, and saw that they are signed to Grace, from the models I presume. They must be modelling dresses she has made. I was about to leave when I noticed a drawer in the sewing-table. I felt uncomfortable to be opening it, though I recalled, in a curious flashback, how I'd never had any scruples prying into Tilda's things. I opened it, expecting to find pins and suchlike. It was full of letters. They were airmails, all addressed to Grace at her old pre-war address, which had been crossed out and the Blockley address put on in a different hand. I hesitated. I looked at the date of the first— the letters appeared to be neatly placed in order— and the last. The first was dated June 1946, the last March 1950. I could hear Will coming up the stairs, so I closed the drawer, but not without secreting that last letter in my pocket. I met him on the stairs, telling him everything looked perfectly normal.

We went down to the kitchen together. Eileen was feeding Sam, and Will made me a cup of tea. What do you think, Eileen? I asked her. Eileen shook her head and said she had no idea what could have happened, nothing had been unusual. Mrs Baron had seemed just as usual—it was a complete mystery. I thought Will looked relieved when she said that. He said he was going to report Grace as a missing person to the police. He'd already tried, but they'd said to wait at least twenty-four hours. I think now that he is right. Something is very wrong. I left his house feeling guilty about the letter in my pocket.

**30 August**

The police sent someone to see me today, a very bored young policewoman who could hardly muster the energy for the questions she'd been sent to ask, all very routine and obvious. She made it clear that some kind of domestic dispute was thought to be the most likely explanation for my sister's disappearance—Usually is, she yawned. She wanted to know if I'd ever heard Mr and Mrs Baron arguing, and whether Mrs Baron had ever reported any fights to me. I said no, she hadn't, and that I doubted if my sister and brother-in-law had ever seriously argued in their lives. Both, I said, were of a gentle disposition, neither of them in the least aggressive. All the time she was with me I was thinking about that letter I'd taken. It's in French, and my French is rusty, but with the aid of Connie's dictionary I think I've made out most of it and it shows Grace has more secrets than that of Claudia's paternity. She certainly never mentioned this man, Henri, as he signs himself. He was obviously in love with her, and from what I can piece together they must have been lovers, but I don't think he is Claudia's father. He refers to other people who also want to know where Grace is, and there's a bit about 'all of us who suffered together in that terrible time having to bear the consequences'. But Henri says he is going to find

443

Grace even if it takes him the rest of his life, so there is no point in her hiding. He says she has nothing to be ashamed of: everyone did what they had to do to survive. But that last letter, or the last in that pile, was written in 1950, five years ago. How can it have any relevance to Grace's disappearing now? It can't, surely. I wish there was someone I could discuss it with. Not Will, though maybe he knows all about Henri. Unlikely, considering he knows nothing about Claudia's father, which suggests to me there have been no real confidences.

## 31 August

Esther phoned. The police have contacted her and George, part of checking known relatives. I ought to have told her before this but I didn't want to worry her. We discussed the whole thing, and it was a relief to have someone to talk to. Esther may be irritating but at times of strain she is better than nobody, and surprisingly sympathetic these days, since Harry came home. That ghoulish side to her isn't as evident as when she was young, maybe because after Harry's experiences she knows now how people in distress feel. Anyway, we talked for ages. I didn't tell her about the letters, though. Grace might want those kept private. In fact, I dread having to admit I found them, and that I have read one, but I'll have to, when she gets back. As Esther pointed out, no bodies have been found so the worst cannot have happened. Oddly enough, I don't for one moment think Grace is dead. I think Will entertains such horrific scenarios, though. He fears she's been kidnapped or abducted. He says Grace would never be so cruel as to put him through this. I can't help agreeing with that, but on the other hand I don't agree with his kidnap or abduction fantasy. Who would kidnap her? Why? I tried to comfort Will by pointing out that kidnappers do it for money, and no one could have thought Grace was worth much, and even if they had, they would have sent a ransom note by now. There was nothing I could say to make abduction by some lunatic seem unlikely. But lunatics *are* lunatics. All I said was that there was not a shred of evidence that Grace had been captured against her will.

## 1 September

Grace's car has been found in Dover. In perfect condition. No signs of any struggle. My heart contracted when I heard the word Dover—it made me think instantly of the cliffs—but no body has been found and the coastguards have assured Will, who thought the same as I did, that if she had thrown herself off the cliffs her body would most certainly have been found by now. In any case, the car was nowhere near the cliffs; it was in the town. It looks more and more as if Grace chose to drive off, for whatever reason, and that no one else is involved. The police are less interested now, not that they seemed terribly interested in the first place. They have towed the car away. Will has asked me to go with him down to Dover to search for Grace. Eileen will stay with Sam. I feel so reluctant about going but I don't like to let him

445

down. He wants to search every hotel and boarding-house in Dover, showing Grace's photograph. He is now convinced she has had some sort of breakdown and may have forgotten who she is. At least this theory is preferable to the abduction one and tortures him less. So I am going to go, though it worries me that there will be nobody in my house if Grace should try to contact me, but I suppose that is not very likely as she hasn't done so yet. And if Will is right, if she's lost her memory, she'll have forgotten I exist. I try to imagine not being able to remember anything at all and I can't. Memory is so much a part of identity. It's eerie to think of having no memory. I felt, those months in Blockley, that Grace was working ferociously hard to kill certain memories, and that she thought she'd succeeded. If, now, she has indeed forgotten who she is, will she be in a state of terror and panic? But she drove her car, parked it neatly in a public place, and has survived three days without accident, so she is in some kind of control. Grace has my house key, she's always had it, just as I have hers. I am going to write a note, saying where I've gone and why, and leave it prominently displayed, just in case she comes here. But how can she, if she has lost her memory.

**2 September**

Tense day with Will. We drove here, to Dover, and booked into an hotel, and then spent the whole afternoon going into all the other hotels, about twenty of them, showing Grace's photograph. Reactions varied enormously. Some receptionists were most helpful, peered at it for ages, thought long and deeply, called for other staff to join them, and then regretfully shook their heads. Others were suspicious, or bored, or both, and I felt angry with them. I began to see why Will wanted me with him. I am the respectable middle-aged woman who makes his inquiry seem sincere, and I am calm whereas he is all too clearly distraught. I insisted that we paused to eat something after an hour of this—we'd left London at eight in the morning and had had nothing at all to eat or drink the whole day. Will just pushed his sandwich about but he drank the tea, and I think the break steadied him. Off we went again, until we'd visited all the hotels listed in the town guide. He wanted to go out this evening to search places of entertainment but I could see no sense in that. I cannot imagine that Grace, in whatever state, will be out on a dark autumn evening looking for entertainment. But he went. He can't keep still. He feels better prowling around. I settled down here in this rather dismal hotel bedroom, wondering how long this will continue. I feel so detached and I think Will finds me cold and unsympathetic. He expects me to be in a state, as he is. He came near to accusing me of not caring about Grace but I didn't bother to refute this suggestion. Grace knows I care, that's all that matters. It is just that I cannot be doing with histrionics.

**3 September**

Terrible day, from every point of view. Torrential rain and a howling wind so that we were soaked before we'd checked the first half dozen bed-and-breakfast places. The rain was the sort that stings, and it drove against us with such force, coming straight off the sea. My umbrella was blown inside out and I had to abandon it. Every time we rang a doorbell, and the door was reluctantly opened, we presented such a wretched picture and were given short shrift. The photograph of Grace is beginning to look dog-eared, especially after it was twice dropped on a wet doorstep. It was all so depressing and also pointless, I felt sure. I tried to say so at lunch-time but Will grew quite fierce and insisted there was nothing else we could do. To my alarm, he started worrying aloud about what to tell Claudia, who comes back with her friend's family the day after tomorrow. He is right, of course. Claudia will have to be told something, and she will take it very hard. Then Will asked if I would be there when she arrived home and do the telling. He says it would be better coming from me: he would be unable to keep his fears out of his expression and voice. I can see that this is true, but all the same I don't want to be the bearer of such tidings. Will says I have known Claudia since she was 4 and have a better understanding of her. I don't think that is correct. I don't think anyone except Grace is close to Claudia. She is so reserved, almost inscrutable, and I am never at ease with her. But I suppose I will have to do what Will asks. At any rate, I am going home tomorrow even if he stays. I've agreed to go to his house to relieve Eileen a little, though it isn't something I have much enthusiasm for. Sam is sweet but he is exhausting and I feel I've done all that, done the looking after small children. The thought of school starting again in three days' time dismays me—I will not be able to concentrate on anything if Grace has not returned.

## 4 September

Left Dover early afternoon, by train, leaving Will to continue his pathetic search. He suggested that I drove Grace's car but I didn't feel up to it. More than that, I felt superstitious about taking over her car—ridiculous, but a strong feeling that it would bring bad luck. Went to my own home first and had a bath and changed my clothes, then drove over to Will's place where Eileen was very glad to see me. There were no messages. She, too, is concerned about the return of Claudia tomorrow, telling me that the girl had taken some persuasion to go on holiday with her friend—the first real friend she's made—because she's never left her mother before, not even for a night. Grace has apparently tried to persuade her to accept invitations, not that there have been more than a couple, but she had never agreed until now. I remembered that when Grace and Will married they didn't have a honeymoon but went to Sardinia later with Claudia. How odd. But then, this being the case, isn't it surely a sign that Grace will return for Claudia? If, as Eileen says, she urged Claudia to make the huge step of going away without her wouldn't part of her persuasion have been that she'd be right here when she returned? Grace knows better than anyone her daughter's dependency on her and would surely never let her down. But on the other hand, maybe it shows that Will is correct to believe Grace has had some kind of massive breakdown—in her right mind, she wouldn't let Claudia return to find her missing. Eileen and I went over all this then I insisted she had a day off, well, an evening, and she phoned a friend and went out about six o'clock, after she'd put Sam to bed (thank heaven).

This left me alone in the house, except for the sleeping baby, and I was irresistibly drawn to Grace's sewing-room and those damned letters. I took the whole drawer out and only then saw that it was twice the length I'd realised—pulling it out that first time I'd taken the thick piece of wood at the back to be the end of the drawer but it isn't. The drawer runs under the whole length of the table and is divided into two compartments. There were more letters in the back section. All in French. All from Henri. The date of the last one was two days before Grace disappeared. I know I will have to tell Will. Even before I'd hurriedly read them, trying simply to get the general sense, I knew that. I read the most recent letter, the crucial one, carefully, though with no dictionary to hand I made a poor job of it. So far as I can make out, Henri has discovered where Grace works. He says he has never given up his search and his love for her. He says ten years is too long to punish him and he doesn't know why she has made him suffer when nothing that happened was his fault: it was the war. He asks for one meeting with her, just one chance to see her beautiful face again, surely she can grant him that. Then I think the tone changes, his words sound threatening. He writes that he knows the truth about the child and one day she will need to know and he hopes he will not have to be the one to tell her. So it seems that here in these letters is some kind of explanation, or the beginnings of one, for why Grace left so abruptly. Did she go to meet Henri? Or to evade him? I can't work out what she is so frightened of, but maybe I am missing vital clues. The postmarks on the letters show them to have been sent very regularly since 1946. I am certain no letters arrived while Grace and I were living together in that cottage in Blockley. The first arrived there, if it was the first, after I'd returned with the twins to London. And she has kept his letters, as though they are precious or at least significant. I will *have* to tell Will, and perhaps the police. It is all so complicated, so hard to understand, so much is at risk.

**5 September**

Grace arrived home this morning, at ten o'clock, in a taxi.

**6 September**

The events of yesterday were so dramatic that I couldn't think about describing them, everything had to settle, and I am not sure it has done so even now. Grace came into the house looking pale but quite composed. Eileen and I heard the door open and thought it was Will returning, but there was the quick pitter-patter of high heels on the hall floor and then in came Grace, straight over to Sam's high-chair in which he was sitting, eating toast. He screamed, Eileen and I exclaimed, Grace picked him up and cuddled him and then she wept a little

451

and used his bib to wipe her face, and then she said would one of us make her some coffee, she'd be grateful. Eileen made it, and we sat in stunned silence, waiting, while she drank it. The waiting went on and on, and finally I could stand it no longer and said, Grace, for heaven's sake, where on earth have you been, we've been terrified . . . Don't, she said, and, I know, I'm sorry. I didn't mean it. Then she asked where Will was and I said he was on his way back from Dover where he and I had spent two days searching for her after her car was found. She closed her eyes and groaned. Yes, I said, the car, you can imagine what we feared. She said she was sorry, and then asked Eileen if she'd put Sam down for his nap, but of course the baby wouldn't be parted from her and she herself had to go off with Eileen to settle him. It seemed ages till she came back and I was beginning to feel angry with her and working myself up into a great state of indignation now that the relief of seeing her back, apparently unharmed, had passed. At last she came into the kitchen again, without Eileen, and said she didn't know where to start, she didn't know how to explain, something had just come over her and she'd had to get away and she knew it was inexcusable to have gone off like that. She thought maybe she'd had a breakdown—she couldn't even remember driving to Dover, or leaving her car there—she would go to the doctor's. On and on, and all of it lies. I let her ramble on, watching her wander about her own kitchen fiddling with things, and then I'd had enough. What about those letters, I said. What letters? was all she would say. The ones in your sewing-table drawer, from Henri, I insisted. Who is Henri? I asked her, and told her not to lie. It was strange how afraid I felt, asking that question, demanding an answer, and yet dreading what I thought could be the only possible reply. What a mess this is, I kept thinking, what a mess, how many lives are spoiled—because, of course, I assumed she must love this Henri and had gone to him and now her whole life was going to be turned upside down. Was she now going to leave Will for Henri? He would be devastated. It seemed to me so wicked of Grace to wreck what I'd thought was a happy marriage, one I'd envied, and make so unhappy a husband who had made her feel secure, and, worst of all, damage her children's future. All this was going through my head as I watched her and the tension was unbearable. She told me to sit down. I sat, and glad to, my legs quite weak all of a sudden. I thought she might be going to say that I had had no right to read her letters, but she didn't. She spoke very quietly, in a composed way which surprised me and made me feel my own voice and manner had been strident— it was as though she were the elder sister and I the younger and the one in the wrong.

She said Henri was a man she'd known when she went to Paris to work in 1938. They hadn't lived together ever, but they were in love and she thought that if it had not been for the war they would have eventually married. Then the war came. Paris was occupied. They got separated. Something terrible happened. She had Claudia. Then she came back to England. I knew the rest. She hadn't forgotten Henri but she never expected to see him again, nor had she wanted to. Nothing that had happened had been his fault but he belonged to the past and she'd wanted to forget

453

she'd ever been in France. He'd written to her after the war and his letter had been sent on and she'd written back, just once, telling him how she felt and that the clock couldn't be put back. But he wouldn't accept this. He went on writing. When she left Blockley, his letters had gone on being forwarded for as long as her redirection arrangement worked and after that they had stopped, or perhaps had been returned to him. She'd thought that was the end. But then he'd seen her name in a fashion magazine and had started writing to her through it. She'd asked them not to forward any more letters but by then he'd discovered where she worked and wrote to her there. She'd written back, telling him she was now happily married and asking him to stop writing. He'd agreed, on condition she met him just once. So she had. They'd met in Dover, and he'd driven her to an hotel a few miles away. Afterwards, she hadn't been able to find her car and realised it had probably been towed away, but she didn't try to trace it—she was in a hurry to get back for Claudia. She'd come back by train. It was all over. She was very tired. She would tell Will everything. She knew she should have told him before. She knew she'd behaved foolishly. She'd panicked. She should have left some sort of message, she should have made something up. I am writing this in the way she spoke, in a flat, staccato, almost monotone fashion. It took my breath away. There were so many gaps in this unsatisfactory tale that it hardly made sense to me, and yet she seemed to think she'd told me all she needed to. I wanted to press her, but on the other hand there was that same reluctance to do so which I always felt with Grace. 'Something terrible happened' was not enough, but if I asked point-blank what this was, I would feel brutal. Grace had never asked me details about my affair with Robert or about our baby and what happened, though I knew Tilda had told her something. She'd always understood that this was my 'something terrible' and that I didn't want to talk about it, ever. So I should respect Grace's privacy. But all the same, because of her disappearance there were consequences going right back to her 'something terrible' which surely couldn't be kept to herself. What would Will say? How much did he know? I felt I shouldn't be there when he arrived back. I said I was going home. I said I hoped everything would now be all right. Grace said it would. She saw me to the door. She looked drained, very, very tired and sad and I wanted to embrace her but didn't. I should have done. Whatever the ins and outs of all this, she is miserable and has been through a hard time, and it is not over yet.

**9 September**

Silence from Grace, and from Will. Not a word. I presume he is back, and Claudia too, and that they have talked and something has been decided. I suppose I feel mildly upset that they have not thought to tell me how things are. Quick enough when they need me—no, no, I mustn't say that, they are the words of bitterness and I have nothing to be bitter about. It is none of my business what they have said to each other and how things have been resolved. If they have, as I hope.

455

## 10 September

A note from Will, thanking me for all my help, and hoping to see me soon. That's all. I tore the note up. So many things I want to know and which are surely askable, such as why did Grace keep Henri's letters if he meant nothing to her? I feel so intensely irritated not to know. I will ask. I think I am entitled to ask. The next time I see Grace I will ask.

\*     \*     \*

*If Millicent did indeed ever ask Grace to solve these mysteries she did not note down the answers in any diary. But what she quotes from Henri's letters does suggest that Claudia's father probably was a German. Why else would the Frenchman say that he knows the truth and he hopes he will not have to be the one to tell it to Claudia? More significantly, perhaps, Millicent reports that Henri, in this same letter, tells Grace she has 'nothing to be ashamed of' and that 'everyone did what they had to do to survive'. But then there are the burn marks Millicent noted on her sister's arm which suggest that, whatever her relationship with Claudia's father, she may have been tortured at some stage. What may have happened, of course, is that her original German protector left Paris, or was killed, and from being protected Grace went on to be persecuted. By 1943, the Germans were arresting huge numbers of Parisians for Gaullist, communist or anti-German activity and Grace could have been rounded up. Having had a baby by a German soldier would not have saved her—85,000 babies were fathered by Germans in France during the war, making her plight not uncommon.*

*At any rate, Millicent seems never to have been told the truth and this fact creates a permanent distance between her and her sister which never entirely disappears. She tries to be sympathetic towards Grace, but her lack of trust, or what she sees as a lack of trust, hurts her. A great keeper of secrets herself, she resents Grace firmly choosing to keep this darkest of secrets.*

*But they do see each other again, very soon, ten days after Grace's return home. Millicent goes to lunch—though there is a long entry in which she debates whether she should, because she is feeling so aggrieved—and is astounded at how normal everything seems in the Baron household. Neither Will nor Grace makes any reference whatsoever to the events of 28 August to 5 September, but she realises this may be because Claudia is present. Millicent makes a determined effort to rise above her resentment by focusing on more important issues. Chief of these is her growing interest in the anti-H-bomb movement. At the time of Harry's involvement in the Korean War, she had of course written of her fury at the thought of another war in which the H-bomb might be used but this hadn't at the time led her into allying herself with those who protested against it, though she does record reading John Hersey's* Hiroshima *(a book published in 1946 which is a factual account of the deaths of those killed) and wishes she could stop the use of bombs. Then in March 1955, she picks up a copy of the* Hampstead & Highgate Express *while she is visiting Daphne, and seeing the headline 'H-bomb Must Be Banned' and reading of the start of a campaign against it, she wishes she could be a part of it. On*

457

*26 August, just before Grace's vanishing-act she actually attended a meeting in Golders Green, held in a Methodist church hall, to discuss what can be done about trying to get the H-bomb banned. She found herself rather embarrassed to be there and sometimes uncomfortable at the company she was keeping, but her wish to try to do something grows stronger. Millicent continues to attend meetings. She is pleased to be one of the silent, solid supporters without whom the leaders emerging cannot make any headway. The next two years, 1955–7, pass without any dramas, with the twins at university and using the house merely as a base. Then her big moment comes on 12 May 1957 when she is proud to be one of the 2,000 women who marched in silence throughout the streets of London to Trafalgar Square to be addressed by distinguished speakers (among them Vera Brittain whose* Testament of Youth *Millicent has read and admired).*

\*     \*     \*

## 13 November

Connie rang, a rare treat, and I told her I'd attended the meeting about the H-bomb, managing, I hope, to make it sound amusing, though really it was more embarrassing than funny. There was something so terribly British about us all—not a fanatic among us, but instead sixty or so people, overwhelmingly respectable in dress and bearing, all being polite to each other. The hall was draughty, the seats uncomfortable, and the windows hadn't been cleaned for months. The man

458

who addressed the meeting, aged about 50, told us he was an accountant and that he'd never done anything like this before, and said how relieved he was to see that far from being hotheads we all appeared to be sensible people who had been brought together through a sense of outrage over what governments might do with a nuclear bomb. At that point, the only light in the hall, weak in any case, went out. Much laughter, then a search for a new bulb followed by another search for the fuse box when the bulb didn't work. By the time our accountant friend was speaking to us again we were restless and bored. He wasn't a good speaker. A very ordinary man, but then who am I to talk? That was the point about us all, surely. It was what should have been inspiring.

## 1 December

A better meeting tonight, and a very different collection of people. Not so many of my own age and some of them excellent speakers. One young woman, who reminded me of Connie, had obviously done some proper research and quoted all kinds of statistics to do with radioactivity which, though I didn't take them all in, sounded impressive, not that I think any of us needed to be convinced that an H-bomb exploding would cause horrific and lasting damage. But I liked her combination of passion and logic. We applauded her wildly.

## 13 May 1957

Too exhausted last night even to think about writing in this diary, but I ought to have done because thinking about the events of yesterday kept me awake in spite of my exhaustion. I seemed still to be marching, in perfect time with complete strangers to my right and left. We were absolutely silent from the moment we set off, and except for our feet and the rustling of some of the black sashes we all wore there was no sound until it started to rain heavily and even then the noise as the rain hit the pavements in torrents only seemed to make our lack of noise more significant. I had dressed sensibly, wearing a long waterproof coat and wellington boots and a large waterproof hat with a wide brim which was a godsend because it not only kept my head dry but also my shoulders. I looked a sight, but I didn't care. I'd made my sash out of black nylon, not very pretty, but it was light and even when sodden didn't burden me. I tied it across my body and then in a bow at the side. It was incredible how, without much actual organisation, we all lined up, hundreds of women all together, and set off, those with banners mainly in the front. Most of these were crudely made, and the lettering on them soon began to run in the rain, but still the simple words Stop The Tests and Save Your Child could be read. I felt so proud of us all, making this silent, dignified protest prepared to march through London and get soaked and think it worthwhile. Most of the women were, I am sure, like me and had never done anything like this before. I tried to concentrate, as I marched, on the thought of those who had died in the last war but that was a mistake, it only choked me with emotion, and it was foolish because it is too late for them. We were marching for the next generation, for Connie and Toby, and Claudia and Sam, and their children. It was strange how, even surrounded by hundreds of others, I felt isolated, not in the least submerged in the crowd. We were all individuals, people of no consequence but not a mindless mob, not folk following the herd. We all knew why we were there. I heard onlookers say as we passed by, What are they doing, what is going on? and I thought how too often I have been in that position, not knowing what governments were doing in my name. I was tired of feeling bewildered and outraged and spineless. It helped yesterday to march in those atrocious conditions, and listening to the speakers when we got to Trafalgar Square I felt inspired to continue. The newspapers today say there were about 2,000 of us marching and even more standing in the Square.

**14 May**

Connie telephoned, highly delighted because she says she saw my photograph among the marchers in a newspaper. I didn't see it myself, but she was adamant it was me and described my outlandish hat most convincingly. She said she was proud of me and that if she'd been at home she would have joined me. I like the idea of that, Connie and me, niece and aunt, two generations marching together. It was what I wanted to do as a girl, become involved in protests against war, but Father dissuaded me. I wonder what he would think of me now. He'd be scandalised, probably, he'd say I was making an exhibition of myself and that I should be at home, running my household like a dignified woman.

## 15 May

How famous I am becoming. Harry turned up at my door today, grinning from ear to ear and saying he'd come to ask for my autograph after seeing my photograph in the paper. He stayed for tea and became serious over it. He is such a thoughtful young man, and of course his terrible experiences in Korea have changed him. I asked him how he was feeling and he said he still has stomach problems but that he has recovered well, considering. Esther had told me that he hardly ever talks about it, and doesn't like to be pressed, so I didn't ask questions. He is going to agricultural college in the autumn, wants to be a farmer and in time take over the family farm. It was nice of him to call. Before he left, he seemed to linger in the hall, as though he was reluctant to go or wanted something. He stopped in front of the photograph I have hanging just behind the front door, of George on his 18th birthday. That's Dad, isn't it? he said, and I nodded. He stared at it for ages as though he couldn't quite believe it. I've never really known what happened to him in the war, he said, just that he was injured and invalided out. I hesitated, not wanting to tell him anything George himself had not done. I said that yes, he'd been injured, shot, and had his arm broken, and he'd been gassed. Harry said nothing. I never guessed what he'd gone

462

through till Korea, he said at last, and even then I wasn't wounded. Now I know how he feels.

**25 May**

Went to visit Toby, on my day off, before his term ends. I am alarmed to hear he has changed his course from medicine to sciences. He has suggested I visit before, but somehow I've felt diffident about turning up, ye ancient maiden aunt, worrying that he might be embarrassed by me, though he's never given the least hint of this. Anyway, I went and was glad, though at first memories of being there before, with Daphne, and thinking of all that had happened since to hopes and ambitions, well, it made me a little melancholic for a while. Hope Toby didn't realise and that I managed to keep the melancholy out of my face. He has rather a poky room but the college itself is splendid. We walked along the backs and then had a picnic lunch. I'd said he was to choose a restaurant and I'd treat him but, surprisingly, he'd shopped and had a basket stuffed with treats and insisted we should have a picnic and then he'd take me in a punt on the river. Truth is, he isn't very good at punting and I was sure we'd capsize, but no, he kept us afloat, just, though I hung rather grimly on to the sides.

Toby doesn't talk much. It seems to me that he used to be just as much of a chatterbox as Connie but now he has become rather quiet and rarely initiates any conversation. Would this have happened if Tilda had been alive? A silly thing to wonder, of course it would, his reluctance these days to talk has nothing to do with his mother's absence. In fact, Charles was not much of a talker either. Charles was mentioned several times in the course of the day, twice by me, once by Toby. I shouldn't have said his father would have been disappointed that he'd dropped medicine. I couldn't help saying that he was looking more and more like his father—he blushed furiously at this— then that Charles had once capsized a punt and half drowned Tilda. I don't think he likes me volunteering this kind of thing. He always frowns and looks away, whereas Connie leaps on any little titbit and wants more. The difference between men and women? More prejudice. I noticed Toby didn't seem to know anybody. He didn't greet anyone we met in the grounds of his college, and he wasn't greeted by anyone. Maybe he hasn't made any friends, or maybe they just were not around today. I feel a little anxious about him and must talk to Connie. I thought it permissible to ask if he missed her and was surprised how quickly and strongly he denied it, almost as though I'd insulted him, or had implied he couldn't stand on his own two feet.

He's coming home for two weeks at the end of term and then spending the rest of the vacation in Alaska, on some expedition. I'm glad he won't be on his own. He used to be every bit as sociable and popular as Connie, but not now, so going with a group is the best thing. What a worry children are, even when grown up, and I am only an aunt. I realise I want Toby to have a girlfriend and be happy and do well and get a good job and marry and settle down, and it is all quite ridiculous when I, of all people, know that life is full of shocks and surprises and it's no good planning and having cosy

464

fantasies of a perfect future for one's children. It's strange the way I worry about Connie far less and yet she's the girl and life is harder for women. But Connie is full of spirit and can cope with anything, and when I went to visit her was in the thick of everything and surrounded by chums. If Toby looks more and more like Charles, Connie looks less and less like Tilda. Twice people thought I was her mother and I must say I could not help being flattered. Connie is the daughter I would like to have had. I said that to her once. But you *do* have me, she said, seeming quite hurt, I *am* your daughter, how could you not think so? I was touched, but not fooled. I know the difference. I love Connie dearly, and I am close to her (I think) but Tilda was her mother and in many ways even after all this time she still is. But Toby is the one who might be a different boy if his parents had lived, and if he had had Jack as an influential big brother. I never think of him as the son I almost had. Never. I feel distant from him and it worries me. Have I failed Toby?

# 8 July 1957

Daphne has suggested that we go on holiday together, somewhere interesting and sunny as she puts it. My instinctive reaction was to say no, emphatically, but she pre-empted me by telling me not to say no automatically and to think about it. Holidays have always been a problem to me when I have to think of taking them alone. I want to be bold, and go off and do adventurous things but increasingly I have not the nerve. I can't believe I ever went to Paris on my own all those years ago. It is embarrassing to be alone, one is so conspicuous, and eating especially makes me uncomfortable and self-conscious. One is a target, though of course of a different kind to when one was young. I did it in Paris all those years ago but shrink from doing it now. A companion solves so many problems, though that can be embarrassing too, knowing what people think if they see two women together. Well, let them think, that doesn't bother me. But would Daphne and I get along? I said that to her. What after all do we have in common? Nothing, except for a history. Precisely, said Daphne, and that is why it would work. We know each other, and all about each other, and there need be no pretence, we are frank and outspoken together. I said to her that I couldn't imagine that she could not holiday alone, or else in a group, since she is fearless in all situations, unlike me, and a very social animal with hordes of friends. She said she was tired of her friends, male and female, and felt too sad to be alone on holiday, she would be preyed upon. That made me laugh, Daphne, preyed upon indeed, the very idea. So I seem to have agreed, with the proviso that I vet where we will go and that it cannot be anywhere which costs much money. I emphasised that I am poor, and she said, oh stuff. But I *am* poor. I realised the other day that really I am, except I own a house, which of course in London is something. But the income I have had all these years from Mother's shares, or rather Harold's, to pay bills and meet ordinary costs of living, is small. I should never have sold so many of those shares—it was foolish. I can't bear to see how much they are worth now. But I had no option, I needed so much money last year to re-roof the house and have it rewired, and then the car packed up and even this second-hand Ford cost such a lot. I have looked after the twins these last few years on *their* money, from their trusts, and now they are at university they need it themselves. I don't think either of them realise my financial situation and I will certainly not draw attention to it. If I am very, very careful I can still manage. But this holiday Daphne proposes will be an extravagance. If I did not earn a little from my teaching I could not indulge myself.

**15 July**

Daphne has come up with such absurd holiday suggestions. Nepal was one, trekking in the Himalayas. Has she ever been climbing? No. Nor has she ever walked anywhere if she could drive. And as for me, my walking experiences hardly equip me for the Himalayas, though compared to

467

Daphne I would rate as a Sherpa. The next was Australia, the Great Barrier Reef and the interior—ridiculous! The cost alone is prohibitive. Daphne pooh-poohed this, saying she will pay, but I am not having that. Really, I don't care if the whole idea falls through. I am quite content pottering about in my garden and have no great urge to get away.

**20 July**

I have agreed to go to Greece, on 5 September for three weeks. A much more sensible suggestion and in fact I feel enthusiastic. It will be a good combination of sightseeing and relaxing on beaches. Daphne is in charge of our itinerary, probably a fatal mistake, but I shall inspect it carefully in due course. We are to start off in Athens and then go to several of the islands. Daphne couldn't possibly stay in one place more than two days and plans what she calls island-hopping. I hope these hops will not be too exhausting. When I told Connie where we were going she approved and said how romantic. Not, I fear, in our case, though of course she'd meant romantic in the broadest sense. It made me remember Robert though, and his ambition to sail among the Greek islands. Two middle-aged ladies—well, I am more than middle-aged—doing it is not quite the same thing. I hope I am fit enough. I think I am, so long as I take care of my back.

468

## 16 August

Daphne says we must wear shorts and shirts and carry swimming costumes and that is all. She acts as if we are 16. But I have bought two pairs of shorts and hate them both. Shorts are ugly, it seems to me. It is not that I have bad legs—nothing wrong with my legs even at the mighty age of 56—but that I seem to have put on weight round the hips for the first time in my life, and shorts make me look fat and heavy. Oh, such vanity; but I do mind. I think I will exchange the beastly shorts for light, loose trousers, and ignore what Daphne says. I have bought myself a camera. Dreadful extravagance, but I have always wanted one of these modern Instamatics and I would like to try to take some photographs. I like to think I might have an eye. And I have bought a good pair of sunglasses, since I know the bright sun of Greece will make my eyes water, and a floppy hat. I am being quite childish about this holiday. I am trying to remember when I last did anything as exciting and it is a very long time ago indeed. Connie's and Toby's generation are so fortunate. Already the two of them have travelled to so many countries and think nothing of it. Do I envy them? Yes, I envy them.

\*       \*       \*

*The holiday is a success. Millicent's pleasure is evident in all the diary entries, which detail every aspect of it, from the island scenery to the historic sights in Athens. She thinks she could live on Corfu, the last island they visited, and for a while entertains a fantasy of buying a humble little stone house in*

469

*Nissaki and supporting herself by teaching English. She feels young again, wears her shorts (she evidently only took one pair back to the shop) and is quite delighted imagining herself as a beatnik. She and Daphne don't so much get on well as co-exist, leading separate lives but sharing living quarters. Daphne sleeps all morning, totters out to drink and eat at midday, sleeps again in the afternoon then spends long evenings in the taverna keeping what Millicent refers to as 'highly doubtful company'. She herself, on the other hand, is up at dawn to walk on the beach before she swims most of the morning, with interludes reading in the shade—she has taken Iris Murdoch's* Under the Net *with her, Doris Lessing's* Martha Quest *and Tolkien's* Lord of the Rings *(which she abandons). She joins Daphne for lunch, has a siesta, then is out taking photographs in the late afternoon. She does go with Daphne to eat at the taverna, but comes back to their rented house early and reads again. At the end of September, as they prepare to go back to London, she has some reflections to make about the whole experience of the Greek islands.*

\*　　　\*　　　\*

## 25 September

I feel sad to be leaving this island. I think of my London street, the general grey of it, the hard pavements, the traffic, and I think of the rain and cold and the lowering skies so much of the year, and I am appalled. Daphne, oddly enough, is quite happy to return. I thought she was having a wonderful time but maybe not. She says I have *led*

470

*the wrong life* and that I should have been born an island urchin whereas she has metropolitan stamped through her like a piece of rock. I have thrived, but she has not. She hasn't tanned as I have, in fact she looks pale and a little drawn and not as though she has been on holiday in such perfect weather. She says she feels tired. Too much drinking, I think. How she can drink all that retsina and ouzo I cannot imagine. Twice she's been sick, but this hasn't stopped her going back for more, and she has an awful cough but won't stop smoking. If I point out that it is the drinking which is making her sick she hurls at me the usual jibe, that I am prim and school-marmish and asks me to stop being judgemental. So I do, I have. It doesn't hurt me any more when she says such things. Here I don't feel in the least prim or school-marmish, and I know I don't look it.

**1 October**

An awful dreariness hangs over everything. Bad luck to come back from such a wonderful holiday to cold, wet weather and so many small things which have gone wrong. Some guttering has fallen off the new roof in a storm and a cat has got into my garden and wrecked what remained of my plants. I seem to take delight in nothing. Is this the beginning of old age? Yet I didn't feel it in Greece. Go back there, then, my irritable self snaps, but that isn't the answer. The truth is, and it must be faced, I am bored. My life seems to lack both point and pleasure. Pleasure—is life about the pursuit of pleasure? Once I thought it was meant to be about

471

more than that. What all this introspection amounts to is a restlessness, a refusal to be satisfied with ordinariness. Endless expectations which aren't realised. Oh, I annoy myself. If this is going to be the aftermath of every holiday, I had better not take any more.

## 5 October

Toby has been here briefly, a pause before going back to Cambridge. He is a strange young man. All he wanted to talk about was some rumour that the Russians are about to put a dog into orbit. I wish Connie had been here at the same time so that we could have discussed him. He has grown a beard which because it has come out red makes him look very fierce. I do wish he would shave it off, but he says he doesn't intend to unless it turns out there is some college rule forcing him to. He seems to have grown even taller, but maybe he simply looks taller because he is thinner. Not much emerged about his Alaska trip. Not much emerged about anything. He has become singularly uncommunicative. He showed no interest in my Greek holiday. The truth is, he has become a morose boy and I don't know what is the matter with him. I tried to talk to him about his future, but he seemed to think this was some kind of impertinence. He shrugged and said repeatedly that he doesn't know what he wants to do, but he is glad he gave up medicine. He can't see the point of being a doctor: doctors know so little and their work is miserable stuff, he says. But on the contrary, I said, their work is worthwhile and full of purpose. Making sick people better, what

472

could be more satisfying? Toby said doctors make more people ill than well, which exasperated me. It occurred to me more than once during these interchanges that Toby doesn't like me. That is what seems to come off him, dislike. I intend to bear this with dignity.

**2 November**

Phone call from Daphne, whom I have not seen since our holiday, though I have called her several times and got no reply. Could I come over, she asked in her most plaintive voice, one I know well, one which makes me wary because she puts it on when she wants something—her special little-girl voice. I said it was late and dark and I really didn't feel like driving to Frognal. Couldn't it wait until tomorrow? She said she supposed so in such a sorrowful voice, not at all like her—usually a refusal to answer a summons results in passionate persuasion—that I weakened, while resenting her power over me. I drove to her house in a bad temper, prepared to be very cross with her, but when I saw her I must say I was taken aback. This was no pretence. She looks quite dreadful, terribly thin and her colour is alarming and her cough frightful. She was huddled in bed, her hair all lank, and looked as though she hadn't moved from it for a week. There were plates of half-eaten sandwiches on the floor and mugs of cold tea and the room stank of stale cigarette smoke. I scolded her to hide my alarm and bustled about clearing up and then went off to her kitchen to make a hot drink. It was nine o'clock by then and too late to ring her doctor, but I decided to stay the night and do so first thing.

A bad night, the spare bed uncomfortable and Daphne's cough making sleep impossible. I rang her doctor at eight in the morning and, thank God, got Dr Harding, a woman. I say thank God because by then I had seen the blood Daphne was coughing up, blood and mucus mixed, quite horrible, and I was terribly afraid of its significance. I was right to be. Daphne is now in hospital and, though no diagnosis has yet been made, I think it is fairly obvious what it is going to be. I think Daphne knows too. She said nothing and I said nothing as we travelled in the ambulance but she held out her hand and I took it. I saw her into the ward, by which time she had her eyes closed and was completely withdrawn. I hope she won't stay in this ward long. She requested a private room but there isn't one available at the moment. I do so hate hospitals. Tilda could never understand why. Daphne hates them too. We used to agree that happiness could be defined as walking out of a hospital. She, of course, had so much of them after her accident whereas I have never been in one as a patient in my life, except that once, and it was only for such a short time it hardly counts. I don't recall much about it at all. Daphne has put me down as next of kin on the admission form. I am not kin but I suppose I am all the kin she has. I have just rung the hospital but there is no news: she is in that cliché state, as comfortable as can be expected. Luckily, today was not a teaching day, though if it had been I would have had to take the time off, whatever chaos it caused at school.

## 4 November

Couldn't write a word yesterday and even now I find it hard. This diary is of so little use when I most need it. Daphne has a tumour on her left lung. Look how cowardly I am, even in private. The doctor has made it plain that he expects to find it is malignant, or in other words that she has cancer and the lung will most probably need to be removed. My head was spinning with all the implications of this, but I could only frame idiotic questions of no importance and failed to ask what really needs to be asked: is her life in danger, can she survive with one lung? And crowding in on this was the other question, which I can never ask. Will she be able to live alone after this operation?

## 5 November

Daphne has been moved to the Royal Marsden in Fulham. I am not sure why, except that apparently Dr Harding has told her that the Marsden is the specialist hospital for cancer and she has the best chance of the right treatment there. But there isn't at the moment a private room available here either and, worse than that, she is in a ward which is full of what even I can see are terminal patients because the terminal ward is being decorated. When I was there today, for the whole two hours I stayed, a woman sang Happy Birthday, Dad, over and over again, humming the tune every now and again in a low drone. Daphne says she's called Brenda and that last night she got out of her bed, trailing drips and tubes, and danced up and down

475

the ward singing and had to be forcefully restrained. She has a brain tumour. Well, said Daphne, brightly, my brain is fine. Before I left, Brenda had changed to singing No control, going out, no control going out. It is barbaric, how can my poor darling friend get better here? What a terrible place. I hate its long, tiled, gloomy corridors and its endless flights of stone stairs. I got lost on my way out and began to panic, I felt like a little mouse, trapped and scurrying around. This won't do.

## 6 November

Arrived at Daphne's bedside to find the ward quiet, thank God, but then I realised why. In the next bed to her was an old lady being given the last rites. The green curtains were drawn round the bed, and we could hear the priest reciting the doleful words. Then at the end of the ward, in a small cubicle near the nurses' station, another man was saying prayers over the now immobile and silent Brenda. Daphne was laughing, it was just so very dreadful. I found it hard to sit beside her. She told me not to look so bloody miserable and I said, how could I not, and she said she wanted me to cheer her up and be my sensible self at which point, quite disgracefully, I burst into tears, the worst thing to do. I controlled myself quickly but the damage was done. Daphne amazed me. She was so calm, said she was prepared for the worst and felt philosophical now she was actually in hospital. It was the weeks before that had wrecked her, the worrying, the suspicions she'd had, even before we went to Greece, that was

476

the bad part. Now she feels in good hands and has given herself up to fate. I left her feeling ashamed of my tears when she herself is so brave. I will do better tomorrow, though in fact I won't see her tomorrow because the operation is in the afternoon and I am not allowed to, so will not have a chance to redeem myself. Poor Daphne, to be going through this ordeal and no one to cherish her except me.

**8 November**

Daphne is finally in a private room, at last. She was sitting up today, so at first glance she looked much better. Not at second glance, though. She has all sorts of tubes coming out of her, which I try not to look at. She was sleepy, even if propped up as though sitting, and only opened her eyes fully when I crept in and said hello. She did try to smile but her face hardly moved. It was so awkward, such a strain. What to say? I was lost, muttering on about the weather and the traffic and other banalities. I ran out of steam so quickly. The words 'how are you feeling' choked me and I could not say them. I didn't know how long to stay. After a while, I got up and tip-toed round the little room, fiddling with the flowers, playing with the cord of the window blind, the feeling of being trapped growing and growing. I saw her hand move on the white sheet, opening and closing over and over again, and I suddenly sat down again and put my own hand into hers. It seemed such an intimate gesture, more so than a kiss. I thought she seemed to like it, and I put my other hand over our joined hands and held them tight. That was how the nurse found us. She came in to take readings of some sort or another. She looked at me so pityingly and then was gone.

An hour I sat there and then I released her hand and it flopped back onto the sheet. She was asleep. There was no point in staying. I crept out as I had crept in and felt so weary. And now I am overwhelmed with misery, not all of it on account of Daphne. I wish I had some religious faith, I wish I was a Christian, like Mother and Tilda, but I have not and am not, and at a time like this, it is a loss. I dread going to the Marsden each day. My footsteps slow down as I reach the hospital and I experience all the symptoms of panic and have to force myself up its steps. But Daphne has no other visitors. Where are all those friends she was forever referring to? If they have shown concern, I know nothing of it, but then maybe they are unaware of what has happened. I suddenly thought today of Jimmy. I wonder if I should try to find his address and tell him, but it is so long since they were divorced and he is in America and what good would it do? I worry about what is going to happen if Daphne is discharged and I know that my real worry is for myself and my fear that I will have to look after her. Well, I will, of course I will, but it is a daunting prospect.

**11 November**

Grace came. It is so long since I have seen her. She brought little Sam and it was a pleasure to see him, such a bright, glowing, healthy boy, a smile always on his face. Grace said I looked depressed. I know she meant old. I told her about Daphne and she was all concern, genuine I am sure. When I said I was visiting every day, Grace said that was good of me but was it really necessary? Daphne isn't family after all. She said it gently but I was angry and told her that Daphne meant more to me than some of my family. She took this to be a reference to herself, I think, and flushed, so I added rather feebly that I had known Daphne since she was 17 and we had been through a lot together and she had no one else to care for her. Grace said she was lucky to have me with my highly developed sense of duty. That's what she called it, *my highly developed sense of duty*. I flared up and said duty had nothing to do with it and that if I was motivated by anything it was by affection and loyalty. Grace said she was sorry if she'd upset me, but then spoiled her apology by wondering aloud if Daphne was as reliable as a friend as I was, would she do the same for me? But, of course, she added, I had family to care for me, should I need looking after. She said that bit hurriedly. I laughed, maybe a little bitterly, and said my family need not worry, I would never call on them. I have always been independent and I always will be. That is what my life has been about, *standing on my own two feet*, and it is not going to change just because I am growing old. I am ashamed of that outburst now. So pompous. And Grace left soon afterwards.

I started wondering about the truth of my fine words. What if I am ill? Can I indeed remain independent? I will try to, desperately hard. I ought to think about it carefully and try to provide against being ill and unable to manage. I wonder if I would kill myself. It is such an act of courage not

479

cowardice and I don't think I have that courage. My mind is full of such wretched thoughts and it is not healthy. I go to the Marsden, I sit uselessly with poor Daphne, I come home exhausted in every way, and then I sit and muse about death. What an awful stage my life seems to be at.

\*     \*     \*

*These kind of entries continue during the rest of 1957 and into 1958 as Millicent masterminds Daphne's convalescence with her customary efficiency. She finds a nursing home for her friend to go into and then engages a nurse and a housekeeper for when she returns home. Since Daphne is wealthy, money is not a difficulty, but finding kindly and sympathetic people who are trustworthy is. Daphne is not an easy patient and for six months Millicent is at her beck and call trying to make the support system work. Connie, on her rare visits home, is concerned that she is wearing herself out and there is one entry in which Millicent expresses her fury that her niece has called her a martyr. But then, in March 1958, Daphne has a relapse, is readmitted to the Marsden, and on the 20th she dies. Her death is sudden in spite of the long preparation for it, and Millicent is stunned. She writes that it is as if she were a ship and all the wind has left her sails and she is becalmed. She can hardly manage to arrange for Daphne's cremation and sees no point in a funeral, but then the absence of ceremony in turn depresses her. She finds herself sitting slumped in a chair, day after day, making no effort to do anything. It adds to her depression that Grace and her family go to live in New York, which is a shock to her. Fortunately, Connie comes home at this point for the*

480

*Easter vacation and galvanises her aunt into joining her on one of the Aldermaston marches.*

\*      \*      \*

**2 April 1958**

What a determined young woman Connie is, so full of energy and ideas, making me ashamed of my listlessness and apathy. The very air in the room seems electric when she comes into it and, though she makes me feel weak she also perks me up, something passes from her to me and I am the better for it. From the moment she arrived home she began shaking me up, asking me what on earth I thought I was doing letting myself go in the way I obviously have. Look in a mirror, for God's sake! she shouted, and promptly marched me into the hall and pointed at my reflection in the mirror there. Who is that? she demanded. Who is that miserable-looking creature with bags under her eyes and no colour in her cheeks and chopped-off hair? Do you know her? Because I don't. She exaggerated, but not much. I do look awful, no wonder I avoid mirrors. My hair is turning grey and has become so dry and brittle, but then I have taken no care of it. And it is too short. I don't suit it so short. Even my skin isn't anything to boast about any more. I sighed, and Connie started again, this time on my clothes, asking how I had come to live permanently in tired old skirts and hopelessly old-fashioned *patterned* blouses. This is how she carries on, hectoring and accusing by turns, and she won't listen to my excuses and what I have been through

481

and how useless I feel, and how there is no point in anything. Oh please! she says. I had no idea what she was talking about when she mentioned the letters CND. She asked if I was the same woman who had boasted about having gone on the women's march only two short years ago. She wants me to go on a march with her now—a three-day affair. I don't think I am up to it. I said this and was told by Connie not to talk such nonsense. She reminded me that I am 57 and not 97 and made me look out my walking boots and my rucksack and in general tried hard to work up some enthusiasm in me. I am not sure that she has succeeded but I did feel a little leap of hope that all is not after all doom and gloom.

## 9 April

This was nothing like the women's march, goodness me no. For a start, there were as many men as women and some of them decidedly odd-looking characters who, I fear, were more with us for the fun than out of conviction, but really I have no right to say that. Then there was the age range, so many young people, which is a very good thing. Lots of Connies, all eager-faced and bouncing along, full of energy. There was a lot of singing too, songs I've never heard, and a lot of shouting, mainly of slogans which were a little hard to make out. Connie stayed with me, though I was slow, and linked arms and I didn't feel in the least self-conscious. She was cross with Toby because he didn't join us, and would accept no excuses from him. He wants to get a first and says he must study hard, which seems to me worthy and not at all like a feeble excuse, but Connie is disgusted with him, says he is selfish and stuck in an ivory tower and she doesn't know what is wrong with him. She says she is not going to get a first and doesn't want to and wants to do something worthwhile. Where have I heard those words before . . .?

\*     \*     \*

*At the beginning of the 1960s, a big change comes over Millicent's life. She retires from teaching at 60 (in 1961) and immediately feels at a loss (though she takes up some voluntary work). From this point on, Connie begins to dominate in her diaries. Almost every entry for the next decade seems to relate in some way to her, even when events such as the Cuban Missile Crisis or the assassination of President Kennedy are being recorded: it is what Connie thinks about them that is important. What Connie says, what Connie hopes, what Connie is going to do—it is as though Millicent no longer has a mind of her own. Connie influences how she dresses, what she eats and what sort of car she buys. 'She drags me into modern times', Millicent observes, and sounds pleased. But she also worries about her niece, whom she considers rash, and though she admires Connie's political activism (which of course she contrasts with her own passivity when young) she fears it will lead her into trouble. Her fears are justified. Connie is arrested for the first time in October 1961 when she takes part in a sit-down outside the Russian Embassy. Millicent, who has refused to join her, alleging that she doesn't understand this protest or the point of a sit-down, even though Connie has apparently argued for its validity, is appalled. She pays Connie's fine on that occasion, terrified she will otherwise be sent to prison (though in fact no one is imprisoned). She suspects her niece's career will suffer if she becomes known as a trouble-maker and pleads with her to be sensible and not so flamboyant if she has to take part in these protests. Connie, who is herself a teacher by now, rejects her aunt's advice. She is teaching in a school in Paddington, in the area where Millicent once worked in the 1930s, in a secondary modern with a large proportion of immigrant children whose English is poor and she has herself started extra classes for them after school. She is living with three other young women in a run-down flat on the edge of Paddington/Kensington. Millicent visits quite regularly, taking treats with her (cakes she's baked and that sort of thing) and, though she admires Connie's dedication, she frets that the kind of work she is doing and the kind of life she is leading are going to ruin her health. She describes Connie as frighteningly thin and looking much older than her years (she was 24 in 1961). Millicent spends a lot of diary time in the mid-sixties, wondering where Connie gets her passionate convictions from and also pondering over what she sees as the lack of both pleasure and fun in her life. She is perturbed, too, about the lack of what she calls (knowingly imitating her own mother) 'romances'—Connie has friends who are men but so far as Millicent can tell no love for any of them. She knows Connie is not a virgin and that she is on the Pill, which she considers a good thing (and wishes it had been available in the 1920s for herself) but she is saddened that no one Connie really cares for has come into her life.*

*     *     *

## 24 April 1967

I made Connie angry yesterday, though I am sure I never intended to and, frankly, I think she took offence without cause. All I happened to say was that I was surprised she wanted to live with Caroline, Jane and Judy in the way they did and she flared up, as only she can flare up, and said she didn't like my insinuation. I said there had been no insinuation and she said of course there had, I was plainly criticising her friends and the flat and behind the criticism she perfectly well knew lay this ridiculous old-fashioned wish that she should have a nice young man and settle down with him in a semi and have 2.1 children. She maintained that I was always hankering after such a dull life for her. Well! I protested mightily, said never for one moment had I wanted such a fate for her and how could she think I did when she knew from my own life I didn't think marriage and children the be-all and end-all for a woman. I decided to take offence myself. I protested that I was hurt that she had me down, obviously, as an embittered spinster trying to live the life she had really wanted through a niece. It was Connie's turn to cry Nonsense (which I'd made it, deliberately) and to swear she'd never thought me embittered, but that nevertheless, when I thought I was being subtle or discreet, I was neither. Fact is, said Connie, you *do* wish I had a lover, you *do* disapprove of casual sex, you *do* think I and my flatmates live in appalling squalor, and you *do* wish I taught in a *nice* school. I stared at

485

her, and then asked very quietly what was wrong with that, any of it. Connie snapped, 'Everything.' She added that my generation had spent our youth being obedient and living according to the dictates of our elders and had never risked anything. Her way of life, she said, was infinitely richer. She was doing work that mattered and not shrinking from making her opinions known, and as for men, they had their place and their uses and they weren't important to her. She is happy and fulfilled, she says. I don't believe her, but was too afraid of starting her off again to say so. How can she be happy when she is so worn out? How can coming home after an exhausting day to a filthy, untidy, comfortless home make her happy? How can spending every spare minute she has shouting outside embassies—now it is the Greek Embassy, because of the Colonels' coup—make her happy? And how can these one-night stands, as she calls them, make her happy? Maybe I was never entirely happy myself, but I was happier than Connie when I was 30, in spite of many blows of fate.

## 25 April

Lay awake last night wondering whether it is true that I was happier at 30 than Connie is now. I can't remember what on earth I was doing when I was 30. All these diaries I've kept, and I can't remember. There is the temptation to look out my diary for 1931 and find out, and yet that is an awful thought, embarrassing for some reason. I don't think I could bear to read something I wrote all those years ago. Inevitably, it will be gauche and trivial, and the knowledge that, even so, it will have been the truth at the time is no comfort. I have never intended to read my diaries. I like to record things, to try to give shape to what happens (or does not) to me, but I don't want to read them. Nor do I want others to read them, whatever anyone might think. No, I am not going to look myself up. I ought to be able to remember where I was and what I was doing even if I cannot recall what state of mind I was in or what my feelings were. I think I had just moved from Brighton to London, or if I hadn't I was about to. And I'd given up teaching and was training to be a social worker. What was the name of my superior? Can't remember, and it isn't important. So, at Connie's age I was in love with Frank, and Frank (as well as Percy) was in love with me. Am I right therefore to declare I was happier than Connie is now? Yes. I still think so. She doesn't realise how daring I was in my own time, what with my career and my lover. She thinks she and her friends are the first women to enjoy the advantages of both. She thinks me almost Victorian, a blushing maiden in my youth, knowing nothing of sex and doing no more than tinkle on the piano and dust furniture. It is provoking. She is indeed more emancipated than I ever was, by her education alone, but I was not entirely shackled. Yet, happy . . . ? Ruthless honesty compels me not to be absolutely sure. I know I would find a great deal of anguish in my diary for 1931, frightful stuff I daresay about Frank, and my attraction to him, but lack of real love for him—and then all the guilt about poor Percy. I wonder what happened to Percy. I feel that, unlike Frank, he may not have survived the war. I could have found out, but I never tried to, and I knew no one except Charles who knew him and who might have told me of his fate. I shall tell Connie what thoughts she has given rise to when next I see her, and put her right about a few misconceptions.

## 2 May

Connie came for lunch. I prefer her to come to me rather than my going to that flat. I don't think she comes out of duty, at least I hope not. She was in quite a calm mood for once and looked not quite so harassed, though I didn't comment on her appearance, remembering as I do how it irritated me when Mother made comments about shadows under my eyes and so forth, and required explanations for them, and then praised on other occasions my so-called bright eyes and glowing skin and wondered if they were due to a 'romance'. So I said nothing. She has had her lovely hair cut and shaped in a geometric way. It gives her head a sculpted look which I don't quite care for, but at least it is tidy. I told her about the time I had my hair cut off and what a big event it was and how Tom hated it and preferred it long. Connie kindly indulged me and asked me to remind her who Tom was, she wasn't sure she'd ever heard of him, and professed to be interested in the answer.

Then it came out that she has a favour to ask. Could she move in here for six months? Well, of course, I'm delighted, and said so, but wondered why she wanted to. It seems the lease of the flat has run out and the rent to renew is more than any of them can afford, so they are all going their separate ways. Connie says she wants to find something on her own but can't do that quickly and needs time. She asked, jokingly, what the rent here would be, and what rules there were. This brought on a discussion about money which I would rather not have had. Connie suddenly asked me what I did for money and I said I had plenty of money and tried to move the conversation to other matters, but she persisted, asking how could I possibly claim to have plenty. Where did it come from? Part-time teaching couldn't have earned me much. I thought about saying that my financial affairs were none of her business but instead said my mother had left me some shares which had always given me a sufficient income. Connie stared at me with the strangest look on her face and I thought at first she was going to berate me for being a capitalist pig, she is always attacking capitalist pigs, but she didn't. She asked suddenly if I had brought her and Toby up on that income. I said there had been no money problems, which she said was evading the real question. I was obliged to remind her about the money I'd been granted from hers and Toby's inheritance, which I had asked them to agree to, to cover various things as they grew up. But she said she wasn't fooled—she knew I must have spent a very great deal of my own money on her and her brother and it should be paid back. I said that was nonsense, I wouldn't hear of it, there was nothing to pay back. Well, said she, I am going to pay a proper rent now and look after bills while I am here. You can save it if you want for your old age. I do wish she wouldn't say things like that. I do wish she wouldn't mention money. Later, she returned to this same distasteful subject, asking me if

Daphne had left me anything. I was shocked, and said no, certainly not, why should she have. In that case, Connie asked, where had her money gone, who had inherited it, and her flat? I told her I had no idea, it was of no interest to me, but that knowing Daphne it had probably been left to some charity and that that was a good thing. I said, I suppose a little accusingly, that she seemed very interested in money. What is wrong with that, she said, money is important, especially to women, money is independence. Well, really, as if I of all people do not know that. Then Connie said that in my case, having an unearned income, however small, had been my undoing, *it had ruined my life*. It was very hard to keep my temper. I managed to ask her, tight-lipped it is true, how she came to that interesting conclusion. She said I had been able to chuck my job as a social worker and by doing so had wasted my brain. I thought about pointing out that I had 'chucked' it, as she so elegantly put it, first of all because there was a war and then to look after her and Toby, and then that, however lowly she considered it, I had resumed teaching. But I didn't. I just tried to look rather sad and yet dignified, and kept silent. I was pleased to see this made Connie uncomfortable. She said sorry and came and gave me a hug and told me it was just that it had always seemed a shame to her that someone as clever as me had never used her ability, or not for any length of time. My potential has been wasted! I said it probably had been but that it hadn't been very great in the first place and I had done some worthwhile things. Connie said maybe, but that she couldn't imagine how I now put my days in. I said like millions of other women, looking after my house and garden—she snorted with derision—and doing voluntary work of one sort and another, taking the library trolley round at the hospital and helping in the Save the Children shop—more snorts, though not so loud—and reading and listening to music and walking. She said I made her despair. But we parted friends.

## 3 May

I know Connie does not mean to despise me, or make me feel ashamed, but that has been the effect of yesterday's diatribe. I found myself lying awake thinking, for some reason, which must have a connection though I can't identify it, of the time I kept a record for Mass Observation. The ordinariness of my day never seemed pathetic then. I remember feeling quite excited at what I had to describe. But I wouldn't be able to feel that now. I have watched myself all day today and not been pleased. Connie is right, now that I no longer teach even part-time, my doings are trivial and few, my pleasures modest. Yet I am not bored any more, not exactly, and that restlessness I once felt so constantly is not there, or not today. It happened to be my afternoon for taking the library trolley round at the hospital and as ever I felt a degree of satisfaction doing it. Connie might sneer at this, but she doesn't understand what goes on, how I enjoy helping patients choose books and feel quite triumphant when I persuade a reader of silly romances to try something more interesting. Also, going round the wards when I hate hospitals so much is hard for me and I feel that by doing it I am overcoming fear. I like it when I can conquer small terrors. No, Connie would not understand that. I think she thinks that I am lonely, that is what is at the bottom of all this. She cannot see how, though I am alone most of the time, I am not lonely. There is a difference. I do miss Daphne, though often even when she came back from America, I did not see her for weeks or months, but I don't crave a best friend, or a companion. I think maybe I have become horribly selfish, and have grown used to the self-indulgence of living alone, but is that so terrible?

## 1 June 1967

It is very peculiar having Connie back living here. The noise! And I don't even mean her records blaring away, I mean ordinary noise, the constant banging of doors and clattering down the stairs and the unnecessary scraping of chairs. She cannot even eat her cereal quietly in the morning—the spoon bangs, bangs, bangs against the side of the bowl. When she leaves the house peace settles over it as if after an earthquake, and I stand quite still for a while savouring it. She comes home so late, but at least then tries hard to be as quiet as possible. She seems to lead such a hectic life, when she eats I don't know. I had envisaged suppers together, even looked forward to cooking for her. I have a recipe for a chicken, mascarpone and mushroom gratin I want to try—it's not worth making for one—but I can never get Connie to guarantee to be here. She says I am not to get food in for her, she will fend for herself. So far as I can see, not much fending goes on. Nor much grooming. I offered to do her washing, or rather to load the machine for her and hand-wash delicate items, but she laughed and said she didn't need a washerwoman and, in fact, in the two weeks she has been here, she has never used the washing-machine. She washes her smalls and drapes them over the bath and that is that. The rest of her clothes, which seem to consist of those horrible denim trousers and black cotton T-shirts, remain uncleaned. She does have one dress, which she wore one day, if it can be called a dress. It is white, extremely short, sleeveless, very plain, with a

493

round neck edged in red. It is lucky she has good legs. Heaven knows what her pupils think of her.

## 15 June

Connie brought a young man home with her last night. We have discussed this. Of course I want her to have her friends to stay, I want her to feel free to have whom she likes when she likes. But it brought back memories of her teenage years when she was always staying out late and scaring me and trying to make me let boyfriends stay the night which I never would allow. We had such arguments. But bringing male friends home now is to be expected. I am even glad of it. I was curious this morning to meet her friend. It being Sunday, she was not going to work and so had no need to get up and it was midday before she emerged, yawning mightily. She ignored me—I was chopping onions and had the wireless on so she could be forgiven for thinking I was concentrating—and trudging over to the kettle, boiled it and made herself a cup of instant coffee (hers, I don't use it). I put the wireless off and said good morning then altered this to good afternoon. No response. Then I heard movement on the stairs. The most extraordinarily ugly man came into the kitchen, quite massive and hairy with a beard and matted-looking long hair. I was so shocked I simply stared, very rudely. Hi, this creature said, any chance of coffee? Connie handed him her half-drunk mug. He accepted it, tasted it, shuddered and said, I meant *coffee*. So I made him some. Connie muttered 'snob', and he said wanting proper coffee was not snobbish. No one introduced

494

us. I thought that quite remarkable. I looked and looked at Connie, but she seemed in a daze. I coughed, but her attention was not to be drawn. I felt like a servant in my own house, not a comfortable feeling. In the end, I went into the garden and started dead-heading roses. I had closed the door to the kitchen but the window was open and I could hear raised voices. Shortly afterwards, I heard the front door slam. On I went, clip, clip, and finally Connie appeared at the door. Sorry about that, she said, he's gone now. And that is all she told me. She went back to bed without another word. I went out to the park, glorious day, and when I came back about four o'clock, she had disappeared. I find her behaviour extraordinary. If I had not brought her up myself I would think she had never been taught any manners at all.

## 1 July

Connie asked me what I was going to do about holidays and I said nothing, I don't need holidays and I don't want one. The mere mention of the word holiday makes me think of Greece ten years ago and Daphne and it is upsetting, not that I said so to Connie. Then it turned out that she was wondering if I would care to join her at a workshop in Brighton. I didn't understand the word 'workshop', but apparently it only means a sort of conference. Why it can't be called that I don't know. It is a workshop to raise women's consciousness, a three-day event at which there will be speakers on a variety of topics. I asked what kind of topics and she showed me a list. There were titles like Violence in the Home and What Can be Done About It. I said I didn't think I would enjoy that sort of thing very much, and Connie exploded, saying enjoyment was not the point, surely I could see that. I said, in that case, what *was* the point, and she said to change things, to make society better and safer for women. Well, that is all very worthy but hardly a holiday. I said it didn't really interest me, I didn't see how I fitted in or why she'd suggested this workshop to me, and she groaned and held her head in her hands and said sometimes I am unbelievable, and that it is women like me, utterly passive politically illiterate women, who are responsible for the state of things. I said I thought I had done my bit, I had gone on the women's march, but she interrupted me saying she was bloody well tired of hearing about that pathetic march and hearing me boast about participating, and that if I went on to also add that I'd joined CND and been on *one* Aldermaston march she would scream. Constant action and participation were needed to combat male power. Really, there was no point arguing with her, so I didn't.

**25 July**

Connie has gone off to her workshop, dressed as if for battle in trousers and denim jacket, very military-looking, and the house is quiet. The phone has been ringing constantly, with her friends calling to make plans and discuss tactics, and the living-room floor is littered with pamphlets and bits of paper with notes on. Connie is, it seems, the mastermind, responsible for having invited the speakers and for making sure enough women turn up to hear them. I tried to show an interest but she has been very aloof and cold towards me and has ignored my inquiries. I have scurried about my own home feeling humble. It is a relief to be once more on my own and feel what Connie calls the 'vibes' change. Everything is rush, rush with her, she moves at such speed and with such violence, jumping downstairs, slamming doors, and swearing as she goes. I do object to the swearing, there is no need for it. I have never liked swearing and have never had to live with it, not even during the war, not to the extent Connie swears and certainly not containing the f and c words. Damn and bloody and bugger were the worst then, apart from Christ and hell. I told her one day that she was foul-mouthed and it did not become her. She laughed, and hugged me. That is the confusing thing about Connie. She is so affectionate and sweet under her aggressive surface.

## 26 July

Toby rang today, wanting to speak to Connie. I told him where she was and he said he would ring back after she returned, and was about to hang up, but I protested and said he could talk to me for a while, surely. I haven't spoken to him for months and haven't seen him for well over a year. I'm afraid I pointed that out rather reproachfully and gave him what Connie calls a guilt trip, but I can't hide that I am hurt by his lack of contact. It is not that I am a crabbed old aunt wanting gratitude for services rendered in the past, but I don't like to think he cannot spare five minutes to talk to me. I wish I understood what his work consisted of and could ask intelligent questions and get closer to him that way, but I don't. Connie says she doesn't think anyone understands it, it is much too complicated. All she knows is that his research is to do with nuclear power and she wishes it was anything else but that. If only he had become a medical doctor like his father and not a physicist. I asked all the same how his work was going and he said slowly. I let that go and asked if he was well, and he said yes, but he was troubled with bad headaches, probably because there is a lot of eye strain involved in his work. Conversations have been like this for years now with Toby, I ask questions, he replies, and then he waits. He never asks me anything. I tried to open this stilted exchange out by telling him about his sister's dedication to the feminist cause but he just grunted. Then I thought to inquire why he wanted her, was it for anything in particular, could I perhaps help. Astonishingly, he said he thought he should tell her he is going to America, to San José in California, to work and live, next month. I asked, calmly, whether he didn't think I would want to know too. Why hadn't he told me? There was a silence, though I didn't feel it was caused by any embarrassment on his part; it felt more like surprise that I should want to know. I asked him if he was emigrating, or was this temporary, and he said it was permanent, he was emigrating. And then I had to drag out of him the reasons, which seemed to be only that the work opportunities are better. I can't wait for Connie to get back so that we can discuss this.

## 29 July

I should have asked Toby if he would prefer to tell Connie his news himself, but I didn't, and so worried about whether or not I should. In the event, she was hardly through the front door, looking exhausted and dishevelled, I may say, and not as though she had been at the seaside in this glorious weather, before he happened to ring. I hovered in the kitchen, half listening, waiting for her reaction and rather dreading it—she can be so violent and I don't want her to break with her twin or say anything she may regret. However, she received his news calmly, almost indifferently. They only talked a bare three or four minutes. I expected her to come and discuss what Toby had said, but she went upstairs straightaway to have a bath, and I was left feeling a little cheated.

When she came down, I was the one who had to ask what she thought. She shrugged and said it wasn't exactly unexpected, opportunities were much better for scientists in the USA, and she knew Toby had been approached before and was tempted. All he's got in his life is work, said Connie, so he might as well go where the best facilities are for doing it. I said it wasn't very patriotic of him. Patriotic? she echoed, over and over, as though I'd said something incredible. But I stuck to my guns. Yes, I said, patriotic, leaving his own country to take all his skill to America when he owed his entire education to Britain. Connie laughed, but not with real mirth, or it didn't sound like it, and said I was so insular it was ridiculous, and that patriotism had caused two world wars which was quite enough. I tried to insist that there is nothing wrong with loving one's country and being devoted to its welfare, but she waved her hands about in that exasperating way she has and said there was everything wrong with it. I started to say that during the war—but she leapt up and put her hand over my mouth and said why didn't I do something useful like making her a snack. So I did. But after we'd eaten, I couldn't resist asking if she was not just a little upset about Toby emigrating. She said no, that she no longer had much feeling for him and he had none for her. This shocked me. But you are *twins*, I said, and you were so close as children, quite inseparable, where on earth has all that gone? She said it was just that they'd grown up and twins were no different to anyone else in that respect whatever people thought; there was nothing shocking about growing apart. I insisted there was, and that it was sad, and she said it was only I who was sad. There was a pause, and then she said she felt Toby was a damaged person. She didn't know what exactly had damaged him, it was too facile to say it was their parents' death, though maybe that was at the root of his detachment. She asked me to recall how he had suddenly changed in personality in adolescence, gone quiet and withdrawn and moody, whereas before he had been so energetic and lively. And yet nothing had happened specifically to cause this. I do remember, it is true what she says, but that doesn't explain why *she* became so separate from him. It worries me. It isn't right somehow. What have any of us got to be sure of but family? I sound like Mother—how she used to annoy me when she said that.

\*        \*        \*

*This seems an odd thing for a woman like Millicent to have written, a single elderly woman who, though always involved with family members (and who had of course in many ways sacrificed herself to family responsibilities in taking on her sister's children), could not be said to have a life revolving round them. But Connie's apparent lack of emotion about her brother's decision to emigrate clearly upsets her and makes her wonder if somehow it is her fault. Although she is not a mother, she wants what most mothers want, to see their children close to each other and the family unit tight. But she shows herself to be marvellously undemanding of Connie when she might with justification have made claims on her. Connie after all is the only member of her family with whom she might see herself having a future. At the beginning of 1968, when her niece moves into a flat of her own (in Shepherd's Bush, an area her aunt considered 'seedy') Millicent accepts that she will want to have a private life so she is pleasantly surprised when Connie keeps in close touch and shows no sign of doing so simply out of duty.*

*Increasingly, the diaries for 1968 to 1970 demonstrate how Connie continues to influence her aunt in all kinds of ways, keeping up a determined campaign to make Millicent do something more than potter about her house and garden, give her time to voluntary work, and read. She doesn't see this as scorning her aunt's way of life, or as trying to humiliate her, though Millicent certainly feels this is implicit in all the lectures about wasting her brains, but as trying to make her aunt see that some use can still be made of her intelligence. It is all part of Connie's feminist credo to make Millicent look at herself and, even at her age, fulfil her potential.*

\*       \*       \*

## 10 December 1970

Connie burst in today waving a newspaper cutting
and looking ferociously determined. I assumed she
was about to bombard me with information about
the latest insult to feminists, but no, it was nothing
like that. It turned out to be an advertisement, or
rather an announcement, about this new so-called
Open University. Connie says it must have been
thought up with me in mind and insists I must
enrol. She says it is what I have been waiting for all
my life, as if she would know, for heaven's sake. I
am much too old to become a student. But Connie
got all excited, the way she does, and said she
would never forgive me if I didn't take this
opportunity and study for a degree. What on earth
would be the point, I protested, and that brought
forth more passion, about how education was a
point in itself and surely I saw that. I said I would
go so far as to send away for details and then think
about it, but of course I only said that to calm her
down and change the subject. But after she'd gone,
Idid read the notice several times, and slowly I am
beginning to wonder if I am not after all attracted
to the idea. It is not the thought of having a degree
which attracts me, I am too old to long for such a
symbol of achievement, but that I have always
wanted to *study* properly, in a disciplined way, and I
have never had the chance. No, that is not true, I
have had the chance in that I have had the time

and been near libraries and could have at any point in the last twenty years decided to educate myself further. What I have lacked, I suppose, is motivation and guidance. Doing a degree course at home would give me both. I wonder if I could do it.

\* \* \*

*Millicent went further than just wondering, sending off for details as she had said she would. At first, she is rather bewildered and finds the information about the different 'disciplines' (as they were called) confusing. Everyone had to do a Foundation Course and once she has grasped how it was organised she decides she might as well attempt that and then decide whether she wants to do, or is capable of doing, the six courses necessary to gain a degree. She elects to study Humanities, which had five disciplines that attracted her: History, Literature, Philosophy, History of Art and Music Appreciation. In February 1971 she duly registers as an Open University student (one of 24,000, of whom 40 per cent had no academic qualifications at all). She waits anxiously for the post to bring the first weekly 'unit' and is vastly relieved to find she can do the necessary exercises easily, gaining high marks from the beginning. Just as Connie had hoped, the studying gives a particular kind of disciplined structure to her life which it has lacked. It also gives her some excitement. She discovers a real interest in philosophy and reads far more than she is required to, and through the History of Art assignments she is stimulated to go to some London art galleries she has never visited. But the thought of attending the Open University Summer School (compulsory) in August worries her. She doesn't want to be with other students or take part in group activity, and she is embarrassed about what she calls her 'great age' (70 in July). But there is no way out: she has to go to the new East Anglian campus for one week.*

*       *       *

## 5 August 1971

Am I mad? I feel as mad as Connie, all het up and excited. I remind myself hourly that I am 70 years of age and it is not appropriate to be in such a state just because I am going to summer school. I worry that I will not be given my own room, though I have been assured that I will. I simply could not go back to sharing, living in a dormitory, even for a week, the way we did in the WAAF. I need my privacy, and not just for the good of my soul. I would not wish, now, to undress in front of others. It is not that I am prudish, but that my body is no longer a sight I welcome and I do not care to show it to others. It is sad, all this shrinking and ageing of the flesh. People still say I look younger than my years, they have always said it, but it makes no difference because even in my late fifties, the insults of ageing had begun. I remember putting a bathing costume on in Greece and being transfixed at noticing for the first time the way the flesh on my thighs fell away in slippy little lumps, and hating the sight. And the way my hands, the backs of them, developed these ugly dark brown splotches. How vain this sounds, but it is not—I am merely facing up to the various disintegrations taking

504

place. I wonder if most of the students will be old and feel as I do. I doubt it. Probably I shall be the oldest. Well, I shall be dignified about it. I shall not attempt to be chummy with those much younger than myself, nor shall I behave in an unseemly way. I am there to discuss our studies, not to form relationships.

## 8 August

Took a long time deciding what to wear before I set off today. I wear trousers a great deal these days—ever since I retired from teaching I've tended always to wear them if I am not going anywhere. They are so much more sensible for pottering about the garden. But I didn't feel comfortable about wearing them to go to this summer school. I suppose I wanted to look dignified, smarter, more my actual age. So I bought a new dress and jacket from Marks & Spencer's. It's a rather attractive coral colour—now that my hair is white I can wear pinky shades—and looks fresh and cheerful. I wore Mother's pearls with it, and her clip-on earrings. Connie says pearls are a joke, but I like them and my neck is not *too* scrawny yet, so I don't mind the attention the pretty pearls draw to it. It's strange the way growing older doesn't mean I don't care about how I look—I always thought that when I was old I wouldn't care, but I do. At any rate, once I was satisfied with my appearance, I set off.

Drove to Norwich with no difficulty. I am so glad I can drive and still feel perfectly confident in a car. I cannot imagine how I would have managed if obliged to use trains and take taxis or buses. It would all have seemed too much bother and would have discouraged me from travelling. I feel, too, that I can escape easily if I wish to. And I might. First impressions are not cheering, though I do have a small, cell-like room to myself, as promised. These new buildings are horrible, the whole university about as far from dreaming spires as possible: dreadfully ugly, like concrete garages, and the classrooms boom even when only one person speaks, never mind when the two dozen in our group all start talking. The day seemed long, nine to six, and I was fatigued by the end. We gathered in a cafeteria-type place this first evening, terribly uncomfortable plastic chairs, and everyone seemed awkward and unsure, even the tutors. There are ten men and fourteen women, not counting the tutors. All much younger than myself, except for two of the men who I would guess are either my age or older. We sat in a circle and introduced ourselves. It was impossible of course to take everyone's name in or where they are from but I did register that the men who are my contemporaries are called Robert and Malcolm, Robert from London and Malcolm from Nottingham. It was explained how the school would operate and time-tables were handed out. There seems plenty of free time and mention was made of gathering in the bar before supper each evening. I don't know that I shall do that, though I don't want to be stand-offish. One of the women started talking to me while we ate after the introductory talk. She is called Claire, mother of two, always wanted to go to university but never had the chance, yet she is only 42, so it seems to me she could surely have had the chance, but I said nothing. She naturally asked me about myself. I always hate that. It is silly, I know, but I don't like giving my age or saying I am a single woman—it makes me sound pathetic. There is never anything to say after I have said that. Claire asked me if I had had a career and to shut her up I said I had been a teacher, and that helped, she was instantly satisfied, has me pigeon-holed now. Claire has found the assignments tough. She has so little time to do them, what with having to look after the children and her husband and home and working part-time as a doctor's receptionist. I admire her, and said so, but already she bores me. Always my trouble, too easily bored, fatal to socialising. I hope I didn't show it.

## 10 August

I think one thing is becoming clearer each day and that is that this summer school does not in any way, so far as I can judge, prove a help to studying. Precious little studying goes on. I could understand more after sitting on my own in my room at home reading the texts than I have done here sitting with others discussing them. Yet people like Claire seem excited by this group participation. She is constantly exclaiming at how helpful and enlightening she finds other people's observations and says again and again how glad she is that she came. I am not sure that I am glad. In so many ways it has proved a waste of time, and the fact that I have time to waste is no consolation. This school is all about socialising, as I suspected. There is a great deal of pairing off in the evenings and I imagine this is leading to rather more than platonic relationships. This makes me sound a prig, but I don't disapprove in the least, for what after all has my life taught me but to take one's chances when they come. Do I really mean that? I think so, but maybe not entirely. Chances have to be weighed. Being entirely spontaneous is never wise. Lord, how portentous I am becoming. I should remember Frank and what a chance I took then.

## 11 August

Went for a walk this evening. Too beautiful to stay in my cell and I've lost all interest in being with a group. Unfortunately, or I thought it was unfortunate at first, I met Robert, who had had the same idea. I saw him ahead of me and I tried to walk very slowly so that I would never catch up, and I had seen a path veering off to the right which I was going to take when I reached it, but he chose to sit down on a bench just near it and it was impossible for me not to be noticed and impossible to pretend I didn't know. I think he was as embarrassed as I was. I had to stop and say good evening, and he stood up, very gentleman-like, and I said please would he sit down, I was just having a walk and didn't want to disturb his reverie. I was then going to walk on, but he nodded at the river in front of us and said it was such a perfect view, didn't I think, and somehow I found myself sitting beside him staring at the view. It was, as he said, very lovely, the river at this point broad and fast-flowing and on this night catching the reddening rays of the setting sun; and beyond the river, on the far bank, there were three weeping willow trees gracefully bowing before a stone wall that enclosed a churchyard. Robert, who is Bob (unlike my Robert, who was never a Bob), said it did him good, scenes like this. He said it wasn't that he felt Wordsworthian about it, but that it reinforced his belief that essentially the world is a beautiful and peaceful place and he needed that solace. We sat quietly for a while, without even exchanging pleasantries, which I was glad of, and then he said he was going to walk on before the light faded and I found myself rising and walking with him, though I had not been specifically invited to do so. He has a limp. I'd noticed it on the first meeting, as everyone was bound to. I thought initially that maybe he had arthritis but then I decided it was too pronounced for that. When we started walking together he apologised for his slowness and said I should not feel inhibited about walking faster and leaving him behind. I said something about it being an evening made for sauntering, ambling, and not rushing. A war wound, he volunteered, though I'd betrayed no curiosity about the cause of his limp. I was beaten, he went on, not shot, by the Japanese, in Changi, have you heard of Changi? I felt a little leap of alarm, though what I was alarmed about I'm not sure, there was no need or justification for alarm of any kind. I had to clear a sudden thickening in my throat to manage to say that yes, I'd heard of Changi. Then there was a choice. I didn't have to explain the reasons why, I could easily, being the age I obviously am, have heard of it through what was written about it at the time and afterwards, but I chose to volunteer the information that my Robert had died there. I called

509

him my fiancé. Nothing wrong with that. Bob asked his regiment and when he died, and I had to tell him that though I knew his regiment I couldn't recall exactly when he was killed except it was in 1943. So, Bob said, was it malnutrition, was it cholera, typhoid, what was it? I told him.

He stopped walking and closed his eyes and gripped my arm tightly. I wished I had said nothing. It was the strangest feeling, an overwhelming feeling of *shame* that I had told him at all. I felt that by telling him I had made something intensely personal into something public. I disliked his distress too. It irritated me. It seemed so melodramatic. Then, when I saw he was weeping, I was appalled and furious and wanted to get away and never see this stranger again. I said I must be getting back and he said he was sorry, he'd been overcome, he'd thought about Changi every single day since he'd left it and, when I'd told him about Robert, he had been right back in the hell of it in a moment.

I was obliged to walk back with him since he still clutched my arm like an ancient mariner, and I hated being with him. He asked for more details but I said I couldn't talk about it and he said he quite understood, but I don't think he did. How could he understand something I don't understand myself? He then talked about his own life after Changi, which was preferable, but I took none of it in, except that he is a widower with three grown-up children who are good to him. He asked if I had married and I felt the familiar resentment when I said no. Then a truly humiliating thing happened. We were entering the block where we both have our rooms and Chris Downey, one of the tutors, was coming out. Oh, she said, beaming, you two have got together, how nice. I was mortified—the assumption! I tried to have a sense of humour about it and said something about how ridiculous people are, but then Bob said shall we go to the bar and have a drink, and I realised he was not mortified but rather pleased. I said I was sorry, I was tired and must go to bed. I bade him a very formal goodnight.

## 12 August

There was a note slipped under my door some time last night. The moment I saw it, a white folded sheet of paper lying very obviously on the wooden floor, I knew who it would be from and what it would say. I ignored it for a while. I washed and dressed, and then finally, when I was ready to go for breakfast, reluctantly picked it up and read it. I admit I was agreeably surprised at how Bob expressed himself. Very simply, very straightforward in tone. He said he realised he had upset me and he was sorry for it and he had been a blundering fool and had been unable to control his own emotion which he had inflicted upon me. He would not behave so crassly again, and hoped I would share another walk with him before the week ended but would quite understand if I did not feel so inclined. I was, am, impressed that he took blame upon himself when of course he had nothing to blame himself for. I didn't want to accompany him on another walk but on the other hand I felt I had been unkind and had seemed cold and uncaring and I was sorry too. I thought, I must not be schoolgirlish about this. I must act as becomes my age. So I made a point at breakfast of joining Bob at his table and being pleasant. There were others there, and I wasn't going to mention his note or his invitation in front of them, but as the group broke up and we all began to make our way to our respective classrooms I said quietly that it would be a pleasure to walk along the river this evening, but perhaps rather earlier. I even managed to make a joke about what Chris Downey would be bound to think if she saw us. We arranged to meet straight after supper.

I rather dreaded the whole idea, but in fact I enjoyed the walk and his company. He is a very intelligent man. I'd been aware of this in our tutorials, the way he spoke, showing a keen mind, but I was even more struck by it in our conversation. Whereas I tend to speak before I think and so am constantly having to qualify what I say, Bob takes time to consider his own thoughts before sharing them. This makes him a slow talker but once I'd got used to the delays I adapted to his manner and it had a good effect on my own. It turns out that he is an engineer, recently retired. He is studying for an OU degree because once he'd left work he was bored and wanted to fill in the gaps in his education. He admitted he found the course easy, not particularly challenging, and like me felt this residential school was mostly about socialising. Nothing wrong with that, he said. I said I was rather anti-social, and he said, a little pompously, I thought, that I shouldn't be, socialising was important, not just for the individual but for the community and for the future of the world at large. I said did he mean no man was an island, that argument, and he said not exactly and we had an interesting discussion about what he did mean. The time flew. It wasn't such a beautiful evening, the sun went behind clouds around seven o'clock, and there was a stiff breeze. But it was invigorating, the walk, the talk, everything.

## 15 August

Last day of this school. Most people seem very sorry it is over, which makes me wonder what dullness they are going back to. A great deal of swapping addresses and telephone numbers went on but I wasn't asked for mine, I am relieved to say. I had worried that Bob might request it and suggest that we should, as they all put it, 'keep in touch', but, thankfully, he didn't, correctly gauging, I should think, what my response would have been. Instead, he wished me luck with my studies and said he knew I would get a degree with no difficulty at all.

## 16 August

Home. Thought all the way back of Bob and his parting words. He looked so distinguished, dressed to return to his home, wearing a suit, unlike the other men. He, too, had driven here and we walked to where our cars were parked together. He insisted on carrying my suitcase which I did not want him to do because of his limp and because he had a bag of his own. I'm old-fashioned, he said, I carry ladies' cases. I told him my niece would say that I was a woman and not a lady and entertained him briefly (I hope) with Connie's rules about vocabulary in this new feminist age. When we'd each opened up our cars, he put my suitcase in the boot, closed it firmly, and then held out his hand. I shook it. He said it had been a very great pleasure meeting me and that he was sorry it hadn't been for longer than a week. Was that a hint? Possibly, but if so, one to which I did not respond. He stood for a moment looking at me rather searchingly, I thought, and then asked if he might be permitted to say he thought I was courageous and he admired me. Well, it was an absurd thing to say, and quite inexplicable. I felt it was somehow patronising, because of course it is he who is courageous, with his war experience. I suppose I must have shown my annoyance, because as I said goodbye and got into my car he came to the window and said very quietly that what he'd meant was that it was rare to find a woman perfectly happy to stand on her own two feet and at peace with herself. That, he ended, took a certain kind of courage. Does it? I can't see how it does. It isn't as though I chose to, as he referred to it, stand on my own two feet. But he undoubtedly intended it as a compliment, so I must try to take it as such, I suppose. It certainly couldn't have been merely flattery because flatterers always have a motive and since Bob will never see me again he can't have had one. He wasn't the sort of man I expected to find attending a summer school, since he is already well educated. I could see that a couple of women there, in their mid-fifties, I think, were eyeing him as a good catch. I find myself speculating now as to what his dead wife was like and what his own life is like now. His surname is unusual, double-barrelled and odd. I looked in the phone book for it and found it easily. The only one there. Mine is so common, there are scores of Kings.

## 25 August

Connie came to ask how the summer school had gone and I found myself telling her about Bob. I thought she would tease me, and laugh, and was prepared for it, but she didn't. She sighed and looked at me as though I am an exasperating child and said I was impossible and should have been given a good shaking years ago. Oh, and why pray? I asked, and she said I knew perfectly well. I liked Bob and was interested in him and I was simply incapable of making the effort I was obviously longing to make, and it is all to do with my foolish pride. I asked what effort and she said the effort of friendship, of making the running, of developing a relationship. She alleged that I knew I wanted to see Bob again but, for reasons she failed to understand, but reasons which she suspected had always been the same, I refused to admit it. Nonsense, of course. I tried to explain that though I was interested in Bob, which was why I'd told her about him, and though I had thought about him since, that didn't mean I wanted to see him again. If someone were to come and tell me all about him, and if I could be a fly on the wall of his house, then I would enjoy learning more about him, but I did not, definitely do not, want a relationship of any kind and that is the truth. Relationships are a

515

bother, I said, new ones, I mean. I have enough in my life as it is, I don't want any more, thank you. And you criticise Toby, Connie said. You say that about relationships, and yet you are the one appalled and worried because Toby is so emotionally isolated. Then she said a shocking thing: maybe he got it from you, she said. Maybe you brought him up to think relationships are too much bother. I didn't know whether to laugh or cry. I stared at her, incredulous, thinking that any minute *she* would burst out laughing and say, oh, for heaven's sake, she was joking. But she didn't. She just sat there, meeting my stare. Finally, I managed to pull myself together and tell her I thought she was being both silly and cruel. On the contrary, she said, she was following my example by being honest. She'd thought this for a long time, that the way I'd always been so solitary, almost glorying in my independence, almost boasting that I had no need of a partner, and having virtually no friends, except for Daphne, and certainly no male friends, had probably sent out messages to the growing Toby. But what about you, I protested, if it didn't send out messages to you, why did it send them to Toby, not that this whole theory isn't ridiculous. She said my intense reserve *had* sent messages to her too. Why did I imagine she was now 34 and had never had a successful relationship? I was angry by then. Is this about blame? I asked. She said no, of course not, it is about how patterns of behaviour are perpetuated. We looked up to you, Toby and I, we thought of you as a saint and we wanted to copy you—I stopped her there. I got up and said this was clap-trap and I'd had enough of it. It is all this American

516

influence she is under, these stupid books she reads, in which what happens to you is always someone else's fault. I turned my back on her, and heard her flounce out without saying goodbye.

But she did ring, as soon as she got home, to apologise, though it was rather a half-hearted apology, I must say. I accepted it, a little coldly. Love you, she muttered before she put the receiver down. She is always saying that, at the end of every phone conversation. I think I am supposed to say the same back but I never do, I won't have love reduced to a banal pleasantry. Really, Connie is a very upsetting girl, I don't know what will become of her. She gets these strange notions in her head and nothing will shift them. I always have the feeling that though she is strong she could be led by someone stronger. She has so much passion in her, and rage, and it has never quite found the right direction. She's looking for it, a cause I suppose, and then she'll give her all to it.

\*       \*       \*

*Millicent's comments were more prescient than she could possibly, in 1971, have realised. The next decade sees Connie becoming more and more involved in feminist political activity. Whenever she comes to see her aunt, she brings magazines with her which completely baffle Millicent, who records her astonishment at the front cover of* The Red Rag *(price 10p) which read 'A magazine of Women's Liberation—Inside: Unions, Orgasms and More'.* Spare Rib *she finds easier to cope with. By this time, of course, Millicent is an old woman and the tone of her diaries has changed.*

*The entries from 1971 onwards become rather stilted, with only rare expressions of emotion—for example, when Mrs Thatcher becomes Prime Minister in May 1979. Millicent, though not a Tory, is impressed and rather thrilled to think a woman has risen to this eminence—'she must have such determination' she writes, and contrasts it with what she sees as her own lack of it. Otherwise she herself is discontented on the whole with what she records and goes through one of her phases of wondering why she is carries on with her diary at all, coming up with a new reason: because she wants to 'get to the end', still writing it. Other people, in these years (1971–1981) 'get to the end'. She records their deaths formally. George dies in 1973, Esther in 1975, and Stephen (their eldest son) is killed in a car crash in 1979. She writes to her nephew Harry, telling him he will always be welcome in her home, but by then he has married and has his own home. Rather surprisingly, she does not go on to gain an Open University degree, discontinuing her studies after she has completed four full units, and with only two more to go. The reasons for this are not entirely clear, but may have been partly due to difficulties with writing because of arthritis in her hands. She doesn't, though, see this as a failure and emphasises that she has thoroughly enjoyed studying and that a degree would have meant little to her. With no descriptions of her studies to write about—and she has written about them in often tedious detail—her diaries once more falter and the content reverts to notes about her garden, her house and very little else.*

*But then, when the Walk for Life march to Greenham Common from Cardiff took place in the summer of 1981, Millicent's diary takes on a new lease of life. Connie goes on the march. She is one of the hard core of supporters who sets off on Thursday, 27 August, from outside the City Hall to walk the 120 miles to Greenham, the site of the proposed American Cruise Missile base. Once there, she stays, one of the founders of the peace camp which is to become so famous. Millicent was beside herself with worry, sure that Connie is getting caught up in something that will lead her into real trouble.*

## 3 September 1981

There is nothing in my newspaper about Connie's march, and nothing is shown on the television news. I cannot decide if that means it has fizzled out or not. If it has, Connie will be furious and start ranting about the male-dominated media, but at least it will mean none of my fears will be realised. I said to her that she seemed to think she was some kind of suffragette, fighting for a worthwhile feminist cause, and she said she was fighting against the use of nuclear weapons and that this was a far greater cause. But throwing up a comparison with suffragettes was a mistake—I shudder to think that it may have put into her head ideas of chaining herself to railings somewhere. It wouldn't do her, or her protest, any good, but it might land her in prison and that would be the end of her career. I think her career may be over anyway. Term starts tomorrow, and where is she?


## 5 September

Four women have chained themselves to the perimeter fence of the base at Greenham. My heart missed a beat when I heard it given out on the wireless. Is Connie one of them? No names were given. There are other women there making a dreadful keening noise. The place is swarming with police. They say a letter is being delivered to the base's commander. Connie will doubtless be in the thick of it. I ought to admire her and all the others for doing what I have never done, but somehow I can't, I find this kind of display embarrassing. I couldn't do it, exposing myself to ridicule and contempt.

## 6 September

Television coverage at last of the Greenham women, and thank God, Connie was not one of those chained to the fence. One of the women was quite old, in her seventies I would say. It looked a lovely day and the common very green and attractive. Part of the letter delivered to the commandant was read out, a bit about the women protestors representing thousands of ordinary people who are opposed to nuclear weapons. Here we go again. Well, I am one of them and I should be grateful, as Connie is always telling me, that such action is being taken on my behalf. But does it do any good? What I have to face is the shaming fact that, even if it could be proved that it does, I could not go and chain myself to a fence somewhere in Berkshire. What does that say about me? I'm afraid I know only too well.

## 9 September

Connie is back, but only to announce that she is returning to stay there, to live in a tent on Greenham Common. I asked about her job, and she said she had already given in her notice. But you will be letting the children down, I said: you are supposed to give at least half a term's notice.

She just waved her hands about and said it couldn't be helped, what she was doing was far more important for children all over the world. I think it is disgraceful, to leave her school in the lurch like that, but she is oblivious to such responsibilities. She is, I suppose, inspired, her eyes blazing with excitement and conviction, her cheeks flushed and her body bristling with energy as she described the camp to me. She declares she has never known such wonderful women, all of them feeling as strongly as she does, all of them quite ordinary and prepared to sacrifice the comforts of their normal lives to make this protest. I felt she was looking at me accusingly when she said there was one woman there who was over 80, enduring the pain of arthritis but determined to join in. I said how brave. Then I asked what everyone was going to do for supplies, and what about lavatories and washing facilities—the camp would not be very pleasant, it would be rife with disease, if this was not thought about. She laughed and said it was all being organised, I needn't worry. She is quite prepared to go to prison. I accused her of actually wanting to, of hankering after martyrdom. Oh, I didn't want us to argue but that was what we were doing. I tried to stop it, but I couldn't. Before she left, to get ready to go to the camp for heaven knows how long, I managed to persuade her to promise to ring me once a week. I pleaded. I said I would not be able to sleep for worrying about her. I said she could make it a reverse charge call. Very reluctantly, she agreed to *try* to ring regularly, but wouldn't commit herself to once a week. I have to be content with that.

522

**20 September**

Ten days, and at last a call from Connie. She sounded cheerful, and was full of how I'd approve of what was being done in the way of organisation. She says a small village is springing up, and that there is a communal shelter erected out of tarpaulins and branches in which there is a cauldron hanging over a fire for cooking. It sounds ghastly, but she says good stews are made and nobody goes hungry. The local people are being wonderful and several of them have made their bathrooms available and she'd had two baths herself which she was sure would please me with my mania for cleanliness. I asked her what exactly she did all day and she said she was always frantically busy, mainly preparing statements for the media and duplicating posters and leaflets. I had so many questions to ask but she had to go to a meeting. I suppose I must be grateful that she has rung at all.

**1 October**

The weather is dreadful, and of course I think of Connie, sleeping in a tent in all this rain and cold, and not even a proper tent if newspaper descriptions are to be credited. The things they live and sleep in are called tipis, like wigwams, and some of the women aren't even in these but in 'benders', bits of sheeting pulled over branches, totally inadequate to protect them now winter is coming. Connie's fine words about organisation are belied by the pictures I have seen, acres of mud everywhere and not a sign of any shelter worthy of the name.

**6 October**

I read today that the Post Office says it is prepared to deliver letters to the camp. I like the idea of writing to Connie, though I fear she will have no interest in anything I have to say, and if I use a letter to tell her to keep warm and dry and to eat properly she will likely ignore it. But still, I will attempt to communicate with her. It will make me feel that she is not lost somewhere, out of my reach.

**7 October**

Wrote to Connie, addressing it to the communal tent, Greenham Common Peace Camp. Of course, writing it I could not help remembering when I last wrote to a camp, and how pointless that turned out to have been.

**9 October**

Such a shock today. I opened my newspaper to see staring at me a photograph of Tom, just as he was when I knew him. It was his obituary. Before I could read it, my eyes went straight to the little bit of factual information they always give at the end: yes, he had married, twice, and had two sons and a daughter. He'd gone into the Foreign Office after

Oxford. There was a tribute to how he had overcome the loss of his arm and had, in spite of it, been a keen tennis player. His life, in this account, sounded happy, but it made me sad, looking at his boyish face. I wonder if Phyllis is still alive. I wonder if I should write to her, but I don't have an address.

## 12 October

Connie got my letter, and seemed amused and pleased that I'd written, testing the Post Office's promise. She wasn't on the line long, there was a queue behind her for the telephone, but she urged me to go to a rally which is going to be held in Trafalgar Square on 24th of this month. I said I would go.

## 24 October

Being old is a great handicap when trying to cope with crowds. I am not frail yet, I do not need a stick, but even so I worry about being knocked down in a crush and about whether I have the stamina to make my way through it. I went early, knowing I had to be sure to get a position where I could lean on something, and chose the steps of the National Gallery in front of one of the pillars. It meant being quite a distance from the speakers at the rally, so I couldn't hear very well. My mind wandered. I found myself looking at all the enormous crowd of people, thousands and thousands of them, the most I have ever seen gathered in one place, and wondering how many were there for the entertainment, and how many by accident, and how many out of real conviction. And then I fell to studying individuals near to me, watching the expressions of a young man and woman arm in arm leaning on the same pillar, quite vacant, dreamy expressions, almost bored, indeed both of them yawned a good deal, and I was fairly sure they were only there for the spectacle. I waited for ages, a full hour afterwards, before trying to get home. The dispersing of the vast throng was in fact quite orderly with nothing for the mounted police to do. I was so tired by the time I got onto the bus but felt pleased I had made the effort. Connie won't see the effort involved, I'm sure, but I hope she will be pleased.

## 25 October

Connie rang to see if I had gone to the rally so I was glad I had. But far from being pleased with me, or giving an 80-year-old any credit at all for braving the hordes, she was annoyed that I couldn't report what the Greenham woman's speech had been about. What is the point in going at all if you don't hear what is said, she shouted. She grudgingly left the subject and moved on to tell me that the camp is growing bigger, with people arriving all the time, which is making the running of it more difficult. There are constant arguments about how things should be done, and a good deal of tension between the men and the women. She wishes a women-only rule had been made right at the beginning. I said I didn't see why men didn't have their part to play in a peaceful protest but she retorted that it was men who made the nuclear weapons in the first place and men who would be in charge of deploying them and, frankly, men were to blame for the whole mess we are in. It is when Connie says things like that that I lose patience with her.

## 2 November

Sent Connie a parcel. She will laugh at its contents but I don't care. I put in some thermal underwear and a scarf I have knitted, and some thick socks, and then a box of her favourite biscuits and some soap. I shouldn't have included the soap, but it was very nice soap and nice soap is such a comfort, I always think. It was quite a big parcel. The woman at the Post Office saw the address when she was weighing it and asked was it to my daughter and I said no, my niece, and she looked at me closely and said why do they do it. I was about to say I didn't know and then I thought no, I can't say that. So I gave her a little lecture and it was rather gratifying to see her nod her head at the end.

## 21 November

Connie is on picket duty. She says pickets are now posted twenty-four hours a day to stop the 'benders' and 'tipis' being removed by the council. It seems every now and again men appear to clear the common, which they have no right to do. I don't like the sound of this. Connie could get hurt.

She is quite likely to get into fights. She told me not to be silly.

## 22 December

An excited and, for once, long phone call from Connie, all about what she calls the first positive action. It seems she woke up yesterday to find some land next to the camp had been bulldozed ready for some pipes to be laid. These pipes, for sewage, were to go through the camp into the base. She was asked to move the tipi she shares with two other women but she, and they, refused. She says the workmen were more embarrassed than anything. She and her friends then sat down in front of the mechanical digger being used and said they wouldn't let the pipes be laid because to do so would prolong the existence of the base. The workmen gave up straightaway. Connie was beside herself with joy, seeing this as a great triumph. Well, really. How can preventing the laying of necessary sewage pipes be a triumph? Connie says it is a rehearsal for the inevitable coming confrontation. I asked if she was coming home for Christmas. She said of course not, how could she think about Christmas when all this was happening. I almost said she might think about me, but I didn't. I would never plead loneliness.

## 1 January 1982

A Happy New Year call early this morning from Connie. She'd been up all night, walking round the nine miles of the fence and hanging messages on the fence and on the trees. I asked what on earth these messages said and she rhymed off several, Dare To Hope was one. They also called out to the soldiers in the base, urging them to think about the significance of it and what sin they were being called on to commit. I'm sure all that would be heard would be a general caterwauling which would be much derided, but it seems to have made Connie amazingly happy.

## 15 February

The Greenham camp has become women-only after a violent confrontation between the men and the women there. Connie reports, I think with satisfaction, that the men have all gone. She thinks the policy of non-violence will have more chance of success now, with the police and council officials less likely to use strong-arm tactics against women. I would not be so sure. It is perhaps the very presence of men that has prevented attempts to remove the camp already.

## 23 March

I was waiting for this. I knew it would happen: Connie has been arrested, yesterday. There was a blockade of the base, with hundreds of the women massing in front of the gates and refusing to move. As soon as some were bodily lifted away, others took their place. Connie, of course, returned again and again to the fray and I expect argued with the

Americans all the time. She and thirty-three others have been arrested and charged with obstructing the highway and must appear in court. She says I am not to worry, she will not be imprisoned, but I am frantic with worry. What kind of life is she leading, what will happen to her when all this is over? It is not as though she is a silly teenager. She is a woman of 45 years of age who ought not to be spending her days like this, and with worse to come. When I say this to her, she says that at least she will have stood by her principles and tried to do something, and I know that she means to point out that I never have.

## 4 April

Interesting visit from Harry. It is ages since I have seen him and he has changed in appearance, seems much heavier and is losing his hair. But he looked well and is very happy with his wife Joanna and two children, a boy and a girl, whose photographs he showed me. It was a relief to have someone to talk to about Connie. He listened very patiently to my tale of woe about her being arrested and how she was obsessed to the point of madness. He said he rather admired her and all the women there, which surprised me. I asked him why and he said he thought the power of a peaceful massed protest had never, so far as he knew, been put to the test in any kind of sustained way and that it was worth a try.

Then he changed the subject to ask how I was, and inquired if I needed anything. That was thoughtful of him. He asked about Toby too, and was astonished that I never hear from him, and about Grace and her family, not knowing they had gone to live in New York. In short, Harry showed himself to be almost the only concerned family member. I wish Connie was married and had two children and was enjoying life, like Harry. He invited me to go and stay with him and when I said travel was beyond me now, he said he would come and get me any time I liked. I am almost tempted. I shall think about it. I was sorry to see him go. After he left, I thought how I should like to leave him something when I die, but I have nothing meaningful except this house and that is left to Connie. I must select some memento, perhaps a piece of furniture that belonged to his grandparents, perhaps the two oak chairs actually made by his great-grandfather.

**26 April**

I wonder if Connie knows that we are at war in the Falklands and what she thinks of this 'victory' of ours, recapturing South Georgia. I can hardly bear to read about what is going on—war, war, war, and our woman Prime Minister the most warlike of all.

**29 May**

Phone call, at last, from Connie: she is fine, or so she says and, though she was one of those who lay down in the mud to obstruct the bulldozer trying to clear the site, she was not arrested this time. She described the scene vividly, the awful fear as this gigantic bulldozer moved slowly towards her, the ground vibrating as it advanced and the noise deafening the nearer it got to her, spraying her and the others with mud and grit so that they had to keep their eyes tight shut and rely on their other senses to know what was happening. It stopped inches from her and when she opened her eyes she found she was staring up into its metal jaws and she did not dare move for the dread of catching her clothes in them. Then the council workmen came, aided by policemen, and dragged her out, swearing at her as they did so. But her protest had been effective. The camp stays and she is jubilant. She said why do I not come down and visit her. It will change your mind, she said. I find myself wondering if it would. Maybe I should go. But oh, the journey would be so tiresome. I wouldn't want to go by train and be without my car at the other end, but it is quite a long way to drive, and my car is old. I am not sure I am up to it. I will think about it.

*          *          *

*All summer Millicent goes on thinking about it, with constant encouragement from Connie, but does nothing. Finally, near the end of the year, she feels she should make the effort, even though it is winter and not the best time either to drive or to be away from her home. She asks Connie to try to find a small hotel near the base, or as near to it as possible, because she certainly does not intend to sleep in a tent. She then plans her route meticulously, and goes to her GP and to an optician the week before to check her health (pronounced A1, except for the arthritic thumbs) and has her car serviced. Then mid-morning on 11 December, she sets off, the car equipped with all manner of emergency provisions. Included in her luggage is the scarf Robert gave her on her birthday in 1939, the last present from him, though she is not at all sure when it came to the test that she can bear to tie it to the base fence (and she later doesn't mention whether she actually does or not).*

\*     \*     \*

## 11 December

I don't know why I was so nervous about this journey. I arrived perfectly fresh, and not in the least tired, by lunchtime. But still, taking it easy, even absurdly easy, must be a good thing. This hotel is pretty dreary and the food poor, but it is warm and clean and the staff friendly. It was a straightforward journey until about five miles from Newbury, when the traffic began, a long line of vehicles moving very slowly. I got sandwiched between two vans and had to be careful not to stall, which was a strain. The van in front of me was crammed with women, far too many of them. I could see them crouching through the two back windows. They seemed to be singing but, though I could hear them banging on the roof of the van, I suppose in time to whatever they were singing, I couldn't hear the words. They made me nervous, though. I do worry that this is going to be a rowdy affair. If so, I shall leave. I felt very conspicuous, sitting alone in my car. The women in the van waved at me and smiled and put their thumbs up but all I could do was nod. Had some difficulty finding the hotel and felt quite exhausted by the time I had parked the car.

There was a message from Connie waiting for me, saying she couldn't leave the camp, there was too much to do, but that she would meet me at the main gate in the morning at 10 a.m. Her note said not to bring my car but to get a taxi and she would organise a lift back for me. I don't like the idea of not having my car available. I will be dependent on Connie and have no way of escaping. However, she must have a reason for forbidding the car, so I have booked a taxi. I shall take care to ask the taxi driver if there is any chance of getting in touch with him later. There must be a telephone box somewhere near the camp, because Connie often rings from one.

## 12 December

It is late, I am worn out, but I will not be able to sleep until I have set down something of what I saw and heard and felt today, however much it hurts my hand to write. I am on what Connie calls 'a high', uninfluenced I may say by either alcohol or drugs.

It was a damp, misty morning, with the miles of fencing round the base arising eerily from the ground, the only thing of any height it seemed for miles around. I was surprised by how high this fence was, and how barren the land it enclosed, with nothing but grey cement visible inside it. The taxi driver set me down as near to the main gate as he could get and I stood for a moment looking at all the tents in front of it and the women around

534

them, most holding mugs of steaming tea. Connie was there, waiting for me, and the minute she spotted me rushed forward to embrace me, seeming quite thrilled to claim me. She introduced me to so many women but I didn't take in any of their names, and then we set off to walk to a section of the fence which was to be ours, though I am not sure who decided it would be, Connie probably. There, attached to the grey wire about four feet off the ground, were photographs of Tilda and Charles and Florence and Jack, all mounted on a piece of white card, and underneath the words 'NO MORE BOMBS, R.I.P. London 1942'. My eyes filled with tears and I could not speak. For so long now I have thought I am beyond tears, ever since Daphne died I have never cried, I have no more tears, they will not come. I have shed too many in my life and always in private, always secretly, but standing there I wept. I was dreadfully embarrassed, but I don't think anyone noticed my distress, not even Connie. There was too much going on, with women on either side pinning the most extraordinary items to the fencing, not just photographs but banners they'd embroidered and poems they'd written out, and ribbons and flowers, and even teacups. Some women were weaving coloured strands of wool through the fencing, making something ugly into something pretty and others were fixing coloured Cellophane across the gaps so that suddenly, with the light coming through it, it looked like stained glass. There was a little girl not far from where we were who was helping her mother fix some baby clothes to the fence, tiny white lacy garments, and I wondered about their significance.

More and more women arrived until we were two deep next to the fence, and then someone began singing and simultaneously hands were held out and grasped and we all pushed along to make room so that this great line of women were soon holding hands in an unbroken cordon round the base. At least, we couldn't know it was unbroken but after about half an hour a woman came running behind us shouting, It's complete, it's complete, we've done it, we've done it! No one wanted to let go. Slowly the line I was part of began to move to the left, I moved with it, supported by Connie who held my hand in such a way that my elbow was held too. The ground was uneven but nobody fell. I don't know how far we walked, but eventually we came to another gate where a blockade was going on and the movement, the lovely, swaying, gentle progress stopped. The line was not broken, but we stood still because there was a fight, or what looked like a fight, going on. I didn't want to see it, and kept my face towards the fence, but Connie twisted round and yelled 'Bastards' at the men trying to drag some women away. I think if she had not had me with her she would have broken away and joined in. I saw, in the distance, inside the fence, some men come out and stare, but they did not come near. Connie asked me soon after the line had begun moving again and we had passed the gate, if I wanted a rest. She said we could leave the line and come back to it, and so I decided that it would be sensible if I did sit down for a while, though I had not thought of doing so until that moment. She took me to a tent she seemed to know, where there were some plastic garden chairs grouped outside and I sat there, my legs feeling suddenly shaky, and she disappeared inside and brought out a flask of tea. Oh, it was delicious! I was quite revived and eager to return to the line, but Connie wanted me to see what she called her home before we returned. Again, I felt tearful, though this time managed to prevent the tears escaping. It was so pitiful, that tent, the canvas sodden from all the recent rain so that if touched anywhere it dripped, and the horrible squalor of sleeping bags and dirty-looking blankets, and an unpleasant, bad smell, fuggy and close, hanging inside. And here Connie lived, it had been her home all these months. We went back to join the line but after another hour of slowly circling the fence Connie said she would have to leave it to do some important planning. She wouldn't tell me what this planning was for, but since it meant her going off she thought I should go back to my hotel or she might lose me and I'd have to get myself back, which might prove difficult. So I was brought back by a young woman going to Newbury to pick something up. She drove like a maniac, but I arrived here in one piece. There is a television in this bedroom and I have just watched the coverage of the Greenham event. It showed the base entirely encircled by what is believed to be nearly 30,000 women of all ages from all over the country. And I was one of them.

**13 December**

Just as well I booked in here for tonight too. Couldn't possibly have driven home today. I feel drained. Yesterday, I felt elated and, until the very end, hardly tired at all, but today I am worn out and stiff and my back pains me. I think of Connie and others in their awful tents and wonder how they stand it. At least in the war we had dry huts to sleep in and proper beds and hot showers and baths available.

I didn't go out to the camp today and didn't really expect Connie to come to me, but she did, briefly, mid-afternoon. She had a hot bath in my bathroom here and looked much the better for it, especially after she'd washed her hair. She seemed excited about something. I thought at first it was a kind of retrospective excitement but no, it wasn't, it was because of something planned for New Year. She says that whatever it is will be spectacular. I begged her to be careful. We parted good friends. She asked if I understood more now and I said I did, coming had made the difference she had said it would. And I told her I was proud of her and that if I'd been forty years younger I would have stayed and joined her. Now I am bothered by having made such a boast. Would I have crawled into that ghastly tent and endured all the privations simply to join in this protest? I suspect not. Connie is the stuff of heroines, and I am not.

## 14 December

Home, and glad to be. An invitation to spend Christmas with Harry and his family was waiting for me. He encloses details of which train I could get and he will meet me, or offers to drive up and collect me. Well, I wouldn't put him to such bother. I think that if I really wanted to I could probably

538

drive. I had no need of that stop on the way to Newbury, and with a rest could easily have managed another hundred miles, I'm sure. I will think about it. Connie will not be coming back, that's certain, so I have no need to think of her.

*      *      *

*Rather to her own surprise, Millicent does decide to accept Harry's invitation, though she doesn't drive but goes by train and is met by him. She spends five days with the Kings, from 22 to 27 December, and is enchanted by Harry's wife Joanna and his two children, Martin, aged 8 and Frances, aged 6. Their family life deeply impresses her and, inevitably, she records in her diary the contrast with Connie's Spartan existence. She feels guilty sitting in front of a roaring log fire, waited on hand and foot, after a magnificent Christmas dinner, thinking of Connie. Harry and Joanna seem so content with their lives, though she doesn't think them smug, and she knows they would never do what Connie is doing. They are more like her, she thinks, ordinary people who, though they care about others and about the future of the planet, are too wrapped up in their own lives to want to make public protests. She realises, too, that she is mentioning Connie all the time, and talking too much about Greenham. Afterwards she feels ashamed and, when she gets home, records that she has written in her letter of thanks that she is sorry to have done so. But it sticks in her mind, the huge difference between Harry's ideal family life and Connie's lack of one, and she comes near to deciding, rather unfairly, that her niece's involvement arises out of discontent and a desire to give herself some sense of purpose. Harry and Joanna, she reflects, don't need that. Their own family gives it to them.*

\*　　　\*　　　\*

## 31 December

Oh, heavens. Connie phoned to tell me to be prepared for dramatic events. She said that I was to tell no one—as if I had anyone to tell—but that she and some other women are going to climb over the fence and enter the camp. The press has been alerted and there will be full coverage. The action will start at dawn tomorrow, so I should listen to the wireless and watch television later on. All I could think of as she talked was that horrible fence, so tall, so strong. How will they get over it? She says they have got ladders and hidden them in the bushes and it will be easy. Will it? I don't think so. And how will they get over the top? I can't remember if there is barbed wire or spikes on top but I do recall long prongs bending outwards at intervals. I asked what they were going to do if they got over and she said paint slogans on the silos, that kind of thing. She doesn't seem to have thought that the fence may in some way be alarmed. I have visions of alarms going off and armed soldiers rushing out, or dogs. Oh, I wish I had not been told until it was over, but Connie seemed to think I would appreciate this advance information.

## 1 January 1983

Connie has been arrested, again, and for something far more serious. This time she will be sent to prison. I am sure of it. I am so agitated I can hardly bear to take in what happened. All I can absorb is that Connie was one of the women who climbed the fence and then danced on top of the silos before the police arrived and arrested her and forty-three others. I should go down there at once, but she says there is no point and I am not to think of it. They are to appear before the Newbury magistrates in two days' time. I feel she should have her own solicitor but she maintains she has no need of one. All she wanted to talk about was how glorious the break-in had been. They had had to be so quick getting the ladders up and then flinging an old carpet over the top so that they could safely get over. No one spoke, everyone concentrated on negotiating the fence, but once over they all yelled as they went up the muddy slopes of the silos, yelled and sang, elated to have done it. Eventually they were forcibly hauled down by policemen and ejected. It was pretty rough but she had no complaints and she'd expected to be manhandled. For some reason, she has given a false name to the police, lots of them have, to cause confusion. She has promised to ring me after the 3rd.

## 3 January

Connie and the others have not been charged under the Official Secrets Act, even though they penetrated into a high-security area, but with a breach of the peace. I am relieved to hear it. Maybe now she won't be sent to prison, maybe she will just be fined. I suspect she will refuse to pay a fine but I will pay it for her. It will make her angry, but I cannot have a niece of mine going to prison. I have not told her what I intend to do. Instead, I am going to go to the trial next month. I am quite determined to be there.

## 6 February

I don't think Connie saw me. I had some difficulty getting into the courtroom. It is not large, but I managed in the end, my age and respectability doubtless helping. It was all very interesting and I quite forgot to be anxious.

But today my head spins with the strain of trying to take in everything I've heard, much of it distressing since it consisted of details of radiation sickness and death through nuclear fall-out. The defence case seemed powerful to me, but not, alas, to the magistrates. It was so upsetting, watching a dozen policemen march into the courtroom before the verdict to pen in the women in the dock, no need for this, surely, they have not murdered anyone and were not likely to try to escape. I saw Connie and others climb onto chairs so that they stood above the policemen. She was found guilty of a breach of the peace, as they all were, and sentenced to prison for fourteen days. I had been prepared for the worst, though not expecting it, but even so I was shocked and felt quite faint. I tried to get near to Connie but she was herded off very quickly into a van and I had no chance to speak to her. I asked a policeman where the women were being taken and he said to Holloway, where they belong. I beg your pardon, I said, my niece is one of those women and she is from a good family and has done what she did for all our sakes and should be thanked for it and not imprisoned. I don't know what came over me. Move along, grandma, he said, laughing.


## 20 February

Never did I think that I would go through the gates of a prison either as a prisoner myself or as a visitor. I found it hard. The building itself intimidates me and I felt weak and nervous going into it. Because of my age, the warders were kind to me, one of them taking my arm to help me along though I had no real need of it. I suppose I simply looked frail. Connie was cheerful and not at all intimidated. She said I looked dreadful and told me to sit down and relax and she would do all the talking. She is in a cell with three other women, one a companion from the camp and the other two in on drug charges. Her main complaint was how long they'd been kept in reception when they arrived, three hours sitting in nothing but a dressing-gown, and they were all so tired. She's still tired, and finds sleeping difficult because of all the noise at night, endless bangings and crying out, occasional piercing screams, and the seemingly endless patrolling of the warders. She said the days pass quite quickly and of course there are only eleven more to get through. I dared to ask what she was going to do when she was released. She looked astonished at my question. She is going back to Greenham, of course. So, it will all begin again. But there was no point arguing. Before I left, I pleaded with her to come and spend at least one night with me, in comfort, before going back to the camp. She has said she will.

## 2 March

Connie is free. It hadn't been certain at what time she would be released so I did not meet her. She arrived here quite flushed and triumphant after some sort of reception party outside the gates of Holloway. The press were there and she'd been presented with flowers and someone had given her a lift, telling her they felt privileged to have the opportunity. Quite the star, I must say. She was on the telephone instantly, making lots of calls and sounding over-excited, I thought. I looked at her while she was talking and thought how she had aged. No doubt about it. In the last two years, she has aged about ten. Greenham has done that to her, dulled her skin and etched these lines and made her lovely hair lank. How she would shout at me if I said this aloud. I suggested that while she soaked in the bath I might wash her clothes, as she seems to have no others with her, and she could wear some of mine till they are dry. She said if it made me happy, I could go ahead. So I did. Dear Lord, those clothes! I washed them by hand, since most seemed to be woollen, and the dirt and dye which came out of them turned the water black. Her undergarments are disgraceful, in tatters, and the woollen tights she wears under her trousers so full of holes they are useless as coverings. It was a fine, windy day and I hung everything in the garden to dry but felt pangs of embarrassment at the thought of neighbours seeing such doleful garments. I said nothing about their state of course. I know only too well what the answer would be. Then I cooked a splendid dinner, plenty of meat to build her up. I know most of the women at the camp are vegans or vegetarians and Connie gets no meat even though she still eats it. Strange how, unlike me before I went to Italy, she has never been a vegetarian. She tucked in very satisfactorily. We had a bottle of claret, Harry gave it to me and I have been saving it, and then whisky afterwards, in front of the fire. Connie became very mellow then, not surprisingly. She thanked me, said it was always a comfort to know I was here and that she could always come to me. But then she asked did I still keep my diary. She wanted to know if I'd recorded what was happening at Greenham. I said naturally I had. She nodded, said she was glad. We're making history there, she said. I didn't quite like her tone, but made no comment, though I was tempted to remark that Greenham might at the best rate a footnote and at the worst be forgotten if overtaken by greater events. But Connie was in full flow, carrying on to declare that Greenham would be seen to represent ordinary women everywhere. I think I have heard this before, but then anyone living as long as I have is bound to have heard most things before. She said I was very quiet. Was that because I was not admiring enough? We sat up till midnight, though I was ready for bed long before. She hugged and kissed me before she went, in a way she hasn't done since she was a little girl but then Greenham has seen a growth in such embracing. You are so small, Aunt Millicent, she said, I always forget how small you are, and I'm sure you've shrunk. I said very probably, old women do. You're not old, she said, and I told her not to be so silly, of course I am old and my time is nearly up. She seemed shocked, and held me at arm's length and examined me minutely. No, she said very firmly, your time is *not* nearly over, you have a diary to keep up. So we parted laughing.

## 5 March

Connie stayed three nights after all. There was some urgent phone call summoning her to a meeting and she came back from it very self-important, saying she had things to organise here in London before going back to Greenham. But we had no more cosy evenings. She was out each night and I hardly saw her. Now she has gone back, loaded with all kinds of things needed at the camp. I ran her to the station and couldn't park and so our farewells were hurried. I watched her stalk down the concourse, full of confidence and with never a backward look.

\*     \*     \*

*After this, Millicent does not follow Connie's fortunes at Greenham quite so intently—it is as though she has become weary of the subject. But she does describe in some detail Connie's second arrest, when she is one of the 187 women who cut through sections of the fence round the base with bolt-cutters in*

*October 1983, and then writes intermittently about Connie and the others who carried on right up to 1987, when NATO finally agreed to get rid of the missiles. The diaries from the end of 1983 to 1987 are thin. Partly this is due to Millicent's arthritis, which for years had been bad in the joints of her thumbs, and partly to a growing loss of interest in recording her own life 'up to the end'. She worries about what this 'end' will be like, what is going to happen to her, how she is going to manage in old age if she goes on living until she is 90 or even older. Her general health is still good, as it always has been, but she catalogues failing faculties ruthlessly. In 1988, she gives up driving which distresses her greatly, and makes a significant difference to her much-valued independence, but she is forced into this after two dizzy turns while at the wheel. Nothing happened, she didn't have an accident, but she feels nervous afterwards and thinks of these 'turns' as a warning she ought to heed. The dizziness is due to raised blood pressure, quite easily corrected, but she doesn't resume driving. In 1989, she has a fall, nothing serious, but her left arm is never quite right afterwards—she wrenched it in the fall and it remains painful though nothing is broken or fractured. Her eyesight begins to deteriorate in 1989 and for the first time she has to wear spectacles, and in 1990 she suffers a partial hearing loss in her left ear. The writing in her diary is still quite clear, but from being neat and small it grows large and runs over the lines of the pages. Also in 1990 there is a particularly poignant entry about her teeth.*

## 6 April 1990

What a miserable business growing very old is proving to be. I thought I would keep my own teeth until the very end, but I have had to suffer the humiliation of having my top teeth extracted, or almost all of them, only the wisdom teeth and a molar each side left. What a miserable business. Mr Dawson said I had been unfortunate: after a certain age teeth don't usually deteriorate but my old amalgam fillings had caused an infection and loosened the teeth and there was nothing he could do to save them. He assures me that the plate he is making will serve me beautifully, but I doubt it. I cannot bear to look at myself, my mouth now slack and ugly. Heaven knows, it is bad enough looking in the mirror, anyway, and I try not to. I can eat, my bottom teeth suffice, but it is awkward. Luckily, I have very little appetite now. Soup does me fine for the moment. Teeth, eyes, joints—all collapsing and the sudden heart attack I would have preferred is less likely all the time. I dread finding myself in an institution. I won't let it happen. Yet I know, even as I write this, that I may not have the power or means to prevent it. It agitates me to think this. I feel decisions about my future ought to be made now, and by me, before it is too late. But like most people, because it is all so painful to contemplate, I defer it. I let time roll on, I lull my fears with a false sense of security, a foolish *que sera sera* attitude.

\*     \*     \*

*But Millicent's worries about having to go into an institution are, happily, never realised. She never imagined she would ever leave her London house, where she has lived after all from 1936 (with an interruption of course during the war years), but in 1992, Harry and his wife persuade her to move to a cottage near to them. Although she doesn't write about it much, Millicent says she thinks about it long and hard before deciding to agree. The plain fact is that she has no other family except Grace, who is still in New York, and Connie and Toby, with whom she has lost contact, and no close friends. Her neighbours seem to change all the time and she knows she could not depend on them in the future if she should become housebound. She doesn't want to depend on anyone but knows it is likely she might be forced to. She also acknowledges that since she has stayed more and more in the house, London's amenities now mean little to her. She no longer goes to the theatre or is able to roam the parks and squares as she once did.*

*So, in 1992, at the age of 91, she sells her London house and moves to the country. Harry and Joanna arrange everything for her and it is not nearly as traumatic as she has anticipated. In fact, she records in her diary that she feels she has been given a new lease of life. Her cottage delights her and she even quite likes being part of a village. People are kind to her, and Joanna and her children visit every day, if just for a few minutes. The only person apparently not happy about the move is Connie, but then Connie is becoming stranger by the minute. The entries about her are short and sound very controlled, though it is not exactly clear what is being controlled—anger, perhaps? Or alarm?*

**20 June 1992**

I wish Connie would not keep telephoning if she is
going to be so unpleasant. I have invited her to
come and stay so she can see how comfortable and
content I am but she says she hasn't time.

**25 June**

A glorious day, roses fully out and cascading down
the back wall of the cottage. Only a letter from
Connie spoiled the day. I didn't want to open it,
but felt obliged to. I think being with this group has
unhinged her mind. She rants on about my being
taken advantage of and I cannot imagine what on
earth she is talking about. Such a contrast with
Toby's reaction to my news. I never expected him
even to acknowledge the letter I sent, telling him
where I was going, but he has responded
immediately, full of approval and enthusiasm for
the whole idea of the move. Maybe he is happier in
California—he sounds so much more like the
young Toby, cheerful and forthcoming again.

**4 July**

What does Connie want from me? Money?
Possibly. She may think now that I have a great
deal, knowing as she does what I sold my house for.
I suppose this ridiculous commune, or whatever it

is, needs money. Well, it will not get mine.

*     *     *

*Other entries about Connie are equally cryptic. Previously, Millicent has mentioned, in the late 1980s when her Greenham protest came to an end, that Connie went to the north-west of Scotland with a group of other women. She was going to write a history of Greenham Common while living with these other feminists in a self-sufficient way, growing their own food and so forth. Millicent gives this idea six months, but Connie stays (though no book seems to have been written, unless it was published under another name). Communication has become infrequent until Millicent writes to say she is moving to be near Harry. Then she records that an avalanche of letters descends on her. Why Connie, who hasn't seen her aunt for years by then, should object so violently to this move is a puzzle. Millicent may have been right, it may indeed have been to do with money. Connie hasn't worked since 1981 and cannot have much left of her own money. She may think Harry is trying to get Millicent to leave him an inheritance Connie regards as hers. Whatever the reason, it is sad to witness the drifting apart of aunt and niece. But on the other hand, the emergence of Joanna as a support for Millicent balances this. She likes Joanna very much, finds her kind and gentle, rates her an excellent wife and mother, and most important of all utterly happy with her life. In 1995, when Millicent finds writing too painful to struggle on with, she asks Joanna to become her amanuensis.*

*     *     *

551

## 1 May 1995

This diary is now being written for me by Joanna
King, wife of my nephew Harry, my hands being
too arthritic to make writing anything but a chore. I
can still write but am finding it painful. I am sitting
with my eyes closed in an attempt to pretend I am
alone though I am very aware of Joanna opposite
me writing this down. I don't think it is going to
work, though that will be through no fault of
Joanna's, of course. Speaking is not the same as
writing, it was the writing itself, the very formation
of the letters, which led me on. I don't like the
sound of my voice either. This will never do.
Joanna, we will stop, I will wait until I feel I need
my diary.

## 16 June

This is another attempt to *speak* my diary and if it
fails to satisfy me I shall not try again. I have never
written down dreams. It always seemed such a
waste of time, especially as that is what dreams are
in my opinion, waste matter—Joanna, you need not
write this down—the waste bin of the mind. But
this last six weeks I have been so bothered by the
same dream that I know that if I was keeping my
diary myself, I would be bound to describe it. I
dream I am marching, a very pleasant feeling in
itself at my age, very enjoyable to feel my legs
moving so freely and painlessly, and the energy of
the marching invigorates me and I know I am

552

smiling. I am marching with many, many other people, men as well as women but mostly women—though no children I notice, where are the children if there are so many women?—at any rate, I am marching with hordes of others but I have no idea where to. We are not in uniform, we do not carry weapons, this is not an army, this is not a war dream. And there are no banners, nobody is shouting out slogans, there are no signs that this is a protest march. I march all night but I am never tired. Sometimes, I see the marchers, including myself, from above. There is no end to us, behind and ahead, still we come, a never-ending stream. Joanna, that is from a hymn, is it not, life like a never-ending stream, something like that?

# AFTERWORD

The hymn Millicent is probably thinking of is 'O God, our help in ages past', where in verse five 'Time, like an ever-rolling stream, / Bears all its sons away'. There is a note after this, saying that Millicent decides not to go on because trying to speak her diary does not feel comfortable. Harry then suggests a tape-recorder, so that his aunt can have the privacy she feels essential but, though she tries this, it is no more successful—the two existing tapes are mostly full of her fussing about whether the tape-recorder is working, and whether her voice is loud enough. But the failure of these methods focuses attention on what is going to happen to her diaries and, as related in the introduction, that is how I came into the picture.

So, the diaries end, after all those years, not with a bang but with something of a whimper. They fade out with a dream. But of course when I'd finished studying them, Millicent was still alive and had promised to let me visit her again to ask her questions arising from them. I was looking forward to this, and spent a long time deciding which areas to concentrate on, feeling that if I bombarded her with what were essentially trivial inquiries, to do with dates and places and names, then she might not have the energy to satisfy my curiosity on deeper issues. Most of all I wanted her to concentrate on the *significance* to her of her diary throughout her life, and especially at times of crisis, those periods when she simply stopped writing it. The gaps spoke louder to me than the entries before and after, and though I worried about how painful it might be for her if I probed these areas, I wanted to do it. I also very much wanted, perhaps most of all, to get her to decide whether she felt she had indeed taken wrong turns in her life, and if so at what stage. Had life, in her opinion, been a series of choices, or did she see it as a random affair, a matter of being dealt a certain set of cards and her only choice that of how to play them? All the other people I'd known who had lived to almost a hundred, including my own father, had been remarkably firm believers in what is called 'fate' and I'd always found it interesting that this didn't depress them, but instead appeared to please them. I guessed because it freed them from responsibility.

When I was ready, I made an appointment through Joanna to visit Millicent again. In fact, Joanna herself drove me down, picking me up after another trip to see her sister. I was relieved to hear from her that Millicent was still in good health, though she had been having some trouble with breathing and was becoming a little bit forgetful. This last bit was not good news, since I wanted her to do a great deal of remembering, but Joanna assured me it was just normal forgetting of names and nothing approaching senile dementia. On the drive down she asked if there had been any great surprises in the diaries and I said it depended what one already knew. Since I had known nothing, beyond the fact of Millicent's age and status, everything had been a surprise. I hadn't, I said, expected her to have had love-affairs of the kind that she did, wrongly thinking that she would have been too respectable and that for women of her generation it had been a case of nice girls didn't.

Joanna said she was glad that Millicent had had lovers. She'd always thought it odd that Millicent had never married because even now it was obvious that she'd been pretty and lively, and Joanna had always imagined she must have had a fiancé who was killed in the war. I told her then a bit about Robert, but not about the baby in case Millicent wanted that kept private till after her death. But then Joanna asked a question I'd given a lot of thought to: when, on the evidence of the diaries, had Millicent been at her happiest and her unhappiest? The first part was the easiest to answer—she'd been at her happiest, I was sure, during the beginning of her love-affair with Robert—but the second was harder. There were many times, I knew, when Millicent had been wretchedly unhappy—on the death of her father, after her miscarriage, and after several other deaths—and, apart from those tragedies, there were the miserable years teaching in Brighton and enduring lonely years in Blockley. She had had quite a lot of unhappiness in her long life and yet her spirit had never been broken, she'd never succumbed to despair.

Millicent was standing looking out of the window when we drew up and rushed to open the door but it wasn't us she was so enthusiastically waiting to welcome but her beloved diaries. Helping her to stack them back in their cupboard was touching—she almost stroked each exercise book as she put it on its shelf and smiled with enormous satisfaction when the task was done and she had closed and locked the door. She asked me how long it would take for me to edit the diaries. I said, now that I had read them all and selected and photocopied the entries I wanted to use, it was a question of shape, of making sure that my own contribution provided a framework for her words. It would, I reckoned, take me about a year. I thought she might think that was far too long, but on the contrary she was pleased, saying that, as she'd told me at the beginning, she didn't want the book published till after her death, so the longer it took me, the more likely she was to have departed this life.

We then went back into her sitting-room and settled down with some tea and she told me to 'fire away'. I fired, and almost immediately became aware that for all her outward brightness and apparent coherence, Millicent's mind was not nearly as sharp as it had seemed when I first met her. I hadn't then, of course, been subjecting her to detailed questioning, but even so I estimated there had been considerable deterioration. It didn't matter that she couldn't recall names, or even that when names were mentioned they seemed to mean nothing to her (though that was more alarming), but it was so disappointing that she couldn't begin to discuss emotions and feelings at crucial periods of her life. When I tried, as delicately as possible, to talk about the loss of her baby she looked shocked and said, 'Did I have a baby? Are you sure, dear?' When I produced the relevant pages I'd photocopied, and read them out to her, she became agitated and I ended up apologising and consoling her, regretting I'd ever tried to bring the subject up. After that, I was much more careful, sticking to the less traumatic mysteries, such as why did she not go ahead and gain her Open University degree. She was happy enough to offer explanations here but, even then, there was a lack of conviction in her voice. I knew there was no point hoping for enlightenment on sensitive matters, and our conversation quickly degenerated into general chat. 'Well, you know everything about me now,' she said, 'my whole life, every little detail, is in those diaries.' It would have been cruel to disagree, but I left full of regret that Millicent was not ten years younger and able to supply vital information as a kind of codicil to her own diaries.

A month later, she fell and broke her hip. On 13 January 2000, the anniversary of her father's death, she died. At her own request, there was no funeral. If there had been, I would have gone to it, longing as I did to meet Connie and any other members of the family who might have attended. In her will, Millicent had left everything equally divided between Harry, Toby and Connie, with a small legacy to Julian, Alfred's son (whom she had never met and knew nothing about). In an earlier will (in which Connie alone had been left the house), the diaries had been bequeathed to Connie, and this bequest still stood, which surprised me. Joanna told me that when Connie came down from Scotland to collect them, she told her of her aunt's agreement that I should edit them, and that after her death they should be given to a university archive, but as far as she knows Connie has not yet deposited them anywhere. Connie has not contacted me.

I hope she will indeed entrust the diaries to some responsible person and that they will be treasured. They tell the story of an unremarkable life and yet what Millicent King experienced in her very ordinariness was shared by so many of her generation. To me, she is as symbolic, in her way, as the unknown soldier: the Unknown Woman of her times.

# ACKNOWLEDGEMENTS

The following books (as well as many contemporary newspapers and magazines) proved useful during the editing process.

*Women and the Great War*, (ed.) Joyce Marlow (Virago Press, 1998)

*Greenham Common: Women at the Wire*, Barbara Hartford and Sarah Hopkins (Women's Press Ltd, 1985)

*Few Eggs and No Oranges: a diary showing how unimportant people in London and Birmingham lived through the war years, 1940–1945*, Vere Hodgson (Persephone, 1999)

*The Long Road to Greenham: Feminism and Anti-Militarism in Britain Since 1820*, Jill Liddington (Virago Press, 1990)

*Lesser Gods, Greater Devils*, Arthur Lane (Allen Lane, 1993)

*Occupation: The Ordeal of France 1940–1944*, Ian Ousby (Pimlico, 1998)

*Wartime Women: An Anthology of Women's Wartime Writing for Mass-Observation, 1937–45*, (ed.) Dorothy Sheridan (Heinemann, 1990)

*Bombers and Mash: The Domestic Front 1939–1945*, Raynes Minns (Virago Press, 1985)

*Wartime Jottings of a WAAF Driver 1941–46*, Diana Lindo (Woodfield Publishing, 1992)

*Goldsmith's College: A Centenary Account*, A.E. Firth (Athlone Press, 1991)

*Paris in the Third Reich: A History of the German Occupation 1940–1944*, David Pryce-Jones

(Collins, 1983)

*The Thirties: A Dream Revolved*, Julian Symons (Faber and Faber, 1975)

*A Woman's Place, 1910–1975*, Ruth Adam (Persephone, 1977)

*Penelope Hall's Social Services of England and Wales*, Penelope Hall (Routledge Kegan & Paul, 1983)

This book began as described in the first two pages of the introduction, but I never did meet the woman in question. She cancelled our meeting at the last minute because of some family objections. I was already so looking forward to her diaries that I decided to overcome my disappointment by pretending I had indeed obtained and read them. The result is fiction. The real 'Millicent' has since died, and though her diaries exist, I have never read them.